SON OF SIMON

THOMAS FINCHAM

A MYSTERY NOVEL

Son of Simon
Thomas Fincham

Visit the author's website:
www.finchambooks.com

Contact:
contact@finchambooks.com

PROLOGUE

UNKNOWN

In the middle of the black ocean, a white boat floated on the still water. Three men stood around another man. He lay on the boat's deck, bleeding from the side of his head. His prescription glasses were next to him. The right lens was cracked, and the frame handle was broken. He was alive, but barely. He moaned and groaned. He begged for help. Instead, the three men covered his mouth with duct tape and tied his arms behind his back. They attached weights to his ankles and wrapped his body in a blue tarp. For good measure, they attached more weights at the end of the tarp. They then lifted the man up and hurled him over the side. He fell in the water with a loud splash. They watched as he disappeared into the darkness below.

When they were satisfied the ocean would not spit him out, they started the boat and pulled away.

ONE

SIMON

I'm the good guy.

Trust me.

It may be hard to believe once you know what I've done, but I had a good reason for doing it.

I had a life that was perfect. At least, I thought it was perfect.

What was perfection, anyway? There was no way anyone had a perfect body, but millions of people believed such a thing existed. Chiseled abs. Muscular arms. Toned chest, perhaps.

What about a perfect face? A strong jawline for men? Big round eyes for women? What was it then?

Perfection was in the eye of the beholder. We meet someone and instantly feel they are perfect for us. That he or she is our soulmate, put on this earth just for us.

When the honeymoon phase is over, we begin to see the porcelain skin we so admired at the beginning was covered with wrinkles and warts. And those who were able to accept this other phase—the not-so-rosy side of married life—they were the truly happy ones.

Many don't, though. That was why half of the marriages ended in divorce, and it got worse with each passing generation.

Why was that? Maybe we were more enlightened about what was important in our lives. Marriage, children… They were a thing of the past, and the future was more about one's personal growth.

The dead man's body was two feet away from me as I sat on the edge of the bed. I don't really know his name. But I wonder if he had a family of his own. A wife. Children, even. And I'm torn by what I've done.

He didn't leave me with much choice, though.

I had warned him not to make a move. But he did.

The man's gun was in his coat pocket. The coat was on a chair in the corner of the room. The man was able to reach the coat and pull out the weapon.

I was justified in pulling the trigger. My life was in danger.

There was another option, though. An option that would've avoided the man's death. I should not have come here in the first place. But more importantly, I should not have come with a weapon.

I was the reason for his demise. I was a murderer. Whether my act was pre-meditated or not was up to the lawyers to decide.

I could very well walk away from this mess. At the moment, no one knew I was even here—except for one person.

This person knew my reasons. I did it for him.

Would I do it again—take a man's life—if given another chance?

The quick answer would be: no. But the more complicated answer would be: I don't know.

We, humans, were complex creatures. We did bad things for all the right reasons. Was my situation one of those? I hoped so.

I'm not a killer. But I have killed.

I always thought I was living a beautiful life, but now I think I was living a beautiful lie.

My gun was on the table next to the bed. The man's gun was on the floor next to the chair.

I pulled my cell phone from my pants pocket. I stared at the black screen.

I still had a choice. I could stuff my gun in my jacket and walk out of the room. Maybe I could even get away with it. I remember reading some statistic that, on average, only sixty percent of all murders were resolved. And that statistic was even lower in some parts of the country.

Was Arlington one of them?

I'm not sure, and I don't really care.

Even if the police never solved who killed this man, I would always know it was me. Carrying that weight would be far worse than spending my life locked up in an eight-by-ten cell.

Were prison cells really eight-by-ten?

Again, I'm not sure, and I don't really care.

What I do care about is doing the right thing.

I swiped my finger across the phone, unlocking it.

I took one last look at the body on the floor.

I then dialed a number.

TWO

Three Weeks Earlier

HELEN

She sat at the edge of the bed with a gun in her hand. She knew this weapon inside out. She had to. As a detective for the Arlington PD, her Glock 22 was her best friend.

Helen Sloan was only a couple of months away from retirement. At the age of fifty-five, she was qualified for a full pension. She'd already been on the force for thirty years. When she'd first joined, she never thought she'd reach retirement.

She wasn't worried about getting shot and killed in the line of duty. She figured she'd quit being an officer long before that.

She was always stubborn, though. Her dad taught her and her siblings to never quit. "Life wasn't meant to be easy or fair," he'd say to them. "It's filled with hurdles and tragedies, and you have to just make the best of it."

In her line of work, she'd seen her share of tragedies. Some so profound that it was a miracle she had any faith left in humanity.

Her first case involved the death of a bus driver. The driver was in his early thirties. He had a beautiful wife and three wonderful children at home. His biggest mistake was being in the wrong place at the wrong time. The passenger he stopped to pick up was an ex-con in a hurry to meet his parole officer. The ex-con had been in and out of prison for a variety of offenses. And on that day, he was angry that the driver was ten minutes late.

Ten minutes!

That was all it took for the ex-con to walk up to the driver and fire three rounds into his head. The driver died on the spot.

The ex-con was given life without parole. The CCTV camera on the bus had caught the horrific act. Not to mention, there were a dozen people already on the bus. The ex-con had little choice but to plead guilty. The alternative was a trial, which would have resulted in him getting the death penalty.

Helen never understood why that ex-con let his emotions get the better of him. Why he let ten minutes ruin his entire life.

Maybe it was the fact he had a handgun in his backpack when he decided to take the bus that day. A gun he illicitly obtained, because as a parolee, he was forbidden to own firearms.

What if he had no gun on him? Would that have prevented him from letting his anger get the better of him?

She didn't know. She did know that, while people killed people, guns or no, guns made killing a whole lot easier.

She checked the time on the alarm clock next to her bed. The clock had been a wedding gift from her in-laws. Even after all these years, it was a surprise that the thing still worked.

Maybe products of the past were made to last, she thought. *Unlike now, when everything's cheap and disposable.*

She'd been up at the crack of dawn. In fact, she hadn't slept a wink all night.

She'd tossed and turned in bed. She'd tried reading a book, but nothing calmed her mind. She'd even gone downstairs and made a cup of chamomile tea for herself. Tea usually put her right to sleep.

But not last night.

She took a deep breath and shut her eyes.

She could feel her heart pounding inside her chest. She was already on several medications for a variety of ailments. High blood pressure. Joint pain. And now anxiety.

The first two were due to her age and the pressures of the job, but the last one had cropped up recently.

She had sensed her time on the force had come to an end. She'd given everything in the line of duty. She was divorced, and she rarely got to see her daughter and one grandchild. She'd sacrificed a lot.

And for what?

She was alone in a big house, and soon, she would be without a purpose in her life.

Her detective badge was on the side table next to the bed. She was proud of it, but at the same time, she was burdened by it. The responsibility had become too much to bear. But it was all she'd ever wanted.

Detective Helen Sloan of the Arlington Police Department.

It always had a nice ring to it. But now, more so than ever, it felt hollow. As if it had lost its power.

Her cell phone buzzed, and she quickly answered.

"I'm on my way," she said.

THREE

HELEN

She followed the Ford sedan's GPS like a talisman; it was the only thing keeping her from getting lost. She was never good with directions. In fact, she was the worst. She couldn't tell the difference between north and south. Prior to the GPS, she relied on road maps. She'd bought so many maps over the years that they used to take up all the space in her front passenger seat. But even they didn't prevent her from going in the wrong direction from time to time. The only way she was able to get by was because of her photographic memory. She would use certain locations as markers. A gas station, or a park, or a school playground, anything that could help her along her route. If she got lost, she could always drive to the marker and find her way back.

Once, while driving to a crime scene, she remembered an old bakery. Several weeks later, when she returned to the scene, that bakery had been replaced by a hair salon—a fact she was not aware of. Helen drove for more than half an hour before she realized where she was.

Her ex-husband, Paul, on the other hand, was great with directions. He knew what roads lead to where and how they all connected with one another. Like all newlyweds, they were broke, and so Paul decided to drive a taxi at night to pay the bills. It required him to know the city streets inside out. He passed the taxi cab exam on his first attempt, which was rare at the time when most people had to do it several times.

When the electronic GPS came to the market, she was first in line to get one. She couldn't live without it. Apart from the Ford's GPS, she also kept a separate GPS device as a backup. And as a backup to a backup, she also used her cell phone's GPS on rare occasions.

She pulled into a quiet street. She saw a police cruiser up ahead. A uniformed officer was standing next to the yellow police tape. She waved her badge.

The officer held up the tape for her.

She spotted a white Chevy sedan and frowned. She parked behind it and got out.

The man standing next to the sedan was tall, had a heavy mustache covering his upper lip, and deep-set eyes.

"What're you doing here, sarge?" Helen asked, walking up to him.

"I came here to speak to you, detective," the sergeant replied.

She smiled. "You could have just called. I mean, we all have cell phones now. Unless you're one of those who think cell phones cause cancer. If that is the case, you should wait until you are back at your desk to use a landline."

"Funny," he said, not smiling. "But this is important, and I wanted to tell you in person."

The smile fell from her face. "You can't fire me. I'm retiring soon." She suddenly thought about her pension. If she was let go, she could lose all those years of service.

He shook his head. "Of course, I'm not firing you. You're my best detective."

"Nowadays, people are fired for the smallest of offenses. Substance abuse. Sexual harassment. Unlawful use of force," Helen said.

"Those are *not* minor offenses," he countered.

She grinned. She was trying to lighten the mood. The sergeant's sudden and unexpected appearance was making her feel uneasy. Especially today.

He said, "I need a favor from you."

"What kind of favor?"

He paused, waiting to see what her reaction would be. "I've got a newbie I want you to partner with on this case."

"No way!" she said, shaking her head.

"He was top of his class."

"I don't care. I'm not a babysitter."

"Just give him a chance."

She looked him directly in the eyes. "Sarge, I'm gone soon, and…"

"And that's why I need him to tag along with you. I want that knowledge and experience passed on to the next generation. You're the most senior member in the department."

"I'm old now, am I?"

"You know I don't mean that," the sergeant said. "I still believe you've got a lot of good years ahead of you. But it was *you* who had come into my office and told me you wanted to retire."

She shrugged. "Yeah, I did."

"I never asked you then, but why decide to call it quits now?"

She looked down at her shoes. "It just feels like the right time, you know."

"I know that feeling," he said. "If I didn't have a son going to med school, I'd be lounging on some Caribbean beach with a Mimosa in my hand."

She raised an eyebrow. "I never took you for a Mimosa drinker."

"I'm not much of a drinker, to begin with. The wife loves them, so I give her company whenever we go on trips. My point is, teach the kid a few things before you leave, okay?"

Helen bit her bottom lip. "I don't know…"

"It's a simple case," he added.

"How do you know?"

"Drunk guy found stabbed on a park bench. Probably a bar fight turned fatal. Plus, all those years ago, *I* took you on as my partner, remember? You were one of the youngest graduates, and you were a woman. I was told that was a bad combination. But I listened to my instincts, and you and I had some great years as partners, didn't we?"

She smiled ruefully. "We sure did."

"Just give him a chance. You might actually like him."

Helen sighed. "All right, fine. But he better not get in my way."

FOUR

HELEN

She left the sergeant and walked further down the road. The area was surrounded by commercial buildings and office towers. On the side of the road was a bench. Next to the bench was a bus shelter.

Leaning on the bus shelter was a man.

He quickly straightened up when he saw her approach.

"I'm Michael," he said, extending his hand. "You must be Helen."

"*Detective* Sloan," she said, shaking his hand.

His face flushed. "Um… yes, of course."

He had neatly combed hair, unblemished skin, and soft eyes. He was wearing a suit that looked like it belonged to his father. And his tie was loose around his neck, probably because he didn't know how to tie one properly.

I could be his mother, she thought.

"The sergeant didn't tell me your name," she said.

"Oh, right. It's Michael James Porter."

"You prefer I call you Michael James Porter?"

"Michael is fine."

She then turned her attention to the body on the park bench. "What have we got here?"

"Victim's name is Derek Starr. I found a wallet in his pocket. He's thirty-eight. Married…"

"How do you know he's married?" she asked, interrupting him.

"He's got a wedding ring on, so I assumed…"

"Never assume anything," she said. "He could be separated or even divorced. Some men, and even women, continue to wear their wedding rings even after the end of their marriages."

"Really?" Michael said, surprised.

"My ex-husband took his off after one year."

"And what about you? You waited one year too?"

She held up her left hand. The gold ring was still visible on her ring finger.

"I'm confused," he said. "Why still wear it when you're not married?"

"I can't speak for others, but for me, it's a reminder of a life I once had."

"Aren't you worried men won't ask you out if they see that?"

She smiled. "Who says I want men to ask me out?"

His brow furrowed. "Don't you?"

"At my age, you don't want to be wading through the dating scene. Plus, once the men find out I'm a grizzled homicide detective, they quickly move on. I hear retired teachers and nurses make the best companions for men of a certain age."

"I didn't know that."

"That's what I heard. I can't say if it's true, though," she said. "All I look forward to at the end of the day is a glass of wine and a good book."

"Okay, sure."

"What else can you tell me about the victim?" Helen asked, getting back to business.

"He's got two kids," Michael answered. "And before you say how I can be sure, I can't. I just saw photos of a boy and a girl in his wallet."

"Any photo of the wife?"

"There is one."

"So, we can assume for now that he's married with kids."

"Okay. And also, there was still cash in his wallet."

"So, robbery wasn't a motive," she said.

"Nope."

Derek Starr was wearing a black business suit and no tie. His shirt collar was unbuttoned, and there was a dark stain on his white shirt. *Likely from where he was stabbed*, Helen thought. His eyes were closed. His head was bowed, with his chin touching his chest. To anyone passing by, he could pass for sleeping—unless they saw the blood. He was also gripping a beer bottle in his left hand.

"How far is the nearest bar?" she asked.

"I saw one about a block away when I was driving up here," he replied.

"Maybe he had a few too many to drink. And maybe he got into it with someone at the bar. And maybe that someone decided to teach him a lesson once he left the bar," Helen suggested.

"I don't know about that," Michael said.

She turned to him. "What makes you say that?"

He pointed to the victim's shoes. "Those look like real leather. And they look like they are custom made."

"Okay, so?"

"Look at how scuffed they are."

"What's your point?"

"These shoes cost a lot of money, and anyone who owns them would know how to take care of them."

"How does that help us?" she asked, feeling annoyed.

"If I had to take a guess, I'd say, he was dragged to this spot."

"Dragged?"

"Yeah. The sidewalk is cement, but the road is concrete. Those shoes could only look like that if they were dragged across concrete."

She stared at him. "You know a lot about shoes?"

"I'm a collector. I started when I was a teenager. I own a hundred pairs. Most are basketball shoes, but as I've gotten older, I've splurged on some dress shoes as well."

"All right. So, he was dragged, but from where?"

He shrugged. "Maybe from the bar?"

"Well, let's go take a look," she said.

FIVE

SIMON

"You're nothing more than thieves," he said with tears in his eyes.

I was seated in a posh conference room on the top floor of a glass office building. My firm, Harris & Harris, occupied two offices on the executive level, which gave us access to the conference room, as well as a private gym with a shower and other amenities. Just the monthly rent for space was more than what the average person made in salary.

I'm Simon Harris, and, along with my brother, Gabe, we are partners at a private equity firm. Hence the title of our firm.

Gabe was seated next to me. He had perfectly coiffed blonde hair, pale blue eyes, and a dimple whenever he smiled or laughed. I, on the other hand, had receding dark hair, brown eyes, and the beginning of a double chin.

I was a good four inches shorter than my brother. He was five-foot-eleven. I was five-foot-seven. Gabe was also two years older, but he was more than a brother to me. He was like a father.

Our father had founded the firm when we were just kids. He wanted his children to take it over once he was gone. The best way to do that was to name it Harris & Harris after his two sons.

Gabe Harris Sr. died at the age of forty-two. The same age I was now. He was working at his desk when he'd suddenly had a heart attack. He was found several hours later by his secretary. Gabe Sr. never took much care of his health. He drank a glass of scotch daily, and he smoked a pack of cigarettes on top of that. He also worked twelve hours a day. He was always in his office going over the financials of all the businesses he had invested in.

Our firm invested in struggling businesses, and we made them profitable. We then sold the businesses to the competition for even more money.

The man across from us at the conference table was Dimitris Diakos. Dimitris was a short, stocky man. He had a round face, a round body, and pudgy hands. Dimitris owned an olive oil processing and distribution business. His family owned land in Greece, which provided the best olives in the Mediterranean. Dimitris's olive oil was used by restaurants, hotels, and bars throughout the city. In most cases, he was their main supplier. He had a plant in Arlington that turned the imported olives into oil. At the peak of the business, they had eighty employees. But with competition increasing and costs going up each year, the company had gone into deeper and deeper debt.

That's when we showed up. We saw value in the company, and we made a deal with Dimitris. We bought fifty percent of the company for a third of the price, and we also took control of all the decision making. Dimitris wasn't happy when he made the deal. But what choice did he have? He was desperate, and we were vultures circling to attack.

"You stole my business," Dimitris said, pointing at both of us.

Gabe leaned forward and smiled. "We had an agreement, Mr. Diakos. That agreement was that we would do *whatever* necessary to make the business viable again."

"You also took my family's land in Greece," he said.

"The land was owned by your company. When we invested in your company, we also took control of the land."

"That doesn't make sense."

"Why doesn't it?" Gabe asked. "Your most valuable asset is not the plant that processes the oil. It's the land that produces the olives. Without the olives, there is no oil."

"But it's been in my family for generations. My mother has a house on that property."

"I'm sure with the money you're getting, you can buy her a nicer house."

"She's eighty-seven!" Dimitris snapped. "She's lived in that house her entire life. She'll die if she finds out what has happened."

"I'm sorry," Gabe said, "but the land, including any property on it, is now owned by Terra Oils Incorporated."

Dimitris's face turned beet red hearing that name. "You had no right to sell my company to… to… to *them*."

"They are one of the largest olive oil manufacturers in the state. They have distribution channels throughout the country. They'll take your brand and put it in places it never had a chance of getting into. We are talking giant grocery locations."

I was letting Gabe do most of the talking. I was never good with confrontations. Plus, Gabe was better at keeping his emotions in check. My first reaction in a situation like this would be to either run away and avoid the situation or start yelling back and make the situation worse. The latter was not something I did often. I wasn't aggressive by nature. In fact, I was timid if you asked anyone who knew me. I preferred that everyone got along. Maybe that's why Gabe made the day-to-day decisions at Harris & Harris even though we were fifty-fifty partners. He was also in charge of acquisitions, while I handled the administrative part of the venture.

"What about the rest of my employees?" Dimitris asked.

"It's not up to us to decide what happens to them," Gabe replied.

"You've already fired half of them."

"We had to make the business leaner. This required us to cut some costs."

"These people were like my family. Some had been with me since the day I started the business."

"They were all given a nice severance package."

"Okay, but those packages don't last forever. I know a couple of people who still haven't found work after you let them go, and that was months ago."

"Again, difficult decisions had to be made, I'm afraid."

"What am I going to say to them and their families?" he asked.

"You tell them you had no choice. The business was already struggling. And I should remind you. You came to us. Not the other way around. We saved your company from going into bankruptcy. And in the process, we did what you were unwilling or incapable of doing. We made the business profitable again."

"You didn't have to sell it," Dimitris said. "We could have bought it back from you down the road."

"We are not in the business of managing companies. We invest to make a quick return. And then we move on. Which is something I would also advise you to do," Gabe said.

Dimitris stared at us in silence. He then lowered his head. He suddenly looked defeated. My heart went out to the man. He was sixty-four years old. He'd spent his whole life building the business. And now it was gone.

Gabe pushed the white envelope toward him. It contained a check for the portion of the sale of the business to Terra Oil Incorporated. "That's more than enough money for you and your family."

"How long will it last?" Dimitris asked.

"It's up to you how you spend it."

Dimitris grabbed the envelope and stood up. He then said, remorsefully, "I just wanted to leave something behind for my children. My son was supposed to take over the business. He knows it by heart. He warned me not to get involved with you people, but being a stubborn man, I never listened to him. I was wrong."

He wiped the tears from his face and walked out of the conference room.

SIX

HELEN

The Bearded Tavern was a short walk from where Derek Starr's body was found at the bus stop. The interior of the bar was dark and dingy. It didn't help that everything from the tables to the chairs to the bar top was a shade of charcoal. The lights were yellowish and dimmed low. Also, the bar had very few windows. Those that existed were covered in drapes.

Helen understood why bars were purposely kept dark. It confused patrons as to the time of day. It made them stay longer and drink more.

The bartender was true to the name on the bar. He sported a long grayish beard that went down to his chest. He wore a baseball cap, and both his arms were heavily tattooed.

"What can I get you guys?" he said in a gruff voice.

Helen and Michael flashed their badges. She said, "We found a man down the road and were wondering if he came in here for a drink."

"He got a name?"

"Derek Starr."

"We get a lot of regulars, but I can't say I know that name. Is he in trouble?"

"He's dead."

The bartender's bushy eyebrows shot up. "Oh."

Michael sifted through the wallet in his hand. He then pulled out a driver's license and held it up for the bartender to see.

The bartender squinted. "Yeah, I think he came by last night."

"Around what time?"

"I don't know, maybe eight or nine."

"Was he alone?"

"Yeah, he was."

"And what else?"

The bartender shrugged. "He ordered a pint. Drank it at the bar and then left."

Michael jumped in. "Did he also get a bottle of beer?"

The bartender shook his head. "No. Like I said, he ordered a pint, and that's all."

"Did he talk to anyone?" Helen asked.

"No. He kept to himself."

"Have you seen him in your place before?"

"Actually, when I think about it, that was the first time he'd been here."

She thought for a moment. "Do you have security cameras?"

"Sure, I do. You wouldn't believe how many times drunk people tried to rob me."

"We want a copy of the footage."

SEVEN

HELEN

They walked back to the bus shelter.

Michael said, "I don't get it."

"Get what?" Helen asked.

"The thing about the beer bottle."

"What beer bottle?"

"The one in the victim's hand."

"Okay, what about it?"

"It feels like it was staged."

"Staged?"

"Yeah, like the victim was made to look like he'd gotten into a bar fight or something."

"He did go to that bar down the street, you know."

"Yeah, but the bartender said he ordered a glass pint, so where did he get the bottle of beer?"

Helen opened her mouth and then shut it.

"Why have another beer when he'd already had a drink at the bar?" Michael said, his voice tinged with excitement.

"Maybe, later on, he decided to get some more," she suggested.

"It still doesn't answer where he got the bottle, though."

"Perhaps, he had a case in his car."

Michael's eyebrows shot up. "So, where's his car then?"

Helen stopped and turned to him. "The sarge thinks I could teach you a thing or two about an investigation. But it looks like you could teach me something instead."

"I didn't mean... to step on your toes..." he stammered.

She smiled. "It's good that you're asking all these questions. I do the same thing. But in my case, I ask myself these questions. So, it's kind of refreshing I don't have to have conversations in my head."

They reached the bus shelter and found the medical examiner had already bagged the body.

"I assumed you guys were done with it," he said.

Robert Liesk had thinning hair, a protruding belly, and he wore round spectacles. He also had on a white lab coat. Helen had known Robert for over two decades. He never got married, and he lived alone. He'd asked her out once, right after her divorce, but she'd turned him down. It wasn't that she didn't find him attractive. It was just that she wasn't interested in a new relationship. Her divorce, although amicable, took a toll on her. Robert was also a good friend, someone she could lean on during tough times. And she didn't want to jeopardize her friendship, if the relationship turned sour.

"You in a rush to take it away?" she asked him.

"I've got two other autopsies on my schedule, so yeah, I kind of want to get out of here."

"You just want to get them done so you can finish your Taj Mahal."

Robert was obsessed with puzzles. He could be found in his basement each night with Beethoven playing in the background while he hovered over a giant table, putting all the pieces together. After completing hundreds of 2D puzzles, he'd moved on to 3D models.

"The Taj Mahal has over a thousand pieces, mind you," he said. "And I'm happy to say I'm halfway through it. When I'm done, I'll invite you over for a glass to celebrate."

She and Robert shared an affinity for fine wine. His wine cellar held close to a hundred bottles. She'd been to his place a few times to taste some of the vintages, and she could honestly say Robert had a knack for picking the best wine.

"You let me know once it's done, and I'll be there," she said. "Now, what can you tell us about our victim?"

"He was stabbed twice. Once in the torso and once in the stomach. Even before opening him up, I can tell you, the knife likely cut into his vital organs. During my preliminary examination I saw no other visible marks on his face, hands, or anywhere else on the body. Which leads me to believe he died from the trauma caused by the stab wounds."

Michael said, "Can you tell us if he was stabbed at the bus stop?"

"Are you asking me about the time of death?" Robert said.

"Um… I just want to know if he was stabbed somewhere else and dragged to this spot."

Robert rubbed his chin in thought. "He didn't bleed out here, I can tell you that."

"I knew it!" Michael said, snapping his fingers. But when he saw the look on Helen's face, he quickly sobered up. "I mean, that's what I was thinking, too."

She asked, "You think the victim may have been killed elsewhere?"

"That's a possibility," Robert replied. "The average human body has close to one-point-five gallons of blood. People bleed out a *lot,* unlike in the movies, where if a person is stabbed, all you see is a stain on their clothing. You can expect a puddle underneath a person who's been stabbed in the torso and stomach."

They mulled this over.

Helen said, "I won't keep you long. I know you've got a puzzle to get to later. But let us know your findings when you're done with the autopsy."

"You'll have a report first thing in the morning."

"Thanks, Robert."

EIGHT

LEO

He squinted behind the dark glasses. He was in a black GMC Canyon truck about a block from the bus shelter.

He went by the name of Leo. No one, except for one person, knew his real name, and Leo preferred it that way. He had spent the better part of the last decade creating his alter ego.

He was close to six feet in height. The two-inch heels in his boots pushed him up to that level. He had broad shoulders, muscular arms, and a toned stomach. He ate a high-protein diet, and he had worked out daily for the last three years. He had gone from a scrawny one-hundred-and-fifty pounds to slightly over one-ninety. He had also tanned his skin, which was now light brown.

In order to transform himself completely, he had shaved his head down to the skin, and he'd grown a heavy beard. On top of that, he preferred wearing his sunglasses at all times. Even indoors, if possible. He was doing everything he could to hide the person he was before his life had fallen apart.

The extra body mass, facial hair, and bald head were crucial in building his new persona; it made him look intimidating.

He had debated getting his arms and chest inked with prison tattoos. But he worried about their permanency. After he'd completed his mission, he would shed the extra muscles, lose the beard, and grow the hair on his head back. He would also ditch the heeled shoes and stop tanning. In short, he would go back to being who he once was. And the tattoos wouldn't be something he could easily rid himself of. Also, there was a strong probability that others could remember the tattoos and use them to identify him.

Anonymity was paramount in what he was trying to do.

In the distance, he saw the two detectives speaking to a man in a white lab coat. Leo had been here before the police had first shown up. In fact, he was the one who'd called nine-one-one. He made sure the call was short and that he muffled his voice. He'd also worn gloves, so none of his prints were on the phone.

He had seen the detectives go to the bar down the block. He wasn't concerned about what they'd find there. If everything had gone according to plan, nothing would lead back to him or his associates.

After the body had been hauled away, the detectives got inside a Ford sedan and drove off.

Leo put the car in gear and left the scene. He didn't follow the detectives. That was not part of the plan. Instead, he drove a mile down the road.

He slowed when he saw a skinny man standing on the corner. He was smoking a cigarette. The man had on a brown leather jacket, a white t-shirt, and pristine white runners. The man lowered his sunglasses when he spotted the truck pulling up.

The man flicked the cigarette away and got in the passenger seat.

"Everything okay?" the man said.

"You did good, Tyrel," Leo said.

Tyrel grinned. "Of course, I did."

As part of his new persona, Leo had spent a good deal of time with drug dealers, hustlers, and gangsters. Tyrel wanted to be one of them. But he wasn't one of them. Behind the bravado, Leo saw a scared kid.

Tyrel had just turned twenty. He had grown up in the projects. His father was serving time in prison for armed robbery. His mother was on social assistance. She was busy raising Tyrel's four other siblings. Each of them had different fathers. Tyrel was estranged from his mother. She was angry at him for not getting a stable job and helping her raise her children. As far as she was concerned, he was dead to her.

Tyrel didn't care. For the past four years, he'd been staying at a rundown apartment with another guy. They survived by selling stolen goods out of the back of the guy's van. Tyrel had a feeling the guy was cheating him out of his rightful share. But Tyrel couldn't say anything. The guy was in charge. And so, Tyrel was now looking for something bigger. Something where he could make more money.

That's where Leo came in. He was able to get Tyrel out of his current situation, which in turn, made Tyrel beholden to him.

"Come on," Leo said. "Let's go celebrate. You've earned it."

Tyrel had a big smile on his face. "Damn right, I've earned it."

NINE

HELEN

Lynn Starr wiped her nose with fresh tissue. She had shoulder-length hair with blonde highlights. Her nails were painted red, and she wore a knee-length blue dress. She was also petite. She had been crying from the moment Helen and Michael broke the news of her husband's death. At one point, Helen feared the woman would pass out. Michael had sensed the same thing. He had quickly gone to the kitchen and brought her a glass of water.

Helen saw genuine concern in Michael's eyes.

Derek Starr had gone out after a long day at work. He was still in his business suit when they'd found him on the bench. Like most men, he probably wanted to let off steam. A glass of beer would've done the trick.

Instead, he was stabbed and left for dead.

Helen knew the Starr's had two children, a seven-year-old and a five-year-old. Fortunately, both were at school at the moment.

She would need to be strong for them. She was now their sole provider.

Helen felt a knot in her stomach. The pain on Lynn Starr's face was heart-wrenching. Helen had been the conveyor of bad news dozens of times. That was part of the job. But that didn't mean she enjoyed it. On the contrary, it was the one thing she would not miss when she retired.

She felt the weight of each investigation. Some unsolved cases still haunted her. She would stay up at night, staring at the ceiling, going over every aspect of the murder. She desperately wanted to provide closure to the victim's families, and she felt personally responsible when she could not.

Helen could see the same pressure in Michael's eyes now. He was searching for some way to tell the widow everything would be all right. But until they solved this case, Helen knew that would not be possible.

She said, "Mrs. Starr, do you mind if we ask you a few questions?"

Lynn Starr looked up at her. Her eyes were raw. She sniffled and then said, "Yes… okay."

"How long have you and your husband been married?" Helen liked to start off by asking simple questions—ones the bereaved could easily answer while in a state of shock. This way, she could ease her way into the more difficult questions—ones about infidelity or betrayals.

Lynn Starr smiled. "It would've been eight years this July. We met two years before that. I was working for a travel agency. Derek was flying out a lot back in those days. And while his company covered his travels, he didn't like going through their secretary. Instead, he would call me and ask me to get him the best deals on a flight. He later told me his company paid a stipend for each trip, and if Derek could find a cheaper flight, he could pocket the difference. I spoke to him on the phone so many times that one day he showed up in person where I worked. It was around the time of the holidays, and he said he wanted to give me a Christmas card for all the money I'd saved him over the year. We got to talking, and soon he asked me out." She paused and looked down at the tissue in her hand. "He proposed to me at the airport. He got the ticket agent to make it look like there was an issue with my booking. I was then escorted by a customs agent to a room. I didn't know what was going on, but when I got to the room, I saw him down on one knee, holding a ring. There were boarding passes for all the flights I'd booked for him taped to the walls. He wanted to keep them to remind him of how our relationship had started. He loved going out of his way to surprise me."

Michael said, "We're really sorry for your loss."

"Thank you," she said.

Helen said, "Did your husband have any enemies? By that, I mean, did anyone want to hurt him?"

Lynn Starr shook her head. "No. Everyone loved Derek. He was always the life of the party."

"What did your husband do?"

"He worked as an account manager."

"For which company?"

"Chester & Associates."

Helen looked up at Michael. She could see he was thinking the same thing. Chester & Associates had been in the news lately. Helen didn't know all the details, but there was a big scandal brewing.

She asked, "Was your husband having any trouble at work?"

"He never discussed work with me. He said everything he did was secure and confidential. And he was bound by non-disclosure agreements. But yes, he was under a lot of pressure lately." She paused and then asked, "Do you think someone from his work hurt him?"

Helen shook her head. "We have no reasons to believe this at the moment. We are just trying to get a full picture of who your husband's been in contact with and what was going on prior to his death."

There was a moment of silence.

"Could your husband have gotten into an argument with someone at a bar?" Helen asked.

"Derek never got into fights," she replied. "He was very agreeable by nature."

Helen couldn't think of anything else to ask.

She pulled out her business card. "If you think of anything that might help us, please give me a call. Again, we are so sorry for your loss."

Lynn Starr took the card and nodded.

They walked to the front door.

Michael stopped and turned to face Lynn Starr. "We will do everything possible to find your husband's killer. I promise."

Lynn Starr smiled. "Thank you very much."

TEN

SIMON

I dribbled the ball between my legs and then turned left. My defender was stuck to me as I made a move to the basket. He took a swipe at the ball, but I shielded it with my body. He hit my arm as I threw the ball up; it hit the backboard and went in.

"Foul and the basket!" I roared.

"I barely touched you," he said.

I held up my arm. There was a red mark just below the wrist. I have pale skin, so I bruise easily, which helped to plead my case.

Jayson Roberts shook his head in disagreement. Jay was a good three inches taller than me. He also had long arms and long fingers. Perfect for dribbling the ball and blocking a shot. He had a dark skin tone, hazel eyes, and a trimmed afro.

I'd known Jay since we were in fifth grade. His family had just moved into the neighborhood. His dad worked for a pharmaceutical plant, and his mom was a physiotherapist. As I was never the most popular kid in school, or even in my own class for that matter, I always had difficulty making and keeping friends. Maybe my teacher so sensed my inability to socialize that she made me responsible for getting Jay up to speed in the class.

Jay didn't need any of my help. He was smart enough to pick up whatever we were learning. But for some strange reason, we formed a friendship that lasted to this day. We found out we liked the same kind of music. The same kind of movies. Even our interest in food was very similar. We both hated pickles, and we made sure to remove them from our burgers whenever we were at a fast-food restaurant.

We were at a stage when most people started having a midlife crisis. They changed jobs or entire careers. They ended their marriages and moved on with someone younger. Or they just bought themselves a fancy car.

Jay and I were still a couple of years away from hitting middle age. But I had already started questioning everything about my life. *What am I doing here? What is my purpose in life? Is this all that there is?*

On the other hand, Jay seemed even more content as he got older. He was married to a wonderful woman named Yvonne. She was a kindergarten teacher. And together, they had two beautiful daughters.

Jay beamed whenever he spoke of his wife and children. They were his pride and joy. They were what gave him a certainty in an otherwise uncertain world.

It also helped that Jay loved what he did. He worked as a lawyer for an organization that took on cases of inmates who were innocent of the crimes for which they were convicted. So far, he had exonerated six people. The process was long, requiring hundreds, if not thousands, of man-hours. The courts were quick to convict someone, but it took forever for them to overturn that conviction. For that reason, Jay's organization only took on a couple of cases at a time. And they relied heavily on donations to make sure the cases did not stall. After all, a wrongly accused person was rotting in prison while the real culprit was living a life of freedom.

I went to the free-throw line and made the shot.

Jay was still irked that I had called a foul. It was his turn. He dribbled the ball from left to right. He then took a step back and hit a three-point shot; it went straight through the net.

"Bang!" he said.

On the next play, I made the same move, and this time Jay stripped the ball cleanly off me.

He then dribbled the ball behind his back, spun around, and hit a fadeaway shot off the backboard.

"Game!" he yelled, raising his arms up to an imaginary crowd.

I wiped the sweat off my forehead and grimaced. "You got lucky today," I said.

"It seems like I'm lucky all the time."

"I'm just a little winded, okay?"

"Whatever. You're just a sore loser."

We walked off the court and up to the bleachers. I pulled out an energy drink from my gym bag and took a long sip.

"That stuff's not good for you, man," Jay said.

"All the pro athletes drink them," I said with a shrug.

"It has a lot of sugar and salt."

I made a face. "When did you become so health conscious?"

"When I turned forty." He pulled out a bottle of water. "This is all you need."

"Well, my stuff helps to repair the muscles and heal the body."

"They say that only for the commercials. A good night's rest is all you really need to repair and heal your body. Did you know that most athletes nap right before a game?"

"I didn't know that."

"They do."

"But I see them drinking this stuff during a game," I said.

Jay smiled. "You see the logo on the cup, but you don't really know what they are drinking, do you?"

I opened my mouth but then shut it. *He has a point*, I thought.

We sat down on the bench. A couple of kids had already taken possession of our basketball net.

I didn't care. I was beat.

Jay took a sip from his bottle and asked, "So, what's wrong now?"

ELEVEN

SIMON

"What?" I said, twisting my face. "Nothing is wrong."

"Listen," Jay said. "I've known you most of my life. In fact, come to think of it, I've known you longer than I've known Yvonne."

"You make it sound like we are *really* old."

"We're not young anymore, that's for sure," he said. "What I'm trying to say is that I know when something is bothering you or when you are feeling guilty about something."

I raised an eyebrow. "Now I'm guilty?"

He stared at me a moment and then sighed. "We've been best friends for a long time, so I'm just going to say it: I bet you screwed someone over, and it's eating away at you."

"How do you know I screwed someone over?"

"Okay, let me put it this way. For the past three months, I get no calls from you, not even a text message. Then today, out of the blue, you want to drop by to play ball. You know I come to this park regularly to shoot hoops. You could've come by any time before."

I shrugged. "I was busy, you know."

Jay said, "I bet there is a donation check in your wallet made out to my firm."

My eyebrows shot up. "How do...?"

He smiled. "Do you remember last Christmas when you unexpectedly wanted to go for a drink?"

My brow furrowed. "I did?"

"Yep. I had family over to my house for the holidays, but seeing that you are my best friend, I dropped everything, and I went to meet you at a bar."

"I kind of remember it now," I said

"What you probably don't remember is that when I got to the bar, you'd already had a few too many drinks. You had given the bartender a big tip in advance and told him to keep the liquor flowing. Anyway, when I showed up, you gave me a big hug. You seemed *way* too happy to see me."

"I was probably drunk," I said.

"Drunk as a skunk," Jay said. "Anyway, we got to talking, and suddenly you burst into tears. And you started blubbering like a kid. It was as if you wanted to let everything inside you out—like a dam bursting."

I was horrified at what I was hearing. What had I told Jay that I maybe shouldn't have?

He smiled. "Don't worry. You didn't say anything I didn't know or didn't have any idea of before."

"What did I tell you?" I said, afraid to ask.

"You mentioned you and Gabe help businesses stay afloat. Which I already knew from you. But you also mentioned what you really do was screw them over in the process."

I had no response to that.

Jay continued. "You talked about some tech company and how you sold the patent against the company founder's wishes. You weren't making much sense, but you were pretty torn about it."

I remember that company. MT Solutions had developed a device that enabled the user to control multiple devices using Bluetooth technology. It wasn't revolutionary. Other companies had done the same thing. But what made it unique was the fact that the AI was sophisticated enough to adapt to newer versions of any device. Which meant you never had to upgrade the software.

Ever.

This could work in other industries, but not the tech industry. The business required users to constantly purchase newer products each year. Companies already had working models of phones with bigger screens, better cameras, high-processing speeds, but they chose to release them one step at a time. They wanted repeat customers. And if they gave them all the bells and whistles at once, those customers could wait years before they changed their devices.

The owner of MT Solutions had come from humble beginnings, and he wanted to change the way the industry worked. He was concerned about how wasteful society had become, and he wanted to provide a product that could last a very long time. Consumers wouldn't have to part with their hard-earned money each year just to have a functioning product.

But by being too focused on that one product, the company was bleeding money. They'd already gone through all the funds raised through angel investors. And that's where Gabe and I came in.

Gabe knew the money wasn't in production itself but the patent to the AI. We made an offer, took control of the company, and then proceeded to sell off its valuable asset. Our firm made a lot of money, and so did the owner. It was capitalism at its best.

So, why was I so broken up about it that I had called my best friend to confess my inner turmoil while in a drunken stupor?

Because the company we sold the patent to buried the AI so it would never see the light of day. That AI could've impacted that company's bottom line going forward, and it was better for them to just make it disappear.

What Gabe and I had ignored understanding was how important this AI was to the owner of MT Solutions. He had spent years laboring over the AI while living in a tiny house with his parents and five other siblings. The AI software was his dream. His reason to leave his family behind and come to America.

While he was now a wealthy man, his purpose in life had been taken from him. Sure, he could now provide a better life for his family in his home country. That was never out of the question. He knew money made the world go round. But it was the way we went about it that broke him.

During our initial meeting, he had specifically told us the AI patent was not for sale, and we had verbally agreed to it. Or, at least, Gabe had. The owner had failed to put this in writing. He believed in a handshake and a person's word. A big mistake on his part. And a shrewd move on ours. We took advantage of his faith in us and used it against him. By giving us control, we did whatever benefited us the most.

Some would argue—and I did the same—that had we not stepped up, the company would've eventually gone into receivership. And the AI software would have died with the company. But what no one knew, except for Gabe and me, was there were other companies—mostly non-profits—who were willing to buy our share of MT Solutions in order to continue its mandate of providing a sustainable product.

Instead, we chose an option that gave us a better return on our investment.

I looked down at my shoes. "I'm sorry if I unloaded on you at the bar that day. It was probably an embarrassing situation for you."

"You were pretty inebriated, that's for sure," he said with a laugh. "And you also told me how much you loved me."

My face turned red. "I did?"
"Numerous times."

My embarrassment deepened. Not because I had professed love to my best friend, but because I didn't remember any of it.

Jay then leaned closer. "At the end of our conversation, right before I drove you back to your house, you handed me a check for ten thousand dollars."

I remembered writing it. I was at home. Alone. Sitting in front of the TV when I made the decision to do it.

"The money was greatly appreciated. And I can assure you it did a lot of good for our cause. We were able to hire someone on a part-time basis," he said. "But as your friend, I have to tell you that you can't buy your way out of a guilty conscience."

He was right. It felt like blood money to me. And by donating a portion to various charities, I was trying to cleanse myself of it.

Jay leaned in again and asked, "Now, is there a check in your wallet, or not?"

I reached into the gym bag, retrieved my wallet, and pulled out a check made out to Jay's law firm.

"Oooh, that's a lot of zeroes," he said, eyeing it.

I held the check in my hand. "You sure you want it? I mean, you know how I earned it."

"If that money helps me get an innocent person out of prison, then my conscience is clear. It's up to you to decide how you want to live your life."

I handed him the check. "Thanks for a good game. Next time I'm kicking your butt."

He laughed. "Keep dreaming, buddy."

TWELVE

HELEN

They were driving back from the Starr residence when Helen turned to Michael and said, "You shouldn't have said what you said."

Michael frowned. "What did I say?"

"You *promised* the grieving widow that you'd find her husband's killer."

"What's so wrong about that?"

"You might not be able to honor that promise."

Michael scoffed. "I think you're being too presumptuous. We've only just begun our investigation."

She asked, "Do you know how many murder investigations went without an arrest in the last decade?"

He shrugged.

"Close to fifty percent."

"I didn't know it was that high."

"And if you dig deeper into the numbers, that's two hundred and fifty thousand cases."

Michael's mouth dropped.

"That was my reaction too when I'd first heard it," Helen said. "That means we have close to a quarter of a million murderers roaming the streets right this minute. If knowing that doesn't scare you, then nothing will."

Michael stared out the window in silence.

They drove for several minutes before he turned back to her. "I was only trying to console her."

"I know you were. But giving someone hope when you aren't sure you can deliver is another thing."

"I believe I will solve who killed Derek Starr."

Helen could see he truly believed this. She then said, "It's one thing to *want* to make the world a better place. It's another thing to actually *make* it happen."

"Is this your way of preparing me for what lies ahead as a detective, or have you given into cynicism?" he asked.

"Both," she answered. "I was once naïve like you. I believed that crime never paid and that good always triumphed over bad. But in our line of work, when you see evil every day, you can't help but wonder if you've made even a small dent in the universe."

He said nothing.

She said, "As you go through your career, you'll see how hard it is to close one investigation. And when you do, you can't celebrate because there are dozens more that need to be resolved. To make matters worse, the cases keep piling up each and every day. It's like people can't stop hurting each other even for a second."

She was talking more to herself than him.

Helen then said, "I just hope you don't make the same mistakes I have. I made promises too, and I still haven't been able to live up to them."

They drove in silence for several blocks.

Michael pulled out a black object from his coat pocket. Helen saw that it was a 7-inch tablet.

"You carry that with you all the time?" she asked, curious.

"It beats walking around with a laptop."

The department had given each detective a brand-new laptop. Helen used to keep it in her Ford. But one day, her car was broken into. Fortunately, the laptop was in the trunk, or else the thief would have taken off with all her notes on the cases she was working on. As her job required her to be all over the city—especially in neighborhoods that were deemed unsavory—she had decided to keep the laptop at home. She kept mental notes of everything that occurred during the day. If she was overloaded with information, she had a small notepad in her pocket to jot it down on. At the end of the day, she would transcribe her notes onto her laptop. Those notes were vital when closing a case.

Michael plugged a USB drive into the back of the tablet and began swiping the screen.

"What're you doing?" she asked.

"I wanted to see what was on the CCTV camera footage the bartender gave us."

"You don't think I want to see what's on the footage, too?" she asked.

"Oh right. Sorry. I just wanted to get a jump on the investigation."

She pulled to the curb and parked. "Let's have a look."

"Now?"

"Yes."

"You don't want to wait until we get back to the station?" he asked.

"Listen, I didn't mean to berate you about what you said back at the Starr residence. If I was your age, I would've said the same thing. So, let me help you honor the promise you made to her."

Michael looked at her.

Helen gave him a smile.

"All right," he said.

He pressed a button on the tablet, and the screen instantly filled with a black and white image.

They could see the interior of the Bearded Tavern. The bartender was behind the counter, tending to several customers seated at the bar.

One of them was Derek Starr. He was dressed in the same suit he would later be found wearing at the bus stop. Starr had a pint in front of him. His head was low, his eyes on his drink. Next to his glass was his cell phone. In the low lighting, it wasn't easily visible at first glance. But whenever he swiped his finger over the screen, the phone would suddenly come to life.

Every so often, though, Starr would turn and look in the direction of the bar's front door, as if he was waiting for someone to walk through and greet him.

Half an hour passed before he got up off the stool and left the bar.

"Did you notice something?" Michael asked.

"What?" Helen replied.

"He doesn't have a bottle in his hand, nor is his glass empty. He doesn't appear to be drunk if you ask me."

Her brow furrowed. "Your theory might be right," she said.

"What theory?"

"His murder might have been staged."

THIRTEEN

COLE

He was five-ten, with dark curly hair, brown eyes, and he had just turned twenty-one. He was wearing a hard hat, solid steel-toe boots, and an orange reflective safety vest.

Cole Madsen worked for BB Construction. The company primarily focused on residential properties. They built town, semi and detached houses. Their recent project involved the construction of forty townhouses in an undeveloped area of Arlington.

Cole watched as a cement mixer poured concrete into a giant hole. Cole was grateful to get on this project. Construction work was hard to get these days. Even if you got on a project, the work might not last long enough to keep a steady income coming in.

They were in the process of laying the foundation for each of the townhouses. It would take six to nine months from now until the houses were ready to move into, which meant Cole could rely on being employed for at least that long.

There was a crew of ten on-site at the moment. Cole was the youngest, and as such, he was always sent to pick up lunch for the team or do whatever errands they asked of him. He didn't care. He would clean the portable toilets, just as long as they paid him.

"Hey Cole," the guy next to him said. His name was Jimmy, and he was the one who had gotten him the job. Cole had met Jimmy at a bar. Cole had just passed the legal age to drink. Jimmy had come in after a long shift, and they got to talking. Jimmy was only a couple of years older than him, but it seemed like he had been working all his life. Cole was unemployed at the time, and when Jimmy heard Cole's story, he decided to speak to his supervisor about bringing Cole aboard.

"What's up?" Cole asked him.

"I think the boss wants to see you," Jimmy replied.

Cole looked in the distance and saw their supervisor was standing on the steps of his makeshift office.

Cole left his spot and walked over to him.

"We'll talk inside," Bob Golden said. He was a short, burly man. He had hairy arms, a hairy chest, and a silver head of hair. Big Bob, as he was affectionately called, also wore a ten-thousand-dollar emerald ring on his finger. The ring was a gift to Big Bob from a grateful client. The client's project was behind schedule. The client hired Big Bob to take over the project. Big Bob completed it in a quick turnaround, and he did it under budget, something unheard of in the construction industry. The ring was a reminder of a job well done. So, Big Bob always wore it, even during the times when he chipped in by getting his hands dirty.

"Take a seat," Big Bob said.

Cole took off his hard hat and sat across from him at a small table. The table was covered with blueprints, invoices, and stationary.

Big Bob leaned back on his chair and said, "Cole, I'm afraid I'm going to have to let you go."

Cole blinked. "What did I do wrong?" he asked.

"I know about your mom, and I know how much you need the money to help her, so this wasn't easy for me to do. But you have to understand. BB Construction isn't all mine anymore. I have bosses on top of me now."

Cole knew that BB Construction had been bought up by another company. Big Bob still controlled half of BB Construction, though. But the acquisition helped him bid for bigger projects. Developers were willing to give him the contracts if they knew he was backed up by a larger company with deep pockets.

Big Bob picked up a piece of paper in front of him. "Cole, your test came back, and it showed that you had traces of cannabis in your system at the time of the testing."

Cole's mouth dropped. "I only smoked it a few times, and I told you that when you asked me about it."

"You did, but upper management isn't happy to see something like this."

Cole was silent.

Big Bob said, "As you know, each new hire has to go through a drug test. It's not something I like doing, but it's what the state regulators demand. They want to make sure you are not under the influence of any narcotics when handling large machinery."

"But I don't handle any machinery."

"I know, and I told my bosses the same thing."

"You can do another test," Cole offered. "You can do it now if you like. And I bet you won't find anything on me."

"I believe you, but that's not how it works," Big Bob said. "These tests go directly to human resources. They work with the union to make sure every crew member is clean. You can take it to the union if you like. But I can tell you. The union doesn't fight in these types of cases. You can do just about anything on the site, apart from hurting someone really badly, and the union will back you up. But in your situation, you are still on probation. This means management can fire you for any reason they want."

"I really need this job, boss," Cole pleaded.

"I know you do, and that's why I hired you, but my hands are tied. I'm sorry."

Cole knew there was no point in pushing this. His time at BB Construction was over.

He got up.

Big Bob said, "I'll leave you on the payroll for the rest of the week. It'll help when we issue your final pay."

"Thanks," Cole said.

When Cole came out of the portable office, Jimmy came over. "Why did the boss wanna see you?" he asked.

"I'm fired."

Jimmy's eyes widened. "For what?"

Cole told him.

"That sucks, man."

Cole nodded.

"Hey, listen," Jimmy said. "Why don't you drop by the bar later? I'll meet you there after the shift. Let me buy you a beer at least."

"Sure," Cole said.

FOURTEEN

HELEN

Chester & Associates was a large accounting firm in Arlington. They had over a hundred employees, and they specialized in taxation, auditing, and management consulting. Their headquarters was located in a twenty-story glass office tower, with the company occupying the uppermost levels.

Helen and Michael took the elevator up to the eighteenth floor. After introducing themselves to the woman behind the desk, they were promptly escorted to a room at the far end of the hall.

The room had floor to ceiling windows with a clear view of the waterfront. While they waited, Michael looked out the window.

"You know, my parents weren't happy when I joined the department," he said.

"I wouldn't be either if I were them."

He turned to her. "You really don't like your job, do you?"

"I never said that. I love being a detective, but I would prefer to shield my child from what I see every day on my job. A lot of it can make your stomach churn."

"But we make an impact in people's lives," he said.

"There are other ways to make an impact in people's lives, you know. For instance, my daughter works with kids who are on the autism spectrum. Some of these kids don't even know how to properly dress themselves. She teaches them how to perform basic tasks so they can one day become independent adults."

"That sounds amazing."

"Her eyes light up when she talks about them. Their small victories are her victories."

Michael thought about what she had said and turned back to the window.

"What did your parents want you to do?" Helen asked.

"Both my parents are academics," he replied. "They were hoping I'd pick a field of interest and specialize in it."

"You could've become a teacher," she said. "Teachers make the biggest impact on a young person's life."

"True, but I can't see myself having to deal with thirty kids in one class."

The glass door opened, and a woman came in. She was dressed in a dark business suit, and she had on heels. In her hand was a white folder.

"I'm Beverly Schlesinger. I'm the Vice-President of Human Resources at Chester & Associates." She held out her hand. They shook it.

"I was hoping we could meet with Mr. Brian Chester," Helen said. She knew the company was named after its founder and president. If anyone knew everything about the company, it'd be him.

"I'm afraid Mr. Chester isn't in the office today, but I'll be more than happy to answer any of your questions. Please have a seat."

They sat down at a glass table. Beverly said, "Now, why is the Arlington Police Department so interested in our firm?"

"We are here regarding one of your employees."

"You had mentioned that to our secretary on the phone, but I still don't know how this has anything to do with us."

"Your employee, Derek Starr, was found murdered this morning," Helen said matter-of-factly.

The color drained from Beverly's face. She placed a hand over her mouth to stifle a reaction.

"We spoke to his wife, and she mentioned that Mr. Starr was stressed about something at work," Helen said.

Beverly paused to compose herself. "I'm not sure what to tell you, but I mean, we're all stressed at work. That's the nature of the job."

Michael asked, "Could this have anything to do with what's being reported on the news?"

"What do you mean?"

"From what I can find browsing the internet, it looks like your firm is under investigation from not only the FBI but also the Securities and Exchange Commission."

"I agree we've gotten some bad press of late, but what does this have to do with Derek?" Beverly asked.

"That's what we're trying to find out."

Beverly licked her lips. She then said, "I can't discuss anything related to any ongoing investigations. If you want, I can forward you to our legal department. But as far as Mr. Starr is concerned, I've looked into his HR file, and there are no red flags. He was an exemplary employee. In fact, he was one of the firm's earliest hires. I can't imagine what happened to him had anything to do with our firm."

"Probably not," Helen conceded. "But we still have to see if there are any connections to his death."

"I understand, but I can assure you, no one at Chester & Associates even knew he had died until you just told me."

Helen had made sure the news outlets hadn't leaked out Starr's name until she had personally broken the news to his wife. But it was only a matter of time before the media did. As of right now, he was just someone who'd been stabbed after a night out at a bar.

Beverly said, "A lot of people knew Derek. He was one of our longest-tenured employees. They'll all be distraught at the news. We'll have to schedule a therapist to come and help them deal with this tragedy."

"Yes, of course," Helen said, disappointed their visit didn't lead anywhere. She pulled out her business card. "If there is anything anyone knows that might help us in our investigation, please give us a call."

"I will," Beverly said.

FIFTEEN

SIMON

I pulled up into the driveway in my black BMW 5 series. I'd gotten the car right after Gabe and I had completed our last deal. The car wasn't my idea, but my wife's. Vanessa thought I'd earned it after working so hard for so long.

Frankly, I've never cared much for cars. I never saw the appeal. They were tools used to get from one place to another. That's it.

Obviously, cars, like houses, were a status symbol. If you drove an expensive model, this projected an image that you were well-to-do, someone who was successful. And the more you made, the more luxurious your cars became.

On the other hand, Gabe knew more about cars than I did. Not in the sense of what kind of transmission or engine a car had, more in the sense of what kind of car one should buy as they moved up the social ladder.

I parked next to a white Mercedes SUV. It belonged to Vanessa. I'd given it to her as a birthday gift. I didn't surprise her by driving it up to the house and unveiling it to her. She told me what she wanted, and I got it for her.

Vanessa worked for a non-profit that focused on the wellbeing of children in poorer regions of the world. They were, unfortunately, struggling the most. Civil war. Famine. Corruption. You name it. These places were hit with it.

I could see how our lifestyle may give people the wrong impression. Vanessa was asking people for money to help the needy while she lived in relative comfort. I had asked her the same thing once before, and her answer was that the biggest donors were not the average person but people with wealth and money. By living among them, she could convince them to divert some of their charitable efforts toward her and the organization. Unlike what you saw in the movies, people with affluence gave away a substantially larger amount of their money than those who weren't in the same position.

In all fairness, Vanessa took a small salary for her work with the non-profit, so pretty much I was paying for everything else. And I liked the fact that she helped people. I mean, I don't consider what I do helping in any way. Mine was pure business. How much can I get back for what I've invested.

I put the BMW in park, and got out. The house was close to five-thousand square feet. It had four bedrooms, five bathrooms, a swimming pool in the backyard, a gym and sauna in the basement, and it came with a nanny suite. As we don't have any children, the suite is currently being used as extra storage.

I entered the grand lobby. It had a massive chandelier, which cost thirty-thousand dollars to build and install. I thought it was a waste of money, but Vanessa thought it would raise the value of the house in case we decided to sell it down the road. The floors were covered in Italian marble, and most of the furniture was imported from all over the world.

The house was far too big for just two people. We both worked long hours, and so it was empty most of the day. But Vanessa was happy, and as they said, a happy wife is a happy life.

I went into the kitchen, and there was no one there. Even the family and living rooms were quiet. Vanessa loved to cook—I was glad because I couldn't cook to save myself—so either she was behind the stove whipping up something delicious, or she was curled up on a chair in the family room with a book in her hand.

I walked up the spiral staircase and went into the master bedroom.

I nearly lost my breath at the sight of her. She had on a backless black dress. Her smooth blonde hair, which was usually tied into a ponytail, flowed down her shoulders. Her green eyes were accentuated by dark mascara. And she had on bright red lipstick.

She was sitting in the make-up chair when she caught me staring at her through the mirror.

"You okay there, big boy?" she said with a grin. "You look like you've never seen a girl before."

I smiled. "Not a girl this beautiful."

She got up and walked over to meet me. I am five-seven. Vanessa is two inches taller than me. Some men would find that awkward or intimidating, but not me. I felt there was more of her I could love.

She kissed me and then made a face. "Oh dear, I got lipstick on you," she said.

I didn't bother wiping it off. "Good. I always wanted to see how I looked with make-up."

She smiled. "Now go and get ready. We're already running late."

I frowned. "Late for what?"

"We're going out to celebrate the closing of your big deal. Didn't Gabe tell you?"

"No."

"Well, I just spoke to Deidre, and they are meeting us at that restaurant we were always thinking of trying."

"What restaurant is that?" I asked.

"You know I'm not good with names. It's the one that's supposed to have the best calamari."

My shoulders sank. "I don't feel like celebrating."

"You always say that, but once you get out, you end up having a good time."

"Yeah, sure, after I get a couple of drinks in me." I then pulled her closer to me. I grinned. "Why can't you and I celebrate alone tonight?"

She stared at me. I could get lost in her eyes.

"How about this? We go and try to enjoy ourselves, and after dinner, you might get a reward yourself," she said with a wink.

"I like the sound of that," I said, still grinning.

SIXTEEN

HELEN

The Arlington PD was located in a red brick building that was once a community center. When the city decided to go on a hiring spree, they needed more space to house the new recruits. They also needed a prime location that would enable them to cover a wider area for policing. After an exhaustive search, the city chose the community center. The building was already in dire need of repairs. Most of the HVAC systems had to be upgraded. The oil furnace was costing the city twice as much to heat the interior, so that had to be changed as well. The plumbing consisted of clay piping that was installed decades before, which made the sewage back up on a regular basis.

It took two years and millions of dollars in taxpayer money to convert the community center into a place where the police could serve the people of Arlington properly. The force had over five hundred police officers and over a hundred civilians, all working under one roof.

The homicide unit wasn't at the top of the police food chain, so to speak. That was the drugs and narcotics unit. They were the ones who were on the news on a regular basis, busting gangs and hauling cash and drugs into the division. And so, the top floor of the building was given to the narcs, while the lower floor belonged to the homicide unit.

Murders took a long time to solve. It was also not very glamorous. Detectives didn't normally pose with the suspects who were charged with the murder. The narcs, on the other hand, proudly showed off for the cameras the cash, drugs, and weapons they had seized.

Helen never cared who got the most publicity. The only thing she cared about was doing her job. But that didn't stop her from putting up a fight to get a cubicle by the windows when the department first moved into the new building.

She felt she'd earned it. After close to thirty years on the force, and most spent in homicide, it was her right to get first dibs on where she sat on the floor. Plus, she was on her way out, so she wouldn't be holding the spot for years to come.

As a newbie to the unit, Michael was relegated to the middle of the floor, surrounded by other cubicles and no windows to glance out of if he was in the mood to do so.

They were seated behind her desk, going over the investigation, when she asked, "Who called it in?"

"According to the nine-one-one dispatcher, the call had come in from a pay phone two blocks from where we found the body," Michael replied.

"And let me guess, the caller didn't leave a name."

"You guessed right," he said. "Do you want to hear it?"

Her eyebrows shot up. "You have the recording?"

"That's the first thing I requested when I got to the scene."

She smiled. "Well, aren't you the eager beaver."

He shrugged.

"All right. Let's have a listen."

He pulled out his cell phone, pressed a few buttons, and held it out for her. She put the phone to her ear.

Dispatcher: 9-1-1. Do you need police, medical, or fire?

Caller: Police.

Dispatcher: And what is the trouble?

Caller: There is a man dead at a bus stop.

Dispatcher: Where are you calling from?

[the caller gave the name of the intersection]

Dispatcher: I will send a cruiser right away. Can you…?

The caller hung up.

Helen returned the phone to Michael. "Not much to work on, I'm afraid."

"That's what I thought, too. And if you listened carefully, the caller's voice sounded far away, like he was cupping the end of the phone to muffle his voice."

Helen shrugged. "That's nothing to be suspicious about. A lot of people don't want the police to know who they are. Even if they have nothing to do with the crime, they just don't want to be bothered by it."

"Maybe that's why the caller didn't use his cell phone."

"That would be my guess," she said with a shrug.

"Or," Michael said, "he could be the killer."

"What?"

"Yeah, he could be the one who murdered Derek Starr."

Helen crossed her arms over her chest. "I would like to hear this explanation."

"Think about it," Michael said. "The caller never said he'd seen a guy bleeding at the bus stop. He said there was a *dead* guy at the bus stop. How would he know Starr was dead? Unless he was responsible for the murder."

Helen laughed in disbelief. "That's the most absurd thing I've ever heard."

"Is it?" Michael said. "I mean, when I showed up at the scene, I actually thought someone had made a mistake because Derek Starr looked like he was asleep on the bench."

"I thought the same thing myself," Helen said, conceding a point.

"Exactly," Michael said, clapping his hands together.

"Don't get too excited," she said. "What would be the benefit for the killer to make the call? Tell me that."

Michael fell silent.

She said, "I don't think we can glean too much from the call. Clearly, the caller had seen the blood on Derek Starr's shirt. The caller had probably even gone up close to check up on him. And when there was no movement from Starr, he proceeded to inform the authorities." She turned back to the notes on her desk. "While I applaud you in thinking outside the box, I don't believe the caller is our killer. If he was, then he should be on *America's Dumbest Killers*."

SEVENTEEN

SIMON

The dinner was far better than I'd expected. We were in a French restaurant that was, according to the Michelin Guide, rated a 3 star. I don't know much about the grading of restaurants, but I'm told that's like a gold standard for the industry.

I don't even know what anyone at our table ordered. All I know is that it cost a pretty penny, and it was all being paid for by my older brother.

Gabe was beaming from ear to ear. He'd already ordered a second bottle of champagne for the table. Gabe worked hard, and he played hard. In our twenties, when neither of us was married, he'd suddenly hop on a plane and go to Vegas for the weekend. Or jet off to some island in the Mediterranean. Or even some music festival in Europe. Gabe was always spontaneous. It helped that he was an extrovert. Something I was not.

I've always wondered how two brothers could be so opposite.

I never liked being the center of attention. If there was a dance, I'd be the guy in the corner observing all the dancers on the main floor. Vanessa thinks I'm anti-social, but I'm not. I like the company of other people. It's just that I don't like being surrounded by people I don't know. I'm not much of a small talker, and so it takes a lot of energy for me to start up a conversation or even sustain it.

If Vanessa wasn't dragging me out to various social events, I'd probably be cocooned in my house. Vanessa inspired me to be a better man. She loved and believed in me. She pushed me to get out of my shell.

I always wondered how someone like me managed to snag a woman like her. Vanessa could've been a model. In fact, she had modeled for department store magazines when she was younger, displaying the latest outfits that were on sale for that week, but she didn't turn it into a career.

I couldn't take full credit for meeting Vanessa. That privilege went to Gabe's wife, Deidre.

Deidre was just as gregarious as Gabe. She had dark hair, dark eyes, and high cheek bones. She, too, could have been a model if she'd chosen to become one. Deidre had a smile that could disarm anyone.

Gabe had known Deidre since they were teenagers. They were the typical high school couple. Gabe was the quarterback for the football team, while Deidre was one of the team's cheerleaders.

Their wedding had close to five hundred guests, and it cost nearly a hundred grand. They had two beautiful children. Charlie was ten, and Lilly was seven. I adored my niece and nephew. I loved when they called me "uncle."

I'd always dreamed of becoming a father, but when the doctors told us Vanessa couldn't have kids, I pushed that dream away. We'd discussed adopting, but with both our careers eating up so much of our time, that topic got pushed aside as well.

I had resigned myself to the fact that I would never be a parent. And I was okay with this because I had Vanessa by my side to share our pain together.

I'd never had much success with women, for obvious reasons. I've always been shy, and I've been told I don't take rejection easily. Most of my relationships didn't move past the first date, and if they did, they wouldn't last more than three months. When I look back now, most of those relationships fell apart for one reason or another. Either I was too needy, or they were.

I've always held onto this romantic notion of what a family should be. And yes, men weren't too far apart from women in what they wanted. They, too, desired a situation that gave them comfort and security.

In my case, I wanted a house with a large back yard, with two kids—ideally, a boy and a girl—and a pet. I'm allergic to dogs, so I'd go with a cat or even a hamster. Any animal would do to round out the family nucleus.

We'd play board games on weekends, have pizza and movie nights, or even go ice skating during the cold winter months.

This might not come as a surprise, but I'm a lousy skater. And my first date with Vanessa was at a skating rink. Gabe was so sick and tired of listening to me moan about my lack of a love life that Deidre— by then his wife—had set Vanessa and me up on a blind date.

I made a complete fool of myself that night. I fell on my face and my butt a dozen times. But through it all, Vanessa kept helping me get back up. That's when I knew she was the one. She never laughed at my awkwardness. She encouraged me to keep trying.

As I looked at her across the table, my heart swelled with emotion.

I was truly the luckiest man alive.

EIGHTEEN

COLE

Jimmy tried to cheer him up, but Cole wasn't feeling it. He had a great chance to build something—a career even—and now it was gone. He was certain that after the townhouse project, Big Bob would pick him for another.

Cole was eager to learn. He just needed a chance. And he blew it by smoking weed the night before he started his first day of work. He had never worked on a construction site before, and he was nervous. His other jobs had been working at an electronics shop, at a fast-food restaurant, and even a gas station. The construction position was going to be his highest-paying job so far. The union had negotiated a standard hourly rate for each of their members, so Cole didn't even have to haggle over the pay. All he had to do was show up on time, do the job that his supervisors wanted him to do, and collect his paychecks.

Jimmy assured him that he'd help him find more work, but Cole knew that would not be easy. His next employer would want to know why he was let go from his previous job. Cole could make up a lie, but the moment they contacted BB Construction, they would have to tell them the truth.

Cole felt like he had let everyone down.

He had taken the job for his mom. The moment she was diagnosed, she had to stop working. She was now relying on him to run the house.

Jimmy had gone out on a limb for him. Big Bob trusted Jimmy, and Cole had betrayed that trust by going into work with marijuana in his system.

After two beers, Jimmy had to go home. He had another shift in the morning. Jimmy told him to give him a call if he needed anything.

Cole knew he wouldn't be calling him any time soon. They weren't really friends. Jimmy had his own group he hung around with. They were mostly people from BB Construction. Now that Cole was no longer part of the crew, he didn't have anything to contribute to their meetings.

He waved goodbye to Jimmy and decided to leave the bar as well.

He felt like crap as he walked down the street. Getting fired was never easy, especially when you were desperate, to begin with.

Cole had seen his share of difficulties in his short life. He knew the value of money. He couldn't count the number of times he and his mom had moved. It felt like every two years, they were packing up and driving someplace new. Their travels had to do with whatever work his mom could find.

Things were tough growing up. He'd spent most of his childhood being alone at home, watching TV to pass the time. His mom would leave prepared meals in the fridge for him, which he would eat throughout the day.

He never blamed his mom for leaving him by himself because he knew she had no choice. She was working, so they had a roof over their heads and food on the table.

He would stare at the clock, and he would pray for it to speed up. He couldn't wait for his mom to burst through the door with a smile on her face, which she always did. She would hug him and give him dozens of kisses. He would protest and tell her to stop, but deep down, he loved every minute of it.

When she was home, it felt like she'd never left. She would turn on some music, and together, they would make dinner. She would sing to him. She would even dance. Those were the happiest moments of his life.

But when she got sick, it felt like a cruel slap to the face.

She'd already been through enough. It wasn't easy raising a child on her own. But now that he was an adult, he thought their luck had finally turned.

It hadn't.

Instead, he had to abandon his dream of going to college and giving him and his mom a chance at a better life.

He turned the corner and kept walking.

He saw a park up ahead. It was dark at this time of the night, but he knew where he was going.

He kept moving deeper into the park until he saw movement up ahead. He then saw a silhouette underneath the lamplights. When he got closer, the silhouette morphed into a man.

NINETEEN

COLE

The man was wearing a hoodie, a puffy jacket, baggy jeans, and basketball shoes. His name was James Packer, but he liked going by the nickname, Buddy.

A smile broke across Buddy's face when he recognized who it was. "Cole, what're you doing here, man?"

"I came to see you," Cole said.

"Last time you came by here was when there was snow on the grass."

"Yeah, I've been busy."

"So, how can I help you?"

"I need a hit."

The smile faded from Buddy's face. "Everything okay?"

Cole looked away.

"Is it your mom?"

Buddy had been raised by a single mother, too. Like him, he and his mom had moved around many times as well. Most evenings and weekends, they would play video games in Buddy's room. When Buddy's mom died, Cole and his mom took him in. He stayed with them for over a year.

"She's still the same," Cole said with a shrug.

"So, why do you need a hit?"

"I just got fired."

Buddy's brow furrowed. "I heard you'd started doing construction or something."

"I did."

"So, why'd you get fired then?"

"For smoking weed."

Buddy's eyes widened. "Are you serious?"

"I am."

"And you want more?"

Cole shrugged. "I figured, what's the worst that can happen now? They can't fire me twice."

Buddy made a face. "Where'd you get your supply from?"

"I got it from you, man."

"You had been keeping the stash for that long?" Buddy asked, surprised.

"I don't smoke it every day."

"But you got fired because of it?"

"I needed to let off some stress."

"Well, that sucks."

Cole pulled out some bills. "How much is it going for?"

Buddy shook his head. "I ain't gonna charge you. You're family."

They found a bench and lit up.

The drug business was notorious for violence. Each gang had marked their territory, and if you took even a step into their turf, they retaliated with force. Buddy wasn't affiliated with any gangs. That's why he sold his goods in the park.

Buddy blew out thick smoke. "So, what're you going to do now?"

Cole took a toke and his eyes immediately watered. "Wow, that's strong."

Buddy grinned. "It sure is. The best on the street, if you ask me."

Cole coughed, controlled his composure, and then took another toke. He didn't want Buddy to think he couldn't handle the stuff.

"Do you need a partner?" Cole asked.

Buddy stared at him. "You mean, selling weed?"

"Yeah. I mean, together, we could double whatever business you're doing now."

Buddy shook his head. "No way, man. You're not cut out for this business."

"How hard is it to sell this stuff?"

Buddy fell silent.

"Listen," Cole said. "I didn't mean no offense, but don't people come to *you* instead of you going to them?"

"Sure, people seek me out, but you don't know if the person buying the weed is an undercover cop or not. Plus, some people don't have the cash, but they still want the goods. You know what I mean?"

Cole knew. Robbery and assault were common on the streets. People got beat up just for wearing the latest smartwatch. And when it came to drugs, you could get shot.

"So, why do you still do it?" Cole asked.

"I'm expecting a kid, man."

"Really?"

Buddy nodded.

"Congrats."

"Thanks."

"Where're you staying these days?"

"I'm living with my girlfriend at the moment. Her parents are letting us stay in the basement rent-free until the baby arrives."

"When is the baby due?"

"In three months. And then we gotta find a place to rent, you know."

"Does your girlfriend know what you do?"

Buddy smiled. "She used to be one of my clients."

Cole laughed. "That's crazy, man."

Cole took one last long toke and prepared to flick the stub of the joint away

Buddy said, "Blow it out and put it in your pocket."

"What?" Cole said.

"This is a public park. If people see toke stubs on the ground, they'll know something's going on, and next thing you know, the cops will be driving around during the night. I like this spot. My customers know where to find me, and if things get dangerous, the park is open and has lots of exits for me to make a run for it."

Cole nodded and put the stub in his pocket. He then stood up. "Thanks for the smoke," he said.

"Hey, listen," Buddy said. "I know a guy who might be able to help you get out of your current situation."

"Who is he?"

"He's a new client of mine."

"What does he do?"

"I never asked him, but I know he's looking for people. I'll give him a call for you if you want."

"That'd be great. Thanks."

TWENTY

LEO

He hung up the phone with a frown on his face. Although things were going according to plan, there was still a possibility for it all to derail. They'd been planning this for years. This was personal. Something they had no choice but to do. The world was filled with injustices, and he never expected they'd find themselves at the end of one.

Some would argue he'd wasted the last ten years of his life. But he would counter that when you love someone so much, you will do anything for them.

What happened tore his family apart. He began to withdraw from everything and everyone. He began to drink more. He then dabbled in recreational drugs—anything to dull the pain.

The drugs and alcohol only made things worse.

Instead of solving the problem his family was suffering through, he became the problem. They had to divert their attention to him, to help him grieve *his* loss. Which only made him angrier. He was never the bedrock of the family. His older brother was. But after he was gone, Leo was expected to take over. But he was weak. He was always the sensitive one. And he let his emotions destroy whatever relationships he was involved in, put a rift between him and his remaining siblings, and led him to end up homeless.

He'd spent countless days sleeping on park benches and alleyways.

If it weren't for another person, he would've died on the streets. He would've been another statistic. A person who'd let his vices destroy him.

This person pulled him out of the pits of hell, guided him to sobriety, and told him the only way out of his misery was revenge.

His family had been wronged. *He* had been wronged. And if he focused his energies on going after the people that hurt him and his family, the fire that was burning a hole inside him would simmer down.

The pain would never fully go away. It never did when someone had endured tragedy. But it would get better.

That was why he was the face of the operation while this other person worked behind the scenes. There was a lot at stake for both of them. Neither wanted to go to prison. But neither was willing to let this plan fail.

They'd gone over every scenario. Looked at them with a microscope. Made sure that none of it ever came back to bite them. Their plan was sound, but there was a huge part that required human involvement.

There was one thing they knew for sure. People didn't always follow instructions. And even if they did, there was still the potential of them making a mistake. And if that mistake was monumental, then there was nothing he or this other person could do to fix it.

They had a backup plan for such situations. In case things fell apart. But they'd been working on this for so long that to not see it through until the end would be worse than never doing it in the first place.

They weren't going to get another stab at it. This was their one and only chance. And *he* had to make sure they didn't fail.

Once everything was over, when they'd succeeded in their mission, maybe then he could start his life over again.

That brought a smile to his face.

TWENTY-ONE

SIMON

I was glad Vanessa convinced me to come to the restaurant. We laughed. We drank. Gabe told a few stories from our childhood. Most were about me. Normally, I would be embarrassed and irritated, but as the audience was our wives, I didn't take any offense.

I'd known Deidre back when she started dating Gabe in high school. And Vanessa was my wife. I believed she should know everything about me, warts and all.

Before we got married, Vanessa had asked one thing of me. She wanted me to always be honest with her. Her father had cheated on her mother. But it was not his philandering ways that broke her mother. It was his constant lies.

He would tell her that he loved her and would stop seeing other women and that nothing else mattered but her and the kids. But behind her back, he would keep cheating on her.

It took Vanessa's mother eleven years before she finally had the courage to leave her father. She regretted not leaving sooner. Her youth and beauty were behind her, and so were the suitors looking to be with her. Plus, she now had three kids to take care of.

Had she not believed his lies and seen him for what he was, a two-timing scoundrel, she would have walked away with just Vanessa, her oldest child at the time. She adored her other children as every mother did, but she would have had them with a man who cared for and respected her. Instead, she spent the remaining years of her life bitter about how her husband had robbed her of the opportunity of living a different, perhaps even better, life.

Vanessa didn't want that for herself. If I was cheating on her, she wanted to know the truth. This way, I had a better chance of keeping her than if I lied to her. Because once the truth came out, which it always did, I would lose her for good.

I had promised her and myself I would never break my wedding vows. And I never have. Vanessa was my heart, my soul, my everything. It sounds mushy, but I don't know any other way to describe it. She is my Yin to my Yang.

Okay, I'll stop with the clichés now.

Outside the restaurant, we waved goodbye to Gabe and Deidre and made our way to our car, which was parked on the opposite side of the parking lot.

I was smiling as we held hands and walked.

"I know what you're thinking," she said.

"What?" I asked.

"You're thinking about your special gift once we get home."

I blinked. "I had completely forgotten about it," I said. But then my smile turned into a grin. "Now that you mention it forget speed limits. I'm getting us home in record time."

She laughed. "Okay, then what were you smiling about if not that?"

I faced her and wrapped my arms around her. "I was thinking how blessed I am to be with you."

"Well, you should feel lucky," she said, teasing. "I'm still a catch in many circles."

"Yes, you are," I said and kissed her.

We turned and walked up to my BMW. I pressed the key fob, and the car beeped as it unlocked. Vanessa opened the passenger side door and got in. I walked around the vehicle to the driver's side.

I grabbed the door handle.

I caught something moving in the corner of my right eye.

Before I could see what it was, I was pushed up against the door from behind.

The next moment, I felt a sharp pain across the side of the head. My ears began to ring loudly, and I was instantly disoriented.

A searing pain shot up through the side of my body, just below my ribs.

Someone's punching me!

My knees buckled, and I tried to hold on to the side view mirror to stay up.

I then heard a scream.

Vanessa!

I don't know what came over me just then, but I swung my elbow behind me. By doing this, I lost my grip on the side view mirror. As I fell to the ground, I took one more swing, and it connected with something fleshy.

I hit the concrete, my head inches from the BMW's front tire.

I was then able to face my assailant.

He was wearing a hoodie, and his face was covered by a balaclava.

He balled his fist, and he hit me squarely on the mouth.

I tasted blood.

My upper lip was split open.

He raised his other hand up, but when he brought it down again, I was ready for it. I blocked his attack with my forearm, and I managed to get a grip on his left wrist.

My only thought was: *I can't let him keep hitting me.*

He tried to shake me off, but my grip held. He kicked me, his boot hitting my torso, but I didn't let go.

I then heard sounds. They were screams and shouts.

My assailant yanked his hand back. My fingers slipped off his wrist.

I watched as he disappeared from view.

I lay on the cold concrete for seconds, which felt like minutes.

I then saw a shadow fall over me. It was Vanessa.

She had a look of fear and concern on her face.

She said something to me, but my ears were still ringing.

I caught the movement of her lips. *"Are you okay?"*

"I'm fine," I said.

I felt more shadows over me. Someone strong pulled me up to my feet.

"You okay, buddy?" I heard a man's voice ask.

"I'm fine," I said, not looking at him.

"You're bleeding," Vanessa said.

I touched my upper lip; it stung.

We were suddenly surrounded by more people.

I heard more voices.

"*What happened?*"

"*Is he all right?*"

"*Did someone call the police?*"

I suddenly wanted to get away from there. Get away from all the commotion around me.

"Let's go home," I said to Vanessa.

"But you're hurt," she said.

"*Please,*" I begged.

She saw the look in my eyes. I was scared and in shock. "Okay," she said. "Get in the car. I'm driving."

TWENTY-TWO

HELEN

She unlocked the front door and entered. She punched in the alarm code on the panel next to the door, waited for a second for the alarm to disable, and then shut the door behind her.

She was exhausted, both mentally and physically.

The Derek Starr investigation was still in its infancy, and she was already feeling the pressure. More so now than in any other investigation.

Maybe it was time to call it quits. Retirement was something she'd thought of for a long time. She just couldn't decide on the right day to hand in her badge and gun.

Speaking of which, she thought.

She walked over to the kitchen. Her lockbox was atop the fridge. She entered the pin code and then placed her weapon and badge inside.

With age, she had begun to forget all the passwords and PIN numbers one had to know in order to function in this day and age. There was one for her email. One for the debit and credit cards. One for her home alarm. One for her laptop—the list went on and on.

In order to make it easy to remember, she used her daughter's date of birth as a numeric combination, and for the alphabetical password, she used a variation of her first name, Emily.

There was no way she would ever forget her only child's name or DOB. That was the one thing that was forever ingrained in her mind.

One time, after a long and draining day at work, she couldn't remember the code to her home alarm, even though it was just four digits. Was it month and then day? Or day and then month? Or was it month and last two digits of the year? After three failed attempts, the siren activated, waking every neighbor on the street.

She then had to call the alarm company and provide a security word that only she would know. The security word was, obviously, Emily. Only then did the alarm become disabled. However, by then, all the neighbors were out, wondering what was going on.

In order to avoid future embarrassment, she hung a calendar on the wall next to the alarm panel. On it, she had scribbled in blue ink: DAY/MONTH.

That way, she would never forget it was the day Emily was born and the month she was born.

She closed the lockbox and then opened the fridge. If she was hoping to find something edible for dinner, she was sorely disappointed.

She barely had time to do groceries, forget preparing a meal. She was never good behind the stove, to begin with. Her ex-husband, Paul, was the one who did most of the cooking when they were together. When it was her turn to cook, she'd order takeout instead. Emily loved those nights when they'd eat pizza, Chinese, or even Indian food for dinner. And Helen couldn't blame her. Paul wasn't a great cook. He did it out of necessity. There were only so many days one could eat out. Fortunately for them, when Emily was just a baby, Paul's mother would come over and cook meals that'd last for days.

When she was certain there was nothing in the fridge, she moved her attention to the freezer. Fortunately, she found a box of chicken nuggets and a bag of French fries. While she did not know how to cook, she did know how to follow instructions on the side of a box.

She preheated the oven and then placed a tray of nuggets and French fries inside. She then headed down to the basement. In her cellar, there were bottles upon bottles of red wine. She looked at the label of each bottle, even though she knew the contents of her inventory by heart. She liked the feel of the bottle in her hand as she pondered which one to savor tonight.

She'd dreamed of moving to the south of France. She would purchase a vineyard and spend the remaining years of her life tending to it. But she knew she would do no such thing. Her daughter was in Arlington, and so was her grandchild, Lucy. She'd already missed too many important events in Emily's life, and she was not about to do the same for Lucy's.

Helen had a laundry list of things she wanted to do once her career was over and done with. She'd make more of an effort to connect with Emily. They were never close to begin with, and with time passing by, they were becoming more distant. This was Helen's fault, not Emily's. As a parent, she should have invested more time and energy in her child's everyday life. Instead, she was busy running after bad guys. She never realized that she had sort of become a bad guy in her own daughter's life.

When she'd made her selection, she took the bottle upstairs.

She checked the oven, and when she was satisfied the nuggets and fries were just right, she transferred them from the hot tray to a plate. She grabbed the bottle of wine and moved to the kitchen table. She didn't open the bottle, though. That was for later.

She slowly ate the nuggets and fries. They were bland even with a side of ketchup. Once done, she grabbed the bottle and an empty glass and went upstairs. She changed into something more comfortable and plopped onto the bed.

She finally opened the bottle and poured half a glass of red wine.

She picked up a book on the other side of the bed. *The Searching Man* was about one man's journey through life in search of meaning and purpose. It was written in the first-person. She'd read all the author's previous books, so she was eager to see what he'd come up with in his new release.

She took a sip from the glass and flipped to the page she'd stopped on the night before.

This was the time she most looked forward to all day. She didn't care about the investigations she was working on, or what was even happening in the world, for that matter.

All she cared about was that she had a good glass of wine, a good book to get lost in, and her bed to keep her warm and comfortable.

TWENTY-THREE

SIMON

I lay in bed as I stared out the window. The blinds were open just an inch, allowing a burst of morning light to stream through.

I was in my bedroom. I'd had a fitful night's sleep. My mind had kept going back to the ordeal from the night before.

Vanessa wanted to drive me straight to the hospital. She thought I needed stitches to seal the cut on my upper lip. But I had protested. I wanted to go home. I wanted to hide. I wanted to erase what I'd been through.

The bleeding had stopped by the time we got to the house. The cut wasn't as bad as we'd thought it was. She applied ointment, so the wound didn't get infected.

I had managed to take a hot shower. My entire body hurt when I did. I saw bruising on the side, just below the ribs. But I was relieved there was nothing broken. I'd been through my share of mishaps, so I knew when something was broken or not.

Gabe was the adventurous type, and as the younger brother, I wanted to be just like him. If Gabe got a skateboard, I got one, too. If Gabe went rollerblading, I did, too. That didn't mean I was good at either of them. I'd had a concussion, a dislocated shoulder, had one of my fingers snapped in half, a hairline fracture in my ribs, and even a broken hand.

Hearing this, anyone would think I was fearless. On the contrary, all those things were due to me being clumsy and stupid. Just because Gabe could jump his bike over a set of cement stairs didn't mean I could do that too.

Also, a lot of the injuries happened because Gabe and his friends goaded me into doing those stunts. Gabe never wanted me to tag along with him when he went out. He only did it because our mother told him to. Instead of making sure I stayed out of trouble, he and his friends got me into even more trouble.

They used me as the victim of his pranks. They'd make me go up to a girl and tell her I loved her and I wanted her to have my babies. The girl wouldn't take too kindly to such an affront. Not only would I be embarrassed as Gabe and his friends would holler and laugh at me, but I would also be left with a mark across my face from where the girl had slapped me.

After the shower, Vanessa had given me painkillers, and I'd gone straight to bed. Right before I had succumbed to the meds, I had thought about my special gift after dinner.

My face flushed. I had gone through a traumatic event, and the only thing on my mind was whether I'd get lucky or not.

I looked at the other side of the bed. It was empty.

Vanessa had a fundraiser to go to. I'd asked her to stay and be with me. She kissed me and told me she'd come home early. She even promised to make me my favorite meal: steak and mashed potatoes.

While I was disappointed that she wasn't here with me, I understood why she left. Desperate children in poor countries relied on the money raised by the non-profit. Their suffering was much worse than what I'd gone through.

I was a grown man. I was shaken by what had happened last night, my ego bruised by the beating I'd taken. But I would survive.

I decided to stop feeling sorry for myself and get up.

I went into the bathroom. I cupped cold water in my palms and splashed it over my face. My eyes were red and tired. A few more hours of sleep would fix that.

My upper lip, on the other hand, was purple and swollen. It looked like a bee had stung me. It hurt when I tried to smile.

I dried my face and went downstairs.

TWENTY-FOUR

SIMON

The house was dark and empty. I quickly opened the curtains and let the strong morning light brighten the space.

I then went into the kitchen. I smelled coffee. Vanessa was an early riser. She liked to do an hour of yoga before going to work. She would always brew an extra cup for me.

I filled my cup from the coffee pot.

I spotted a note attached to the fridge:

Babe. I haven't forgotten about your special gift. Luv. V.

I smiled. Vanessa always knew how to make me happy.

I then saw my cell phone on the kitchen counter. I must have left it there before going up to shower. I remembered there was blood on my clothes and I couldn't wait to take them off.

How hard is it to remove blood stains from a white shirt? I wondered.

I hated having to throw out a four-hundred-dollar dress shirt, but that's what I would have to do.

There was still a thirty-percent battery on the phone. I swiped left, entered my PIN, and a photo of Vanessa and me came up on the screen. It was taken during our honeymoon. We'd gone on a trip through the Greek islands. That was almost fifteen years ago. We looked like young lovebirds. My hair was thick and black, and my skin was tanned and smooth. Vanessa didn't look like she'd aged one bit. If we decided to re-create this photo now, I'd look like I was her creepy uncle.

I shuddered at the thought. Mental note: start working out and eating healthy.

There were several missed calls and voice messages on my phone.

I checked the first one. It was from Gabe.

"Hey man, I just heard what happened from Vanessa. I hope you also got a punch or two in there. Let that guy know you can't mess with the Harris boys." Gabe was always trying to make me stronger—a fighter. In truth, I did get my attacker with my elbow. "Don't worry about coming down to the office," he said. "You've earned a break. I'll try to drop by the house later today. No. Wait. I think Charlie has soccer practice today. Vanessa told me you didn't want to go to the hospital, so I'm guessing it's not so bad. Maybe I'll see you at the office then."

I shook my head. My brother wasn't great with sympathy, or other emotions for that matter. At our dad's funeral, I remember he didn't shed a single tear, even though dad and Gabe were very close. Dad was grooming him to take over the firm from a very young age. They'd spent more time together than I ever got with our father.

The next message was from mom.

"Darling," she said in a faux British accent. My mother wasn't born in England, nor was she raised there. She was born on a farm in Missouri. She'd get up at the crack of dawn to milk cows or feed the chickens. Her childhood was hard and rough, and she would spend her adulthood trying to erase her past. "I'm terribly sorry to hear what happened. You need to go to the police and tell them everything. You need to also go to the hospital and get yourself checked out. If you want, I can set up an appointment with Dr. Hershfield." Dr. Hershfield was my doctor since I was a baby. He was now seventy-two years old. He only came to his clinic twice a week. Even then, he was only there for a couple of hours. Why he hadn't retired was beyond me. It wasn't like he needed the money. Dr. Hershfield owned a house in Arlington, one in the Hamptons, and another in Florida. "You have to document everything you went through. Your physical and emotional pain. *Everything.* If we find who did this to you, we will sue them for every penny." I rolled my eyes. My mom was overly dramatic. She was always concerned for mine and Gabe's well-being. But she was even more concerned about compensation for even the smallest slight. We had lawyers on retainers because of her. "Once you feel better, you should come see me, but not today. I've got a bridge game with the girls, okay? Love you."

I shook my head again and put the phone away.

I suddenly felt a headache coming on.

TWENTY-FIVE

HELEN

She returned to the Arlington PD. She found Michael slumped over his desk. Papers were scattered everywhere. She glanced at the garbage can next to the desk. Coffee cups were piled high.

His hair was disheveled, and there was drool forming next to his open mouth.

At least he's not snoring, she thought.

Her ex-husband was a snorer. He could wake the neighbor's cat if he got loud. Helen, on the other hand, was a light sleeper. She would get up at the slightest movement or noise. She tried plugging her ears, purchasing a special mattress where one's tossing and turning didn't affect the other sleeper. She'd even gone so far as to get a white noise machine. Anything to drown Paul's snores and his constant movement on the bed. In the end, she ended up sleeping separately in another room.

Their friends and family thought that was the cause of their marriage ending. Helen begged to differ. In fact, she believed that was the reason her marriage lasted as long as it did. They both woke up fresh, and they weren't at each other's throats from not getting a good night's sleep. In some cultures, couples slept in different beds from the very beginning. It didn't mean they didn't love or couldn't be intimate with each other. It just meant they understood each person had a different sleeping pattern than their significant other. Some got cold in the middle of the night, while some got hot. Some tossed and turned the entire night, while some slept in the same position through the night. Also, the duration of sleep was a factor. Some went to bed early and woke up early. Others liked to stay up late and sleep in.

She stared at Michael. He looked so peaceful asleep. She decided not to disturb him. There was still time before the division was filled with detectives and other staff.

She turned to go.

His head snapped up like a jack-in-the-box.

He blinked several times, wiped the drool from his chin, and then began typing on his laptop.

"Are you okay?" she asked, stunned at what had just happened.

He turned to her. "Why wouldn't I be?" he replied matter-of-factly.

"Um... I mean, a minute ago, you were passed out."

"That?" he said. "I was just resting my eyes."

She looked around at his desk. "You spent the entire night here?"

"Not all of it at my desk," he replied. "I caught some sleep in the lounge."

The division had a private area with a kitchenette and seating arrangements. It wasn't uncommon to see people napping on the couches or snacking at the various tables.

"I admire your dedication to the job," she said. "But if you want to be productive, you need to be in your own bed. It doesn't compare to what we have in the division."

"I'm fine," he said. "The coffee from the vending machine isn't so bad."

"I'm sure it tastes great, but wait until the caffeine wears off and you crash."

"I won't crash. If I do get too tired during the day, I'll take a power nap."

Helen had heard of people who only slept four hours at night but took naps throughout the day.

Maybe Michael's one of them, she thought.

"Okay, so, did you find anything while you were here?" she asked.

TWENTY-SIX

HELEN

Michael searched around his desk, picked up a piece of paper, and held it up for Helen. She took it.

"The reason I ended up staying behind last night was that the victim's phone records came in."

They'd contacted Derek Starr's service provider. Most providers wanted a warrant, and even then, they made a fuss about their customer's privacy. According to Helen, privacy ended once the person was dead. Especially if that person was murdered. In Starr's case, they didn't have to subpoena the records, and they didn't even have to wait long for them.

"Anything caught your attention?" she said, glancing at the phone history.

"On the day Starr was murdered, he received several calls from a private number. In fact, he received a call from a private number right after he left the bar."

Helen's eyes narrowed. "How can you be so sure?"

"I checked the footage from the bar. And if you look carefully, he leaves the bar and stops at the front door. The door has a glass pane. You can see him standing there with his hand over his ear. I checked with the phone log and the time matched."

"You think it's the same person calling from the private number?" she asked.

"That'd be my guess."

Helen thought this over. "So, you think Derek Starr was waiting for this person at the bar?"

"That would be my guess, yes," Michael replied. "But that's not the interesting part."

"What is?"

"How did the caller know to call him right before he left the bar?"

Helen's eyes widened. "Because the caller was watching him?"

"Exactly," Michael said.

"Are there cameras outside the bar?" she asked.

Michael shook his head. "There had been so many fights between drunk patrons on the streets that the bar owner decided to remove the cameras. He didn't want to get involved in any police matters. Just so long as the fights weren't inside his bar, he didn't care."

"We can contact all the businesses in and around the bar," Helen said. "I'm sure they'd have security cameras. One of them must have caught someone waiting for Derek Starr to come out."

Michael shook his head. "There used to be a bowling alley across from the bar, but it's been closed for a good year now. There was a 'for lease' sign on the side of the building. So, I contacted the real estate company on the sign, and they said the owner hasn't put up CCTV cameras on the property. There's no point because the building's empty."

"What about any other businesses?" Helen asked, sounding disappointed.

"There's a laundromat next to the bar on the right, which doesn't have any security. I checked. And on the left of the bar, there's another empty store. Whoever picked the bar to meet Derek Starr—"

"Assuming Derek Starr went there to meet someone," Helen interjected. "Let's not get too ahead of ourselves."

"Yes, assuming he did. Then that person chose the bar for a reason. He or she knew there'd be no one around to record what happened next.'"

Helen crossed her arms over her chest. "I'm impressed," she said. "So, what's your working theory then?"

"I think someone lured Derek Starr to that bar."

"Why?"

"I'm not sure yet, but that person purposely didn't show up."

"Why didn't they?"

"They knew the bar's security cameras would have caught them."

"Okay, keep going."

"And when Derek Starr left the bar, this person followed him and then made their move. They attacked Starr and left him at the bus stop to die."

Helen mulled this over. "Seems a bit of a stretch."

"Sure, but it isn't entirely implausible, is it?"

"No, it isn't," she conceded. "Not bad for a rookie."

Michael finally grinned.

TWENTY-SEVEN

COLE

He had his hands in his pockets as he made his way through a department store's parking lot. The store was still hours away from opening, so the lot was empty, except for one vehicle, a GMC Canyon truck.

As he got close, both the driver side and the passenger side doors opened. Two men came out. One he recognized as Buddy. The other man, he'd never seen before.

The man's head was shaved clean. He had a heavy beard, and he wore dark sunglasses. Underneath the denim jacket, Cole could tell the man was well-built.

Buddy turned to the man and said, "He's the one I was telling you about."

The man didn't take off his glasses, but Cole could feel his stare bore into him. "Search him," the man said.

"What?" Buddy said, blinking.

"I said search him," the man growled.

"But I know him."

"I don't," the man shot back.

"He's a friend…"

"He could be wearing a wire."

"I'm not," Cole said.

"If you're not," the man replied, "then you wouldn't mind letting us take a look."

Cole looked at Buddy.

"I'm sorry, man," Buddy said, his tone apologetic. "We just have to make sure."

Cole shook his head and pulled off his jacket. He placed it on the hood of the truck. He then pulled up his shirt, exposing his bare chest and stomach.

"Happy?" Cole asked.

"Sure," the man replied with a nod.

Cole pulled his shirt down, grabbed his jacket, and put it back on.

Buddy then said, "Cole Madsen, this is Leo."

"Why are you here?" Leo asked.

"I'm here because Buddy told me you could help me."

"How?"

"I guess I need a way to make money."

Leo shrugged. "There are many ways to make money. It just depends on what you're looking for."

"I need money fast."

"You're desperate?"

Buddy jumped in. "Like I told you, Cole just got fired."

"Why doesn't he just get another job?" Leo countered. "That's what most people do when they're laid off."

"Yeah, I guess I could," Cole said. "But I need serious cash in a hurry."

"Why?"

Cole hesitated.

"Listen, kid," Leo said. "Do yourself a favor and go home. You don't want to get involved in something unless you're a hundred percent sure. Because once you're in, there's no going back."

Leo turned to get back in the truck.

"My mom's sick," Cole blurted.

Leo stopped and faced him.

Cole said, "She's not doing well. The meds she needs cost money. I was able to pay for them through my construction job, but now it's gone."

"Where's your father?" Leo asked.

"Never met him. He ran off before I was born."

Leo paused. Cole could see he was running something through his head.

Leo then said, "Okay, I'll give you a chance, only because Buddy recommended you."

"I do," Buddy said.

"But," Leo said to Cole, "if I find out you are playing us, I'll put a bullet through your head."

Cole swallowed.

"What we ask you to do, you do it. No questions asked," Leo said. "If you're uncertain right now, then you should go back to where you came from and forget we ever had this conversation."

"I can't go back."

Leo came closer. His face was inches away from Cole's. "Do you understand the path you are heading into?"

"Um… I think I do," Cole said with a shrug.

"This is not the time to be uncommitted, kid," Leo said. Cole could smell his breath. "This is the time to make a firm decision." For good measure, Leo lifted his jacket up. Tucked between his belt and shirt was a gun. "Are you in, or are you out?"

Cole took a deep breath. "I'm in. Just as long as I get paid."

Leo smiled. "You pass our test. You'll get paid all right."

TWENTY-EIGHT

SIMON

I was sitting at the dining table with a cup in my hand. It was my favorite cup. Vanessa had given it to me on our first-year wedding anniversary. Across the side of the cup, it read: "Greatest Husband of All-Time." She also bought me a set of golf clubs. She thought it would be good for me to learn the sport. A majority of business deals happened at the golf course. Gabe was always looking to find ways to play a few holes. If the weather was clear, he wouldn't show up at the firm until midday. He said it gave him the opportunity to build relationships and also get an advantage over the competition. And I had to agree with him on that. There were numerous times when he'd return from a round of golf and tell me to start looking into one business or another. And within a short time, we'd be investing in that business.

I tried my hand at golf, but I found I was terrible at it. My swing was awkward, and I would get frustrated when the ball would find its way into the bushes, trees, or the water. I later realized I didn't like the idea of chasing a tiny ball around a large area. Instead, I preferred chasing a large ball in a small court. Hence, my love of basketball.

The golf set was now collecting dust in the garage. However, the coffee cup was used each and every day, sometimes to Vanessa's dismay. The cup had a dark stain in the spot where I filled it up each day. I tried scrubbing it off, but the stain seemed like it was permanent. Vanessa has offered to buy me a new cup, but I've told her strictly not to. The next cup couldn't beat the one I was using. What would it say, anyway? "Best Husband in the World?" I'm already the Greatest Husband of All-Time, you know.

That's my problem. I tend to get attached to things and people. I have had one best friend since grade school. I've been married for a decade. And I have no intention of moving out of this house anytime soon.

I am a creature of habit, and I like things to stay the same.

It's probably a coping mechanism on my part. I don't deal well with change. I set a routine, and I follow through with it on a regular basis.

The cup gave me comfort. It was a reminder of all the good times I've had while sitting at the table, enjoying a moment of silence, and ruminating on my life.

Today I needed the cup more than any other day. The events of last night were a shock to my otherwise structured life.

Nothing exciting ever happened to me. Sure, Vanessa and I had gone on exotic trips, but those trips were in a controlled environment. We always tried to get a tour guide or be part of a travel group. If we went to a resort, we preferred to stay within the resort's boundaries. We rarely ventured out. And even if we did, we wanted our guide to take us straight to our destination and then back to our hotel or room.

Some would argue that we never really got to see the real place. And I would agree with them. When I think about it now, we only went to those countries to show our friends that we'd been there.

We rarely spent time interacting with the locals in order to experience their culture. Taste their food. Speak their language.

Vanessa was always in a hurry to get from one place to the next. She didn't like to stop and, sort of, smell the roses. To her, life wasn't about memories but more about documentation. She liked to take photos of all her experiences. If we went to a nice restaurant, she would take a photo of the meal and post it on all her social media accounts. If she bought a new pair of shoes, she did the same thing.

We had more photos of her in various poses than of us together. For instance, at the Louvre in Paris, she made me take photos of her standing in front of the glass pyramid outside the Louvre. Then another of her from the side next to the structure. Another with her back to the camera but looking over her shoulder. Another of her holding her arm up as if lifting the glass pyramid in her palm. And so on, and so forth. I must have snapped close to fifty photos. How many of those ended up on her social media account? I have no idea.

If it were me, one photo would have been sufficient. Me outside the Louvre. And that's it. I mean, it's not like I would ever go through all of them. By the time I'm old, I'll be more preoccupied with something else in my life. Most likely, it'll be regular visits to the doctor.

Speaking of doctors, I had told Vanessa I would get myself checked out by our family physician. But I won't.

I feel fine.

The bruising around my face was subsiding. I expect it to be completely gone in a few days.

However, there was something else that I needed to do.

During my struggle with my attacker, I had managed to get a hold of his wrist. I had seen pale skin, along with a familiar tattoo. But more importantly, I was able to pull something from the attacker.

On the kitchen table lay a watch.

It was a dial watch. The leather on the strap was faded and scuffed.

The watch was a family heirloom, and I knew exactly who it belonged to.

I finished my coffee and stood up.

I wouldn't be visiting my family doctor. Instead, I would be going straight to the local police department and filing a report.

I have no doubt the person responsible for my attack will be in police custody in a heartbeat.

TWENTY-NINE

HELEN

Helen and Michael were at the Arlington PD when Helen said, "What do we do now?"

"What do you mean?" Michael asked.

"I mean, we have no leads, no witnesses, nothing that would indicate why anyone would want to hurt Derek Starr."

Michael was silent.

She continued. "While I agree with you that Starr wasn't drunk when he left the bar, that doesn't mean he couldn't have gone to another bar for more drinks."

"But—"

"And," she said, cutting him off, "during his time at this second bar, he may have gotten into a fight with another patron. That patron later decided to take the fight outside, at which time Starr was stabbed and left for dead."

Michael thought a moment. "Okay, so, let's say that Derek Starr did go to another bar. Which bar then? The bar we went to was the closest to where we found his body."

It was Helen's turn to fall silent.

Michael continued. "Also, if another patron had indeed stabbed Starr, then why leave him sitting on a bench next to a bus shelter? And why leave him with a bottle of beer in his hand? Again, I believe it was staged."

"Why would it be staged? What purpose would it serve?"

"Maybe to send us down the wrong trail."

Helen mulled this over. "You seem like you want to lead on this case," she said.

"I don't."

She smiled. "I'm just teasing you. Most new detectives would've taken the situation at face value. Made assumptions without digging deeper into whether those assumptions held true or not. I'm just not convinced there is anything sinister behind Starr's death. I think there are more pressing cases than finding who killed a drunk and left him by the side of the street."

Michael shook his head. "There's no evidence that Starr was a drinker. He may have had a few drinks that night, but it still didn't explain why anyone would want to hurt him."

"All right, we keep looking, but I can tell you right now if we don't find a suspect or a lead soon, the sergeant will pull us off the case in no time. The department's resources are already stretched too thin. I wouldn't be surprised if we get assigned to a new case in the meantime."

"Then let's not waste any time."

"Okay, then what do you suggest we do?"

"I think we should go back to the bus stop."

Her eyebrows shot up in surprise. "The bus stop?"

"Yeah."

"Why?"

He turned to his laptop. He punched a few keys on the keyboard and then said, "According to the Arlington Transit System, the Route 111 bus drives past that bus stop every hour and twenty minutes."

"Okay," she said, trying to follow him.

"That gives us a window for when his body was moved to that spot."

"Moved?" she said.

"Remember my theory about the scuffs on his fine leather shoes?"

"Sure, I remember. You think someone dragged him to that spot, thus causing damage to the shoes?"

"Exactly. In my opinion, there is no way the driver would have pulled up at the stop, seen Derek Starr sitting there on the bench, and not gone over to check up on him."

"How can you be so sure?"

"Starr's suit jacket was unbuttoned, revealing a white shirt underneath. That white shirt had a large red stain on it. I have no doubt that if Starr was indeed sitting at that bench when the driver had pulled up, the driver would have called nine-one-one."

Helen fell silent. She then said, "I arrived at the scene at eight-forty-five in the morning."

"I got there around twenty minutes before you did," Michael said.

"So, for argument's sake, you were there quarter after eight."

"Sure."

"What about the sergeant? I'm assuming he got there before you did."

"We came together," Michael said.

Helen was surprised. "He gave you a ride?"

"Why do you think I left the scene in your Ford?" he replied. "My car was at the station."

"Good point. Okay, so what time did the first officer arrive, then?"

Michael checked his notes. "He got to the scene at seven-fifty-three."

"A little over twenty minutes before you and the sergeant got to the scene."

"Where are you going with this?" Michael asked.

"Humor me," she replied. "What time did the nine-one-one call come in?"

Michael checked his notes again. "The call came in at seven-forty-eight."

"Around five minutes before the officer got there, correct?"

"Yes."

"We can reasonably say that from seven-fifty-three onward, the scene was secured by the Arlington PD."

"That is correct."

"What time did the bus pass that stop in the morning?" she asked.

Michael turned to the laptop. After a few clicks on his mouse, he said, "That can't be right."

"Tell me."

"The Route 111 bus was scheduled to pass that stop at seven-forty-three."

She crossed her arms over her chest. "That was five minutes before the nine-one-one call. Not enough time for someone to drag a body and leave it at the bus stop, in my opinion."

There was a moment of silence before a smile broke across Michael's face. "That's why my theory makes more sense."

"Which theory is that?"

"My theory that the nine-one-one caller is the killer."

Helen rolled her eyes. "We're back to that again."

"No, think about it. What if the killer had waited until the bus had driven past that stop before he dragged Derek Starr's body there?"

"Why would the killer care to do that?'

"Simple. The killer didn't want to be seen dragging Starr's body to the bus stop while someone was waiting to catch the bus. Nor did the killer want anyone getting off the bus and seeing him with Starr."

"Okay, but there is a hole in your theory."

"How so?"

"The nine-one-one call came five minutes after the bus had left that stop. And the call had come from a pay phone two blocks away. There is no way someone could have dragged Starr to the bus stop and then driven over to make the call in that time frame."

"It's *not* impossible."

"I agree it's not, but you have to also remember, there are two traffic lights on that route. It would be very tight indeed."

Michael fell silent. "What if there is not one, but two killers?" he suggested.

"Okay, now you're making absolutely zero sense."

"Think about it," he said. "What if one of them staged the body and the other made the call?"

It was Helen's turn to go silent.

THIRTY

COLE

He was in the passenger seat of the GMC Canyon as it weaved through traffic. The man who went by the name of Leo was in the driver's seat. They'd left Buddy behind at the department store's parking lot.

Cole had wished he'd come along, though. He knew nothing about the man behind the wheel, except that he could help him earn extra money. Cole had tried to start up a conversation, but the man had only replied with a grunt.

Cole wasn't sure where they were going or what the man wanted him to do. This suddenly made him break into a cold sweat. Instinctively, he began to rub his hands together, something he'd done since childhood. That was why his hands were always clammy. He'd constantly try to wipe them dry. He used to chew his fingernails when he got nervous. He would bite them to the quick. But he forced himself to quit. It wasn't something he wanted to do as an adult.

Right now, though, he had the sudden urge to chew them again.

He shut his eyes to compose himself. He tried to think about his mom. She was in a lot of pain, and he was doing this for her. He wanted to help her get better. And he didn't know any other way to do it.

"Here we are," he heard Leo say, snapping him out of his thoughts.

He opened his eyes and looked around. They were on a commercial street. Cars were parked all along the curb. He spotted several high-end stores. A custom tailor shop for men. A boutique exclusively for women's handbags. A spa. A salon. A jewelry store. Even a pastry shop.

"What are we doing here?" Cole asked.

Leo pointed to the jewelry store. "I want you to bring me something valuable from there."

Cole's eyes widened. "You want me to go in there and *steal*?"

Leo laughed. "No, I want you to go in there and *buy* me a diamond necklace."

Cole knew he was being sarcastic. Cole rubbed his chin. "I don't know…"

"Listen. Didn't you say you wanted to make money?"

"I did. But I never said I'd break the law."

"How else do you expect to make cash fast? Or am I missing something?"

Cole turned to the store. Through the front window, he could see three employees behind the counter, two customers being attended to by the employees, and one security guard by the front door, armed and focused.

Cole said, "I figured you'd want me to sell weed or something."

"We are not into drugs."

"Then what are you into?"

"You'll know if you pass our test."

Cole suddenly felt a knot in the pit of his stomach.

Leo pressed a button and the doors unlocked. "I don't have time to waste. It's your choice, kid. You either do as I ask you, or you get out of my truck. And you forget we ever saw each other or had this conversation."

Cole fell silent. A million thoughts swirled through his head. "I can't go to jail. What would happen to my mom? Who would take care of her?"

"You won't go to jail if you don't get caught," Leo said. "So, don't... get... caught."

He had a smile that made a shiver go down Cole's back.

Cole suddenly felt overwhelmed. He didn't know what to do. A part of him wanted to get out and never see this man again. But another part of him wasn't sure what other option he had.

"All right," Leo said. "I'll do you a favor."

Cole stared at him.

"Only because Buddy recommended you. If you go in there and get me whatever you can get your hands on—I don't care if it's a chain, earrings, pendant, doesn't even have to be valuable—I'll give you a grand in return."

Cole's jaw dropped. "A grand?"

"Yep. If that's not enough of an incentive, then I don't know what is."

"What if I steal a necklace worth more than a grand?" Cole asked.

Leo laughed. "Good luck selling that on the black market. Unless you know people willing to buy an item like that off of you."

Cole could take a necklace to a pawn shop, but he wasn't sure what kind of IDs the shops would want to see. Or if they'd even consider buying an item that was stolen.

"Time's running out, kid," Leo growled.

"All right," Cole said.

"All right what?"

"I'll get you something from the shop."

"Good. Once you have it, you give me a call." Leo pulled out a card with a telephone number scribbled in blue ink on it. "And I'll meet back where we first met. The parking lot of the department store."

Cole took the card. "You're not going to wait for me outside?"

"If things go south, I don't want to be anywhere near here."

Cole knew what he was saying: *You get caught, you're on your own.*

"A grand for sure?" Cole said.

"And much more down the road if you pass the test."

Cole swallowed and got out.

THIRTY-ONE

SIMON

I was in a small room at the Arlington PD. On the other side of the two-way mirror was the interview room. Detective Ken Booker had on a gray business suit, a black tie, and polished leather shoes. He had smooth dark skin and perfect white teeth. Across from him at the metal table was a much younger man. He was short, but with broad shoulders and a thick chest. He wore a tight t-shirt that exposed his muscular tattooed arms. His hair was dark and thick and combed back. His upper lip was cut and swollen.

When I had provided a name to the police, it took them less than an hour to bring him in for questioning.

I was also invited to listen in on the interview.

"Do you know why you are here, Mr. Diakos?" Booker asked.

If that name sounds familiar, it should. The man who attacked me was the son of Dimitris Diakos, the owner of the olive oil business my firm had just sold to a competitor.

I had met Nick a few times when I had visited the company. As part of my assessment of the business, I had toured the facility where the oil was processed and distributed. I found Nick to be deeply loyal to his father. In fact, I got the sense his father was grooming him to take over the family business.

I know Dimitris blamed us for what happened. He accused us of stealing his business. We did not. We saved it. While we may have kept him in the dark about our intentions—we had always planned to sell the company in order to recoup our investment and make a profit—we also made him a rich man.

So, I was surprised when his son had chosen to take his anger out on me.

I knew it was him the moment I saw the tattoo. While I was grappling with him, his wrist became exposed, revealing the heads of several snakes. Nick was proud of his Greek heritage. He had tattooed the head of Medusa on his shoulder, the venomous snakes from her hair flowing down his arm and stopping at the wrist.

I had always found the tattoo jarring. I couldn't imagine staring at something like that each and every day. The snakes were inked green, but their forked tongues were red. Their mouths were open as if ready to strike.

I shudder even thinking about them now.

So, when I saw the tattoo, I knew it was him. Furthermore, the moment Nick entered the interview room, my suspicion was confirmed. During the attack, I had swung my elbow back and hit my attacker. I wasn't sure where I had hurt him—he was wearing a balaclava—but after seeing Nick's split lip, I knew it was the mouth.

"Mr. Diakos," Booker repeated. "Do you know why you are here?"

Nick shrugged. "I don't know."

"Where were you last night at around eight pm?"

"I was at the hospital."

Booker was just as surprised as me upon hearing this.

"Hospital?" Booker repeated.

"Yes."

"And what were you doing at the hospital?"

Nick's eyes turned moist. "My… my father had a heart attack… and I was there with my family to be with him."

I suddenly felt a knot in the pit of my stomach. Earlier in the day, we had given the old man news that the business he had given his blood, sweat, and tears to, was no longer his. Guilt suddenly overwhelmed me.

Were we to blame for what happened to him? I wanted to say no, but I wasn't sure I could.

"How is your father doing now?" Booker asked. I was glad he did, because I wanted to know, too.

"The doctors said we got him help right away, but they still want to run tests on him."

"That's good to hear," Booker said. He then got back to the point. "Was there any time you left the hospital?"

Nick shrugged. "Maybe once."

"What was the reason?"

"I might have gone home to pick up my mom's medication. She wanted to stay at the hospital until she was certain my dad was okay."

"And so, you left the hospital and went straight home, is that correct?"

"Yes."

"Did you go anywhere else?"

"No."

I knew he was lying, and so did the detective. Sweat had broken across Nick's forehead. A telltale sign he was struggling.

THIRTY-TWO

SIMON

"Okay, let's move to another question," Booker said. "What happened to your face?"

Nick's hand instinctively moved to his mouth. He winced as his fingers touched his swollen lip. "I... I ran into a door."

"How did that happen?"

"I was in a hurry to get to my car... and I didn't see the door was closed." More lies, but he was trying.

"When did it happen?"

Nick shrugged again. "A couple of days ago, maybe."

"It looks fresh."

Nick fell silent.

"Mr. Diakos, what if I were to tell you there is a witness who says he saw you outside—" Booker gave the name of the restaurant "—and this witness also describes you as being responsible for an attack on a patron of this restaurant." The detective was careful not to mention my name—*yet*. But I'm sure he would when the time was right. "Also, I am certain if we checked the security cameras around the restaurant, it will confirm this witness's statement."

More sweat broke across Nick's forehead. He swallowed and then said, "Do I need to get a lawyer?"

"You should seek legal counsel if you've broken the law. Have you broken any laws, Mr. Diakos?"

Nick stammered. "I… I'm sorry. I didn't mean to…"

"You didn't mean to do what?"

If the detective was trying to get Nick to confess, he wasn't pushing for it. He seemed comfortable to lay out the facts and let Nick decide his next course of action.

Suddenly, there was a noise.

Nick's hand reached for his pocket. He pulled out his cell phone. "It's my mom," he said. "Can I answer it?"

"Of course, you can. You're not under arrest," Booker replied.

Nick put the phone to his ear. He spoke to his mom in Greek for a couple of minutes and then put the phone away.

"Everything okay?" Booker asked.

Nick smiled. "My mom just told me that my dad will be fine. There was no permanent damage to his heart. The doctors think he can go home tonight."

"Again, I'm glad to hear that. Now let's get back to…"

I tapped the window. Booker turned to the two-way mirror. He was surprised by it, but I tapped again.

"Excuse me one moment," Booker said.

He left the interview room and met me outside in the hall.

"I don't appreciate being interrupted," he said to me.

"I apologize for that," I said. "But I don't think it was him."

The detective's eyes narrowed. "You were very confident just a few hours ago."

"I was… but…" I looked down at my shoes. "I'm not so sure anymore. It was dark, and it happened so fast."

Booker studied me. He then nodded, understanding. "I assume you don't want to press any charges?"

"I don't. Please."

"All right," Booker said. He then opened the door to the interview room. I could see that Nick had his head buried in his hands. "Mr. Diakos, you are free to go."

Nick looked up at him, confused. He then realized what the detective had said and quickly got to his feet. He left the room. He saw me standing in the hall. Our eyes met for a brief second before he hurried away. He probably wanted to get out of there before the detective changed his mind.

I turned to the detective. "I'm sorry to have wasted your time."

He smiled. "We are here to serve the community. If you change your mind, though, you can always file another report."

I knew I wouldn't be filing another report.

"Thank you," I said and left.

THIRTY-THREE

COLE

He watched the GMC Canyon drive off.

A part of him wanted to find the nearest subway and take the first train home. He wasn't a thief. He hadn't stolen a single thing in his life—not even candy. But what choice did he have? It wasn't like there were opportunities knocking on his door. Also, running home wouldn't solve his problem. He needed cash, and he needed it right away. The check from BB Construction wouldn't come for another two weeks at the very least.

He stood across from the jewelry store and planned his next move. All the items were locked behind tempered glass. He couldn't just smash the glass with his fists. He would need something strong, like a baseball bat or a crowbar. And he had neither at the moment. So, the only way to get an item out was if he requested it from the salesperson. If he tried to snatch and run, there was the issue of the security guard.

The guard was a good several inches taller than Cole. He was also close to fifty pounds heavier than him. It wouldn't take much for the guard to subdue Cole. Plus, the guard was armed with a pistol.

What if the guard was trigger happy?

He could argue that he, the employees, and the customers of the store were under threat, and so he had to take severe action by drawing his gun and shooting the would-be thief.

Who would miss me anyway? he thought. *Mom for sure. But who else?*

Cole was a nobody. He was born out of wedlock. He never knew his father. And he barely knew his relatives on his mother's side either. His maternal grandparents were rarely involved in his upbringing. He had an uncle in Texas. The uncle used to own a barbeque restaurant in El Paso. Cole had spent a couple of months there when he was younger. His mom started working for her brother as a waitress. Cole remembered the last time he'd seen his uncle. It was when his uncle and his mom had gotten into a colossal fight. His uncle had accused his mom of stealing all the tips from the customers. She countered that she kept the tips because he'd stopped paying her.

Needless to say, the restaurant didn't last long after his mom left. According to her, her brother was lazy, drunk, and irresponsible. When he'd finally shut down the restaurant, he left behind debts ranging from unpaid wages to his employees, bills to his vendors, and rent to his landlord.

Cole watched as customers went in and out of the jewelry store.

Every inch of the store was covered by CCTV cameras. There was no way for him to distract the salesperson and slip an item into his pocket. The security guards in another room were closely watching what each customer did.

He knew something about the jewelry business thanks to his steady diet of TV as a kid.

He was always curious, and he'd quickly moved on from kids shows to more adult-oriented shows. He loved watching how things were made. Or how industries functioned. And that's where he learned that the salespeople inside a jeweler would only bring out one item at a time for customers to examine. If he wanted to see another item, they would put the first item away and pull out the next. And if he wanted to compare the items, to see which one he would choose from, they would display them all at once. This way, they could keep an eye on all the items.

Even if they didn't follow those procedures exactly, they would never let any of the items out of their sight for one moment.

Cole suddenly felt overwhelmed.

He didn't know what to do.

THIRTY-FOUR

HELEN

Michael's desk phone rang. "Detective Porter," he said. He listened for a few seconds and then hung up.

"Who was that?" Helen asked.

"That was the officer at the front desk," Michael replied. "He's been trying to reach you at your desk, but I guess because you've been with me, you weren't there to answer."

Her eyes narrowed. "Why was he calling *me*?"

"There's a woman downstairs who wants to speak to you."

"Me?" Helen said, surprised.

"And I think me as well," Michael said. "This person has information on Derek Starr."

Helen's eyes widened. "What are we waiting for? Let's go talk to her."

They took the elevator down to the main floor. They found the woman waiting in the front lobby. She was dressed in a pink jumpsuit. Her hair was curled, her fingernails painted pink, and she had on bright pink lipstick. She also had on long fake eyelashes and black mascara. The mascara was smeared, creating dark circles around her eyes. She held a tissue in one hand.

"I'm Detective Sloan, and this is Detective Porter," Helen said. "You said you had information on Derek Starr?"

"You guys are working on his case?" she said, wiping her eyes. They were red and raw.

"We are."

"Then I need to tell you something."

"Why don't we go someplace quiet to talk?" Helen suggested.

They took her to one of the unoccupied interview rooms. Once seated at the table, Helen said, "Can you tell us your name?"

"It's... it's Lainey."

"Okay, how do you know Derek Starr?

"He's a customer, and he's a... um... a friend."

Helen shot a glance at Michael and then turned back to the woman. "First, explain to me what you mean by 'customer'."

"I own a massage parlor in Midtown. And Derek's a regular customer of mine."

Helen knew massage parlors had been given a bad rap. Apart from the massage services, there were other services as well, which included services of a sexual nature. Helen was going to give her the benefit of the doubt.

"Why did Derek Starr come to your location?" Helen asked.

"He came because of a recurring back pain," Lainey replied. "He told me he'd always suffered from back problems, but he had aggravated it after he tried to move some stuff in his garage."

"How long has he been a customer of yours?" Helen asked.

"Two years, at least."

"And how often did he come to your parlor?"

"Once a week."

"And now on to my second question. You said he was a friend?"

"Yes."

"How so?"

"I know what this looks like," Lainey said.

"I'm not sure what you mean?" Helen said.

"I run a respectable establishment. I have customers young and old. Male and female. We help customers manage their pain. There are no other services provided. I want to make that clear."

"Understood."

"At the beginning, Derek used to come for his back. But later on, I think he came because he was lonely and stressed out."

"Stressed out about what?"

"Mostly work."

"Did he tell you what he did?"

"Yes."

"And where he worked?"

She nodded. "Chester and Associates."

"And what was he particularly stressed about?"

"I think there were some things at work he was not happy about. Things he wasn't particularly comfortable telling me. But he did say that he was looking to move to another company."

"Okay."

Lainey looked down at her manicured hands. She then said, "I know this might sound crazy, but Derek was worried that something might happen to him."

Helen and Michael sat up straight.

"Are you saying Derek was concerned that his life was in danger?" Helen asked.

"Yes."

"Please elaborate."

"He told me he was being followed."

"Followed?"

"He said he saw a 4 x 4 truck parked outside his house. Then he saw the same 4 x 4 truck parked outside his office."

"How was Derek so sure it was the same truck?"

Lainey smiled. "Derek lives in a nice neighborhood. Hardly anyone drives a 4 x 4 truck. They own luxury cars. Anyway, Derek mentioned that one day he saw the truck parked outside his office building for several hours, and when he sent security to check up on the truck, the driver drove off."

"That does sound suspicious," Michael said.

Helen asked, "Did Derek, by any chance, get the license plate number of the truck?"

"If he did, he didn't tell me."

Helen said, "You mentioned that Derek was looking at moving to another company. Did he give you the name of this other company?"

"Delta Management."

"Did he tell you what this company did?"

"I think they are also an accounting firm."

"Is there anything else you can tell us that might help find who hurt Derek?" Helen asked.

Lainey shook her head. "I wish there was. I'm going to miss him so much."

She broke down and cried.

Helen knew Lainey's relationship with Starr was more than just friendship. Starr might have been having an affair with her. But that did not change the fact that Starr was dead, and they had no leads and no suspects.

THIRTY-FIVE

COLE

He knew he was wasting time. He couldn't wait any longer. He had to do something, and he had to do it now. He took a deep breath and strode across the road to the other side of the street. He went up a flight of stairs and entered the jewelry store.

The bell chimed above the door as he entered. Cole avoided making eye contact with the security guard, but he could feel his gaze as he moved toward the salesperson, a woman. Her hair was dyed blonde, she had on heavy makeup, and her nails were manicured.

"Welcome to Emperor's Jewelers," she said. "How can I help you?"

"Um… I'm… I'm looking for an engagement ring," Cole said.

The woman smiled. "Sure, we have many engagement rings. Is there a particular type of ring you are looking for?"

"I'm not really sure," he said.

She could tell he was lost, and she was eager to help. She had seen too many bewildered and confused men, looking for just the right ring for their partners. And like a good salesperson, she would show them the priciest ring in the store. And why not? She was paid on commission. However, she was also an astute salesperson, and she could see by Cole's attire and his youthfulness that by trying to sell him an expensive ring, she might not get a sale. Instead, she asked, "Is there a particular price range you're looking for?"

"Um... I would prefer something under one grand," Cole replied.

The smile on her face did not waver. "Absolutely. We have many in that price range. Please follow me."

She took him to where they kept an assortment of rings. Wedding rings. Anniversary rings. Friendship rings. Engagement rings.

She pointed at the glass shelf. "We have rings with a single diamond. Rings with smaller diamonds. Rings with topaz. Diamond. Pearl. With bands made out of gold, silver, or platinum. Depending on your preference, the prices vary. Is there one that you would like to take a look at?"

Cole stared at the two dozen rings placed neatly inside the shelf. He wished he had one that stuck out to him, but they all looked the same. They were magnificent and expensive. In his current condition, it would take him months to save up just to buy one. But he was here for another reason. And the longer he stayed in the store, the more exposed he felt. He shot a quick glance at the front door. The security guard was planted right next to it, and he was eyeing Cole suspiciously. Cole feared breaking into a cold sweat. He took a quiet breath to compose himself.

"Can I see that one?" he said, pointing at a ring that was priced at nine-hundred and ninety-nine dollars.

The saleswoman unlocked the cabinet with a small key, pulled out the ring, and placed it on the glass shelf.

Cole's fingers shook as he lifted the ring up and examined it. The ring was sparkly, and it weighed in his hand.

"Do you have any rings that are a bit cheaper?" he said.

"We had some on sale last week, but they sold out very quickly. Have you considered getting, perhaps, cubic zirconia?" she said.

"My girlfriend… I mean, my fiancé, she wouldn't be happy if I got her zirconia."

"When do you plan to propose to her?" she asked.

"Soon," he claimed.

"How soon?"

"We will be driving to her parents' house this weekend, and I was hoping to make the announcement there."

"Oh dear, if it wasn't so soon, I would've recommended you come back in a couple of weeks. We'll be having the store's twentieth-anniversary sale, so a lot of our items will be marked down."

"Do you guys do installments?"

"Installments?" she said.

"Yeah, where I could, maybe, pay throughout the year or so?"

"I can speak to the manager, and maybe he could help you out."

"Sure, that would be great," he said with a smile.

As expected, she put the ring back inside the shelf and locked it with the small key. He watched as she went to the back of the store and disappeared behind a set of doors. He looked around and saw that the security guard was now preoccupied with something on his phone. He was probably bored, staring at customers all day. Cole doubted if anyone was foolish enough to rob the place in broad daylight.

There was another reason why the guard stood next to the door. He kept an eye on who approached the store. If he sensed that something might be up, he could lock the doors in an instant. It wouldn't be possible for a car to pull up in front of the store, masked men to jump out with weapons drawn, and storm the place without the guard taking the necessary precautions.

Did he know I was watching the store from the street? Cole suddenly thought.

The guard typed something on the phone while keeping one eye outside. The doorbell chimed, and the security guard quickly put the phone away. A woman entered the store. She had on an expensive outfit, with matching shoes, and she was carrying a handbag that probably cost more than Cole ever made in a month. She also looked like she'd just come out of the salon. Her hair was permed, and her nails were done. She smiled at the security guard, and the way he smiled back told Cole she was a regular customer.

She walked straight to the saleswoman behind the counter, and she asked, without skipping a beat, "Has the Cartier watch I ordered arrived?"

THIRTY-SIX

COLE

The saleswoman Cole was dealing with returned with a smile on her face. "I just spoke to my manager, and we would be willing to work out an installment plan if you're interested."

"You know what?" he said. "I think I'll come back later. In fact, I might just bring my fiancé with me. There's no point in me trying to surprise her if she doesn't like the ring."

"That's an excellent idea," she said, putting on a brave face. "Why don't I give you our business card? It'll have my name on it. And when you come back, you can ask for me."

Cole knew she was probably not happy about losing the sale right now, but she also didn't want the sale to go to someone else.

"I will do that, thanks," he said, shoving the card in his pocket and leaving.

On the way out, he smiled at the security guard, who smiled back.

Cole walked back to his initial spot, across from the jewelry store. The trip inside the store hadn't been a complete waste. He suddenly had a plan. This plan wasn't foolproof, but it was the only plan he had at the moment.

He watched and waited with bated breath. Several minutes went by, and nothing happened.

The door for Emperor's Jewelers opened. The security guard held the door as the woman with the permed hair stepped out. She was clutching her handbag tightly as she made her way down the street.

Cole had seen a Land Rover, a Jeep, and an Acura SUV parked along the street. But among them was a Mercedes-Benz. If Cole was a betting man, he was certain that it was her vehicle. The Benz was parked twenty feet away from the jewelry store.

Her heels clicked on the pavement as she made her way to her car. Cole knew he had no time to spare. He raced across the road and got right behind her. She pressed a button on her key fob, causing the lights on the Benz to flash. He heard the doors unlock. She reached for the door handle.

At that moment, Cole made his move.

He took two long strides, reached over, grabbed the handbag, yanked it hard, and dashed off.

All it took was five seconds.

As he ran down the street, he heard her scream. He didn't bother looking back. There was no point. The only thought that ran through his mind was to get out of there as fast as he could. He kept running. His legs burned. But he didn't stop.

It was only when he was a good distance away that he glanced back. When he saw no one chasing after him, he stopped and leaned next to a brick building. He was out of breath, and he was sweating profusely. His heart was beating so fast he thought it would burst out of his chest.

He couldn't believe what he'd done.

He looked down at the handbag he was gripping tightly. It was dark brown and made out of some type of leather. He didn't dare open it. His hands were shaking.

He suddenly felt sick.

I'm going to throw up, he thought.

He inhaled deeply through his nostrils. The last thing he wanted was to empty his stomach by the side of the street.

He spotted a garbage can. He raced up to it, leaned over, and opened his mouth, but nothing came out. He tried again. Still nothing.

He was disgusted at his actions.

He dumped the handbag in the bin and walked away.

He had made his way around the corner when a police cruiser pulled up to the curb, cutting off his path. The cruiser's lights were flashing.

Two uniformed officers jumped out and ordered him to lie down on the ground with his hands out. The officers' weapons were drawn.

He did as he was instructed.

Within minutes, he was handcuffed behind his back and placed in the backseat of the cruiser.

THIRTY-SEVEN

SIMON

I got off the elevator and was greeted with a double glass door with the name "Harris & Harris" printed on the glass. The moment I entered my firm, I heard a gasp. It was our secretary, Amy Joy Novak. She was in her twenties. She had dark hair, hazel eyes, and tanned skin. Her father was Caucasian, and her mother was from the Philippines. Amy Joy was only a part-time employee at the firm. She came in the morning and was gone by midafternoon.

Gabe and I didn't need a full-time secretary. We didn't deal with walk-ins, nor were we a customer-oriented business. We had a handful of people working for us, and almost all of them were on contract. Gabe didn't believe in having employees. He was concerned about the benefits we would have to give them if we hired them on a full-time basis: vacation, medical, sick leave, and even a pension.

Naturally, I disagreed with him. I felt like if we hired someone, we should also take care of them. But he won out on that argument. He wanted to run a lean operation, and the only way to do that was to minimize costs.

I could have fought harder, but I didn't. If Gabe decided to go down one road, there was nothing I or anyone else could do to change his mind. He was stubborn, just like our father. In some ways, when he got angry, he looked like our father, too. To say that I was intimidated by him would be an understatement. I looked up to him. He had helped me through some of the most difficult times of my life. He was my older brother and my mentor.

That didn't mean I let him walk over me. When he wanted to cut Amy Joy's pay because there wasn't that much work for her to do, I had put my foot down. Apart from being our secretary, Amy Joy was also studying to become a lawyer. I knew she liked the flexibility of working for us, and I also knew how much she needed the money. She was a good person with a good heart. Once she passed the bar exam, she wanted to represent the marginalized of society. And I was rooting for her.

"Oh my God," she said, covering her mouth. "Gabe told me something happened to you. I didn't know it was this bad."

My hand instinctively went up to my bruised face. I'd forgotten what I looked like. My visit to the Arlington PD had preoccupied my mind.

"It looks worse than it is," I said.

"Does it hurt?"

"It did last night, but the painkillers really helped." I could try to act tough with her, to show that I could take a beating and still hold my head up high, but knowing my brother, he would've already told her the truth. That I got my butt kicked. Gabe couldn't help but poke fun at me whenever the opportunity arose. I can't say I always got him back. I wasn't very good with comebacks, so I preferred to keep my mouth shut. If I didn't, Gabe would continue making fun of me.

"Why are you back at work?" she asked. "Gabe said you would be taking the day off."

"I got tired of sitting at home alone, so I figured I'd drop by and see what was going on."

She smiled. "Well, I'm glad to see that you're okay."

"Is Gabe in his office?" I asked.

"He's on the phone. You can go in and see if he's done."

THIRTY-EIGHT

SIMON

I walked down the carpeted hallway to where our offices were. Gabe had the corner office, which gave him an unobstructed view of the city. My office wasn't too shabby either. It had floor-to-ceiling windows. Enough space for a desk, several chairs, and even a futon in the corner. I reached Gabe's office, and through the glass door, I saw him pacing the room with a headset on his head. He looked up and saw me standing outside the door. He lifted a finger up as if to say, *I'm almost done*, and continued speaking into the headset.

I turned back to the hallway. The walls were adorned with paintings Gabe had picked up on his travels throughout the world. Some had cost as much as thirty thousand dollars. A waste of money if you asked me. But, according to Gabe, art only went up in value, which made them a great investment. And also, they were a symbol of status.

I didn't have an eye for art. I couldn't see the deeper meaning in most paintings, especially the modern works. They looked like someone had thrown paint on the canvas and waited for it to dry.

I saw Gabe put the headset down and wave me in.

"So how did it go?" he asked with excitement.

"What do you mean?" I asked in return.

Gabe made a face. "Come on, don't be like that. You know what I'm talking about."

147

I knew exactly what he was talking about. Before going to the police station, I had called and told Gabe that I believed it was Dimitris' son, Nick, who had attacked me the night before.

"It wasn't him," I said.

Gabe frowned. "I thought you were certain it was him. Didn't you say you saw the tattoo on his wrist?"

"I thought I did, but it happened so fast. And it was dark."

If Gabe didn't believe me, I couldn't tell from his face.

He turned back to his desk.

I said, "Dimitris had a heart attack."

"Is that what Nick said at the station?"

"He did."

"And you believe him?"

"I do."

Gabe shrugged. "To be honest, I'm not that surprised. The old man took it too personally. It's just business, you know."

"To him, it wasn't," I said. "It was everything to him. He wanted to pass the business on to Nick."

Gabe looked at me. I could tell he was annoyed that I brought this up again. We'd already had discussions like these many times before. Gabe always thought he was helping the struggling business owners, while I thought we were taking advantage of them. Our thoughts couldn't be more different, but in the end, the result was the same. We took control of failing businesses, we turned them around, and made a nice profit once we sold them.

He said, "Dimitris may not be able to pass on the business to Nick, but he can surely pass on the money we made him. If anything, he should be thanking us."

Unfortunately, I didn't share the same sentiment. I felt we were responsible for what happened to Dimitris. And in some way, what Nick did to me was well deserved.

But I didn't say any of that. Not out loud. Gabe was known to hold grudges. He was proud to be a Harris. If I told him that Nick was indeed my attacker, and somehow, the police weren't taking the necessary actions, Gabe would find a way to get him back. He would try to hold back the remaining payments owed to the family for the sale of the business. Gabe didn't care if his little brother got hurt. It was more about his pride. That someone had attacked *his* family. And as the head of the family, he took it upon himself to right what he felt was wrong.

"What are you doing here anyway?" he then said. "Go home and get some rest. I need you back in the office first thing in the morning." He grinned. "I've got some new deals I'm working on. And these deals could dwarf whatever we've made before."

I wasn't in the mood to talk numbers or even money. I had come to see his reaction to what had happened to Dimitris. If I was expecting some remorse or emotion, then I didn't get it.

Thankfully, Gabe's phone rang, and when he went to answer it, I quietly left his office.

THIRTY-NINE

COLE

He was taken to the Arlington PD. He was photographed and fingerprinted. Cole knew the procedure. He had been arrested once before. It involved selling booze to minors. It was a few days after his 21st birthday. A couple of teenagers had approached him outside a convenience store. They wanted to get some beer for a party, and they offered to pay Cole twenty dollars to get them a case. Cole didn't think it was too much of a problem, so he obliged. What he didn't realize was that a police cruiser was parked across the road from the convenience store. The officer saw him handing over the case to the minors. He arrested Cole on the spot. The minors, however, fled the scene. The officer was in his fifties, overweight, and out of shape. He was in no mood to go on a foot chase with sixteen-year-old boys. Instead, the officer took Cole to the station. He was charged with a misdemeanor, and he was given a citation to appear in court. The courts were so backlogged that Cole doubted he would be in front of a judge until sometime next year.

But this was different. Cole knew he was in trouble. He had been caught stealing the woman's handbag. He wasn't sure how much was in her handbag, whether she had cash on top of the Cartier watch. In some states, if the value of the stolen property was less than a thousand, he'd be charged with petty theft, and he would end up serving less than a year in prison if convicted. But if the amount was more than a grand, he would be charged under grand theft, and the sentence would be more than a year.

There were other factors as well. Such as the manner in which the theft had occurred, his criminal history, and whether there were other pending charges against him. Cole wasn't concerned about the theft of the handbag. When the police arrested him, they searched him and came up empty. However, he still had the misdemeanor against him.

After he had been booked, Cole was placed in a windowless room. The walls and floor were made of concrete, and the table and chairs metal. The room was set up in a way to make the interviewee as uncomfortable as possible. The room was also cold, and Cole instantly shivered.

The door to the room opened, and a man in a gray suit, black tie, and polished leather shoes entered.

"My name is Detective Ken Booker," he said. "And you are Cole Madsen, is that right?"

The detective had a white folder in his hand, so he already had that information in front of him. Cole wasn't about to say more than he needed to.

The detective sat down across from him and said, "I'm not going to waste your time or mine. You know why you are here, don't you?"

"I have no idea," Cole said. "I was just walking down the street when the officers pulled up and arrested me. I didn't do anything."

"Is that your official statement?"

FORTY

COLE

"It's the truth," Cole said.

"Normally," the detective said, "I would advise you to get a lawyer. If you cannot afford a lawyer, a lawyer from the state will be assigned to you. But before you go down that route, I will tell you what we know. You were seen entering the Emperor's Jewelers. We have two witnesses who can confirm this. A saleswoman who works at the store, and also a security guard. At the same time, a customer was seen purchasing an expensive watch. And right after she left the store, a person matching your description ran up to her and snatched her handbag. While you were not caught in possession of the handbag, we believe you may have handed the handbag over to an accomplice of yours. If you cooperate and tell us exactly where the handbag is, I might be able to reduce the charge against you. You do know the difference between petty theft and grand theft, don't you?"

"I do," Cole replied.

"I figured that, considering you still have a pending case against you."

Damn, Cole thought.

"Also, the security guard believes that you were scoping out the jewelry store in advance. Perhaps you work for a gang. If you guys were planning to rob it later, then I can even tag on grand felony theft. Which means you could be spending, not just a long time but a very long time in prison."

"How... how long?" Cole asked, blinking.

"Minimum, ten to twelve years. Maybe you could get out in half that time for good behavior. But what are you? Twenty-one right now? So that would be way before your thirtieth birthday. However, someone as young as you might not manage well in prison. In fact, even if you came out a new man, a criminal record might not be helpful in your pursuit of stable employment."

Cole knew what he was doing. The detective was trying to pressure him. Make him feel like he had no other option but to confess. And the threat was working. Cole suddenly felt like the walls were closing in on him. He felt like he couldn't breathe anymore. He placed his head in his hands and shut his eyes.

"Just tell us what you did with the handbag," the detective said. "And who you are working with or working for, and I'll see what I can do to help you."

Cole inhaled through his nostrils and exhaled from his mouth. He looked up at the detective and said, "I don't work for any gang or anyone, and I did not steal that woman's handbag."

The detective didn't seem happy with that answer. He stood up and grabbed the folder. "Can you post bail?"

"How much?"

"The state has set a standard amount of five-hundred for a misdemeanor, but because it's felony theft *and* you also have a pending case against you, it'll be five-thousand."

"Five-thousand dollars?" Cole said, raising his voice.

"It's a second offense in such a short time."

Cole's eyes welled up. "I… I don't have that kind of money."

"Maybe your parents can help you."

"My mom's not in any position to help."

"What about other family?"

"I have no one else."

"Friends?"

"None who have that kind of money."

The detective sighed. "If you can't post bail, you'll have to wait in a holding cell until a court hearing can be arranged."

"When will that be?"

"If you're lucky, maybe later today. Most likely, though, it won't be until sometime tomorrow."

Cole placed his head in his hands and began to sob.

FORTY-ONE

HELEN

Helen and Michael were in a lower level of a commercial building. The office belonged to Douglas Voss. He was the hiring manager at Delta Management. According to Derek Starr's friend, Lainey, Starr was looking to jump ship to Chester and Associates' competition.

Voss had grayish hair, small beady eyes, and a sharp nose. He was dressed in a three-piece suit and was seated behind a glass desk.

He had already heard the news of Starr's death, but he was surprised the two detectives would be at his office.

"I'm not sure how I can be of any help to you," he said.

"We're just trying to get an idea of what Mr. Starr was doing prior to his death," Michael said.

Before going into Voss's office, Helen had told Michael to take the lead. After all, in a couple of months, she would be retired. And it would be up to him to continue the good work at the Arlington PD. Plus, she wanted to see how he handled himself.

Voss leaned back in his chair and locked his fingers over his stomach. "Yes, it's true that Derek approached me about joining Delta Management."

"Did he say why he wanted to leave Chester and Associates?" Michael said. "I mean, he'd been there a very long time. In fact, he'd been there when the firm was first established. And as far as I can tell, he was one of the highest-paid employees at the firm. So, money couldn't have been the issue."

Voss nodded. "It wasn't. I'm sure you guys are aware of what's going on at Chester and Associates, right?"

Michael said, "We only know what we have seen on the news. And according to them, Chester and Associates are under investigation."

"And you know why they're under investigation?" Voss asked.

Michael shrugged. "Not really."

"Then maybe you should go back to Chester and Associates and find out."

Michael said, "Why don't you just tell us and save us the time. Derek Starr is dead. Whatever agreement you had with him no longer exists."

Voss looked away. He stared out the window for what was probably several seconds but felt like minutes. He then sighed. "I always liked Derek. He was a great guy. Fun to hang around with. I can't say that we were friends, but I always got along with him. We first met at a convention in Vegas. It was about how organizations could make money by taking on more advisory roles. The general public thinks the majority of money accountants make is from preparing client's financial statements. But that's only a small portion of it. Big money is in consultation and advising clients on how to structure their business, so it will reap the most benefits. How to take advantage of the tax loopholes in the law. When to preserve their funds and when not to. But more importantly, which emerging foreign markets to keep an eye on and where to invest."

Michael said, "Sure, okay, but you still didn't answer my question. Why is Chester and Associates being investigated?"

"Okay, but what I'm about to tell you did not come from Derek. Nothing private or confidential was ever passed on to me. We bumped into each other at a restaurant one day, and after a few pleasantries, he asked if he could give me a call. I wasn't surprised by this, even though Delta Management and Chester and Associates compete for the same business, because it's not uncommon for either of us to try to poach talent from one another. So, later that day, he called me and asked to meet at a bar."

FORTY-TWO

HELEN

Her back arched when she heard Voss mention a bar. The night Starr was murdered or at least was last seen alive, he was at a bar. Was he there to meet Voss?

Michael was thinking the same thing when he asked, "When did Mr. Starr ask you to meet him at the bar?"

"Probably... around two weeks ago."

Helen and Michael were disappointed at the sound of that. They were hoping to find the person Starr was waiting for at the Bearded Tavern.

Michael asked, "Okay, what did he want to talk to you about?"

Voss replied, "He said the situation at Chester and Associates was fragile. He worried the firm might even crumble."

Helen's eyebrows shot up. "Crumble?"

Voss turned to her. "Yes."

"Why?"

"Have you heard of Fast-Card?"

Helen and Michael shook their heads.

"Fast-Card was started in Denmark. They've been in business less than ten years, but they already control twenty-five percent of all online transactions in Europe and North Africa."

"What do you mean by 'online transactions'?" Michael asked.

"They facilitate payments between vendors and customers. They were initially a cyber-security firm until they decided to leverage that expertise over to digital transfer of funds. They grew so fast in such a short time that analysts began to call them a unicorn. Saying they were special and were somehow a step ahead of everyone else—even ahead of those who've been in the business far longer than them. But from what I've heard, and this is only speculation, they do not control twenty-five percent of the European and North African markets. In fact, there is now a strong belief that they had inflated the volume of transactions they had made, specifically in the African region. When you put all the metrics together, they probably do not even control ten percent of the market. Obviously, this is not something investors want to hear. Especially when you are a publicly-traded company."

"So, what does this have to do with Derek Starr?" Michael asked, confused.

"Do you know who Fast-Card's accounting firm is?" Voss asked.

Michael understood. "Chester and Associates."

"Exactly. And you know who's on the board of Fast-Card?"

"Let me guess," Michael said. "Brian Chester."

Voss smiled.

Helen was dismayed at not being able to speak to Brian Chester when they had visited Chester and Associates. He was out of the country. Probably in Denmark trying to clean up the Fast-Card fiasco.

Michael said, "And you believe Chester and Associates were fudging the numbers for Fast-Card?"

Voss put his hands up in a defensive gesture. "Please don't quote me on this. I'm only saying what I've heard and what I've been told. And none of it was by Derek. I think he strongly believed the investigation would have a severe impact on Chester and Associates. Maybe even charges being laid on those believed to be responsible for the Fast-Card mess. And so, he was just trying to be proactive. He wanted to let me know that if there was an opportunity in Delta Management, he would be interested in joining our team. That's it."

There was a moment of silence as Michael and Helen tried to figure out how this helped them with *their* investigation.

Michael then said, "Did Derek ever mention he felt his life might in danger?"

Voss shook his head. "No. Never. And to be frank, I'd be surprised if he told me that. At the end of the day, we're all mere accountants."

"But as you said earlier, you're also advisors, are you not?" Helen said.

"Sure. But the advice we give our clients doesn't lead to life or death. It's only money."

For some, it could be about life and death, Helen thought, but she decided against saying anything.

They thanked him and left.

FORTY-THREE

SIMON

My conversation with Gabe left me feeling angry, not at Gabe and his lack of emotion about what happened to Dimitris Diakos, but more at myself. I should've known better. My brother wasn't one to dwell on the past. He rarely spoke about our father, even though he and our father were very close. Gabe preferred to focus on the future. There was no point in looking back, he would always say. You can't change the past. But you can always change the future.

I, on the other hand, felt like you can always learn from your past. From the mistakes, you had made. Lessons you had forgotten—anything to make you a better person for the present and the future.

I am not ashamed to say that I let Nick off the hook for what he'd done to me, but it was a small price for what we had done to his father.

Does that make me a pushover? Perhaps. But knowing that I got my comeuppance now, rather than later, made me feel at ease.

I left my office building and walked across the parking lot to my car.

I unlocked the doors with my key fob.

"Simon."

I turned around and froze.

A woman stood a few feet away from me. She was small. Almost frail. She had streaks of white in her hair, and her skin was pale. Even then, I found myself weak in the knees.

"Annabelle," I said, barely getting the name out.

I had met Annabelle Williams over twenty years ago. I had gone to India to find myself and volunteer with a group that helped children in the slums. My father had just died a month before that. And I was lost and confused. I didn't know what my life's purpose was anymore. I knew I didn't want to follow in my father's footsteps, and I was glad Gabe was always supposed to take over where my father had left off. It was only later, after much convincing by him and our mother, that I joined the family firm.

Annabelle had gone to India to help the poor and needy. She'd had a hard childhood. Her family was from South Carolina. She was kind, gentle, and honest. The months I'd spent with her in India were some of the happiest moments I could remember.

It was as if we were meant for each other. She understood me like no one had before. Maybe it was my first true love. Maybe I was just confused. What I do remember was that she had broken my heart.

"I knew I would find you here," she said.

I just stared at her.

She looked down at her clothes. She tried to straighten the crease on her dress. "I never imagined we would meet like this. I look like mess," she said.

"You look beautiful," I blurted. I immediately blushed, saying it.

She smiled. "You were always kind with your words."

"What are you doing here?" I asked.

She looked around the parking lot. "Can we talk? Somewhere private?"

"I'm not sure what is there to talk about," I said. "After India, you disappeared."

Her eyes widened. "What?"

"Yeah, you said you would keep in contact. I gave you my home number. My address. But I never heard from you. In fact, I tried searching for you after I got back home. But there were too many Williams' in South Carolina, and I finally gave up."

She looked confused. "I called you several times," she said. "I spoke to your mother. I even wrote to you."

I blinked. "I never got any letters from you. My mom never told me you had called."

She wrapped her arms around herself. "That can't be right. Your mother said that you didn't want anything to do with me. Even after I told her…"

She fell silent.

"Told her what?"

She stared at me. "You don't know?"

"Know what?"

She shut her eyes tight. Her body relaxed, and I thought she would fall on the ground. I don't know why, maybe out of instinct, but I reached out and held her.

"I'm fine," she said. "It comes in waves."

"What comes in waves?"

"The pain and nausea."

"Why?"

She paused, looking unsure if she should tell me. "Simon, I have a brain tumor."

I wasn't sure why—I hadn't seen her in two decades, she was a stranger to me now—but I felt like someone had hit me with a sledgehammer.

"I'm so sorry to hear that," I said. "I truly am."

She smiled weakly. "I know you are. And thank you."

"There's a coffee shop around the corner. We can go there and talk," I said.

FORTY-FOUR

SIMON

We were seated by the windows. I had ordered coffee, two cream, two sugar, while Annabelle had ordered steeped lemon tea.

The coffee shop was half empty. There were mostly students with laptops and an occasional couple in the shop.

I took a sip from my cup and said, "You had asked if I'd known. What did you mean by that?"

She looked down at her cup. "I always thought you were ashamed of me, and that is why you wanted nothing to do with me."

"Ashamed of you?" I said, surprised. "Why would I be?"

"I mean, you knew about my family. You knew they were poor. My dad left us when I was a child, and my mom did odd jobs just to put food on the table."

"I never cared about that. I even told you that when we were together in India."

"I know you did, but people change, or they come to their senses when they get back with their family and their normal lives."

"I didn't forget you, Annabelle," I said. "I spent years searching for you. The only thing I regret is not hiring a private investigator."

She turned and looked out the window. There were tears in her eyes, and her bottom lip quivered.

Again, I don't know why, but I reached over and put my hand over hers. I was expecting her to pull back. She didn't.

"Just because my family was financially secure and yours wasn't," I said, "that had absolutely nothing to do with how I felt about you."

She nodded in understanding. She then looked at me. "So, your mom never told you?"

"Told me what?"

"About him."

"About who?"

"Your son."

If the news of her ill health hit me like a sledgehammer, the news that I had a son felt like I'd been run over by a Mack Truck.

"My son?" I asked, not believing.

"Yes," she replied. "After I came back to America. I found out I was pregnant. I wanted to tell you. But twenty years ago, no one had cell phones. So, the only thing I could do was call your home. That's when I spoke to your mother."

My head was spinning. "You told her you were pregnant?"

"Of course, I did. Why else would I call? I wanted to share the news with you."

My ears began to ring. I shut my eyes to make the noise go away. I waited a few seconds and opened my eyes again.

"When you told my mom you were pregnant, what was her reaction?"

"At first, she seemed excited, or at least sounded excited," Annabelle said. "But then she started asking about me and my family. In India, you told me it was never an issue with you, how poor we were. So, I told your mom the truth. That we had moved around a lot when we were younger. That I hadn't seen my father since I was a child. That when my mom was out of a job, we were on Social Security. That we had been evicted many times for not paying the rent. Now when I think about it, maybe I shouldn't have been so forthcoming with her. I was emotional then. I was pregnant. My mind was all over the place. I was excited about having a baby, but I was also scared at the same time. I needed help. I knew I couldn't bring a child into the world on my own. My mom was barely able to feed me and my siblings. To ask her to feed another mouth would have been too much. So that's why I kept reaching out to you."

FORTY-FIVE

SIMON

I knew Annabelle wasn't lying. The last two weeks we'd spent together in India, Annabelle had been visibly sick. She said it must have been the local food, and I believed her. In hindsight, the signs were there. The morning sickness. The change in taste and smell. The fatigue. Vanessa was never able to bear children, so I didn't experience any of this with her. But my sister-in-law, Deidre, had shown the same symptoms. Gabe wouldn't stop complaining about it. He couldn't wait for the first trimester to be over so that things could go back to how they were before the pregnancy. I had always found his griping irritating. I thought he was lucky that he was going to be a father, something I would never experience.

I suddenly felt sick to my stomach. "I... I had no idea I had a son," I said.

She looked down at her cup again. "I figured that because of my family's history, you wanted nothing to do with us. And that you had second thoughts about the time we spent together in India. That's why you wanted me gone. Out of your life forever. But in hindsight, I should have taken the money."

I stared at her. "What money?"

"The last time I called your house, your mother offered me money to make me go away."

"What?"

She nodded. "Your mother said you had a bright future ahead of you, and it didn't involve supporting me and my child."

Anger blazed up in me. "How much did she offer you?" I asked.

"I never bothered to ask. I always thought you knew. And I was hurt that you thought you could buy me out. That you could use your money to cut me and your child out of your life."

I balled my fists to control myself. All I saw was red. If my mother was in front of me, I knew I would say things to her that I would end up regretting.

Annabelle saw the pain on my face. She gripped my hand tightly. "It's fine," she said with a soothing voice. "You didn't know, and now I know that you had not pushed us away."

I fell silent. My brain suddenly stopped working. It felt like it had crashed from information overload. I took a deep breath.

She said, "But you can help us now. You can help your son."

I looked up at her with eagerness. "How?"

"He's a good kid with a good heart, but he's done something bad."

My heart suddenly sank. "What has he done?"

"I don't know. He called me from the police department, and he said he won't be coming home tonight. It had something to do with bail," Annabelle said. "Since my prognosis, I haven't worked. The disability checks are barely enough to cover the rent. I don't have the kind of money to get him out. That's why I finally mustered the courage to come see you. I have no one else to turn to."

"I'm glad you came to me, Annabelle," I said. "What's his name?"

"Cole. Cole Madsen."

"You gave him your mom's maiden name?"

"I should've called him Cole Harris, but I was angry at you. I figured, in the end, my mom would help me raise him, so why not continue on her family name?"

I wasn't offended. I was just hurt and disappointed at what *my* family had done. They had kept a secret from me that they had no right to keep. Part of me wanted to storm over to my mother's place and confront her for what she had done. But I had more pressing matters to attend to.

"Don't worry," I said. "I will make bail. I will get our son out."

At the sound of the words *our son*, her eyes welled up, and she broke down crying. I couldn't help it either. Tears flowed freely from my eyes, too.

FORTY-SIX

HELEN

She pulled into the driveway and parked the car. It had been an exhausting day, and she was looking forward to unwinding with a glass of wine and a good book.

As she got out, she saw a silhouette on the front porch. He was sitting on the patio chair. She was not alarmed. She knew who it was.

He stood up when she got to the front steps.

"If I hadn't seen you in that very spot many times before," she said, "I would've thought you were an intruder and shot you."

He smiled. "I wasn't in the house, but outside. Wouldn't shooting me be too excessive in this case?"

"You're still on my property."

"It used to be mine, too."

Paul Sloan was tall, with broad shoulders, a cleft chin, and piercing blue eyes. Over the years, his hair had thinned, and his skin had sagged a bit, but he was still handsome for a middle-aged man.

If they were still married, people would think she was older than him by a good ten years. But in fact, he was older than her by a mere ten months. They had met at a party while at college. He was with his friends, and she was with hers. He always told her that the moment he saw her, he knew he would one day marry her. But she could never confess the same thing. While love at first sight did exist, it took a woman time to decide if she wanted to spend the rest of her life with someone. And it took a good two years and several attempts for Helen to accept Paul's proposal. The first time he proposed to her was on a beach in Punta Cana. While it was a picturesque moment, she told him she wasn't ready. The second time was on a boat in Maui. She again turned him down. The third and fourth times were in Barcelona and Turkey. The proposals were less and less elaborate. Paul would just pop the question out of the blue to see what her response would be.

The fifth and final time was when they were watching TV at home. They had just finished dinner and were enjoying a movie when he turned to her and said halfheartedly, "You want to get married?"

By then, she'd been considering it for some time. She had passed the police academy and was working full-time as a patrol officer. Paul, on the other hand, was teaching English literature at a college nearby. They both had careers they enjoyed and the security that came with them. She couldn't find any reason not to settle down and start a family.

That night when she said yes, he let out a loud laugh. But when he saw that she was serious, he ran upstairs, spent twenty minutes searching frantically for the ring, came back, got down on one knee, and formally proposed to her.

They hugged, kissed, and cried.

That was almost thirty years ago. So much had happened between then and now. They had a girl, Emily, who was named after the poet Emily Dickinson. They moved up in their careers. Paul was a tenured professor and a published author. She became a detective who was months away from retiring.

And they were no longer together.

Such was life.

FORTY-SEVEN

HELEN

"Paul, what are you doing here?" she asked.

"I called you several times," he replied. "I even left a message."

She reached into her pocket and pulled out her cell phone. She saw half a dozen missed calls and even an icon for a voicemail that needed to be heard.

"Sorry, I've just been busy with a new case," she said. "What was so urgent that you had to come all the way to my house to tell me?"

"I came to tell you it's Lucy's birthday."

Lucy was Emily's daughter and their only grandchild. She was turning four. *Or was it five?* Helen thought. She was terrible with dates and ages.

"When is the party?" Helen asked.

"Tonight."

Helen checked her watch. "You mean *now*?"

"Svetlana and I are on our way there right now."

Helen raised an eyebrow. "Svetlana?"

"That's her name."

"Where is she?"

"In the car."

Helen turned and spotted Paul's sedan parked across the street. In the passenger seat, she saw a silhouette.

Helen asked, "How long have you both been waiting here?"

"Only a couple minutes," he replied. "I was actually writing you a note on the patio table when I saw your car pull up." He pulled out a piece of paper from his pocket and held it out for her.

She took the note and unfolded it. It read in bold cursive: *Lucy's birthday. Tonight. Please come.*

"I was going to stick it in the storm door so that you saw it when you got home," he said.

"You've been with Svetlana for how long?" she asked.

"A couple of months now."

"Another fan of yours?"

Women found writers, especially writers who were published, very attractive. There was something alluring about those who could create worlds out of prose. Paul's first two books sold close to half a million copies. He had toured several countries, been to many writer's conventions, and had been invited to speak on many panels. So, it was not uncommon to see him with younger women after he and Helen had separated.

It was not Paul's infidelity that caused the dissolution of their marriage. It was… just complicated.

"No, actually, I met her at a book signing," he said. "She was there to promote her new book while I was there to promote mine."

"Well, that's a first. You usually date groupies or wannabe writers. People who think that by dating a published author, somehow they'll get their manuscripts published, too."

He stared at her and shook his head. "Listen, I'm not here to get into a discussion with you about my love life. I just came to tell you that your granddaughter's birthday is tonight and that it would be great if you were there."

"When have I ever missed her birthday?" Helen asked.

"You weren't there at her last birthday."

"I thought it was on the next day. Plus, I had to show up in court in the morning, and I had to prepare my statements. I was going to be grilled by the defense."

Paul sighed. "There's always some excuse with you."

"Well, I'm sorry that my work is so important. Unlike…" She stopped.

"Unlike mine where I sit behind a desk and make up stuff."

"I never said that."

"But you were about to." He turned to the sedan. He could see Svetlana waiting patiently for him. "Just come. Okay? Both Lucy and Emily would be happy to see you."

He walked down the driveway to his car.

FORTY-EIGHT

SIMON

My meeting with Annabelle left me angrier than before. I was also heartbroken and confused. I was angry that my family had lied to her and betrayed me. I was heartbroken that I never saw my son grow up. I was confused because I realized I still harbored feelings for Annabelle.

She brought out something in me that no one had before. Not even Vanessa.

I close my eyes and sighed. Through all of this, I'd forgotten about my wife.

How would I break the news to her? How would I tell her that I was a father? She and I had wanted to be parents for so long and so badly that sometimes I felt it was the only thing that kept us together. We had shared a single goal: a desire to have a family of our own. Two kids and maybe a pet. We got neither of them. When we couldn't have children, Vanessa didn't want to get an animal. The pet would have been a consolation for what we couldn't create—children. Instead, we focused on our careers and on other parts of our life: travel, friends, hobbies.

I wasn't sure what Vanessa's reaction would be when I told her I had a son. Would she feel inadequate that she couldn't bear my children while I had a child with someone else?

I would tell her it was before I'd met her, and that was the honest truth. Having a child didn't mean we couldn't be together. Things would be a little complicated, but not by much. My son wasn't a child—someone who needed constant care and attention—he was an adult, a grown man.

That thought broke something deep inside me. I was never there during his milestones. I never got to see him walk. Say his first words. Go to school for the first time. Play catch. Or do so many other things that most fathers and sons did.

I wasn't even there for him when he was sick or hurt. I couldn't hold him and tell him everything would be all right.

I wiped tears from my eyes.

I was behind the wheel of my BMW. I had paid for a taxi to drive Annabelle home. She had taken the bus to meet me, and there was no way I was going to let her take public transit. I had debated driving her back myself. There was so much I wanted to ask her. So much I wanted to know about my son. But now was not the time.

I composed myself, started the engine, and drove straight to the Arlington PD.

I walked straight to the officer behind the front desk and announced that I had come to make bail for a Cole Madsen.

The officer checked his records and told me to take a seat in the waiting area.

I sat on a hard plastic chair. I wasn't sure why, but I was nervous. The heel of my right shoe tapped the cement floor uncontrollably. I shut my eyes to make the tapping stop.

I'd been to several meditation classes. I had always been a thinker, worrier, and that had resulted in me becoming anxious quite easily. The meditation helped to calm me down.

I sat up straight with both my feet planted firmly on the floor. I then began to take deep breaths. I inhaled through the nostrils, held it in for ten seconds, and exhaled through the mouth. The trick was not just the breathing, which invariably helped to slow the heartbeat. The trick was to focus on the breathing, visualize the air going into the nostrils and out through the mouth. It was a way to stop the mind from wandering, which wasn't as simple as it looked. But after much practice, meditation became easier.

My eyes snapped open when I heard someone call out my name. I blinked and looked around and spotted a familiar face.

Detective Ken Booker stood two feet away from me. He was holding a manila folder in his hand.

"I'm surprised to see you again today, Mr. Harris," he said.

I stood up. "Yeah, it was a surprise for me, too."

"The officer at the front desk told me that you've come here to post bail, is that correct?"

"It is."

"How well do you know Cole Madsen?" he asked.

"I know his mom, and she asked me for help."

"Have you posted bail before?"

I shook my head.

"The amount isn't as high as in some other cases, but I should let you know that in the event Mr. Madsen fails to appear in court, you forfeit the amount of the bail."

"How much is it? His mom didn't know."

"Five-thousand dollars."

For some reason, I was expecting it to be far more than that. Maybe it was from the movies I'd seen, where the judge bangs his gravel and declares an amount of a million dollars, or something close to that. The defendant would whisper something to his lawyers, and in the next scene, he'd be out free while awaiting trial. No one actually discussed how or who posted his bail. Maybe it was family members. Maybe it was friends or relatives. But a million dollars was a lot of money. Not many people had that kind of money lying around. I guess, in a legal thriller, talking about dollars and cents wasn't as glamorous when you had a bigger mystery to deal with: was the defendant guilty of murder, or was he framed for the crime?

"Mr. Harris—"

Booker's voice snapped me out of my reverie.

"Like I said, it's not a very high amount, but you are responsible for making sure that Mr. Madsen shows up before a judge."

"I understand," I said.

FORTY-NINE

SIMON

"All right," Booker said. "I'll take you to the clerk. I'm assuming you'll be paying by check or credit card."

"Yes, but I wasn't sure what type of payment you took."

"We even take online transfers," he said with a smile. "The Arlington PD is not as behind the times as most people say we are."

I spent ten minutes filling out a variety of forms, signing and initialing several boxes. I also wrote a check for five-thousand dollars.

Once done, Booker took me down the hallway, through a set of heavy metal doors, and down another hallway. He then spoke to an officer behind a desk. The officer was a large man, strong and intimidating. The officer pulled out a set of keys that were hooked to his belt. He then moved to a cell door on the other side of the space.

I was behind Booker, but I could tell there were several people in the holding cell. I wasn't sure which one was my son.

"Cole Madsen," the officer yelled into the cell. Someone stood up and approached the officer. Through the thick bars, I couldn't see his face clearly. My heart started beating faster, and my breathing became shallow. The anticipation was literally going to kill me.

Booker looked at me. "You okay?"

"Yeah, I'm fine. It's just been a long day."

The officer said to the man in the cell, "You're free to go. You just made bail."

A moment later, a young man came out. He was taller than me. Broad shoulders and arms. A hard but handsome face. If you asked me, he looked nothing like me. Except for the eyes. They were unmistakable.

Annabelle had made me promise that I wouldn't tell Cole who I was. She feared he wouldn't take the news too well. He would be angry, and he would lash out. After all, for all those years she had told him his father was gone, probably living in some other country, while I was living in the same city as him. She felt it would be best that she told him herself when the time was right.

I was fine with that. Even I was having trouble making sense of the revelation.

"Who made bail?" Cole asked the officer.

The officer slammed the cell door shut and locked it. "Don't know. Don't care. You can go talk to the detective over there."

That was when he turned and looked in our direction. He recognized Booker, but looked confused when he saw me.

Booker waved him over. As he ambled toward us, Booker said, "I guess you won't be spending the night here or at the state pen."

Cole turned to me. "You posted my bail?"

My throat was dry, but I managed to say, "I did."

His eyes narrowed. "Do I know you?"

"I know your mom, and she asked for my help."

"How do you know my mom?" he asked skeptically.

"I met her in India." I had agreed not to tell him who I was, but I wasn't going to lie to him either. Lies always had a way of coming back to bite you. Plus, this was the first time I'd met my son, and I wasn't going to start off by being dishonest with him. That was no way to begin a relationship.

He nodded. "She did mention going to India when she was younger."

I turned to the detective. "Can we leave?"

"Absolutely," Booker said with a smile. "Just make sure he's in front of the judge when the time comes."

"He will be," I said.

I walked down the hallway, through the set of heavy metal doors, down another hallway, and into the lobby of the station. Throughout this time, I kept staring at my son. The texture of his hair. The slight stubble on his chin. Everything about him fascinated me.

I know that sounds odd, but I don't care. How would you feel and act if you found out that you had a part in the creation of another human being? You'd want to know if he or she looked like you, or if he or she had the same mannerisms as you, or if he or she shared the same hobbies and interests as you.

The next generation was an extension of the first. If you were lucky to have kids, you knew they would continue on your lineage. Hopefully, you would not be forgotten, and perhaps, even fondly remembered.

When we were outside the station, I said to Cole, "My car's over there."

He turned to me. "Listen, I appreciate that you came and got me out, but I'm not going anywhere with you."

"Your mom told me to bring you home."

"I don't know you, man."

"You can call your mom, and she'll confirm what I just told you."

"I'll talk to her, all right," he said, stuffing his hands in his pockets. "But right now, I've got somewhere to be."

"Do you want me to give you a ride?" I asked. I didn't want to see him go. I wanted to spend as much time as I could with him.

"Thanks for your help, but I know my way home."

With that, he walked through the parking lot and disappeared down the street.

FIFTY

HELEN

The birthday party turned out to be more enjoyable than Helen had anticipated. She didn't like large gatherings. She wasn't one for chit-chat, and there were only so many questions she could answer. People found police work fascinating and exciting. They knew only what they had seen from movies and TV series. Investigations were filled with intrigue and suspense, and they were solved within a short period of time. In reality, there was nothing intriguing or suspenseful about them. It was grunt work that required digging through mountains of evidence and going through hours of witness statements. If you were lucky, a clue at the scene or a comment by a witness might lead you to a suspect and an arrest. More often than not, those clues were hard to come by. And those witnesses weren't as forthcoming as the police hoped they would be. People weren't comfortable openly and freely talking to the police, especially if they held a grudge against the victim or if they feared being roped in as suspects on a murder case.

For curious individuals, they wanted to know all the juicy details. What was the most gruesome case she had worked on? How did she link a suspect to a crime? Had she shot and killed someone?

In the beginning, Helen was flattered that strangers were interested in what she did. But over the years, the questions had become tiresome, and she told them she couldn't discuss ongoing investigations. And if they were stubborn and wouldn't relent, she would offer to tell them every sordid detail down at the Arlington PD. They always declined because, like going to the hospital, no one wanted to go to the police station unless it was absolutely necessary.

Fortunately for her, Emily and her husband, Tim, an oncologist, had decided to hold the party at home, and they only invited immediate family. Helen, Paul and Svetlana, Tim's parents, and Tim's sister and her husband. Tim's sister had kids the same age as Lucy, so the kids had a lot of fun together. They were all dressed up as their favorite animated character. The kids had cake and cheese pizza, while the adults had cake and pepperoni pizza.

At the end of the party, Helen decided to stay behind and help Emily clean up. Tim took Lucy upstairs to bed.

"I'm sorry I didn't come with a gift," Helen said.

"I'm just glad you came," Emily said as she loaded the dishwasher.

"Tell me what Lucy wants, and I'll order it online."

"It's fine, mom. You don't have to get her anything."

"No, I want to. Tell me."

Emily shrugged. "I don't know."

"You're her mother, and you don't know what she likes?" Helen said, annoyed.

Emily stopped what she was doing. "Do you really want to know what she likes?"

"That's what I'm asking you, aren't I?"

"She likes that her grandmother calls her to see how she's doing. She likes that her grandmother is at all her important events. She likes that her grandmother spends time with her."

"You're being too overly dramatic," Helen shot back.

"Am I?" Emily said. "Because you know what, mom? That's what *I* wanted growing up. I didn't care for all the gifts you bought me.'"

"What? You were always excited when I got you something."

"Of course, I was excited. I was just a kid. But deep down, I really wanted your attention."

"I gave you as much attention as I could away from my job."

"That's the thing, mom. Your job took so much of your time that you barely had any left for me. And when you did, your mind was still on your work. So, I never really got your full and undivided attention, did I?"

FIFTY-ONE

HELEN

She fell silent, staring at her only child. Emily looked quite like her, but she had Paul's characteristics. She was sensitive. She had what some would call high emotional intelligence. Helen had learned to control her emotions. Her job required her to be focused, impartial, logical. It was the only way for her to do her job properly and not fall apart.

But now that she thought about it, by not bringing home the filth she dealt with at work, she thought she was protecting her family. Instead, she was closing herself off from them. When she was near them, she wasn't really with them. She was someplace else. She was solving other people's problems. She didn't realize she had problems of her own at home.

"Is that why you didn't invite me tonight?" Helen asked.

"I figured you'd to be too busy. Or, you wouldn't want to come."

"I would never miss anyone's birthday."

Emily rolled her eyes. "Come on, mom. You were hardly there when I was young. You missed my recital, my violin concert, my high school graduation. And when Tim and I got married, you left in the middle of the reception."

"I had an important lead to follow up on."

"You always did."

Helen shook her head. "That's not fair, Emily. You make it sound like I was never there."

"Were you?"

Helen thought a moment. "I came to the hospital when Lucy was born."

"I had a C-section, and I was in the hospital for three days because of complications. You came to see me on the last day," Emily said, raising her voice. She shut her eyes to compose herself. She opened them and said, "It was hard not having you around growing up, but at least I had dad. He never missed any of my important events. Not once."

"Before he became a tenured professor, he only taught night classes. The rest of the day, he was home writing his books."

"How many books did he write, mom?"

Helen paused and then shrugged. "He must have dozens of manuscripts in his desk drawers."

"Three. Dad wrote three books. Do you know why?"

"I don't know. Maybe he had writer's block."

"No. He didn't write more books because he was spending that time with *me*. Dad would play games with me at home. He would take me to the playground. We would go shopping together. Watch cartoons together. Have breakfast, lunch, and dinner together. Only time he would write was when I went for my afternoon naps or late at night after I'd gone to bed."

Helen stared at her. "What about when you went to school? Didn't your dad have time to write then?"

"I'm sure that's when he got those books finally written, but that didn't mean he stopped being focused on me. He would drop me off at school, pick me up, help me do my homework, and get me ready for bed. This was on top of everything else he did in the house. He was like a single parent."

"That's sexist. You know that," Helen said. "Throughout history, women have sacrificed their careers for the wellbeing of their family. Now that your father had to do it, you are complaining."

"Whether it is a man or a woman who neglects their family, it still doesn't make it right," Emily shot back. "Children only want to know that they are the center of attention in their parents' world. To them, nothing else matters. Money. Work. Accolades. Those are not important to them. Their parents' devotion to them is." Emily sighed. "Why do you think I decided to take time off after Lucy was born? I know you thought it was a mistake. That I would fall behind in my career, but I'll tell you something. The time I got to spend with Lucy was the happiest time of my life. She would only be young once, and I'm glad I was there to see every bit of it."

FIFTY-TWO

COLE

His arrest and his short time inside a cell had left him shaken and terrified. He wasn't sure if or how he'd get out. His mom must have reached out to as many people as she could for help. Why this man—whom he'd never seen before—chose to come down and bail him out was surprising to him. Maybe he was an old friend. Perhaps, even an ex-boyfriend. His mom never got married, but she'd been with a few men in her time. He didn't hold that against her. She was lonely, and it must not have been easy raising him on her own.

Cole was a troublemaker from a young age. He was rebellious, and he acted out. He never got himself in trouble with the law, but he did get himself in trouble at school. There were too many instances of his mom being called to the principal's office to discuss something he had done in school.

He'd been in detention far too many times to count, and he'd even been suspended on a few occasions.

All through that time, his mother never once yelled at or punished him. Maybe she should have, now that he thought about it. She was more like a friend to him than a parent. And he needed a parent more than a friend.

It would have helped if he'd had a male figure in his life. Someone to put him on the right track when he got off course. A few of his mom's boyfriends tried to enforce some rules on him, but they didn't last long enough to make an impact on him. But more importantly, those men weren't really looking to be fathers. They were only there to give his mom company and to get away from whatever problems they were dealing with. One of them had a drinking problem. He was never abusive toward him, but he did one time hit his mom. She called the cops on him, and she made sure he was charged and sent away. His mom was a fighter before the tumor robbed her of her energy. Another boyfriend had a family. He only came to see his mom for extramarital activity. A third boyfriend suffered from depression. He was a nice guy who always treated him and his mom well. But one day, while going to work, he stepped in front of a train. The doctors thought he'd stopped taking his medications, and the mental pain was too much for him to bear.

All the men in his life never stuck around long enough to forge a lasting relationship with him. The guy at the police station would be gone too. Cole doubted if he'd ever see him again.

Cole also never wanted to see the inside of a jail cell again. For that reason, he decided he wouldn't commit another crime.

He would find another way to raise the cash he needed to help his mom.

But first, he wanted to see someone before he headed home.

He took the bus and got off a block from his destination. He walked down the street and stopped in front of a restaurant. He peeked through the window. The restaurant wasn't busy, but he could see a woman serving customers at a table.

Rachel Moon had red hair, an easy smile, and she had expressive green eyes. Cole had met her in high school. She came from a stable family. Her dad worked in sales for a pharmaceutical company. Her mom was a manager for a department store. She had an older brother and a younger sister. Rachel was in her third year of college, with a focus on health sciences. Her parents were financially secure enough to pay for her tuition. But Rachel was independent. She wanted to pay her own way in life. That was why she worked as a waitress when she wasn't in class. She also tutored secondary school students on the weekends. She was motivated to make something of herself.

He, on the other hand, had no idea what he wanted out of life.

How he and Rachel got together was always a mystery to him. She sat in front of him in biology class. He loved her perfume. It was a combination of strawberries and chocolate. Her hair flowed down her back, and he couldn't help staring at her. He didn't think she had noticed what he did. One day, she turned to him, looked him in the eyes, and asked him what his problem was. Was he a creep? A perv? Or was he just a weirdo?

He was stunned by her directness.

He stammered for a bit, but then something popped in his head. He asked her the name of the perfume she had on. His mom's birthday was coming up, and he wanted to get her the same brand. But he was worried Rachel might think he was a mama's boy if he asked her. It was an obvious lie, of course. Birthdays in his home involved going to a fast-food restaurant. Money was always tight, so gifts were a luxury.

Rachel found that endearing and sweet. She told him the name of the brand—which he never bought, as his mom would've made him return it anyway—and from that day on, they'd started dating.

FIFTY-THREE

COLE

Their relationship was rocky from the beginning. Rachel didn't like the fact that Cole had no plans to go to college, even though he had the grades for it. She knew his financial situation at home, and that he had to work to support him and his mom. She still felt that without proper education, he would be jumping from one job to another. She wanted to be with someone who would work just as hard as her parents had to create a stable environment for their family.

Cole was now ready to do just that. He wouldn't get himself involved with people like Leo. They were criminals. They cared for no one but themselves. When Cole was locked up, he felt all alone. Like there was no one outside who cared for what happened to him. Except for his mom, of course.

He wouldn't dare call Rachel to bail him out. He hadn't spoken to her since their last fight, which was two months ago. He wasn't even sure what it was about, but it was bad. He'd called her many times after, but she refused to answer him. One night, though, she'd left him a voice mail. She said she still cared for him, but she needed space. She wanted to take this time to figure out exactly what she wanted for herself. She told him she'd call him when she got the time.

She never did. And he never bothered to contact her again.

Why did I come here? he thought.

196

He had turned to leave when he heard a voice say, "Cole."

It was Rachel. She was standing outside the restaurant. "I saw you through the windows. What are you doing here?"

"I came to see you," he said.

She crossed her arms over her chest.

"Just listen to me," he said, taking a step closer. "You were right. You were always right. I should be more focused on my future. I can't meander through life without any purpose. I just came to tell you that I'm ready. I'm going to enroll in college the moment the next semester opens up."

Her eyes narrowed. "What about your work?"

"Work?" he said.

"The construction company you work for."

She has no idea I was fired.

"I'm going to quit that."

Her eyes narrowed. "Then how will you pay for anything?"

"I'll get student loans. This way, I can pay full attention to my education."

She stared at him and then said, "Why are you telling me this?"

"I thought it was important that you knew. And…"

She shook her head. "Cole, I'm sorry, but we can't be together."

"Just give me another chance. I can change. I swear."

She sighed. "I'm seeing someone else."

He felt like someone had punched him in the gut. "What?"

"I know I didn't end things properly. I should've called you or told you in person, but as time went on, I just figured you understood."

"Who is it?" he asked.

"Does it matter?"

It didn't, he knew. Whoever it was, it wouldn't change the fact that she would never come back to him. She had moved on with her life.

"I have to get back to work," she said.

He nodded.

Rachel said, "You know, I didn't end our relationship because you didn't go to college. That stuff didn't really matter to me."

"Then why did you end it?"

"I ended it because I couldn't see you waste your life away. You have so much potential in you, even if you never saw it. I did. You're a smart guy, Cole. You just don't know how to apply yourself. You also don't know how to be responsible. Whatever bad that has happened to you, you always blamed it on something else. You never knew your father. Your uncle abandoned you and your mom. Your mom got sick. It was never your fault."

His eyes narrowed. "How is my mom getting sick my fault?"

"The tumor didn't grow in one day. Your mom started to show symptoms *way* before she ended up getting diagnosed. I remember telling you to take her to the doctor, and your response was, 'It's her life, and if she doesn't want to go, then that's up to her'."

He stared at her in silence.

"You were too busy with Buddy getting high to even care," she said. "You got her checked out only when the pain had become unbearable. But by then, the tumor had enlarged to the point that the only way to stop it was to remove it."

"I'm going to get her the operation she needs," he said, defiantly. "I'm going to do everything to make sure that she is better."

"I hope you do," Rachel said. "I really do. But that won't change anything between us. I'm sorry."

He didn't realize it, but tears were flowing down his cheeks. He wiped them with the back of his hand.

"Yeah, I'm sorry too," he said and left.

FIFTY-FOUR

SIMON

My mother lived in a gated community, sandwiched between a forest on one side and a golf course on the other. Each house in the community cost a minimum of a million dollars, with some reaching as high as five million. My parents were lucky to get into the development when it was in its pre-planning stage, which meant they didn't have to pay what it was worth now.

I signed in with the security guard at the main gate. This involved providing my license plate number, the name of the homeowner I was visiting, and the duration of my stay. I was always uncomfortable providing this much information to a stranger. It was no one's business when and how long I spent with my mother. But I understood the reasons behind it. Some of the most affluent people in the city lived here. These people were titans of industry. They also brought with them a host of scrutiny. It was not uncommon to find reporters outside the gates of the community. There were also quite a few members who were indicted on fraud, embezzlement, and various other white-collar crimes. Plus, people with money were always a target, so I felt somewhat secure in the knowledge that my mother was safe.

The security guard was armed. And from what I'd been told, all the guards on shift were ex-military. There was no way an unauthorized person could get in without facing resistance. There had been cases of visitors being disallowed entry because of rude or bad behavior. It didn't matter who they were or who they were visiting. The board that managed the exclusive community were the real decision-makers. They were homeowners who'd been elected each year by the members of the community. The elections were hotly contested, but it was the same people who ended up holding the positions on the board.

My father always believed the elections were rigged. He ran for the board a few times, but he always lost. However, he never dared challenge the election results. People with money tended to hold grudges. And my parents loved living in the community. I think it had more to do with the address. The zip code opened many doors for residents of the community. My parents didn't hesitate to bring that up. Whether it was at the bank, a retail store, or a restaurant, they knew how a few letters and numbers at the end of an address could give them special treatment.

By the time my parents had bought this place, I'd already moved out, so I never got to see the advantage it would've given me had I used it. Gabe, on the other hand, used my parents' address on his bank accounts. He said it allowed him access to more funds when dealing with bank managers.

My father was an avid golfer, and he wanted to be as close to the course as possible, so the house was perfect for what he was looking for. That was before it became *the* most sought-after zip code in the city. My father would play a few holes in the morning, go to the office, and play a few more before sunset. Maybe that's how Gabe got into the sport. Like I said, I'm a basketball fan.

The security guard waved me through. I drove along a winding road and into the community. Each house resembled a mini-mansion, and not one was the same. The community wasn't built by a single developer. Each homeowner bought a plot of land and built their own house to their specifications. Some houses looked like they came from the Victorian era. Some houses looked like they were tiny castles. Some houses were made of glass and steel. Each resembled the homeowners' personality.

My parent's home was more regal. The exterior was white, white Roman columns, white French windows. There were even white Italian statues scattered across the property. It had four bedrooms, five bathrooms, a space for an office, a library, a sauna, a tea room in the back, and it also boasted a large garden and a swimming pool. It had everything a couple, or even a family, with money could ever want.

I parked my BMW next to a water fountain and got out. I walked up to the front steps, and before I could ring the doorbell, a woman answered the door. Rosa was my mother's housekeeper. She was from Guatemala. After my father's death, my brother and I decided that Rosa would live on the property full-time. Prior to that, she used to only come a few hours a day to clean and do other chores around the house.

"Mr. Simon," she said with a smile. "So nice to see you again."

I liked Rosa. She had a pleasant personality. She used to be a teacher in her country. But teachers didn't make a good salary. She had a husband and two children to support back home. Each month she sent them money, and twice a year, she visited them. Her dream was to one day bring them to America, so they could be a family once again.

"How are your daughters?" I asked.

Her smile widened. "They're doing well. And thank you for the gifts, Mr. Simon."

Each year on their birthday, I made sure to send something of value to them. Rosa's daughters were now teenagers. I gave them smartphones, laptops, and anything else that might help them in their education.

"You're most welcome," I said.

"Madam is waiting for you in the tea room."

"Rosa," I said, "do you mind taking a walk outside? I would like to speak to my mother in private."

I was here for a reason, and I didn't want Rosa to be around. I was concerned she would be privy to our conversation. I just wasn't sure how I was going to react around my mother, and I didn't want Rosa to see me like that.

"Of course, Mr. Simon," she said, the smile still on her face. "I think I'll go take a look at the garden. The roses might need extra water."

My mother employed a full-time gardener, but I appreciated Rosa's initiative.

When she was out of sight, I walked past a spiral staircase and straight to the tea room at the back of the house.

FIFTY-FIVE

SIMON

I found my mother seated on a comfortable chair. She was small and slim. She used to dye her hair religiously, but after my father's death, she let the gray come out. Even then, her hair was styled and coiffed. Her skin was tanned and wrinkled, but she always had on lipstick and eyeliner.

She was reading a fashion magazine when she saw me come in. She pulled off her reading glasses and waved me over. "Simon, darling. So good to see you."

She had that same fake posh British accent. It never used to be there until my father started making more money. In the beginning, I found it annoying and downright irritating, but over the years, I've become accustomed to it.

I walked over and gave her a peck on the cheek. I sat down across from her on the chair where my father used to sit and have his cigar.

"Let me get you something to drink," she said with a smile. "Rosa!"

"I asked Rosa to give us some privacy," I said.

She looked surprised. "Oh, okay."

"Mother, I have a few questions I wanted to ask you."

"All right," she said, putting the magazine away.

"And I want you to be very honest with me."

Her eyes narrowed. "What is wrong, Simon?"

My heart was pounding. My hands were sweaty. My throat was dry. I said, "Did you know?"

"Know what?" she said, confused.

"That I had a son?"

She stared at me in silence. I couldn't tell if she was stunned, or if she was contemplating her next move.

She then nodded and said, "I always knew you would eventually find out."

I suddenly felt anger rise in me. "Why didn't you tell me?" I asked.

"I didn't tell you because I wanted to protect you."

"Protect me? Protect me from what?"

"From a life filled with disappointments."

I was suddenly confused.

She looked away. "I always told you that I had met your father at a country club. That he was there to play a few rounds of golf, while I was there to play a few games of tennis. But, that was not the truth. We had, in fact, met at a bar. The bar wasn't far from the university I was attending. Your father, on the other hand, had already finished school and was working for an investment firm downtown. He came up to me and offered to buy me a drink. The next thing I knew, I was in the backseat of a car, and he was on top of me. I had no memory of how I'd gotten there."

My entire body shook. "He... he..."

I couldn't get the words out.

"Yes, he forced himself on me. And right after that, I found out I was pregnant with Gabe. I threatened to take him to the police. In return, he offered to marry me and take care of me."

"Why are you telling me this now?"

"I had hopes and dreams of my own, and being married and having children in my twenties wasn't one of them. That one night at the bar changed the entire course of my life."

"You didn't have to marry him," I said.

"It's not easy raising a child on your own."

The blood rushed to my head. I had to clench my jaw to keep from raising my voice. "But you let Annabelle raise a child on her own."

She opened her mouth but then shut it.

I said, "You robbed me of the opportunity to be with my son."

She covered her face with her hands. "I was only doing it so that you could be free. So that you weren't burdened like I was."

My eyes narrowed. "Like you were?"

She looked up at me. Her eyes were red. "Let me ask you this. What would you have done if you had known you had a child?"

"I would have taken care of him like father had taken care of you and Gabe."

"Would you have married her?" she said.

I opened my mouth, but no words came out.

She said, "You are my son, and I know you better than you know yourself. You've always been sensitive. You've always cared more about others than yourself. You would have done exactly what your father had done. In the process, you would have destroyed all *your* hopes and dreams. I know what I did was wrong, and it's something I've always thought about. That's why I wasn't surprised when you brought it up. But I only did it because I love you, and I wanted to give you a chance I never had."

"It was my decision. Not yours."

"I know. And I'm sorry, Simon."

I stood up. I was angry at her, but at the same time, I felt pity for her. I didn't know that my father had taken advantage of her all those years ago. I know that her love for her two sons was blinding. She would do anything for Gabe and me, even if it meant living with our father so that we would never be burdened with the truth.

"Did father know about Annabelle?" I finally asked.

My mother shook her head. "I knew. And Gabe knew."

FIFTY-SIX

HELEN

The moment Helen got the call, she dropped everything and drove straight over. She was in a rural part of Arlington. Everything around her was open space and farmland. She got off the main road and drove down a winding path until she spotted a structure up ahead.

When she got closer, she realized it was a barn. The barn had seen better years. The roof was missing shingles, and the exterior was rotted and decayed. She was surprised it was still standing.

She parked between a Honda Civic and a beat-up Ford Truck. She got out and walked toward the barn. The barn's double doors were secured by a heavy chain and U-lock.

Maybe the barn has another entrance, she thought.

Michael came around from the back of the barn and waved her over.

"Where is it?" she asked, approaching him.

"Over there," he replied, jabbing his thumb to the right.

She then saw what he was gesturing at. It was a silver Nissan Maxima, and standing next to it was a gray-haired man with a large belly and an even larger beard.

Michael said, "This is Walt Grimsby. He's the owner of the property."

"How do you do," Grimsby said with a nod.

Helen nodded back, but her focus was on the Nissan Maxima. She quickly pulled on a pair of latex gloves and approached the vehicle.

"It's not locked," Michael said from behind her.

She opened the driver's side door and peeked inside. She smelled detergent, ammonia, and bleach. But, there were other smells, as well. She sniffed, and her eyes narrowed. It smelled like booze and body odor.

She eyed the interior. The LCD touchscreen on the dashboard had been pulled out, leaving behind clumps of wires. The glove compartment was opened. Scattered on the passenger seat were several pieces of paper.

She reached over and lifted a colored piece of paper. It was the vehicle's registration, and it was made out to Derek Starr. She sifted through the other contents and found a motor vehicle insurance document, as well as, an invoice from a toll company.

She then placed her hand between the rearview mirror and the windshield. There was nothing there. Anyone using the city's tollbooths would have had a transponder placed right behind the rearview mirror.

She spotted something. A light hit the dashboard at such an angle that she was sure she saw print marks. She got out and walked back to Michael and the property owner.

"We need to get a team over here right away," she said. "We need to pull prints from the vehicle."

"Didn't you smell it?" Michael said. "Looks like someone wiped it clean."

"They did. But I saw prints on the dashboard."

Michael's eyes widened. He quickly pulled out his cell phone and dialed a number. While he spoke on the phone, Helen turned to Grimsby.

"Mr. Grimsby, how long have you owned this property?"

"A long time."

"How long?"

"It's been in the family for generations. We used to grow all kinds of things on the land: tomatoes, cucumbers, cauliflower. And a whole bunch of other stuff." His eyes narrowed in thought. "My parents wanted me to take over the farm. But I had other plans. I wanted to travel and see the world. I left when I was twenty. I worked on cruise ships. I worked as a door-to-door salesman. I sold insurance. I did whatever job I could find. But throughout that time, I never came back here once. I wanted nothing to do with this place. It was my younger brother who took over the responsibility that I had neglected." He then pointed to an area on the other side of the property. "My parents' house used to be over there. A two-story structure. Three bedrooms. One bathroom. No basement. The only thing good about the house was the front porch. It was long and wide enough to hold half a dozen chairs. I remember sitting in the shade of the porch and drinking cold lemonade during the hot summer months. I remember playing cards with my brother there. I remember my mom locking the door when my dad came home drunk. He'd have to sleep on the porch until he sobered up."

Helen wasn't sure where he was going with this, but she didn't interrupt him. He probably didn't have anyone to talk to.

"What happened to your parent's house?" she finally asked.

FIFTY-SEVEN

HELEN

Grimsby blinked, snapping out of his thoughts. "Yeah, the house. One night a tornado came by and tore the house to pieces. My dad happened to be sleeping outside on that particular night, so he managed to get away. My mom and brother weren't so lucky. They were sleeping on the second floor. The neighbors found their bodies about a mile from where the house used to be. I came back for the funeral. I'd never seen my dad so broken up. Even when I had left years before, he had shown no emotion. But on that day, he was inconsolable. I told him I'd stay and take care of the farm, but that made it worse for him. I later found out that my brother didn't like working on the farm, either. He only did it for my father. He wasn't strong enough to leave like I had. And my dad blamed himself for what happened to him. So, while I was back, I was never wanted. Eventually, my dad drowned his sorrows in the only thing that helped him, liquor. When he died, I inherited the farm. But by then, the land hadn't been cultivated in years. Nothing was being grown on it. And with a bad back—an injury I got slipping on the deck of a cruise ship—I haven't been able to do much with it. That's why it looks the way it does."

"Why don't you sell it?" Helen asked.

"I know it sounds weird, but I just don't have the heart to," he replied. "I have some fond memories here. And not so fond memories too."

Michael came back. "The CSU team is on the way."

"How long?"

"They are twenty minutes out."

She turned to Grimsby. "Do you get trespassers on your property?"

"Why do you ask?'

She pointed to an area a couple of feet away from the Nissan Maxima, right next to the barn. "There are a bunch of cigarette butts on the ground. And if you look carefully over there, that's a syringe."

Grimsby's eyes narrowed. "I never noticed that before. I don't come here very often, so I can't say who's been on my property."

"What made you come by today?" she asked.

"I live in a rental five miles from here. Occasionally, I drive by on my way to whatever errands I'm running. When I drove by today, I thought I saw tracks on the property. It had rained a couple of nights ago, and the tracks weren't there when I was here last week. They looked like they'd been made recently. When I went to check, I found the car behind the barn."

"I saw the tracks, too," Michael said, jumping in. "I also saw foot prints. I assumed they were yours."

Grimsby shook his head. "That's a ten-minute walk to the barn from the main road. No way I'm walking that."

"Just as I thought," Helen said.

"What?" Michael asked.

"The Nissan has been wiped down by whoever brought it here."

"Okay."

"But someone else came afterward and stripped the car of its electronics."

"Who would do that?"

"I bet it's the same person who comes down here to light up and get high."

There was a moment of silence.

Michael said, "How do we find this person?"

"I have a feeling that print on the dashboard might lead us directly to him," Helen replied.

FIFTY-EIGHT

COLE

He kicked himself for going to the restaurant. What did he expect from meeting Rachel, anyway? There was no way she was going to take him back. If she'd been remotely interested, she would have answered his phone calls, text messages, and voicemails from months before. That should've been a red flag right there.

People didn't change their minds after time had passed. They only became reaffirmed in their decisions. Rachel knew she didn't want to continue their relationship, and who could blame her? She was right that he barely had his act together.

His mom needed medical attention, and she needed it right away.

He headed back to the spot where he'd been arrested. He spotted the garbage can where he had almost puked.

He looked around to see if anyone was looking and then stuck his hand inside the bin. He rummaged through Styrofoam containers, paper cups, pop cans, and other garbage until he saw it.

He pulled out the leather handbag he'd dumped in the bin prior to his arrest.

It was a good thing he had done that. If the cops had caught him red-handed, his bail wouldn't have been five-thousand only. It would've been an amount far greater than that. He doubted the guy who showed up at the station would've bothered to post bail for him then.

Cole looked suspicious holding the designer handbag, so he hid it inside his jacket and hurried down the street. He kept an eye on his surroundings. He feared being cut off by a police cruiser and getting arrested again. Whatever he had to do, he had to do it fast.

He saw an alley up ahead, and he quickly ducked into it. The alley led to the back of a local business that was filled with garbage bags and other junk, but there was no one around. He quickly unzipped the handbag and opened it. Inside, he saw designer gloves, designer sunglasses, a makeup kit, lipstick, nail polish, and various other items women carried on their persons. He also found a small wallet. The wallet contained several credit and debit cards, along with some cash. He removed the cash and stuck it in his pocket. He rummaged through the handbag some more until he found what he was looking for at the bottom of the bag. He pulled out the white rectangular box and opened it.

Inside was the Cartier watch.

He slipped the rectangular box into the inner pocket of his jacket. He then walked over, lifted the lid of a large metal garbage bin, and threw the handbag inside. He wasn't about to leave the handbag out in the open. If someone found her wallet with the credit and debit cards, they might be inclined to rack up a huge bill.

There was a strong possibility that the woman had already informed her bank of the theft, and they must've frozen her cards. Regardless, he wasn't going to take any chances. The woman had already suffered enough. The Cartier watch must've cost several thousand dollars. There was no way she was going to get that money back.

He felt like a scumbag for what he had done, but he saw no other options. Life was either eat or be eaten. Unfortunately, the woman had become the prey today.

Cole's sympathy for her quickly washed away.

That woman has money and comfort. She has security and stability. And what do I have?

Nothing.

Throughout his entire life, he and his mom had to fend for themselves. There was no one out there to help them. No one who even cared what happened to them. They were at the bottom of the totem pole. They were dirt under other people's shoes. Society preferred to ignore people like them.

Not anymore. I'm going to take charge of my life.

There was no doubt that his arrest and subsequent detention had scared the crap out of him. But that only meant he had been reckless. His first mistake was standing across the street from the jewelry store. Second mistake was going inside the store to scope it out. His third mistake was that he'd made his move too soon.

While the actual theft happened within a flash, he was ill-prepared to make such a move. His face was exposed, and so were his hands.

He bet that right after, the woman must have gone back to the store in a state of hysteria. Everyone heard her scream, including the security guard. She must have told the guard what had happened, perhaps even described her thief. Within minutes, the police had his description. They scoured the vicinity of the theft and, within minutes, caught him a couple of blocks away.

That's what Cole believed had occurred.

He pulled out his cell phone and dialed a number.

FIFTY-NINE

SIMON

After the conversation with my mother, I drove back to my office. I took the elevator up to Harris & Harris' floor. I entered, ignored Amy Joy's pleasantries, and walked straight to Gabe's office.

Through the glass panel next to the door, I saw Gabe on the phone. He was always speaking to one person or another. Always wheeling and dealing, as they say.

I didn't bother knocking. I just barged in.

Gabe was surprised to see me enter. He cupped the end of the receiver and mouthed, "What are you doing?"

"We need to talk," I said.

He removed his hand from the receiver and said into the phone, "Can you hold on one second?" He pressed a button on the base to mute the call. He then looked at me. "Do you mind? I'm on a personal call?"

"Did you know?" I asked in return.

Gabe made a face. "What are you talking about? What did I know?"

"Did you know I had a son?"

He stopped and stared at me. He then reached over and unmuted the call. "Heather, I'm sorry. I'm going to have to call you back." He hung up the phone and leaned back in his chair. He then got up, walked over to a cabinet in the corner, and poured himself a glass of bourbon. He poured one for me, too. He brought it over and placed it at the end of the desk.

"I'm not here for a drink," I said, glaring at him.

"It might help you relax."

"I don't want to relax. I want answers."

He nodded, took a sip from his glass, and sat back down. "Yes, I knew," he said.

My eyes narrowed. I was still standing, and the only thing preventing me from reaching over and punching him was the fact that I'm not a violent person. I'm a pacifist by nature. I prefer discourse over fisticuffs.

I asked, "Why didn't you tell me? Why did you hide it from me for all these years?"

"Mother asked me to," he replied, his tone matter-of-fact. "She said it was the only way to protect you."

I rubbed my temples. I felt a massive headache coming on. "Why do both of you keep saying you want to protect me? I'm not a child."

"You're sensitive."

I looked up at him, the blood rushing to my head. "*Sensitive!* That was exactly the word mother used."

"Because it's the truth. You're different than us. You're different than me, mother, father."

"Speaking of father, did you know what he'd done to mother all those years ago?" I asked.

He took another sip from his glass. "Mother told me, yes."

"Did she tell you before father died, or after?"

"Why does it matter?" he said.

"It matters because you were close to father. It matters because you idolized him like I did. It matters because your loyalty to him never once wavered. Even after his death, you kept his legacy going. You could've sold the firm right after the funeral. The offers were plenty, and there was a lot of money thrown your way. But you wanted to be like father. You molded yourself in his image. So, it matters why you would want to be like him when you know what he had done."

"Would it have changed anything?" he asked.

I looked at him, utterly confused.

He downed his bourbon, placed the glass on the desk, and said, "What he had done was deplorable. He had violated our mother. But there was no going back and changing it. What was done was done. Heck, because of that one action, I was born, so that gave me some solace."

"Did you never confront him about it?"

"It was not my place to question him. It was a personal matter between mother and father, and mother seemed resigned to what had happened, so I didn't pursue it further. There was no point. Father doted on us in his own way. I know he paid particular attention to me. And to be frank, I enjoyed it. He was a man of little praise, so even a small amount of attention was sufficient for me."

"Is that how you justified not telling me the truth?" I said. "That because it had nothing to do with you, you decided to hide it from me?"

He took a deep breath. "Yes, I guess I did."

My eyes fell on the phone on his desk.

Something popped in my head.

"Who's Heather?"

"Who?"

"The person you were speaking to on the phone. You called her Heather."

He shrugged. "It's just a business acquaintance, that's all."

As a partner at the firm, I knew all the people we did business with in case Gabe wasn't available. Gabe was always traveling, so it made sense to keep me abreast of all his contacts.

"Are you having an affair?" I asked.

He leaned over and pointed a finger at me. "That's none of your business, Simon. Stay out of it."

"How many secrets are you hiding?"

"It's complicated," he said.

"You are cheating on Deidre," I said.

"So, what if I am? Did you know I caught her cheating on me first? This is my way of payback. If you're concerned that she'll find out or leave me, she won't. We have a life that works well for both of us. A similar understanding, if you will, that mother and father had. And don't tell me that you and Vanessa don't have secrets you keep from each other."

"I've never cheated on Vanessa. I know she's never cheated on me."

He shook his head. "It's not all about sleeping with other people. There are other secrets that we all keep from our spouses."

"Whatever you have to say, just say it," I said, raising my voice. "Stop trying to protect me."

"You and Vanessa don't have any children. Have you ever questioned why?" he said, his voice rising to match mine.

"We don't have children because we *can't* have children."

"There is a difference between *not* having children and not being *able* to have children. One is a choice, and the other is not."

I stared at him, stunned.

"Vanessa is good friends with Deidre," Gabe said. "They share all their secrets with one another."

"What are you trying to say?" I asked, the words barely coming out of my mouth.

Gabe just looked at me. "Maybe it's something you should talk to Vanessa about," he finally replied.

SIXTY

COLE

He stood in the department store's empty parking lot. The air had gotten cooler. He lifted up the collar of his jacket and stuffed his hands in his pockets.

After he'd made the call from the alley, he headed over to a fast-food restaurant. He had paid for the meal with the cash he'd taken from the woman's wallet. To his dismay, it was only ninety dollars. But then he realized the rich didn't carry cash on them. They preferred plastic. The woman was accustomed to paying for everything by credit. She probably carried the cash in case a small-time vendor didn't take either debit or credit.

Cole had then devoured the meal in minutes. He didn't realize he was famished. His stint at the police station had so preoccupied his mind that he had stopped being hungry. It was only after he had the Cartier watch back in his hands that he felt some sense of calm. It was then that the cravings overwhelmed him.

After consuming the burger and fries, he had lined up again and bought another burger. That was gone within minutes as well. He washed his food down with an extra-large soft drink.

As he waited in the open space, he suddenly wished he hadn't consumed so much soft drink. He would need to use the bathroom soon. But he wasn't about to leave the parking lot. He had come here for a reason, and he wanted to finish what he had started.

He saw a familiar GMC Canyon truck enter the lot; it pulled up to him and came to a stop. He walked over, opened the passenger door, and got inside.

"I was surprised to get your call," Leo said. "When I didn't hear from you all day, I figured you'd gotten cold feet and bailed on me."

"I did what you asked me," Cole said.

"So, do you have it?"

"I do."

"Are you gonna show it to me, or are you gonna make me guess?"

Cole stuck his hand inside his jacket pocket and pulled out the white rectangular box. He held it out for Leo.

Leo took the box and then pulled the lid off. He smiled at the sight of the Cartier watch inside.

"Nice work, kid," he said. "I really didn't think you had it in you."

Cole looked away.

"What took you so long, anyway?" Leo asked.

"Things didn't go according to plan."

"They never do the first time."

Cole turned to him. "First time?"

Leo grinned. "I can tell it's the first time you've broken the law."

"I smoke weed. The law is not something I'm too concerned about."

"Sure, sure, but you've never done anything like this before, have you?"

Cole was silent.

Leo laughed. "I'm just messing with you. You did good. I'm impressed."

"I didn't do it for your praise. Where's my *damn* money?"

"All right," Leo said, still smiling. "You don't have to get nasty, you know."

He reached into his pocket.

Cole tensed up.

"Relax," Leo said. "I'm not going to shoot you. Think about the mess you'd make on my upholstery."

If he's joking, it's not funny, Cole thought.

Leo pulled out an envelope and held it out for him.

Cole took it and saw hundred-dollar bills inside.

"One thousand dollars," Leo said. "Just like we agreed."

"Thanks," Cole said, quickly stuffing the envelope in his jacket.

He reached for the door handle.

Leo said, "Wait."

Cole turned to him and saw Leo holding out the Cartier watch for him.

"What's this?" Cole said, confused.

"Take it," Leo said. "It's yours."

"Why?"

Leo shrugged. "It's a token of our trust. The test was never about money. We have money. It was always about whether you can follow instructions or not. And I can honestly say, you passed with flying colors."

"What am I going to do with the watch? You told me I wouldn't be able to sell it at any pawn shop."

"I know a guy who'll buy it without any questions. I'll give you his name if you're interested."

"I am," Cole said a little too quickly.

"I bet you can get an extra fifteen hundred for it."

Cole liked the sound of that.

"Do you want to make more?" Leo asked.

"What?"

"There's more money if you do exactly what we ask you."

"And what is it you want me to do?" Cole asked.

"First, are you interested?"

"I am."

Leo smiled, put the truck in gear, and pulled out of the parking lot.

SIXTY-ONE

HELEN

The fingerprint from the Nissan Maxima came back with a match. It belonged to a George Rawlings.

Helen and Michael drove to the address on file. Not surprisingly, it was less than a mile from Walt Grimsby's barn.

They drove up to the property through a paved road and parked in front of a Tudor-style house. Unlike Grimsby's plot of land, the area was immaculately kept. The grass was mowed. The hedges trimmed. The flowers watered.

The house was painted white, with the borders around the window frames and the edges of the walls done in dark exposed wood. The roof was steeply pitched, with the masonry chimney prominently visible.

As Helen and Michael got out of their vehicle, the front door of the house opened, and a man stepped into the sunlight. He was wearing a light sweater, striped pajamas, and brown loafers.

"May I help you?" he asked.

Helen flashed her badge. "Are you George Rawlings?" she asked instead.

The man's eyes narrowed. "What has he done now?"

"And you are?"

"I'm his father," the man replied.

"And your name, sir?"

"Bill Rawlings."

"Can we speak to your son, Mr. Rawlings?" Helen asked.

"He's not here at the moment."

"When we mentioned his name, you asked what he had done. What did you mean by that?"

Bill Rawlings looked away.

"Your son is not in any trouble," Helen added. "We just want to ask him a few questions?"

Bill Rawlings sighed. "George has an addiction problem. Unfortunately, this has gotten him into a lot of trouble with the law."

"What kind of trouble, if you don't mind me asking?"

"Shoplifting. Breaking and entering. Depositing fake checks. Anything to feed his addiction. But he's been clean for months. That was the stipulation when I let him back into our house."

Helen didn't know how to tell him that his son had been going onto a neighbor's property and getting high.

"Do you know when your son will be back?" Helen asked.

"I don't know," he replied, shaking his head. "Are you sure he's not in any trouble?"

"Absolutely."

Bill Rawlings paused and then said, "He's got a friend in Uptown. A junkie like him. But George swears his friend is also clean like him. If you're desperate to speak to George, you can check to see if he's at his friend's house."

Helen and Michael drove straight over to the address Bill Rawlings gave them. It was in a seedy part of town. Most of the buildings were social housing. There was graffiti everywhere. Many of the businesses were boarded up, and those that were not empty were cashback operations or motels that charged by the hour.

They stopped in front of a white stucco rowhouse. They got out and went up a set of narrow steps. They knocked on a gray door and waited.

Helen turned back and saw Michael was a few steps below her. He had his hand on his holster.

"I doubt you'll need to pull it out," she said.

"You can't be too certain nowadays," he said.

She could tell he was overwhelmed. The neighborhood didn't convey a sense of safety and security. Helen wouldn't be surprised if the occupants woke up each night from the sounds of gunshots.

In her experience, though, most crimes of that nature occurred in the darkness. There was no threat to them in the middle of the day. Plus, George Rawlings was a junkie. And, they presumed, so was his friend.

Addicts weren't violent by nature. It was their addiction that made them act out. The worst thing they'd do was steal your belongings to sell for cash. Helen firmly believed that's exactly what George must have done with the items he'd taken from the Nissan Maxima.

She knocked on the door again, this time with the back of her fist.

SIXTY-TWO

HELEN

A moment later, the door opened an inch. An eye appeared between the opening. "What do you want?" a male voice said.

"Are you George Rawlings?" Helen asked.

"No." The response was short and abrupt.

"Are you George's friend?"

She was met with silence.

"Can you open the door, please?"

More silence.

"We were sent by George's father. He wants us to bring him back home."

"George is not here," the man said.

"Do you know where he is?"

"I… I don't know."

A loud crash came from inside the house.

"Move!" Michael said as he raced up the steps and past Helen. He lowered his shoulder and rammed into the door. The occupant flew back and fell to the ground.

Michael drew his weapon. Helen did so, too.

He rushed into the house, stepping over the man who'd answered the door, and disappeared down the hall.

"Stay down," Helen ordered the man.

He crawled back up against the wall.

She moved further into the house and then turned right into a doorway she'd seen Michael disappear into.

She was in what looked like the living room. There was a sofa in the middle. A TV was across from the sofa, and in the middle was a coffee table.

Michael was standing next to the coffee table. He was staring at something behind the table.

She leaned over and saw a man wedged in between the sofa and table. He was convulsing. Foam was coming out of his mouth, and there was a needle stuck to his arm.

"He's overdosing!" she said. "Call nine-one-one."

She looked up at Michael. He made no move. It was as if he was frozen. It was probably the first time he'd seen a man in this position.

"Michael!" she yelled.

He blinked and turned to her.

"Call nine-one-one, right now!"

He nodded and pulled out his phone.

Helen knew that most people didn't die immediately from an overdose. It could take minutes or even hours before they succumbed to whatever they'd taken. She reached down and removed the needle from George's arm. She then checked to see if he was breathing. If he wasn't, she'd have to perform mouth-to-mouth resuscitation.

Thankfully, he was. But barely.

She placed her hand behind his neck and lifted him upright.

"George!" she said.

She could see his pupils dilate. His eyes widened, and his eyeballs turned toward her.

"That's good, George," she said, trying to keep him alert. "Help is on the way. But you have to stay with me, okay?"

He blinked and nodded slowly. He was aware of what was going on, but his body was reacting to whatever he had injected it with.

He reached over and grabbed her hand tightly.

She could tell he was terrified.

"You'll be all right," she assured him. "You are not going to die. I won't let that happen."

She could see from his eyes that he believed her.

Michael burst back into the room. "The paramedics are on their way," he said, clutching the phone to his chest.

"How long?" she said.

Michael's eyes were wide. "I... I don't know," he said.

George began to convulse violently. His body was shutting down.

"Stay with me, George," she said. "You have to stay awake!"

Just then, to her relief, she heard the sirens out on the street.

SIXTY-THREE

SIMON

If I was fuming before, I was now downright incensed. What Gabe had said was a gut punch, something that not only took the air out of me, but also deflated me as a person.

"There is a difference between not having children and not being able to have children. One is a choice, and the other is not," Gabe had said.

Those words bounced through my mind like a squash ball bouncing off the walls in a squash court. No matter how hard I tried, I couldn't stop his voice from penetrating my brain. I felt like my head was about to explode.

And the only way to stop it was to confront the matter. I could wait until the end of the day when I had calmed down and discuss it in the privacy of our home. But I felt I'd been lied to far too long, and I couldn't allow that lie to continue for even a second more.

The nonprofit organization that Vanessa worked for was on the twelfth floor of a concrete building. I didn't bother calling her. I wanted to see her reaction when I told her that I knew.

I took the elevator up to her floor, and when I got off, I saw her waiting for me in the lobby.

"Gabe called me," she said.

The anger suddenly boiled over inside of me. Gabe had kept his mouth shut for decades, but he couldn't keep it shut long enough to give me the satisfaction of confronting my wife about a matter that had nothing to do with him.

"I know you're upset with me," she said. "And I know you want an explanation, but please, let's not do it out here. Not in front of my coworkers and my boss. There's a conference room down the hall. We can discuss whatever you want in there."

A part of me wanted to unload on her right then and there. I had earned the right to do so. I was taken advantage of. But I knew I couldn't do it, no matter how hurt I was. I still cared for her. I wouldn't embarrass her in front of her colleagues and superiors.

"Fine," I said.

She looked relieved.

I followed her down the hall and into the room. She moved to the other side of the space, further away from the door, and stopped by the windows. Even though we were not in the lobby, there was still a possibility that our voices would be heard out in the hallway.

I waited for her to speak first. She crossed her arms over her chest and said, "Simon, you have every right to be angry with me."

"*Damn* right I do!" I roared.

She was a little taken aback by my response. She'd never seen me like this. I'd never acted like this before. We'd had disagreements, like all couples, but we rarely raised our voices at each other, and definitely never swore at one another.

She swallowed and said, "Yes, I lied too."

"You lied that you couldn't have children or lied that you didn't want any children?"

"Both."

I shut my eyes and covered my face with my hands. Even though I knew what her response would be, just hearing her confirm it made it more real. I don't know what I was expecting. Maybe that Gabe had heard it wrong. Maybe that there was no truth to what he had told me. But those words out of my wife's mouth broke the trust that was there between us.

I looked up at her. "How could you lie to me?"

"I lied to you because I love you," she said.

"What?"

"I know this sounds weird and confusing, but I knew if I told you the truth, you would've ended our relationship a long time ago."

"Give me some credit, will you?"

"Be honest…"

"I've always been honest with you," I shot back.

"Okay, wrong choice of words," she said. "What would you have done if I'd told you I'm not interested in bearing children, raising them, or having anything to do with them?"

SIXTY-FOUR

SIMON

I blinked. "How can you say that when you run an organization that helps children throughout the world?"

"That's different."

"How can it be? I just don't get it."

"Just because I don't want kids of my own doesn't mean I'm a cold and heartless person. I believe in what we do. I care about these children that we are helping. Without us, they have no hope. No future. Nothing."

I didn't know what to say.

"I've been working for the same organization even before I met you. You always knew that. Maybe that had some influence on your decision to be with me."

It did. I knew how hard she worked to make life better for all those kids. In some way, it glossed over her imperfections. I falsely projected her work onto who she was. I always thought, *If she cared this much for kids she doesn't know, then what kind of an amazing mother would she become when she had kids of her own?*

"You should've told me," I said, lowering my voice. "It should've been both our decisions. I thought we were partners."

"We are partners." She reached for me, but I pulled back. I could see she was hurt by that. She crossed her arms again. She said, "I tried to tell you in so many ways."

"When?" I asked.

"We had so many discussions at the dining table, or whenever we were spending quiet time together."

"I don't remember ever talking about not having kids."

"Remember John and Caroline?"

I did. We'd met them in Saint Vincent. We had gone to the island for vacation, while they had gone there for their honeymoon. We spent two weeks getting to know them. Even after we returned from our trip, we kept in contact with them. But a year after we first met them, they split up. The reason being Caroline was ready to start a family, and John wasn't. The issue had become such a big thorn between them they ended up divorcing.

"You know what your response was when I told you they were separating," Vanessa said.

I nodded. "I said the marriage wasn't going to last anyway if one partner wanted one thing and the other didn't."

"I knew if I told you what *I* wanted, we wouldn't be together for long. And I just couldn't see that. I fell in love with you the first time we were together. I'd never met anyone who was honest, responsible and caring as you were. I blame Deidre. She'd built you up to get me to agree to go on a blind date with you. But you have lived up to it in every way."

I felt a sharp pain in the pit of my stomach. "Why did you tell me the doctors told you that you would not be able to bear children? Why go so far to create such a lie?"

I remember when she had broken the news to me, it felt like someone had pulled the floor from underneath me. I felt like I was sinking deeper and deeper into a black hole. The only thing that pulled me up was my love for Vanessa. I felt, wrongly now, that she was going through the same darkness as me. She wasn't.

She said, "I knew if I told you I didn't want any children, eventually, as years would go by, you would keep bringing the topic up. You would even try to convince me to go through with it. And I was not interested in being forced to do something I never wanted."

"So, it was better for you to continue the lie, to make me believe one thing so that you could keep the perfect life you always wanted," I said. "But what about me? What about the life I had envisioned for myself? Did you ever think about that?"

She shut her eyes. Tears flowed down her cheeks. "I'm sorry, Simon. I'm sorry that I hurt you."

"I'm sorry too, Vanessa."

I turned and walked out of the room.

SIXTY-FIVE

COLE

He was in the passenger seat of the GMC Canyon. Leo was behind the wheel. They'd been driving for almost twenty minutes, and neither had said a word to the other.

Cole had wondered if it was a good idea to keep doing business with someone like Leo. His last assignment had gotten him arrested and locked up. He was certain there'd be a trial at a later date, something he didn't want to think about right this minute.

He was trying to stay focused. He didn't know where Leo was taking him or what he wanted him to do. He had a sense it was something not entirely lawful. Did he want him to jack a car? Break into a store? Or was the next task drug-related?

Cole was beginning to think it was the latter. Drugs were where the real money was. People like him—young, uneducated, without many prospects— were ideal candidates to get into the profession.

Unbeknownst to Buddy, Cole *had* dabbled in selling drugs. But what he did was nothing compared to what Buddy did. Cole sold weed to students and sometimes businessmen. And the transactions were in such low volumes that it wasn't worth getting beat up or shot at for such a small amount.

The last time he tried selling on the streets, a young punk tried to stick him up with a knife. Cole knew he could take him, but the punk was high as a kite. There was no telling how he would have reacted if Cole decided to put up a fight. Instead, Cole decided to hand over the stash.

His supplier wasn't happy about that. But again, the amount was so insignificant the supplier decided to let it pass with a warning for Cole to never work the streets again, or else the supplier would come knocking for the amount Cole lost to the punk.

Cole was more than happy to oblige. He was done dealing, and soon after, he got the job at the construction site. But that felt like a long time ago, even though his firing was only a day or so ago. And since then, he'd met Leo, snatched a woman's handbag, gotten booked at the police station, and was now on his way to another assignment.

"Where we going?" Cole asked, turning to Leo.

"We're almost there," Leo replied with a grin.

They drove for several more minutes before they pulled off the main road and went down a track of gravel toward a patch of water.

Cole could see a bridge up ahead. The path they were on would lead them straight underneath the bridge.

Is this some drug meeting Leo wanted me to be part of? Cole thought.

It wasn't unusual for such meetings to take place away from prying eyes. Dark alleyways. Vacant warehouses. Empty shipping yards. Hidden spots underneath a bridge. They were all ideal locations for exchanging drugs and money.

Cole suddenly had a bad feeling. He stuffed his hand in his pocket and pulled out his cellphone. He glanced down at the screen without Leo catching him. There was no telling how the man would react if he saw Cole on his phone.

The GMC Canyon came to a halt a short distance from the bridge. Leo put the truck in park and said, "That, over there, is where people go to die."

"What?" Cole said, confused.

"It's called Tent City. It's where the addicts and homeless lived. The city knows about it, but they choose to do nothing. It's better to have people like those away from the general population so that they don't become a problem the city and law enforcement has to get involved in. Sort of like, out of sight, out of mind."

"Why are we here?" Cole asked, still unsure.

"We are here because this is your final test."

Cole's eyes narrowed. "You want me to do something in Tent City?"

"Yep."

"Like what?"

Leo reached over and opened the glove compartment. He pulled out a serrated knife and held it out for Cole.

Cole was suddenly scared. "What… is… this?" he stammered.

Leo flipped the knife over so that he was holding the tip of the blade with his fingers. "Take it," he said.

Gingerly, Cole grabbed the handle with his left hand. The knife was heavier than it looked. Light reflected off the edge of the blade.

"What do you want me to do with it?" Cole asked.

"I want you to go in Tent City and stab someone," Leo replied matter-of-factly.

Cole's eyes widened in horror. "What? I can't do that."

"Why not?"

"That's murder."

"It's not when the guy is already dead."

"What're you talking about?" Cole shot back. He suddenly had the urge to drop the knife, jump out of the truck, and run away. But something held him to his seat.

Leo said, "The person we want you to stab is addicted to painkillers and has been for years. He's been in and out of the hospital for a variety of health issues. He's been in jail for vandalism, uttering threats, and a host of other violations. He has no purpose in life other than to feed his addiction. You'd be doing him a favor by putting him out of his misery."

"I don't know," Cole said, shaking his head.

"Listen, if you do this, you'll get ten grand."

Cole's jaw dropped. He looked out the window. A moment later, he turned back to Leo, "How're you going to make money by killing him?"

"His death doesn't benefit us financially, but his death gives us something else."

"Like what?"

Leo smiled. "Your loyalty."

The smile sent a shiver up Cole's spine. "I won't do it," Cole said.

"If you don't do it, there are others who are willing to take your place."

Cole sighed. "I just can't."

"All right," Leo said, holding out his hand.

Cole placed the knife in his palm.

Leo returned the blade to the glove compartment. He then reversed the truck and drove away from Tent City.

SIXTY-SIX

HELEN

Helen and Michael were at a pawn shop not far from where George Rawlings had overdosed. George was alive and in the hospital. The paramedics had gotten there in the nick of time. If they had been late, even a few minutes, Helen was certain the outcome would've been different.

They considered going over to the hospital to speak to him, but that was no longer necessary. Next to the sofa where George had injected himself with heroin, Michael had found a business card.

It was for the pawnshop they were in now.

The man behind the counter was heavyset, balding, and he had a long goatee that fell down to his chest. On top of that, each of his fingers was adorned with gold rings, and heavy gold chains were draped around his neck.

"Can I help you guys?" the man said.

Helen and Michael flashed their badges.

"Am I in some kind of trouble?" the man asked, suddenly tensing.

Michael replied, "We believe a customer of yours brought in an item we are interested in."

"And what item would that be?"

"A GPS console."

The man shrugged. "I have dozens of GPS's. You have to be more specific."

"The GPS was pulled out of a Nissan Maxima."

As an addict, George lied, cheated, and stole to feed his addiction. People in the throes of addiction had difficulty obtaining and retaining employment. Their sole focus was on their next hit, and they did whatever was necessary to get it.

"I don't know anything about a GPS from a Nissan Maxima," the owner claimed.

"The GPS was brought in today," Michael said. "And the person who brought it, his name is George Rawlings."

"That name doesn't sound familiar."

"It should," Michael said. "You're a pawn shop, aren't you? You're supposed to hold people's personal valuables as collateral for the money you loan them, so I doubt you haven't written his name down in your records. Unless—" Michael turned to Helen for dramatic effect "—you didn't write the name down because you knew George Rawlings would never come back to reclaim his item, and the item was most likely stolen. Therefore, you just purchased it from him outright. And if I'm a betting man, you bought it from him for far less than its actual worth."

"That's a lot of assumptions you're making, detective," the owner said. "And to answer your question, the people who come to me are desperate. And I never pay them the market rate for the items they bring to me. The only way to survive in this business is to fleece my clients."

Michael said, "I'm not interested in how you do your business, sir. I'm only interested in the GPS George Rawlings brought to you. Either you bought it, or you're keeping it as collateral; it doesn't matter. What matters is that you should have some record of it. That's the law." Michael leaned closer so that he was inches from the man's face. "Unless you prefer that one of us stays here while the other goes and gets a warrant to search your shop. Your choice."

The man swallowed. "This... GPS... is it that important?"

"It could help solve a brutal murder," Michael said matter-of-factly.

The blood drained from the man's face. "Um... now that I think about it, I might have what you're looking for. Let me go take a look in the back."

"You do that, sir," Michael said with a smile.

A moment later, Helen and Michael walked out of the pawnshop with the GPS console.

They got in Helen's vehicle. Michael started fiddling with the device.

"Doesn't it need to be plugged in?" Helen asked.

"A lot of them have batteries as a backup."

The GPS screen came alive.

"Awesome," Michael said with glee. "Let's see where Derek Starr went on the night of his murder."

Michael scrolled through the device for several minutes. He then pulled out his cell phone and began typing something into it. In the end, he looked up at her, his expression one of deep puzzlement.

"What did you find?" Helen asked eagerly.

"I recognize the address for the bar where Starr had gone for a drink."

"Okay."

"And right after that, there is another address Starr entered into the GPS."

"Great," Helen said with excitement. "Let's go take a look."

"We already did."

Helen's brow furrowed. "What?"

"The last address on the GPS was for Walt Grimsby's barn."

"Why did Derek Starr drive all the way there?" Helen asked, confused.

"I have no idea," Michael replied.

SIXTY-SEVEN

COLE

He slowly unlocked the door and entered. He and his mother lived on the twentieth floor of a high-rise complex. The building was over forty years old, and the years hadn't been kind to it. The windows weren't insulated. The hot water was unreliable. The toilets didn't flush properly. The appliances were old, and they broke down all the time. And water dripped from the ceiling in the bedroom closet.

The hallway carpets hadn't been changed in decades. The paint hadn't been updated in just as long. Only one of the three elevators worked. It seemed like management only made an effort when the situation could no longer be ignored, like, say, when a pipe burst and they knew if they didn't act right away, the cost to fix the problem would be double or even triple.

Cole knew why management wasn't interested in investing in the building. The rents were some of the lowest in the city. And with rent controls, a majority of the tenants refused to move out. Management couldn't physically remove them in order to bring in new tenants and charge them the market rate. They were hoping to make the situation so unbearable that tenants would leave of their own volition.

Cole and his mother had no choice. This was the best they could afford. The unit was one-bedroom. His mom slept in the bedroom, while he took the couch in the living room. He'd always told himself it would be temporary. He had hoped to pull extra shifts at the construction company to get them out of their current living situation. But that was now out of the question.

He carefully went inside and looked around. Normally, he would find his mom sitting in front of the TV, but that was not the case today.

He made his way to the bedroom and found her lying on the bed with her eyes closed.

He then smelled something foul and pungent. He went over and saw vomit on the floor next to the bed.

His mom's eyes opened. "Is that you, Cole?" she said.

"Yeah, I'm home, mom."

"Ignore the mess," she said slowly. "I'll clean it up. I just need to shut my eyes for a minute."

The grimace across her face told him she was in pain.

"Don't worry, mom," he said. "I'll take care of it."

He went out, grabbed a bucket and towel from the bathroom, filled the bucket with water, and came back. He got down on his knees and cleaned the mess. Fortunately, all the rooms had laminate flooring and not carpet, so he was done in no time.

He then sat next to her on the edge of the bed. She looked at him. "Thank you," she said with a weak smile. "I don't know what I'd do without you."

"Did you take your medications, mom?" he asked.

"I think I must have forgotten today."

The pain in her head became so unbearable that it caused nausea and dizziness. The mess was the result of that. It had happened before, so he wasn't surprised by it. But he was worried that her condition was worsening.

"Cole, we need to talk," she said.

"We'll talk when you feel better."

"I might not be around for long."

"Don't say that," he said, his voice shaking.

She reached up and touched his cheek. "There's something I have to tell you, Cole. The person who came to the police station. He's…"

"I know."

Her eyes narrowed. "You do?"

"He told me you met in India."

"Did he tell you…?" Suddenly her face tightened, and she winced. He could tell the tumor was rearing its ugly head.

He reached over and picked up the prescription bottles from the side table. He went out into the kitchen and returned with a glass of water. "You have to take your pills, mom," he said.

He helped raise her head so she could swallow the medications with tiny sips from the glass.

When her head was back on the pillow, she said between shallow breaths, "I need to tell you…"

He put a hand over her lips to silence her. "Not right now, mom. You need to get some rest."

She looked at him, nodded, and then closed her eyes.

He grabbed a chair and pulled it next to the bed. He sat down and spent the next hour watching her sleep.

His mother had given him life. She had provided for him. She had lifted him up when he was down. She had done everything for him. She was his life. He couldn't imagine what he would do without her.

She was his last relation on this earth. If she was gone, he would be all alone.

Tears rolled down his cheeks, and he had to control himself to keep from breaking down. He didn't want his mom to wake up and see him like this. She'd always been strong for him, even during the most difficult times. And he had to be tough for her now that she needed him more than ever.

His eyes fell on the prescription bottles in his hand. The anti-inflammatory drug helped the swelling in her brain. The codeine helped ease the pain and put her to sleep. Without either of them, she wouldn't be able to function properly, or even at all.

One bottle was empty, and the other had a few pills left.

He had the thousand dollars still in his pocket, but he knew the money wouldn't last long. Rent was coming due, and the meds cost a tidy sum. He could pay for one, but not the other.

He covered his face with his hands.

The choice was obvious. He would pay for his mom's meds. The landlord would have to wait. But how long would he be able to push the problems away? How long before he couldn't refill his mom's prescriptions? How long before he and his mom were finally evicted?

He lifted his head up.

He knew what he had to do next.

SIXTY-EIGHT

SIMON

Today had been a series of bombshells after bombshells. The woman who I hadn't seen in twenty years appeared out of nowhere. I was madly in love with her once, and I admit that I still harbored feelings for her. It was obvious how my body reacted whenever I was close to her. My heart would palpitate, my knees would become weak, and my palms would get sweaty. If that wasn't a sign of the impact she had on me, then nothing was.

I thought she had broken my heart all those years ago. In my mind, she was a cruel and calculating person who had toyed with my heart in India. She'd told me things I wanted to hear. That she loved me. That I meant everything to her. That we would be together once we returned to America.

The truth was, she did love me, I did mean everything to her, and she did want to be with me. But she was no villain. The villains were my own brother and mother. This wasn't some Shakespearean tragedy. Two lovers kept apart by their families. This was my life. The lies and secrecy had a devastating impact on me, Annabelle, and our son.

I felt so foolish. Gullible. Naïve. Ultimately, I'd been played. By my brother, my mother, my sister-in-law, and my wife. They were all complicit in holding me back.

My mother didn't tell me about Annabelle because she knew I would've gone through heaven or hell to be with her and our child. While I pitied her for what she had been through with my father, I could not condone what she had done to me. My mother's decision to shield me from the truth altered the course of my life.

My brother went along with the lies because it was the only way to keep me leashed to the family business. That was our father's desire. His last command before he died. The firm he had named after his two sons should be run by his two sons. And knowing how loyal my brother was to our father, he would've done everything to make sure that happened.

My sister-in-law was the one who introduced Vanessa to me. She always knew how much I wanted children. It was obvious the way I doted on my niece and nephew. She knew all along that her best friend had no desire to bear children. No desire to even adopt children. No desire to have a family in the traditional sense.

My wife. The woman who I thought was my soulmate. The one to whom I told my deepest and darkest secrets. The one who I believed was doing the same with me. However, she was in fact lying to me.

That, above everything else, cut deeply.

Vanessa was right when she said I wouldn't have accepted the fact that she didn't want any children. But she should've been honest with me when we first started dating. Deidre had told her everything she needed to know about me. She couldn't argue that she was unaware of this. In fact, on our third date, we were walking on a beach, and I spotted a family making a sand castle together. I said to her how nice it would be that one day we would do something like that as a family. Vanessa had looked me straight in the eyes and, with a smile, told me she hoped for that too. I remember how my heart swelled at the sound of that.

Now I know that was a bald-faced lie. There was no conviction behind her statement. It was only said to appease me. To make me want to like her, love her, marry her.

That brings me to my son. Until this morning, I thought I would always be childless, something I had resigned myself to. But so much time had passed between us. A connection—a special bond that is forged from the moment a child arrives on earth—that was not there. Children, especially those in their early years, are forgiving to a fault. I've seen my niece and nephew be cross with Gabe for something he had promised but failed to do. The moment he would offer them something in return—a trip to the zoo or a trip to the nearest ice cream parlor— he would be back in their good graces.

I doubt I could do that with my son. He was a man, and adults tended to hold grudges for a very long time. It would not be easy for me to get him to trust me, respect me, and ultimately, love me. I fear that boat had sailed. I couldn't win him over by offering to buy him something. His reaction toward me for showing up to post bail was proof of that. There was little gratitude. I wasn't offended by it. I was half expecting it. He had spent most of his life relying on himself to get out of trouble. It must've been a shock for him to see a stranger show that kind of kindness and generosity.

I was a little hurt, though, that he'd refused my offer to drive him home. Then again, I can't blame him. I was a nobody to him. I was someone who had shown up because his mother had asked me to. As far as Cole was concerned, that was the last time he would ever see me.

I wouldn't let that happen. I would do everything to see my son. After all, I had given assurances that he would show up in front of a judge. The five-thousand dollars wasn't important. It was a small price to pay for an opening, however small, into my son's life.

The bail would be my excuse to try to build whatever was lost between us in the last twenty years of his life.

It was the one thing I was looking forward to now.

SIXTY-NINE

HELEN

She was surprised when she received the call. The woman on the other line introduced herself as Michael's fiancée. She said she'd heard great things about her from Michael, and she was wondering if Helen would do her the honor of joining them for dinner.

Michael assured her that he knew nothing about this. It had come as a surprise to him, too. He told Helen she was not obligated to agree to such a request. But Helen did so anyway. It wasn't every day that she got to have a meal at her partner's house.

Michael and Leslie Dobson lived in a brown brick bungalow, in a small town, about an hour's drive from Arlington. It was a quiet town with a tiny police department, no fire station, and no hospital. The closest hospital was twenty-five miles away in another city. The town did have, however, schools, grocery stores, a shopping center, a library, a community center with a basketball court, and the main square that had a skating rink. A place where each year, a giant Christmas tree was lit.

Leslie had prepared a meal that consisted of beef stew, pasta, steamed vegetables, and a side of mashed potatoes.

When they were all seated at the table, Leslie said, "I hope you like it. Unfortunately, I'm not much of a cook, but I'm learning."

"It looks delicious," Helen said with a smile. "And don't worry, I'm not much of a cook either, but I never bothered to learn."

Leslie had short blonde hair, bright green eyes, and a smile that made Helen feel comfortable.

"Michael told me you were a wine connoisseur," Leslie said. "Thank you for the bottle. You didn't have to."

"It was either the wine or a case of beer," Helen said.

"Beer would have been nice," Michael said.

Leslie rolled her eyes. "Wine is just perfect."

Helen jabbed the asparagus on her plate with her fork and asked, "How did you guys meet?"

"You want the altered version or the real version?" Leslie replied.

Michael jumped in. "Let's go with the version we tell everyone."

"She's a fellow officer, Michael. I'm sure she won't judge us."

"I'm not concerned about me. I just don't want her to judge you," he said, looking down at his plate.

"Listen," Helen said. "You don't have to tell me if you don't want to. I apologize for bringing it up."

"No, it's okay. I want you to know," Leslie said with a smile. "After all, you are Michael's partner. And you are responsible for bringing him back to me safely at the end of each day."

"That is correct," Helen agreed.

Leslie said, "I met Michael at the hospital."

"You're a nurse?" Helen asked.

"No. I work for a women's shelter. I help those who've been sexually assaulted."

"Okay."

"I was a victim myself," Leslie said. "I was brutally attacked and left for dead by the side of the road. Michael happened to drive by that night, and he saw me. He was a patrol officer then. He lifted me up, placed me on the back seat of his cruiser, and drove me to the hospital. I can still hear the sirens as he rushed me to the emergency room. The doctors later said if I hadn't gotten immediate help, I would have died from my injuries. Michael saved me." She reached over and held his hand. "The next day, he came to see me. He wanted to make sure I was okay. He then came by every night at the end of his shift until I left the hospital. He then formally asked me out. By the end of this year, we hope to be married."

She smiled at Michael. He smiled back.

"Did they find the person who attacked you?" Helen asked.

Leslie shook her head. "No."

"But I won't stop until I do," Michael said, jumping in.

Leslie beamed. "That's what makes me love him so much. He wants to make the world a better place. He wants to give a voice to victims like me. He will stop at nothing until those who do evil are charged and punished for their crimes. I was so happy for him when he became a detective. I know he can do so much as an investigator. And that's why I don't bother him when he works late."

Helen smiled. "Michael has been burning the candle at both ends."

"He's dedicated to his duty."

"Do you guys plan to have children?" Helen asked.

"Of course," Leslie replied. "What kind of question is that?"

"I'm sorry if that came out wrong. I'm sure Michael's told you I will be retiring soon."

"He did, and congratulations."

"Thank you," Helen said. "I'm not just saying this because I'm in your house, eating your food. I'm saying that because you two are a lovely couple."

"That's very kind of you to say."

"I've had my share of triumphs in my career, but I've also had my regrets. Those regrets were mostly in my personal life. The work can be all-consuming. And because I was chasing every lead, talking to every witness, dotting all the Is and crossing all the Ts, I neglected my daughter, who I have a complicated relationship with now, and my husband, who ended up being my ex-husband." Helen wasn't sure why she was telling them this. Maybe she didn't want them to make the same mistakes as her. Maybe the spark she saw between them jolted something deep inside her, something she'd buried a long time ago. "What I'm trying to say is, cherish the moments you have with each other and with the children you will have one day. Work will come and go, but the memories you share with each other will last a lifetime."

There was a moment of silence before Leslie said, "That's so sweet. I know the only reason you said it is because you want the best for us. Thank you."

Michael nodded.

Helen sighed. "I could use a drink right now."

Leslie smiled. "I think we have a bottle of wine someone brought for us."

Michael grinned. "I'm not much of a wine drinker, but I think today I'll have a glass, too."

They all laughed.

SEVENTY

COLE

"What made you change your mind?" Leo asked.

"I need the money," Cole replied.

They were in Leo's GMC Canyon, and it was parked in the same spot they had been in earlier. Cole could see the bridge's underpass. Just beyond the chain-link fence was Tent City.

"Are you sure about this?" Leo said. "You seemed adamant that you didn't want to do it."

"Like I said, I need the money. It was ten grand, right?"

"That's what I said."

"If I do it, when do I get paid?" Cole asked.

Leo rubbed his chin. "I don't carry that kind of cash on me, so you're going to have to trust me."

"I don't know anything about you. For all I know, you could be a cop."

Leo laughed. "If I was a cop, why would I send you in there to kill a man?"

"Maybe it's a setup," Cole said.

"Why would I set you up?"

"I don't know. You tell me."

Leo shook his head. He then lifted his shirt up, exposing his chest and stomach. "I'm not wearing a wire," he said. "And if you look around the truck, you won't find any cameras or listening devices, okay?"

Cole had already eyed the interior the moment he'd gotten in the truck. He didn't see anything out of the ordinary. *But then again, technology's so sophisticated now. There's no telling where it could be hidden,* he thought.

"You're wasting my time," Leo growled. "Are you gonna do it or not?"

"I am," Cole said.

Leo reached over and pulled the serrated knife from the glove compartment. He flipped the blade so that the handle was facing Cole.

Cole grabbed the blade and placed it in the inner pocket of his jacket.

"How do I find the person I have to kill?" Cole asked.

"There's a reason they call this place Tent City." Leo nodded in the direction of the underpass. "Everyone inside lives in a tent. The person you're looking for, his tent is bright orange."

"How do you know that?"

"We did our homework. We didn't choose anyone at random."

"So why him?"

"Let's just say there is history between us."

"So why don't *you* do it?"

Leo gave him a firm look. "If I did, then how are you going to prove your loyalty to us?"

Who is this "us"? Cole thought. *Maybe Leo works for some kind of organization, like in the movies?*

He felt the weight of the knife in his coat.

Whoever they are, I've got no choice. Mom needs help.

"All right," Cole said.

He got out of the truck.

A strong wind blew across his face, sending a chill through him.

He zipped his jacket up, pulled his hoodie over his head, and proceeded toward the chain-link fence. He didn't bother to glance back at Leo or his truck. He didn't want to psych himself out. He had a simple task ahead of him. The quicker he completed it, the quicker he could be out of there.

The chain-link fence was at least ten feet in height. The fence bordered a vast lot that was mostly dirt, but was pockmarked with weeds and speckled with pieces of cement. He turned left and walked along the fence until he reached an opening. The moment he stepped inside Tent City, he was bombarded with a combination of odors. Sweat, urine, weed, and a host of other foul smells mixed together.

Leo was correct. All he saw were tents upon tents, clustered together cheek by jowl. They came in a variety of shapes, sizes, and colors.

How am I going to find an orange tent? he thought.

Cole slowly made his way into the makeshift community. He saw people young and old, and some in between. Some looked haggard and broken. Some looked like they had just moved in. Their faces did not have the scars from years of living on the streets. They were hoping this was just a short stop as they moved on to better things.

Cole felt like an intruder, but no one paid any attention to him. They were all busy with whatever they were doing. One man was eating something out of a can. Another man was smoking what looked like a joint. A woman was staring at nothing in particular. But most, if not all, residents of the encampment were inside their tents.

Cole was surprised at how orderly the place was. He expected chaos. But every occupant respected each other's private space.

He eyed each and every tent as he moved past them. Dreading, and also hoping to find what he was looking for. He dreaded, because he knew what he was here to do, and hoped, because he wanted to be done with the task.

The longer he was in the camp, the more exposed he felt.

When he thought he had gone as far as he could, he saw it.

The orange tent was in the far corner of the camp.

SEVENTY-ONE

COLE

He swallowed and slowly approached the orange tent. The tent's material was flimsy, obviously some cheap plastic. The bridge protected the people living underneath it, but Cole doubted the tent would be much protection against a strong gust of wind.

Cole knelt down and moved the piece of cloth that covered the tent's entrance. He was expecting to find someone inside. If luck was on his side, this person would either be high, drunk or passed out. It would make Cole's job that much easier. Stab a defenseless man in the chest or back, and run out of there as fast as he could.

To his dismay, the tent was empty.

Crap, he thought. *What do I do now?*

He felt movement behind him. He turned and saw a man standing before him. The man was wearing dirty clothes. His hands were grimy, and so were his fingernails. He had a large unkempt beard, and his hair was matted and long. The man's eyes were glazed, but Cole could tell he was in his senses.

"Who are you?" the man asked. His front two teeth were missing.

"Is this your tent?" Cole asked.

"Who are you?" the man asked again.

Cole unzipped his jacket and reached for the knife. But then he stopped.

I can't do this, he thought. *I can't kill him.*

"I'm sorry," Cole muttered. "This was a mistake."

He turned to leave.

He felt a hand on his shoulder.

"Where are you going?" the man bellowed. He spun Cole around and held him by his jacket collar.

"Did he send you?" the man demanded. His breath was pungent and foul. "Did Brian send you?"

"Who's Brian?" Cole asked.

The man's hands moved toward Cole's neck. "I won't let him hurt me," the man said. "Like he made me hurt Joe."

Cole had no idea what he was talking about, but his grip was strong and tight around his neck.

Cole's hand was still in his jacket when he pulled out the knife. The man saw the blade, and his eyes widened in horror. He released his grip on Cole's neck and swung his left hand across Cole's arm.

The knife dropped to the ground.

The man pushed Cole back. Cole tripped over his feet and fell to the ground. The man jumped on him and pinned him down with the weight of his body.

"This is not how it's going to end for me," the man growled.

The man reached down and grabbed Cole's neck again, but this time he had a determined look on his face.

Cole tried to fight back, but the man was overpowering him.

Cole's eyes watered as air constricted around his throat.

I'm going to die, he thought.

Suddenly, the man released his grip. He looked shocked.

He fell next to Cole.

Cole coughed and blinked.

He saw the knife protruding from the man's back.

How did it…?

"Grab it," he heard a familiar voice say. It was Leo. "Grab the knife."

Cole reached over and pulled the knife out of the man's back.

Click.

He looked up and saw Leo holding his cell phone.

There was another *click.*

Leo was taking his photo.

"What are you doing?" Cole asked, confused.

"This is to prove to the people I work for that you finished the task," Leo replied. "Now, let's get the hell out of here before someone sees us."

Cole stuck the knife in his pocket and followed Leo. When they were back in the GMC Canyon, Leo said, "Give it to me."

Cole looked at him in shock.

"Give me the knife so I can get rid of it."

Cole held the blade out. Leo placed it in a plastic shopping bag and threw it in the glove compartment.

Leo put the truck in gear and pressed down on the accelerator, the tires squealing on the dirt and gravel as he sped away.

SEVENTY-TWO

SIMON

My eyes snapped open. I squinted and looked around. I was in my bedroom. Sunlight was streaming through the corners of the drapes. I moved my hand to the other side of the bed. It was empty. I don't know why I was expecting it not to be.

Last night, when I was in my home office, I heard Vanessa come into the house. I then heard her go up the stairs to our bedroom. A moment later, I heard her coming back downstairs. She must have been dragging a suitcase behind her. She then got in her car and drove off.

I had a feeling she was either going to her sister's place or Gabe and Deidre's.

I wasn't interested in finding out. I hadn't done anything wrong. Why should I go and apologize?

But then again, I knew there was no point for her to apologize to me, either. It would not change the fact that I'd been lied to all these years.

I heard the sound again. It was the doorbell that had woken me up in the first place.

I was still dressed in my pajamas as I made my way downstairs to the front door. I opened it and found Gabe standing outside.

"I've called you a dozen times already," he said, sounding a little annoyed.

Normally, I would make some excuses. Like I had forgotten to charge my phone, or I put it on silent. Or anything else so that Gabe wouldn't be cross with me. Gabe had a temper just like our father, and I didn't want to be at the end of one of his tirades.

Today, I didn't care. There was nothing he could do that could hurt me more than what I was feeling right now.

"What do you want, Gabe?" I said, annoyed in return.

He saw the look on my face and blinked several times. It was the same reaction Vanessa had had back at the conference room.

"Can I come in?" he asked, his voice a little lower.

"Whatever you have to say, you can say it here," I said.

"Come on, Simon. Don't be like that. It's chilly out here."

I sighed and walked back into the living room. I sat on the chair while he came in and took a seat across from me.

"Vanessa's really upset," he said.

So, I was right, I thought. *She did go over and stay at Gabe and Deidre's.*

"Okay," I said.

Gabe said, "We all know what we did was wrong. We made a mistake, and we want to make it right."

"How?" I snapped. "How are you going to make it right, huh? Are you going to give me back the last twenty years of my life?"

"I've come up with a few suggestions," he said. "Like you said, it's been twenty years. That means your son—my nephew—must be in college, right?"

I shrugged. "I wouldn't know. I have no relationship with him, thanks to you and mother."

He ignored my comment and said, "We would like to pay for his education. To help him get a solid start in life."

Anger rose in me. I had to grip the arms of the chair to control my composure. "There is no *we*. He is *my* son," I said through gritted teeth. "You don't get to decide who pays for his education. I do. And as far as having a solid start in life, that boat sailed a long time ago when I couldn't be a part of his upbringing."

Gabe stared at me in silence. He then said, "We want to help, Simon, but you're not making it easy."

I sat up straight and looked him straight in the eye. "What would you have me do, Gabe? Do you want me to go back to how things were before I found out the truth?"

"I didn't mean that. I was just saying that we can get through this as a family."

I laughed. "I'm glad you used the word 'family', because you always had a family. You, Deidre, Charlie and Lilly. I remember all those days you took off from work so that you could take Charlie to a baseball game. Or take Lilly to the stables so she could ride ponies. For their birthday I bought your kids the best gifts an uncle could give them. But I never got my son a single gift for his birthday." My eyes were soft, but my voice was hard. "So, this is *not* something we can easily get through as a family."

I could see that this was uncharted territory to him. If he thought I would bend to his words like I had done before, he was wrong.

"You don't want to make a bad situation worse," he said.

I knew it was a veiled threat. That I better get in line or else.

"The situation is far worse than you think, Gabe," I said, my voice calm.

He stood up. "I guess I can't talk sense into you right now. Maybe you shouldn't come into the office today. Take the day to clear your mind and your priorities."

"My priorities have never been clearer than they are right now," I said. "And I'm glad you mentioned the firm. I'm thinking of selling my share."

His eyes narrowed. Blood rushed to his face. "You can't," he said.

"I can, and I will. There is no one who can stop me."

"I'll buy you out," he said.

I frowned. "There is nothing in our arrangement that says I have to sell it to you. I can always sell it to the highest bidder."

"You wouldn't dare. I would…"

"You would what? Sue me?" I laughed. "Good luck. In fact, I challenge you to take me to court. Maybe then the public will see how we took advantage of the people who just needed a helping hand to save their business."

He stared at me. I could tell I had him. There was one thing Gabe valued above everything else, and that was his reputation. The negative publicity would be something he could not get over so easily.

"Now get out of my house," I said. "Before I call my lawyer right this minute."

Gabe looked defeated.

He turned and left.

SEVENTY-THREE

HELEN

She parked in front of a chain-link fence and got out. She was familiar with Tent City, and she was aware of the problems there. Most residents were addicts, people with mental illness, or those just down on their luck. Fights were not uncommon, but murder was rare.

Homeless people, in her experience, tended to keep to themselves. They didn't go out looking for trouble. Survival was the only thing on their minds. Find a warm place to sleep and food to fill their stomachs.

She'd never been inside Tent City before, but she had been to similar homeless camps. The occupants were wary of the police, and rightly so. Law enforcement, unfortunately, didn't look too kindly on those they believed were vagrants, trespassers, and troublemakers.

That wasn't entirely the police force's fault either. The higher-ups—the politicians and other decision-makers—were the ones who wanted these camps gone. Their constituents thought the camps were a nuisance, an eyesore. If you asked most people, they would say they sympathized with the plight of the homeless, just as long as those homeless did not set up camps near their neighborhood.

Helen was already apprised of the situation, so it didn't take long for her to make her way through the camp to the end of Tent City.

She found Michael standing next to an orange tent.

"You beat me here," she said.

"I was on my way to the station anyway," he said. "A quick U-turn, and I was here in minutes." His brow then furrowed. "Why did we get called into this anyway?"

"We're homicide detectives, aren't we?" she replied. "So, why wouldn't we get called into this?"

"Yeah, sure. But there are other detectives who could've taken this. I mean, we're still in the early stages of Derek Starr's case."

"I was at the station when the call came in," she said. "And I asked for us to be assigned to it."

He looked at her, confused. "Why?"

"I think this case would be perfect for you to take the lead. How complicated could a stabbing at a homeless camp be? We interview any witnesses. We find a motive. We solve the case. Simple."

He thought a moment and then smiled. "Sounds good to me."

Helen turned to the body next to the tent. The victim lay on his stomach. His left arm was underneath him, and his right one spread out. The man's eyes were open and vacant.

"Were you able to ID him?" she asked.

"Alex Ketchum. Forty-six. And according to his driver's license, he had a house in Arlington."

"Is there an address on there?"

"There is," he said, staring at the card in his hand. "But the license expired three years ago."

Helen frowned.

Michael said, "Among his belongings, I found these." He held out a pair of photos. Helen reached over and grabbed them.

The first photo had three kids—two girls and one boy—between about three to eight years old. They were smiling and posing for the camera. The second was of a man and a woman. The woman had long brown hair, rose-colored cheeks, and green eyes. The man was clean-shaven, his hair was combed to one side, and he had a dimple on his chin.

It wasn't difficult for Helen to see the man was Alex Ketchum.

"Our victim had a family," Helen said.

"Probably an ex-wife." Michael held up his hands. "I know. I know. I'm making assumptions, but I don't see a wedding ring on his finger, nor do I think he'd be here if he were still married."

"I can't argue with that," Helen said, still staring at the photos in her hands.

"I also found these," he said, holding up several pieces of paper.

Helen reached over and grabbed them.

The words "I'm a killer" were scribbled over and over in red, blue, and black ink.

Helen looked up. "What does this mean?"

"No idea," Michael replied.

"We should take his prints to see if he pops up in any of the databases."

"You think he could've committed a crime?"

"I don't know, but this could be a confession of some kind."

"Or," Michael said with a shrug, "he could be crazy, you know."

Helen had a feeling Michael might be right. Mental illness was prevalent among the homeless. But she wasn't about to take any chances.

"Any idea of the cause of death?" she asked.

"I haven't checked the body yet. But as I am the lead detective on the case, I nominate you to do the honors," he said with a wink.

She smiled, and then pulled on latex gloves. She could see a pool of blood below the victim's shoulders, which meant the wound would likely be in the lower body. She lifted the victim's shirt up and saw a dark puncture in the middle of the back.

"The victim was likely stabbed," she said. She examined the rest of Ketchum's back. "There are no other bruises and abrasions that I can see, so I'd have to say that wound was the cause of death."

Michael leaned over. "The victim died from a single wound?" he asked.

"It looks deep and wide," she replied, leaning closer. "The knife could have perforated an organ. Help me lift him up. I want to see his stomach." Michael and Helen rolled Ketchum's body onto its side. "Just as I had expected. His shirt has soaked up a lot of blood. So, my theory is correct. The knife must have hit a vital organ, and he bled out."

"So, he didn't die instantly?"

"I can't say, but that would be my guess."

"If that's true, then why didn't he try to crawl away or yell for help? It looks like he died where he fell. Plus, his eyes are open, so that contradicts your theory."

"Not entirely," she said. "Not all people die the same way. I've seen cases where someone was stabbed over a dozen times and still lived to talk about it. And in other cases, I've seen people slip and fall and die right on the spot." She then moved the victim's matted hair across his face. And that's when she saw it. There was a red bump around the temple. "Okay, I stand corrected. After he'd been stabbed, he may have fallen on that piece of cement he is lying next to. The impact on his head may have been the cause of death. Obviously, we'll wait for the coroner to confirm it." She stood up and snapped the latex gloves off. "Who called it in?"

"Another resident of the camp," Michael said.

"Let's go talk to them."

SEVENTY-FOUR

COLE

A sweet smell woke Cole up. He was lying on the sofa in his apartment. He was still dressed in his clothes from the night before, but his boots lay on the floor next to the sofa.

He wished what happened last night was nothing more than a terrible dream. But he knew it wasn't. He could vividly see the man's face.

It had haunted him the entire night.

He'd had a fitful sleep. Once the adrenaline wore off, he was utterly exhausted. He came home and fell on the sofa. But the nightmares kept waking him up.

He dreamed he was surrounded by colorful tents, and no matter how fast he ran or how far, he couldn't get away from them. What made the nightmares even worse, was that every so often, someone would leap out of one of the tents and grab him by his throat. It was then that he would wake up.

He would drift back to sleep just as quickly as he had awoken, but the nightmare would start all over again. He would be surrounded by the colorful tents, people would jump out of the tents and attack him, and in some cases, he would fight back. The only weapon in his hand was the knife. But unlike what happened last night, the knife would be of little use to him. No matter how many times he stabbed his attackers, it did nothing to stop them.

What have I done? he thought.

He shut his eyes. A part of him wanted to break down and cry.

But then he heard his mother's voice. He looked up from the sofa and saw her in the kitchen, standing behind the stove.

"You must've had a rough night," she said.

He swallowed and slowly got up. "Yeah," he said.

She smiled. "Well, I know just the thing to make it all better. I made your favorite. French toast."

So, that's what the sweet smell was, he thought.

She said, "Why don't you get washed up, and I'll finish making breakfast."

He made his way to the bathroom and shut the door. He looked at himself in the mirror. The man looking back was unfamiliar. There was something haunting about his appearance, as if part of his soul had been cut out of him.

Suddenly, something came up in the back of his throat. He turned to the toilet next to the sink and vomited. He quickly turned on the faucet, and prayed his mom didn't hear him. If she saw him like this, she would start asking questions. And he wouldn't have any answers.

Cole hated lying to his mother. She was his one true best friend. But at the same time, he kept things from her. Not because he didn't trust her, but because he didn't want to hurt her.

She knew he smoked weed. The smell was hard to mask, no matter how much deodorant or cologne he sprayed on his clothes. But she rarely asked him about it. She gave him the space he needed. After all, he wasn't a child anymore.

He sensed there was another reason she didn't pry into what he was up to. This hurt when he thought about it. She was preparing him for the time when she would no longer be around.

He rinsed his mouth with mouthwash, cleaned all traces of what had happened, and left the bathroom.

He sat at the kitchen table. His mom placed the plate of French toast, along with a bottle of maple syrup in front of him.

"Do you want a cup of tea?" she asked.

"Sure," he replied, covering his French toast with syrup. "How are you feeling, mom?"

"Much better than last night." She came over and placed the hot cup next to his plate. She then kissed him on the forehead.

He looked at her, confused. "Everything okay?"

"I saw that you'd refilled my prescriptions," she said.

Right before Cole had met up with Leo, he had visited the local pharmacy and used some of the cash from the thousand dollars to pay for his mom's medication

She sat down across from him. "I know you've been taking longer shifts at the construction site just to pay for everything. I just want you to know that I appreciate what you're doing."

A realization struck him.

She has no idea I got fired. I never told her. As far as she knows, I am still gainfully employed.

Suddenly, the French toast tasted bitter. He had lost his appetite. But he didn't stop eating. It would have raised a red flag.

He smiled. "I just want you to get better."

She smiled back. "I know you do."

They ate their meal in silence, and when he was done, he placed the plate and cup in the sink.

He moved back to the living room. He saw his jacket lying on the floor next to his boots.

I must have pulled it off right before I fell on the sofa and passed out, he thought.

He picked the jacket up and rummaged through the pockets. He pulled out his cell phone and checked.

To his horror, there were several missed calls. And they were all from Leo.

"Is everything okay?" his mom asked. "You look like you've seen a ghost."

"It's nothing," he replied, clearing his phone log with a swipe of his thumb. "I forgot today was my day off. I don't need to go to the construction site. And so, I was thinking I would stay home and spend it with you."

The smile on his mother's face widened.

SEVENTY-FIVE

HELEN

Her name was Jenny Paulette. She had dirty blonde hair, a slim body, and pale skin. She was wearing an oversized coat, baggy pants, and black boots. She also wore a baseball cap. From afar, she looked like a teenage boy.

Helen understood the reasons behind her attire. People who lived on the streets were preyed upon. And the statistics were worse for women. They were abused sexually, physically, and emotionally. They were taken advantage of by anyone and everyone. They were truly the most vulnerable of society. Perhaps, even more so than children. Jenny Paulette was no child. She was twenty-six. She had spent the last decade out on the streets. Helen had found out it was a boyfriend who'd steered Jenny into a life of drugs and prostitution. Her story wasn't unique. It was the same story heard thousands of times each day throughout the country: cruel and calculating men taking advantage of young and naïve women.

Jenny had a mother on the East Coast, and a father who lived on the West Coast. She didn't have any contact with either of them, so she had no one else to turn to but herself.

"I kind of like living here," she said.

Helen and Michael were standing outside a beige tent. Jenny was the one who had called nine-one-one.

"How long have you been here?" Helen asked.

"You mean at Tent City?"

"Yes."

Jenny thought a moment. "Maybe less than a year, I think."

"Did you know Alex Ketchum?" Helen said.

Jenny shook her head. "Not really. Mr. Bigshot kept to himself."

Helen's eyebrows shot up. "Mr. Bigshot?"

"Yeah, that's what the others called him."

"Do you know why they called him that?"

"I heard he used to make a lot of money. Had a nice job. A house. A car. I think he was married, with kids, as well."

"Do you know what he did for work?" Helen asked.

"Like I said, I never spoke to him," Jenny replied. "But people talk. Rumors fly like crazy. I mean, there's not much to do here. There's really nowhere else for us to go either. We all tend to stay here. A lot of it has to do with the fact that we don't want to lose our spot. I heard that Tent City used to be way more crowded. People would fight over certain spots under the bridge. If you're in the middle, then you're insulated from the bad weather, so that's prime real estate. That's where you want to set up your tent. If you're new, you'd be lucky if you got something in the corner."

"You said Tent City used to be crowded," Michael said. "What happened to all those people?"

"I wasn't here when it happened, so I'm only telling you what the older folks told me," Jenny said. "There used to be a big drug problem at Tent City. I don't mean there isn't a problem now, but it was worse back then. I heard that one day two guys got into a fight. One accused the other of stealing his stash or something. The next thing you know, one of the guys pulled out a gun and started shooting. Two people got killed, one guy who was in the fight and another guy who jumped in to break it up. The police came down and raided the whole place. They kicked everyone out. They put up barriers around the area. That's why you see the chain-link fence just outside Tent City. Eventually, people started moving back in. But now, you can't just show up and set up camp. A couple of the old-timers will kick you out if they think you are trouble. You gotta be recommended by someone."

"Who recommended you?" Helen asked.

"The girl whose spot I took over," she replied. "I met her at a food bank. She told me about the place. I'd been trying to get in ever since. One day she said she was moving out. She used to be on drugs, but she was clean by then. She said she'd found a job at a shelter outside the city, and people at the shelter were helping her find a more permanent place to stay."

"How did you come upon... um... Mr. Bigshot's body?" Michael asked, trying to move the interview along.

She turned to him. "I was reading my book—I love to read fantasy novels; they take me to different worlds that are more exciting than the one I live in. Anyway, I heard noises, shouts, and then a scuffle or something. I looked out of my tent, and I saw two people running away in a hurry. I'd never seen them at Tent City before, so I decided to take a look at what the commotion was. When I went over to check, I saw Mr. Bigshot lying on the ground. There was also blood. So, I called nine-one-one."

"You have a cell phone?" Michael asked, surprised.

"Everyone in Tent City has one," she replied as if it was a dumb question. "You can get an old phone for, like, twenty bucks. And the pre-paid cards don't cost a whole lot either. I keep it in case things get dangerous around here, you know."

Helen said, "Can you describe the two people you saw run out?"

Jenny made a face. "That's the thing. I didn't really see them too clearly. They were in a hurry. But one of them looked older, I think. He had on a baseball cap and dark sunglasses. The other looked kinda young. He was wearing a hoodie and jacket."

Helen knew that would be of little use to them in finding out who had stabbed Alex Ketchum.

"Thank you for talking to us," Helen said. "We really appreciate it."

They turned to leave.

Jenny said, "I'm not sure if this helps, but I heard Mr. Bigshot yell out a name."

"What name?" Helen asked.

"Brian."

"Brian?"

"Mr. Bigshot thought someone named Brian had sent those two guys to hurt him."

Helen paused to think a moment. "Is there anyone named Brian in Tent City?" she asked.

"Not that I know of," Jenny replied.

"Okay, thanks."

SEVENTY-SIX

SIMON

"I can't believe you said that to Gabe," Jay said with a smile on his face.

I had called up my best friend, and instead of meeting at the basketball court, we were at a coffee shop not far from where Jay worked. I knew how busy Jay was. He was inundated with cases. There were too many wrongfully convicted inmates. And no matter how hard Jay and his firm worked, it felt like they weren't making a dent in the pile of cases. But Jay was undeterred. He always had a positive outlook on life. He never took no for an answer. If a motion was denied, he would file another one. He believed that if he got even one wrongfully convicted person out of prison, then the struggle was worth it.

I shrugged. "Yeah, well, I'd had enough of Gabe and his bullying."

"I always thought your brother was a jerk. I saw how he treated you and those around him. And believe me, I have known you and your family for a very long time. So, I've seen how he behaves firsthand."

"He can be cold, I agree."

"If you ask me, his heart is a couple of sizes too small."

"Isn't that kinda harsh?" I asked.

"It's true," Jay replied. "Remember that time when one of our neighbor's dads committed suicide because the dad had got himself into financial trouble?"

I thought a moment. "I kinda do remember that. He had made a big bet that blew up in his face."

"And you know what Gabe's response was? 'What a loser! If he was smart, he wouldn't have lost all that money in the first place'."

"I can't believe I'm going to say this, but in Gabe's defense, the neighbor's dad got himself into the middle of the Dot.com bubble."

Jay shrugged. He took a sip from his bottled water. Jay stayed away from caffeine and sugars. No coffee. No tea. And no carbonated drinks. I was surprised how he managed to work long hours without consuming either caffeine or sugar.

"But that's not why I called you here," I said. I still hadn't told Jay the reason why Gabe had come to my house in the first place. Only that Gabe was shocked when I told him I was considering selling my share in the firm.

Truth be told, I no longer wanted to be part of Harris & Harris. And it had nothing to do with the betrayal I felt by my family. It was something I'd been thinking about for a long time. Having money is good. Money provides comfort and security. But after a certain threshold, it's no longer enough.

Growing up, I was fortunate enough that my family was well off. I never had to worry too much about whether I could afford something or not. If I wanted something, my parents made sure I had it. But that didn't come without its own problems. When you get something without having to earn it, you begin to lose a sense of purpose.

My life was pre-planned. Which school I would go to: Columbia. Where I would work when I graduated: my father's firm. And later, what type of person I would marry: Vanessa (she was more like my family than I was).

I had put a wrench in the plans by dropping everything and going to India and living in the slums for three months. There, I met a woman who had opened my eyes to new experiences and a new way of looking at the world.

For the first time in my life, I was truly happy and free. I was not shackled by my parents' expectations. I could do whatever I wanted, even if that meant eating two meals a day and tending to the poor and needy.

I was helping people. I was making their lives better. That was what I had agreed to when I joined Harris & Harris. Gabe had convinced me that we were helping owners turn their businesses around. In the beginning, that's what we did, but soon after, it was about making sure the firm stayed afloat and that we maintained our place in society

Somehow, I got sucked into it by my mother, my brother, and my wife. And don't think for one minute that I am blameless. I wasn't some innocent and naïve child. I was complicit in every way. I enjoyed the lifestyle with all its trappings. But I know one thing for sure, with each passing year, a piece of my soul was being stripped away.

"So, why did you call me here anyway?" Jay said.

I snapped out of my thoughts. "What I'm about to tell you is not a joke."

His face turned serious. "Okay."

"Jay, I'm a father."

He blinked for a minute, and then a smile crossed his face. "That's great news, bro."

"It is?" I said.

"I'm so glad that Vanessa's pregnant."

I shook my head. "No. She's not pregnant. I have a son with someone else."

His jaw dropped. "You cheated on Vanessa?"

I waved my hands in the air. "No, no, no. Let me backtrack…"

Jay interrupted me. "Simon, I know how badly you wanted to have kids, but this isn't the way to go."

"Jay, my son is twenty-one years old. It was before I even met Vanessa."

Jay's chin was now touching his chest. "Are you…?"

"I warned you it's not a joke."

"Who? What? Where? How?"

"You know the girl I told you broke my heart in India?"

"Annabel-something, right?"

"You actually remember the name?"

"You couldn't stop talking about her for years after you'd returned from India. How cruel and calculating and evil she was."

"That's not exactly true."

I then spent the next twenty minutes filling him in on the details. How Annabel tried to contact me. How my mother and brother lied to me. Everything.

When I was done, Jay leaned back in his chair and sighed deeply. "Simon, if your life was a movie, it would be a tragedy."

"I hope not," I said. "I still have a chance to rewrite the ending."

"How are you going to do that?"

"I have no idea."

SEVENTY-SEVEN

HELEN

Janet Helmsley had dark hair, olive skin, and hazel-colored eyes. Janet used to be married to Alex Ketchum. She now lived in a three thousand square-foot house that she shared with her new husband, a stockbroker, and her three children. Two were with Ketchum, and the last, a boy, with her current husband.

Helen and Michael were seated across from her in the living room. On the records, Janet was still showing up as Ketchum's next of kin.

When they told her of his demise, she broke down and wept. They were not expecting such a reaction. Divorce usually left spouses bitter and resentful, wishing their exes were dead.

Janet wiped her eyes with the tissue and said, "I'm sorry. I thought I was prepared to hear this, but I'm not."

"Prepared?" Helen said, confused.

"I mean, the way Alex was living, I just knew something bad would happen."

Michael asked, "Are you referring to his stay at Tent City?"

She nodded. "I visited him a few times there. And each time, I was appalled at what had happened to him."

"Your visits to him, were they before your divorce or after?" Helen asked.

"After our divorce."

"May I ask why you would still want to see him, if you were no longer together?"

Janet looked down at the tissue in her hand. "I loved Alex. In some ways, I still do. He was the father of my children, and he was my best friend. It hurt me to see him live the way he did. Dirty. Hungry. Alone." She shook at the thought. "I tried to get him help. For the sake of the kids, at least. They missed him a lot, and they always asked about him. I wanted to get him on the right track, so that he could be more involved with them. I guess, now that hope is forever dashed."

"How did he end up at Tent City?" Michael asked.

"Sometimes I wonder the same thing," she replied. "He was such a wonderful father and a great husband. He lived life to the fullest. When we were dating, he would take me rock climbing, scuba diving, hang gliding—anything to get a rush. I'll admit, I have a fear of heights, and I hated going on some of those outings. But he had a way of convincing you. He knew how to make you feel comfortable. He would assure me that everything would be all right and that he would be next to me throughout the outing. I would believe him. And you know what? I would have a great time. When our kids were born, Alex turned his focus to them. He was no longer the daredevil. He didn't want to do anything that would take him away from our kids. He wanted to see them grow up. I know one time his friends were bugging him to go skydiving, and under normal circumstances, he would've jumped— wrong choice of words—at the opportunity. But he just turned them down. The risk wasn't worth it. He cherished the moments he spent with me and the kids."

"So, what happened to him?" Michael asked.

Janet looked away, and it seemed for a second that her mind had drifted. She then replied, without looking at them, "I always believe it was that boating trip he had gone on with his friends that changed everything. He normally looked forward to getting away for a day or two. To unwind. To be among the guys. But days before that trip, he kept debating whether he should go or not. In the end, his friends convinced him to join them. But when he came back, it was like he was a totally different person. He was distant. Angry. Depressed. He started having outbursts. He would yell at the kids over even the smallest mistake. He would snap at me, berate me, lecture me. But then he would burst out crying like he was a little boy. It would take a lot of effort to console him.

"I tried to take him to a psychiatrist, but he refused. He said he didn't want to talk about it. He started drinking, which he rarely did before, and then he started doing drugs. I first caught him snorting cocaine in the bathroom. He said he was just stressed and he needed relief. He promised to stop, but it only got worse. One time, he disappeared for days. We looked for him everywhere until my brother found him in a crack house. We dragged him to rehab, but a few days later, he ran away from there. For a good month, we had no idea where he was or what had happened to him. Then one day, someone we knew saw him begging by the side of the road. Again, we got him into rehab. When he came out, he was clean. Then the demons came back, and he was at it again. Drugs. Alcohol. And by then, he was sleeping with prostitutes. That was the last straw. As a woman, I could tolerate a lot, but not hookers. I also found out he was draining our life's savings. I worried that we would end up losing the house, the car, everything we had worked so hard to build. After he ran away for the third time, I didn't want to bring him back. I hired a divorce lawyer who found him living in Tent City. I was told by my lawyer that Alex hadn't put up a fight and just signed the divorce papers. I then met Ben, and we got married. He's a wonderful stepdad. He adores the kids as much as Alex did."

"But you still kept going to Tent City, is that right?" Michael said.

Janet smiled ruefully. "I don't know why, but I always held out hope that one day Alex would snap out of whatever trance he was in and be the man I knew he once was. We would never be together again, but I just couldn't see him deteriorate the way he had. It was just too painful."

Janet looked up at the clock on the wall. "I'm sorry, I have to pick up my youngest from daycare and the two eldest from school. I'm not sure how I'm going to break the news to them that their father is dead."

She broke down crying again.

SEVENTY-EIGHT

COLE

He had spent the day locked up in his apartment. After breakfast, he and his mom had watched TV. Mostly game shows and the occasional morning show. Whenever his mom would flip to the news, he would tell her to change the channel. He feared what he would see on the news. By now, the police must have descended on Tent City. They must have scoured the area for evidence. They must've spoken to the residents of Tent City.

Cole was dreading a knock at the door. He dreaded being cuffed in front of his mom and hauled to the police station. He'd already been there once, and he doubted bail would be allowed if he showed up a second time.

What gave him some comfort, though, was the fact that he did not stab the man. It was Leo. He had done the deed. Not him.

Sure, he'd gone there with the intention to kill a man, but he had failed to act on it.

Why did I take out the knife? he thought.

He knew the answer. The homeless man had become aggressive. Cole had feared for his life. Brandishing the knife was an act of self-defense. He never meant to use it against the man. He only wanted to scare him away.

The man had reacted quickly, and before he knew it, the man had pinned him down. There was no telling what the man would've done had Leo not intervened.

I should never have gone there in the first place, Cole thought.

But he did, and now there was a man dead. Cole didn't know anything about him. He didn't know if he had a family. And Cole didn't want to know, either. That's why he stayed away from the news. Guilt was already eating away at him. He didn't want to make it worse.

He had also turned off his phone. He didn't want Leo calling him again. Maybe once he saw no response from Cole, he would give up. That's what Cole was hoping for.

His mom had sensed that something was wrong. She had asked if he wanted to talk about it. He told her that he was just tired. That he hadn't slept well last night. She told him to go get some rest in her bedroom. But he declined. Sleeping was not going to be possible. The nightmares would end up rearing their ugly heads.

Cole was sitting on the sofa next to his mom, watching a cooking show, when there was a knock at the door.

His heart suddenly dropped to his stomach.

The police are here to get me! he thought.

"Who could that be?" his mom asked.

They rarely got any visitors. Never family or friends. Only management coming around for rent, or sometimes kids from other apartments trying to raise money for their school.

Before his mom could get up to answer it, he said, "I'll go check."

He took a deep breath and slowly made his way to the door. He peered through the peephole and then opened the door.

SEVENTY-NINE

COLE

Standing in the hallway was Leo. He had a smile on his face.

"What are you doing here?" Cole asked.

"You weren't answering my calls," Leo replied. "So, I figured I'd come and see you."

"How did you know where I live?"

"I make it my business to know everything about the people I work with."

"Who is it, Cole?" his mom called.

"No one, mom," he yelled back.

Leo said, "Maybe I should come inside and say hello to your mom."

"We can't talk here," Cole shot back. He shut the door behind him and led Leo to the stairwell. He then turned to him. "Listen, what happened last night shook me up. That guy is dead, and for all we know, the police are looking for us."

"Relax," Leo said. "I have connections in the police department. And they have no idea who killed that homeless man."

"What about witnesses?"

"They don't know anything. No one can ID us. Which means we were never there."

"Are you sure?" Cole asked.

"If I wasn't, do you think I would be showing my face in public?"

Cole let out a sigh of relief. "You have no idea how stressed I've been."

"It's not easy killing a man."

Cole's brow furrowed. "I didn't kill him. You did."

"No. If I remember correctly, you were the one who took the knife into Tent City."

"Yeah, but... but I wasn't the one who stabbed him."

Leo pulled out his cell phone and held it up for him. "According to this, you did."

The blood drained from Cole's face. On the screen was an image of Cole holding a bloodied knife next to the homeless man.

"You... you said you took it to show it to your people," Cole stammered.

"I did, and they were pleased by what you had done."

"You have to delete it," Cole said.

"We will when the time is right."

Cole stared at him. "Whatever game you're playing, I don't want to be part of it anymore."

"I thought you wanted to make serious money?" Leo shot back. "I thought you wanted to help your mom?"

Cole shook his head. "Not like this, I didn't."

"You knew what you were getting into when you agreed to go to Tent City," Leo said.

"I know what I agreed to, but I changed my mind when I saw the man."

Leo took a step closer. "Once you get on this track, there is no going back, do you understand?"

"I don't care. I'm done."

Leo smiled. The same smile that had sent a shiver up Cole's spine before. "What do you think would happen if somehow this photo got to the police?"

Cole swallowed. "If... if that happened... I'd tell them the truth."

"What truth would that be?"

"That you killed that man."

"What man would you be referring to?"

"The man in Tent City."

"Do you even know my real name?" Leo asked.

Cole opened his mouth, but then shut it.

"And what would you even tell the police? That you met a stranger a couple of days ago. This stranger made you steal jewelry. He then made you go inside Tent City and stab a man."

"But... I didn't stab anyone," Cole said.

"Repeating it won't change the facts. The murder weapon has the homeless man's blood on the blade and your fingerprints on the handle," Leo said.

Cole's eyes widened. "You also held the knife."

"If you remember correctly, I was wearing gloves," Leo said.

It then dawned on Cole. He'd been set up. Leo had a photo of him at the scene of the crime. He also had the murder weapon in his possession. He had no intention of getting rid of the weapon, like he claimed he would back at Tent City. There was a purpose behind all of this. They were going to use it as blackmail against him.

Leo said, "We are not going anywhere. In fact, we now own you."

Cole felt fear like he had never felt before.

EIGHTY

HELEN

Helen and Michael were back at the Arlington PD. Michael was working behind his laptop when he turned to her, "When we were speaking to Alex Ketchum's ex-wife, we forgot to ask her if she knew anyone by the name of Brian."

"Who's Brian?" Helen asked.

"Jenny Paulette, the woman who called 911 at Tent City, said she heard Ketchum yell out the name Brian."

"Oh, now I remember," Helen said. "We can always call Ketchum's ex-wife to ask, you know."

"That won't be necessary. I think I know who Ketchum was referring to."

Helen looked at Michael. "You want me to guess? Or are you going to tell me?"

"I believe it's Brian Chester."

Helen's eyes narrowed. "Brian Chester is the founder of Chester and Associates. But how can you be sure that's who Ketchum was referring to?"

Michael smiled. "Alex Ketchum was a former employee of Chester and Associates."

Helen's jaw dropped. "And so was Derek Starr."

"Exactly."

"You think there's a connection between the two cases?"

"It can't be a coincidence that a former employee *and* a current employee are suddenly found dead in the span of a couple of days. And to top it off, they were both stabbed to death."

Helen rubbed her chin in deep thought.

Michael said, "Ketchum's ex-wife said that Ketchum had suddenly fallen apart after a boating trip with a group of friends."

"Okay," Helen said, unsure where Michael was going with this.

"So, I did some digging and found out that nine years ago, Derek Starr, Alex Ketchum, Brian Chester, and another man named Joseph Elliott had gone on a boating trip together. But right after the trip, Elliott went missing."

Helen blinked. "Wait. What?"

"Yeah." Michael hit a couple of keystrokes on his laptop. "Elliott was seen getting on the boat with three other men. This was according to another boat owner at the dock. That boat owner also confirmed it was Starr, Ketchum, and Chester with Elliott."

Helen's brow furrowed. "So, what happened to Joseph Elliott?"

"According to Starr, Ketchum, and Chester, after their trip, they had seen Elliott get in his car and drive off. But he never made it to his house that night."

"And the police believed them?" Helen asked skeptically.

"There are no cameras on the dock, but there are cameras in the parking lot. You have to remember it was dark when they returned from the fishing trip. The cameras in the parking lot did capture Elliott's car leaving the lot. In fact, he was seen paying for his parking ticket at the booth."

"The police had visual confirmation that it was him inside that car?" Helen asked.

Michael turned to the screen. "The reports don't say that specifically. Only that someone with his description was seen behind the wheel. But then again, it was dark, so it could have been someone else driving his vehicle."

"Did they find his car, though?" Helen asked.

Michael scrolled through images on his screen. "It was discovered three days later, by the side of the road, several miles from where the dock was."

"What about his body?"

Michael shook his head. "No sign of him. That's why he is still showing up in the missing persons database."

Helen rubbed her temples. "Wait, that doesn't make sense. Why would someone drive several miles from the dock, and then decide to leave their car at the side of the road, in the middle of the night?"

"Good question. The police were suspicious as well. They interviewed the three men who were with Elliott on the night he was last seen by anyone. Their stories matched," Michael said. "According to their statements, they had a great time on the boat. They drank beer, blew off steam, talked about family. And then they came back on land and headed home."

"Did the police check the boat for any evidence of foul play?"

"Give me a minute." Michael worked the keyboard some more. "They did ask to examine the boat, but Brian Chester refused."

"Refused?"

"He was the registered owner of the boat, and he wanted the police to get a warrant in order to search it."

"Did they get one?"

"They did, but by then, it was unnecessary."

"What do you mean?" Helen asked with irritation.

"The night before the police were supposed to execute the warrant, the boat caught on fire. There was nothing left of it by the time the police got to it."

"Did they know how it happened?" Helen asked.

"Like I said, the dock didn't have any cameras back then."

"Why not?" Helen said. "The one place you would have cameras is that dock. Those boats aren't cheap, you know."

Michael checked his laptop one more time. "The company that managed the dock cited privacy issues for not having cameras. Apparently, there was a case of a couple getting too intimate on their boat, which one of the cameras had captured in vivid detail. So, the police had no idea if it was arson. They believe the fire must have started in the fuel tank."

There was a moment of silence before Helen said, "It's time we go and speak to Brian Chester. It seems like he is the last person still alive from that boating trip."

EIGHTY-ONE

COLE

The mood inside the GMC Canyon had suddenly changed. Leo was behind the wheel, with Cole in the passenger seat.

Leo had told him that they were going for a drive. Cole had wanted to tell him to get lost, but he didn't. The balance of power had shifted. Not that Cole had much power, to begin with. It was he who had gone to Leo for help. He needed money, and he was willing to do anything to get it. However, there was always a sense that he had control of his destiny. If he wanted to, he could have refused to steal anything from the jewelry store. He had, in fact, turned down Leo's offer to go to Tent City and hurt someone. It was his desperation and his love for his mother that compelled him to change his mind.

That was no excuse, he knew. People in far worse situations than him didn't start killing just to get out of a bind. That's what psychopaths did. He was aware of what he was doing when he had gone into Tent City.

This was his fault, and no one else's.

Leo, or whoever else he was working with, was now calling the shots. Cole was now a pawn in whatever game they were playing. If he didn't follow their orders, he could end up spending the rest of his life in jail. But there was something else that was deeply disturbing.

Leo had shown little or no remorse for what he had done to the homeless man. He didn't even bat an eye at his death. Cole was worried about what he might do to him if he chose to deviate from his instructions.

Cole had never felt so powerless in his life. And there had been many situations where he was helpless. Single mothers with no support from family and friends weren't in a good position to defend themselves. There were times when his mom couldn't pay rent, and unscrupulous landlords had other ideas as payment. His mom was a proud woman. She would not stoop to sleeping with a landlord in exchange for free rent. There were a few occasions where she and Cole had grabbed their belongings and left in the middle of the night. During those times, Cole wished he had superpowers. Some way to get them out of the predicament they were in. He also wished he had a guardian angel, someone who would step up and remove them from the turmoil they were in.

He had learned his lessons the hard way. There was no one out there that could help them. They were on their own. And now, it was up to him to deal with whatever mess he was in.

"Where are you taking me?" Cole finally asked.

"You eager to be somewhere?" Leo replied with a snort.

Cole turned back to the window. He stared out at the passing cars. He imagined what the people in those cars must be thinking right now. Most were probably returning from work, or buying groceries, or picking up their kids from school. Mundane actions they did on a regular basis. None of them was in his predicament. None of them could be implicated in a murder. None of them could be facing a life sentence. None of them knew what it felt like to be a prisoner in a situation they couldn't walk away from.

"We are here," Leo said.

Cole looked around. They were in the parking lot of an office complex.

Leo pointed at a granite and cement building and said, "We're going to blow it up."

"What?" Cole asked in disbelief.

"We're going to bring that building down to the ground," Leo replied.

Cole blinked. "Are you crazy? You want to kill all those people inside?"

From his observation, the office tower had at least twenty floors, and it probably had over two thousand people working inside.

Leo shook his head. "We're not mass murderers. We're going to do it at night when the building is empty."

"What about security guards?" Cole asked. He knew buildings like this one always had someone on duty at night.

"There's only going to be one person at the front desk," Leo said. "We're going to cause a distraction—we light a garbage bin on fire behind the building to lure him out. When he does, we grab him and tie him up and take him away from the building. Then we blow it up."

He spoke as if this was a run of the mill operation.

"That's insane," Cole said in disbelief. "You will never get away with it."

"You mean, *we* will never get away with it."

Cole stared at him.

Leo said, "You are going to help us do it. And before you say you will refuse, remember what is at stake: your freedom. You deviate from our orders one bit. You will never see your mother again."

Cole was silent.

Leo stared at Cole. "You don't want to be in prison, kid. Trust me. You won't survive. And if you do somehow manage to live long enough being locked up, you can bet they won't let you take a step outside the walls of the prison to be at her funeral."

Cole felt like someone had pierced his heart. Whatever hope he had prior to getting into Leo's truck was now completely dashed.

"I guess I don't have much of a choice," Cole finally said.

"You don't."

Cole stared at the office tower. He could see lights were on inside.

He turned to Leo. "What do you get out of it?"

"Out of what?"

"Blowing up the building."

Leo rubbed his beard. "Let's just say, we've been hired by some people who plan on making a lot of money from the insurance once we complete the task."

EIGHTY-TWO

HELEN

When Helen and Michael had called, Brian Chester wasn't very keen on speaking to them. When they told him both Derek Starr and Alex Ketchum were dead, that got his attention.

Brian Chester had salt-and-pepper hair, smooth skin, and bright blue eyes. He was dressed in a polo shirt, dress pants, and dress shoes.

They were seated in his spacious private office, which had a great view of the city. All the furniture in the office was either imported or handmade. On the walls were photos from the exotic trips Chester had taken all over the world.

"I was saddened to hear about Derek," Chester said. "Now I'm shocked that Alex is gone, too."

Michael said, "They were employees of your accounting firm."

Chester nodded. "Some of my best."

"I heard they were with you from the very beginning."

"I started the firm in my basement," Chester said. "Derek was my first hire. We did bookkeeping, tax preparation, auditing of financial statements, dealing with the IRS, or anything else that required our expertise."

"And when did you move to this office location?" Michael asked.

"Once the business grew, and we started hiring more people, we needed a bigger space. So, I think it was a little over nine or ten years ago."

Helen asked, "Was Joseph Elliott working for you when you moved to this location?"

Chester stared at her. "What does *he* have anything to do with what happened to Derek and Alex?"

"Nothing yet," Helen replied. "We just find it interesting that on the night Joseph Elliott disappeared, he was with you, Derek Starr, and Alex Ketchum. And now, Mr. Starr and Mr. Ketchum are murdered."

Chester's eyes narrowed. "Are you accusing me of something, detective?"

"Absolutely not. We're just concerned that your life could also be in danger."

"Why would it be? I haven't done anything wrong."

"We're not saying you have," Helen said. "We're just trying to see if there is a link between Mr. Starr's and Mr. Ketchum's murders."

"If there is, I don't know what that is, except for the fact they both worked for my firm."

"Don't forget, Joseph Elliott also worked for your firm," Helen said.

Chester fell silent. He then said, "Joe was my best friend. I'd known him since we were teenagers. He used to live around the block from my parents' place. All through high school, we were inseparable. We did everything together. We went on long bike rides, collected comic books, sneaked into movie theaters—so Joe's disappearance was a big shock to me. In fact, I was the one who begged Joe to join Chester and Associates right before we moved into this office. At the time, Joe was working for a large accounting firm in New York. We were managing accounts of many corporations in Arlington. Our workload was so much that I knew I couldn't do it on my own. I trusted Joe with my life and my firm. I offered him a job as an in-house accountant to oversee just about everything at Chester and Associates. When he went missing, it was not only a loss to his family, but, also a loss to me, both personally and professionally. I even put up a large reward for any information on his disappearance."

Helen said, "I understand your connection with Mr. Elliott, but what I found puzzling was why you refused to let the police examine your boat on the night of his disappearance."

Chester's eyes narrowed. "I guess there's no point in me hiding it now. It happened years ago. The reason I didn't let the police go through my boat was that I was afraid of what they would find."

Michael jumped in. "And what was that?"

"Cocaine. I knew Derek and Alex very intimately. You could say we were all good friends. Derek and Alex were senior members at the firm. And Joe, as you already know, was sort of like my right-hand man. All decisions went through him before they came to me. We were all working very hard to grow the firm. I know my name is on the front door, but I really felt like it was a team effort. When you're trying to expand your business, it comes with a lot of stress. So, Derek, Alex, Joe, and I would take trips on my boat to let off steam. So, yeah, I was afraid that the police would find traces of cocaine on the boat, which would put us in a lot of trouble. Having senior management and the CEO of a firm charged with a crime doesn't convey a sense of trustworthiness to clients. And, some of these clients were family-owned companies whose reputation depended on them being wholesome."

Helen said, "I'm sure it must've been a relief when your boat unexpectedly had an accident right before the police were about to search it with a warrant."

Chester fell silent. He then said, "Like you said, it was an unexpected accident. And frankly, no one knows exactly what happened." The phone on Chester's desk blinked. "Is there anything else, detectives? Unfortunately, you've caught me at a very difficult time."

"Does this have anything to do with Fast-Card?" Michael asked.

Chester turned to him but said nothing.

"We know that there is an ongoing investigation of your connection with Fast-Card," Michael said.

"As you aptly stated, it's an *ongoing* investigation, so I can't comment on it," Chester said.

They sensed Chester was in no mood to continue the conversation. They didn't want to aggravate him. He was neither a suspect nor a witness. There was nothing they could do to compel him to keep talking.

They thanked him for his time and left.

EIGHTY-THREE

SIMON

I was parked outside Annabelle's apartment building. When I first laid eyes on the building, I felt a tinge of sadness and pain. The building was falling apart. The exterior paint was peeling. The roof at the entrance was crumbling. The glass on the front door was cracked.

I couldn't believe the condition Annabelle and Cole were living in. Their situation was far worse than what she had told me. I couldn't imagine how they'd managed all those years on their own. Annabelle's family had always struggled financially, so it should have been me supporting her and our child.

That was not to be. Forces outside my control had prevented me from being a father. Perhaps, even a husband. If I think about it hard enough, I would have married Annabelle. At that time, she was the love of my life. And I am certain we would've had more children together.

I took a deep breath to control my emotions.

I have to stop thinking about the past, I thought. *I can't change what has already been done.*

I was here for a reason. I wanted to finally speak to my son. I wasn't sure if Annabelle had told him the truth yet. I doubted that she had, or else she would've called me. After all, she had my number. But she had told me we would have to be patient with Cole.

Cole was already dealing with having a mother who was sick. The revelation that his father was always nearby would be too much for him. Annabelle feared Cole would push me away out of anger. And there was a lot of resentment simmering underneath him.

Cole's childhood wasn't spent like other kids. Playing video games. Going to the movies. Eating out. Having simple fun. Cole's childhood was spent moving from one place to another, always dealing with uncertainty and instability. In short, Cole was always looking over his shoulder for the next threat to him and his mother. He had to grow up faster than other kids his age.

He was also acting out now. I was informed by Detective Booker that Cole was accused of stealing a woman's handbag outside a jewelry store. I would bring my own lawyer to help Cole get through the legal process.

I knew firsthand the advantage children of the rich had. Instead of a sentence that could leave a record, those kids were let off with probation or community service. I hated having to use that influence now. But I would not let Cole rot in jail. No way. No how.

I debated my next move. I could call Annabelle and tell her I was coming up to her apartment and that we should have a family meeting. I knew she wouldn't be too pleased by it, but it was time for the truth.

The longer I waited, the more anxious I was becoming. Annabelle's health was deteriorating day by day. And the sooner Cole knew who I was, the sooner we could work together to get her help.

I then saw a truck pull up to the front entrance. A man was behind the wheel. Next to him was another man. I squinted and realized it was Cole. The man was speaking fast and pointing a finger at Cole. In return, Cole had his head down, and he merely nodded.

A moment later, Cole got out of the truck. He shoved his hands in his pockets and hurried inside.

My face tightened. There was something threatening about the man in the truck.

What is Cole doing with someone like him? I thought.

Maybe it was parental instinct, but I suddenly had the urge to protect my only offspring.

The truck pulled away from the entrance. I decided to follow.

EIGHTY-FOUR

HELEN

"Can you believe that guy?" Michael said, shaking his head.

They had just left Brian Chester's office and were making their way through the parking lot.

"I bet he's hiding something," Michael added.

"Even if he is, we've got nothing on him," Helen said.

"If we gave him a polygraph, the reading would be off the charts."

Helen said, "Before we can give him a poly, we need to charge him first."

Her cell phone buzzed. She answered it, and after a brief conversation, she hung up.

"I have to go," she said.

Michael's brow furrowed. "Everything okay?"

"Yes. Just a family matter. Would you be okay finding a ride back?"

"I'll call for a taxi," he said with a smile. "It's about time I get the department to pay for some of my commuting costs."

She smiled. "Thanks. I'll see you at the station."

She drove straight home. The drive took her close to half an hour, and when she pulled up to her house, she found Paul sitting on her front porch.

"What's the emergency?" she asked, getting out of her vehicle.

He stood up from his chair. "I'm afraid I need a place to stay for the night."

That's when she saw a small suitcase next to his feet.

"I thought about going to Emily's," he said. "But Tim's mom is staying over at their place, and I thought it would be awkward if I showed up looking for a sofa to crash on."

"What happened between you and Svetlana?"

"We got into a fight."

"About what?"

Paul sighed. "I saw her having lunch with someone else."

"I never saw you as the jealous type."

"I thought I wasn't either, but with age, you kind of want to settle down, and I thought she would be the one."

Helen gave him a look. "You do know she is much younger than you, don't you?"

"What does that have anything to do with it?" he asked.

"Women her age also want to settle down. But then, kids come into the equation. I can't imagine you wanting to change diapers at this stage of your life."

"I suppose you're right," he said.

Helen's eyes narrowed. "Wait. Did she kick you out? She's staying at *your* place, you know that."

"I left on my own."

"Why?"

"She was getting a bit... physical."

"She hurt you?" Helen asked, concerned.

"No, but she broke a lot of dishes."

Helen nodded. "In that case, it was smart you got yourself out of that situation."

"I want to give her time to cool off."

"How long?"

"How long for what?"

"How long do you want to stay?"

"Just one night," Paul replied. "I'm hoping I can go tomorrow and work things out with Svetlana."

"All right," Helen said, pulling out her keys. "You can have Emily's old room."

EIGHTY-FIVE

SIMON

I kept a fair distance between my vehicle and the truck. I wasn't sure why I was following it. Maybe I wanted to know who this person was and why he was being so aggressive with my son.

I could tell by the look on Cole's face that he was in some trouble.

Is he involved in a gang? I thought. *Is that why he had stolen that handbag because that's what the gang did?*

I was a bit disappointed, but also relieved. I was disappointed he was involved in criminal activity, but I was relieved that at least it was not drug-related. The sentence for the latter was far worse than the former.

When I entered a sketchy part of the city, I felt uneasy. Most of the shops were closed or boarded up. There was graffiti everywhere. I saw a car with missing tires on the side of the road. I passed by a group of young men standing around a basketball court. They looked at me with disdain and distrust.

I stuck out like a sore thumb in my BMW. I suddenly considered turning back, but I had already come this far. I wasn't going to confront the man in the truck. I didn't know who he was or what he was capable of. I'd already gotten myself pretty badly beaten up. I had no intention of getting beat up a second time in a matter of days.

My only objective was to see what the man was up to. Maybe I could get the police involved in order to extricate Cole from whatever situation he found himself in. It was a long shot, but it was better than doing nothing.

Cole was clearly distressed. And I couldn't imagine something happening to him now, just after I'd found out who he was.

The truck turned into a plaza. I slowed by the side of the road and saw it disappear into the back of a laundromat.

I put the car in park and looked around. All I saw were derelict buildings and vacant lots. I felt exposed sitting inside my luxury vehicle. I feared someone would run up to me and jack my car.

I eyed the laundromat. There was no way I was going to go inside. That would be a reckless move. The shop could be a front for illegal activities. I'd seen documentaries where criminal organizations purchased mom and pop shops to set up their headquarters. The laundromat would be a perfect spot to do just that.

I checked my watch. I would give myself fifteen minutes. If nothing happened, I would leave.

Maybe I would come back tomorrow. Or better yet, I would speak to Cole about it myself.

Before the fifteen minutes were up, I saw a Honda Civic pull into the plaza. A man got out of the sedan, and when he did, I saw a gold police badge was attached to his belt. The man was young, and he quickly adjusted his coat to hide the badge.

He then went inside the laundromat. A moment later, he came out and walked to the back of the building

That's where the guy in the truck had gone, I thought.

I sat up straight in my seat. What were the police doing here? Was the guy in the truck an undercover officer? And what did this have to do with Cole? Those questions and many more swirled through my mind.

I then settled on the most rational explanation. The police were likely monitoring the gang's activities, and, perhaps, the guy in the truck was a police informant. And he was somehow using Cole as bait.

I didn't like the sound of that. Whether that was actually what was happening was beside the point. The alarm bells were ringing loudly inside my head. All I kept thinking of was the guy in the truck, the police officer, and my son. And what the link was between them.

This is crazy, I concluded. *I have no business being here.*

I reached for the button to start the BMW.

I heard two loud bangs, one right after the other. They were so loud that I nearly leaped out of my seat.

A moment later, I saw the truck pull out from the back of the laundromat. It turned into the street I was parked on and roared away.

I waited for the police officer to come running out in pursuit of the truck. But he didn't.

I felt a sharp pain in the pit of my stomach.

Damn, I thought and got out. I ran across the road to the back of the laundromat. The back door was closed, but there were metal stairs zigzagging up to the second floor. The door on that floor was wide open.

I hurried up, the heels of my shoes tapping loudly on the steps. When I came to the top landing, I peered through the door, but I couldn't see anything inside. It was dark.

"Hello," I said. "Is everything okay?"

I slowly took a step inside. My eyes adjusted to the darkness. And that's when I saw a man crumpled in the hallway.

It was the police officer!

There was blood on the floor next to him.

"Are you okay?" I asked, hurrying up to him.

His face was pale, and he was drenched with sweat. I could see that he was still breathing. He opened his eyes momentarily, but then shut them.

I pulled out my cell phone and called nine-one-one. Once I'd told the operator where I was and what had happened, I hung up.

I quickly removed my jacket and placed it underneath the officer's head. I wanted to make sure he didn't lose consciousness.

I then held him and waited for help to arrive.

EIGHTY-SIX

HELEN

She rushed to the hospital the moment she heard the news. Paul had offered to make dinner in return for her letting him sleep over. She was looking forward to a home-cooked meal, like the ones she would have when they were still married. But what her sergeant told her shook her to the core.

She felt like she was in a trance as she drove into the emergency room's parking lot. She quickly found a spot and hurried inside. She flashed her badge, introduced herself, and was promptly informed that Michael Porter had been rushed into surgery.

She spotted her sergeant down the hall. He had a somber look on his face. The sergeant prided himself on the fact he hadn't lost an officer under his leadership. She could tell that he feared today might be that day.

"What happened?" she asked as she approached him.

"A civilian found Detective Porter in an apartment just above a laundromat," the sergeant replied. "He'd been shot twice."

"What was he doing there?" Helen asked.

"That's what I was about to ask you."

"I have no idea. He never told me where he was going."

"Where were you?" he asked.

"I had an urgent family matter to attend to," she replied.

She knew he wasn't going to challenge her. She'd been on the force far too long, and it was not uncommon for detectives to take time off for personal errands. Detective work was an all-consuming job. There were times she would work around the clock, even sleeping at her desk if need be.

"Let's just pray he pulls through," the sergeant finally said.

"Where's the civilian that called nine-one-one?" she asked.

"He's down the hall in the waiting area."

Helen's eyebrows shot up. "He's here? In the hospital?"

"Yes. He wanted to make sure Detective Porter was fine."

"I have to speak to him," she said.

She found him sitting on a hard plastic chair. He was holding his jacket in one arm, and there was blood on his dress shirt. His hair was matted from sweat, and there were heavy bags under his eyes.

"I'm Detective Helen Sloan," she said. "I'm Detective Michael Porter's partner."

"Simon Harris," he said, standing up.

She pointed to his shirt, "Do you need medical help?"

He shook his head. "I'm not hurt. It must've gotten on me when I tried to stop the bleeding, before the paramedics arrived."

"I want to thank you for what you did. You may have saved his life."

"I hope so," he said.

Helen said, "Do you mind if I ask you a few questions?"

"I guess."

"My sergeant told me that you found Detective Porter above a laundromat. Is that correct?"

"Yes."

"What were you doing there?"

She could see him searching for answers. He then said, "I was parked across the street when I heard the gunshots. I went to check, and that's when I found the detective."

"Okay, sure. But you didn't answer my question. What were you doing at the laundromat?"

"If I said I was there doing my laundry, would you believe me?"

Helen looked Harris over. "From the way you are dressed, I don't think you live in that area. And I doubt someone like you needs to go to a laundromat to do your wash."

"You're making a lot of assumptions, detective."

"Assumptions is all I have when I don't know the truth."

"What if I said I happened to be there when I heard the shots," he said.

"You work in the area?"

"No. But like I said, I happened to be there."

Helen sensed he wasn't being entirely forthcoming with her. But she couldn't be angry with him. In fact, if it weren't for him, Michael would…

She didn't want to think about it.

"Mr. Harris," she said. "That's my partner in there fighting for his life. Whatever you have to say, you can say it. I know you didn't shoot him. If you had, you wouldn't have stuck around to save him. So, please, help me understand what happened."

He stared at her and then sighed. "Okay, fine. I was following someone when I ended up at that laundromat."

"Who were you following?"

"I don't know."

"Why were you following them?"

"I don't know."

She felt the blood rise to her head, but she held her tongue. "You're telling me you happen to be at the spot where an officer was shot, and you can't tell me why you were there to begin with?"

"That's exactly what I'm telling you, detective," he said. "But I can lead you to the person who shot your partner."

Helen blinked. "I thought you said you didn't know who it was."

"I can give you their license plate number. Maybe you can use it to find them."

"Give it to me," she said eagerly.

EIGHTY-SEVEN

HELEN

After making a few calls, Helen had put out an APB for the vehicle Simon Harris had given her the license plate number of. She'd asked him to go home and get cleaned up. He'd already done enough. There was nothing more he could do at the hospital. It was now a waiting game. The doctors were doing their best to save Michael. It was their skills and Michael's will to live, that would get him through this.

A part of her felt like it was her fault. So far, whatever had happened was her doing. She'd been distracted by matters other than the investigations she and Michael were working on. She was just focused on getting through the next couple of months.

She covered her face with her hands.

How could this go so wrong? she thought.

The investigations should not have been this complicated. She had let them drag on unnecessarily. She had ignored many of the early clues. Key pieces that could have helped her before Michael had gotten hurt.

Retirement had been on her mind the moment she'd decided to finally go through with it.

It wasn't easy to stop doing what she had done for the last thirty years. Being a law enforcement officer was everything to her. It was her identity. Her purpose in life. But Helen had been preparing for this very moment. She wanted to resolve certain cases and move on with her life. She couldn't hold on to all the disappointments that occurred during her career. The people she felt should've been held accountable for the crimes she knew they committed. And her inability to properly bring them to justice.

Michael was supposed to be the future. She shook her head.

Michael is *the future*, she reminded herself.

She had to believe he would make it through, or else she would never forgive herself.

She spotted someone familiar down the hall. It was Leslie, Michael's fiancé, and she had a frantic look on her face. Leslie saw her, rushed over, and they hugged each other. She then burst into tears. Helen held her tight and cried too.

There was so much emotion bottled up inside Helen. She felt like she had let Leslie down. As Michael's partner, it was her responsibility to watch his back at all times.

"I'm so sorry," Helen said. "He never told me where he was going."

Leslie wiped the tears with the back of her sleeve. "I don't blame you, Helen," she said. "Michael can be stubborn sometimes. If he gets something in his head, he won't stop until he's fully satisfied with the results."

They took a seat and held hands. Helen was not going to leave Michael's or Leslie's side. She would stay at the hospital, however long, to know that he was okay.

They didn't have to wait long. A doctor came into the waiting room and called them out into the hallway.

"You're Michael Porter's family?" he asked.

"I'm his fiancée, and this is his partner from work," Leslie replied.

"I have good news and bad news," the doctor said. "The bad news is that he's lost a lot of blood. We had to pull out two bullets from his body. One had gone through his shoulder and the other through his abdomen. The good news is that both bullets missed his vital organs. He's already on blood transfusion, and we expect him to make a full recovery."

Leslie put a hand over her mouth. "Thank you so much," she said.

"Don't thank me. Thank the person who got him here in the nick of time."

Helen thought of Simon Harris. She'd already asked him to come to the station, and give a full report when he was able to do so. She would find a way to make it up to him, as a way to thank him for what he had done.

Leslie asked, "Can I see him?"

"Not yet," the doctor replied. "He's still in critical condition. But once we move him out of intensive care, you can see him then."

Helen and Leslie hugged each other again. They were relieved that Michael would be fine.

EIGHTY-EIGHT

COLE

After Leo had dropped him off at his apartment, Cole had taken the elevator up to his unit. He found his mom waiting for him. She asked where he had suddenly disappeared to. He made some vague excuse about meeting a friend. She told him she had prepared dinner. His response was that he wasn't hungry.

He had lost his appetite the moment Leo told him what he was planning to do. Whenever Cole thought about it, he wanted to throw up. There was no way you could blow up a building and not hurt anyone. No plan was foolproof, he knew.

Leo may have taken into account the security guard at the front desk, but he failed to mention the janitors that worked throughout the night cleaning office buildings. Most, if not all, were immigrants, looking for an opportunity for a better life. They had no choice but to mop floors, vacuum carpets, and clean toilets just to make a living.

By Cole's estimate, there were likely three or four janitors working inside the building at the same time.

Could Leo get them all out without triggering the alarm? Cole wasn't sure if that was even remotely possible. They would first have to locate all the workers, tie them up, or at least take their cell phones from them, and then get them away from the building. Too much time would be spent making sure not a single soul was inside when the building went down.

And that was another concern he had. He knew that many employees worked long hours, some staying until midnight to finish whatever project, paperwork, or task that urgently needed completion. And, there were also those who would stop by to pick up whatever they'd forgotten in their office.

Did Leo have a contingency plan for all of them?

Cole shook his head. The more he thought about it, the more absurd the entire plan was. Even if they did succeed in leveling the building, he was certain there'd be casualties.

Was the death of one person worth the deaths of many more?

He still had a chance to do the right thing. He could still go to the police and tell them what Leo, and whoever he was working with, were up to. He would have to take responsibility for the homeless man's death. Leo would make sure Cole was punished for his betrayal. But at least Cole would save the lives of countless others.

He put his head in his hands.

He was glad his mom was resting in the bedroom. He didn't want her to see him like this, scared and helpless. The same feelings he would get when he was younger. He wasn't sure how he got through those difficult periods. Maybe it was the fact that he had his mother to pull him out of whatever malaise he was feeling. But when she was gone, who would be there for him then?

He was beginning to think there was nothing he could do to help her get better. His foolish attempt at raising money through illegal means had come to nothing.

After what happened at Tent City, he could be seeing life in prison. But what he was about to do at that office tower would surely see him receive a lethal injection in his arm.

He covered his face and quietly began to sob.

EIGHTY-NINE

SIMON

I opened the door and was surprised to see Vanessa in the hallway. She looked horrified when she saw the blood on my shirt.

"Are you okay?" she asked. Normally, she would rush over and hug me. But today, there was hesitation. There was suddenly a wedge between us.

"I'm fine," I replied.

"What happened?"

I knew I wouldn't be able to explain why I was outside Annabelle's home. What I was doing following the truck. And why I had gone to the back of the laundromat. There were some secrets I wanted to keep to myself now.

"I need to get out of these clothes," I said.

"Why don't you go upstairs and change," she said. "And I'll make hot cups of tea."

I nodded and moved up to our bedroom. I stripped off the bloodied clothes and got in the shower. I let the hot water roll over my body. It was my way of cleansing myself. I wanted to get the smell of blood off me.

I don't know how long I stood under the water, but then I dried myself, changed into something comfortable, and went downstairs.

I found Vanessa at the dining table. I sat down across from her.

She slid a cup in front of me. I took a sip. It felt comforting.

"I'm worried that things are bad between us," she said.

"They are," I admitted.

"Why can't we go back to the way they were before?"

I stared at her. I was too tired to dredge up the lies that she and my family had told me.

She said, "I've been doing a lot of thinking, and I want to make it up to you."

My eyes narrowed. "How?"

"If you want a child so badly, we can adopt."

"No."

"Why not?" she said, surprised.

I said, "If adoption had been a possibility, we would have already done so. We didn't because you never wanted it."

"But I'm ready now."

I shook my head. "No, you're not. You're just saying it to make me feel better. But sooner or later, you'll regret the decision to bring a child into this house."

She stared at me. "Yes, you're right. I don't really want any children. I never wanted them. I felt like they would hold me back."

"That's what I never understood," I said. "Children bring out the best of us, and the worst, as well. But that's what makes life interesting."

She sighed. "You know I grew up with four sisters. My parents wanted a boy so badly that they kept having kids just to get one. My parents had so many hopes and dreams. Things they wanted to do, but couldn't do, because they were busy raising us. I just wanted more freedom in my life. That's all. Is that so much to ask, Simon?"

I shook my head. "Vanessa, I'm not angry that you don't want children. I'm angry that you told me you couldn't have them."

"Would you have stayed if you knew I could, but didn't want to?"

"I don't know," I replied, truthfully. "What I do know is that, all through those times when we kept trying and failing to have a child, I thought something was wrong with me. But then I found out it was you. Or, at least that's what you told me. I then convinced myself it was not meant to be, and I moved on with my life. But to know there was nothing wrong with either of us? That eats away at me whenever I think about it." I looked down at the cup in front of me. "I loved you so much I was willing to abandon the future I envisioned for myself, because I knew it was not your fault. Now I know that it was."

"Simon…"

"Let me finish, please," I said. "If you really loved me, like you say you do, you would have given me some choice on whether we had kids or not. Instead, in order to achieve the future that *you* wanted for yourself, you continued to lie to me."

I stood up, walked over, and grabbed my jacket.

"Is it over between us?" she asked.

I looked at her. She looked so weak and defeated. But I felt nothing. I had given the best years of my life to her. We'd had good times and bad times. I realized now those bad times were unnecessary. While I suffered through all the supposed miscarriages, the disappointments, the dashed hopes, the mental anguish, she was not suffering with me. In fact, she was the cause of my pain.

She had every right not to want children. It was her body, after all. And I would never force it on her. But she had no right to hold me back by resorting to a lie. It was a betrayal of the trust between a husband and wife. It was something I could not easily get over.

"Goodbye, Vanessa," I said and left.

NINETY

LEO

He stared at the phone in his hand. His conversation had left him deeply disturbed. The police were looking for his truck, and they would not stop until they found it. An officer had been shot, and all focus would be on finding who was behind it.

Earlier, after dropping off Cole, Leo had decided to meet up with Tyrel. The plan was in motion, and he wanted everyone on the same page. Tyrel lived above the laundromat. It was rented under a fake name and paid for by Leo. It was supposed to be their base of operations. He was now glad that he didn't leave anything incriminating in that space. Everything was stored in his head.

Humans could not be relied upon. They were prone to making mistakes. Tyrel was no older than Cole. It wouldn't take long for him to slip up and derail what they had been planning for all these years.

Once he'd arrived at Tyrel's place, he had gone into the bathroom to relieve himself. That's when he'd heard a knock at the door. He listened carefully and realized the person outside was a police detective. He wanted to ask Tyrel questions about Derek Starr. The detective had proof that Tyrel was at the same bar on the night Starr was murdered.

The detective had tracked Tyrel's license plate number to the address on file.

Leo had heard enough to know that if he didn't act, the detective would have taken Tyrel in for questioning. And with a little pressure, the detective would have broken Tyrel. Tyrel would've confessed to Starr's murder, and he would have told the detective whatever he knew about Leo.

There wasn't much to tell. Leo was careful not to provide anything that could be used against him. That was why he never left any evidence that could lead back to him. The burner phone he'd given Tyrel didn't have any numbers that could be tracked. All instructions were made verbally and in person. No emails. No text messages. Nothing.

When he saw the opportunity, Leo burst out of the bathroom and fired his gun at the detective. The detective had been taken by surprise. He didn't even have a chance to reach for his weapon. He just crumpled to the floor.

Leo grabbed a stunned Tyrel, got him in his truck, and raced out of there.

He now had to clean up the mess Tyrel had created. His error back at the bar with Derek Starr had come back to haunt them.

Leo knew time was no longer on their side.

He would have to end this tonight.

NINETY-ONE

HELEN

She waited outside Michael's room. He had been transferred from intensive care only twenty minutes before. They were allowing one visitor at a time. Naturally, Leslie was the first to go in.

Helen couldn't imagine what she must be going through right now. She and Michael were supposed to be planning their upcoming wedding. Now they'd be spending that time on Michael's recovery.

She debated whether to stay at the hospital. She wasn't sure how she could face him. The guilt was gnawing at her soul.

The door opened, and Leslie came out. "You can go inside now," she said. "I have to let Michael's parents know that he's out of surgery and doing well. They are getting ready to fly over from Arkansas on the first available flight."

Helen nodded and went inside.

The room was quiet except for the sounds coming from the monitors. Michael's face was swollen, and his eyes were shut. Numerous tubes were attached to his body. He was on oxygen, and underneath his hospital gown, Helen was sure he was heavily bandaged.

Even so, he looked like he was peacefully asleep.

She feared disturbing him, but she wanted him to know she was there. And that she was sorry for what had happened.

She should have returned to the station after letting Paul into the house. That's what she had told Michael outside Chester and Associates' office building. Instead, she decided to stick around the house and enjoy a home-cooked meal and a glass of wine.

She pulled a chair close to Michael's bed and sat down. "Why didn't you call me?" she whispered. "Why didn't you tell me where you were going?"

She knew if he had, she would have talked him out of it. She would've told him to wait for her.

"What were you even doing there? What had you found that was so important you had to go alone?" she wondered out loud.

She watched his face. There was no reaction.

She shut her eyes as tears rolled down her cheeks. "I'm so sorry," she then whispered. "This should never have happened. It's my fault. But I'll make it right. I promise."

She reached over and held his hand.

NINETY-TWO

COLE

He was on the sofa when there was a knock at the door. His body tensed, and he broke into a cold sweat. He pulled out his phone, expecting to see several missed calls from Leo.

There were none.

Who could it be? he thought.

The knock came again. He glanced into his mom's bedroom. She was fast asleep. The medications were working.

He made his way to the door, peeked through the peephole, and then opened it. He recognized the man standing outside. He was the one who had posted his bail.

"What are you doing here?" Cole asked.

"I need to speak to your mom," the man replied.

"She's resting right now."

The man stared at Cole. He then said, "Do you know who I am?"

Cole shrugged. "Mom said you were a friend from India."

The man opened his mouth, but then he shut it.

He then asked, "Are you in some trouble?"

Cole's eyes narrowed. "Who are you?"

"Are you?" the man asked again.

"Even if I am, what does that have to do with you?"

The man took a step closer. "I was here earlier. I came to speak to you and your mom. I saw you get out of a truck. You looked upset, so I followed that truck to a laundromat. I then found an officer lying on the floor, bleeding heavily. He'd been shot twice. I know this because I held him in my arms until the paramedics came. He is now fighting for his life in the hospital."

Cole's mind immediately went to Leo.

Did he now shoot an officer?

The man said, "Whoever you're involved with, they are dangerous people."

Cole was silent.

"I have to go to the police station and provide a statement. They want to know what I was doing following the man in the truck. The bigger question is, what are *you* doing with someone like him?"

Cole never had anyone speak to him this way. A part of him wanted to tell the man off, to get lost, that it was none of his business. But another part of him was somewhat relieved there was someone who was concerned about him.

"I can't talk about it," Cole finally said.

"Listen," the man said. "You have to go to the police and tell them who this man is. He shot a detective, for crying out loud."

"I can't!" Cole said, tears suddenly streaming down his face. He quickly wiped them away. He didn't want the man to see him like this.

"Cole," the man said. His voice was soft but reassuring. "Are you in trouble, son?"

Cole's eyes widened. There was something about the man he couldn't put his finger on. He looked like he genuinely cared for his well-being. Apart from his mom, no one else had paid much attention to him.

For some reason, he nodded.

"Then we should go to the police," the man said. "They will help you."

Cole shook his head. "This guy has something against me."

"Like what?"

"I can't say, but I didn't do it."

"Do what?" the man said, confused.

"I was set up. I swear on my mother's life I would never hurt anyone."

"What are you talking about?"

"If I don't do what this man wants me to do, I could end up going to jail for a very long time."

A look of pain swept over the man's face. He looked deeply troubled by what Cole had just told him.

"Now, please leave," Cole said.

Cole turned, went inside, and shut the door behind him.

NINETY-THREE

HELEN

She didn't want to head back home. She had abruptly left without an explanation, and Paul would ask her what happened. She didn't think she could contain her emotions if she spoke to him. Her visit to Michael's room didn't make her feel any better. Seeing the condition he was in only made it worse.

She decided to drive to Emily's house. She called her and told her she was parked in the driveway.

A moment later, Emily came out of the house and walked over to the car. Helen rolled down the passenger side window.

"What're you doing out here, mom?" Emily asked, confused.

"I wanted to talk to you," Helen replied.

"Why don't you come inside, and I'll put a kettle on the stove."

Helen shook her head. "Paul told me Tim's mom is staying with you guys."

"Yeah, but what does that have to do with anything?"

"Can we just talk? In the car?"

Emily looked around. She then opened the door and got in. "Is everything okay, mom?"

"I just wanted to see you, dear."

"What's wrong?"

Helen bit her bottom lip, trying hard to fight back the tears.

"What happened, mom?" Emily asked, suddenly alarmed.

Helen told her about Michael.

Emily leaned over and hugged her. "I'm so sorry, mom," she said. "I really am."

Helen wiped her face. "I know I wasn't around when you were young."

"It's okay, mom. I'm fine now."

"No, please. Let me say this now before I change my mind," Helen said. "When you were born, it was the happiest day of my life. I couldn't believe I could feel so much love for something so small. You were so beautiful. I always imagined us being best friends. Having long conversations. Going shopping together. Trying out exotic foods. So many things I had planned for us to do." Helen fell silent. "A few months after I had you, I returned to work. I hated leaving you behind, but I knew you would be well taken care of. Paul was a hands-on father. He was aware of your every need. But obviously, he couldn't do it all on his own. There were many occasions where I would watch you so that he could rest. I knew he would need the energy during the times I was away at work. At the time, I was a patrol officer. My shifts were long, and I spent most of my time in my cruiser. One night, Paul called and told me you had a fever, and you had been crying nonstop. I should have driven straight home. But I had another hour or so before the end of my shift. I decided to stick it out. After all, I was the sole provider, and with Paul home with you, we desperately needed the money.

"As I was driving around the neighborhood, I spotted a car idling in an empty parking lot. It was dark when I approached the vehicle. I used my flashlight to shine a light on the occupants inside. There were four people. A man was behind the wheel, with two men in the backseat, and between the two men was a woman. In hindsight, the woman looked too young to be with them. She also looked scared. I asked what they were doing out so late at night. The man behind the wheel said they were just hanging around. I asked the girl if she was okay, but instead, the same man said she was fine. I sensed something was wrong, but I knew if I started digging further, I would either have to take them into the station for questioning, or I could be dealing with a dangerous situation. My only thought at that time was getting home to you and Paul. And with you very sick, I didn't want to be dealing with more paperwork at the end of my shift. I let them go." Helen took a deep breath to prepare herself for what she was about to say next. "Several days later, we got a missing persons report. The same girl I'd seen in that car had disappeared. Luckily, I had taken down the license plate number. We eventually found the car. It had been reported stolen a few days earlier. I knew I had messed up really bad. I spent the next year driving through the neighborhood, hoping to find those three men."

Emily asked, "Did they ever find out what happened to that girl?"

Helen shut her eyes as hot tears rolled down her cheeks. "Many years later, when I'd already become a detective, they found her body wrapped in plastic in a ditch not far from where I'd last seen her. Somehow, her body was still in good condition. We did an autopsy and found out that she had been brutally raped."

"And what happened to those men?"

"Till this day, we have no idea who they were."

There was a moment of silence.

Emily said, "Is that why you were so distant with me? Because you blamed me for what had happened?"

Helen shook her head. "Of course not. I never blamed you. You were just a baby. I blame myself for letting my emotions get the better of me. I blame myself for not doing my duty that night. I blame myself for not protecting that girl."

"Mom, I had no idea you'd been carrying this for so long."

Helen looked away.

"Did dad know?" Emily asked.

"He did."

"And what did he do?"

"He told me there was no way I could've known what would end up happening. That I should forget about it. But I couldn't. I even went to see a therapist, but that didn't help either. I just couldn't make the pain go away."

"Is that why you were always quiet when you were around me?" Emily asked.

"Whenever I saw you, I couldn't help but think of that girl. I imagined what her parents must be feeling right now, knowing she was dead and that they couldn't do anything to save her. But I could have. And I had failed."

"Is that why you cheated on dad?" Emily then asked. "You found someone who was able to console you in your time of need?"

Helen froze. "Who… who told you?"

"There was a brief period where you were really happy, and dad was really sad. I was an adult by then—I think I was already in my third year of college. In a moment of despondence, dad confessed that you were seeing someone else and that you and he would be separating."

Helen swallowed. "I… I didn't know you knew."

"I don't judge you, mom," Emily said. "I love you."

They hugged.

"So, what happened to this guy you were so happy with?" Emily asked.

Helen hesitated a moment. "Like that girl, he too disappeared," she replied. "But unlike her, so far, his body has never been found."

NINETY-FOUR

SIMON

I had gone to the apartment to tell Cole who I was, but when I came face to face with him, I crumbled. I guess I didn't want to make such a life-changing announcement out in the hallway. I had imagined telling him while Annabelle, Cole, and I sat around the dining table. Perhaps, even over a meal.

Wasn't that how they did it in the movies? I thought.

But this wasn't some family drama. This was our lives. And if I didn't handle this situation as delicately as it warranted, I feared I could do irreparable damage to my relationship with Cole before it had a chance to begin.

Annabelle and I had shared some special moments. We had a history together. I was able to go back and see the signs from decades ago.

Cole and I had zero history. It would not only be a shock to him, but he would also deny it, and perhaps, even lash out at me. This was something I wasn't prepared to deal with at the moment.

I had another reason for going to the apartment. I wanted to find out what kind of trouble Cole was in. His lack of specifics told me it was something serious.

Cole was clearly scared. I could see it in his eyes. The mere mention of that man in the truck made him shrivel up like a schoolkid. My desire was to only help him. But I had not earned his trust yet for him to open up to me.

I couldn't blame him. Until a few days ago, I didn't exist to him. And now, suddenly, I was poking my nose into his business. I wouldn't have been surprised if he'd taken a swing at me for asking too many questions. And because he didn't, that further confirmed he was terrified of whatever he was deep into.

I couldn't help but wonder if Cole had hurt someone. He also swore on Annabelle's life that he wasn't responsible for what he was being accused of. I didn't know Cole well enough, or even at all. But for him to make such a statement told me I had to take his word for it. He was telling the truth. Plus, I had no other choice. I couldn't call him a liar. I had no idea what he was talking about anyway.

I'd offered to take him to the police, but he had refused. Whatever this man in the truck had against my son was enough to make Cole even fear the police.

I could end up in jail for a very long time. That's what he'd said to me. If that happened, I knew for a fact that would be the end of Annabelle. She'd spent her entire life raising the boy on her own, and no mother would want to see her son locked up in prison. Especially not someone who was dealing with severe health issues.

But what could I do to help? How could I make things better?

The more I thought about the problem, the more I felt utterly hopeless.

NINETY-FIVE

HELEN

The police found the GMC Canyon in an industrial part of the city. The vehicle was registered to a man in Florida. The man was in his nineties, and he hadn't driven a vehicle in two decades. The only rational explanation was that someone had used the man's identity to purchase the truck.

Helen drove to the scene. She found several fire trucks, along with police cruisers lining the street.

She got out when she saw the sergeant approach her.

"You sure you don't want to take a break?" he said. "I can assign both the Starr case and the Ketchum case to someone else."

She shook her head. "No. I owe it to Detective Porter to solve them. These cases are very personal to me."

He stared at her. She knew if he wanted to, he could remove her whether she liked it or not.

"Fine," he said.

"Where's the truck?" she asked.

"Come. I'll show you." He took her through the side of an abandoned building to the parking lot in the back. "Brace yourself," he warned her. "It smells horrid."

"I've seen my share of car fires, sarge," she said.

"Not like this one."

The smell was unlike anything she'd smelled before. It was like someone had fried meat on an open flame. On top of that, there was the nauseating smell that could only come from burnt tires.

She covered her mouth and nose with a handkerchief.

The sergeant said, "It looks like someone doused the entire vehicle in gasoline and set it on fire. By the time the fire department got here, the flames had reached up to the sky. It took them a good half an hour to get it under control."

She could see the burned-out frame of the truck. But what caught her attention the most was a figure in the driver's seat. The body, or what was left of it, was so badly burned there was no way they'd be able to ID it.

Helen leaned closer and pointed to the victim's head. "What does that look like to you?"

"Looks like a hole in the skull," the sergeant replied. "Likely from a gunshot."

She nodded. "I can see the entry and exit wound. This person was shot at close range."

Still covering her mouth and nose, Helen moved to the other side of the vehicle. She reached for the door handle, but then decided against it. The vehicle was still hot. If she wasn't careful, she could burn her fingertips.

"What are you looking for?" the sergeant asked.

"I want to know if this was suicide or murder."

The sergeant made a face. "It's got to be murder. I can't see anyone shooting themselves and then lighting their body on fire. It's not humanly possible."

"What if they lighted the car *right before* they shot themselves?" she suggested.

The sergeant scoffed. "That would be a stretch, detective."

She pointed to the vehicle's interior. "What does that look like to you?"

The sergeant squinted. On the passenger seat was a lighter. The metal frame was bent and deformed.

"I bet there is a weapon somewhere in the vehicle," she added.

The sergeant turned and waved over someone from the fire department. It took them less than a minute to remove the driver's side door.

Helen moved closer and said, "I see something next to the victim's right foot."

The sergeant instructed a fireman to see what it was. Using a protective glove, the fireman removed the black object and held it up for them to see.

It was a black handgun.

"Well, that's a first," the sergeant said, surprised. He then turned to her. "How did you know it would be there."

"I didn't," she said. "If I'd shot myself, the only place the weapon could've ended up would be on the floor of the truck."

They stared at the burnt vehicle in silence.

"I don't like this," she finally said.

"What is there not to like?" the sergeant said. "The perpetrator knew we would eventually find him. You don't shoot a police officer and expect the department to stop looking for you. He saw this as the only way out."

"But why the fire?" she said.

The sergeant shrugged. "Maybe there was something else he was hiding in the truck. Something he didn't want us to find."

NINETY-SIX

HELEN

She returned to the Arlington PD. She walked past Michael's empty desk, and her heart sank. It was only a few days ago she'd found him with his head on top of the desk with drool coming out of his mouth. He'd spent the entire night looking for evidence that could break open the case. She'd advised him to take it easy, that he had a long career ahead of him, and if he didn't prioritize his life, he would burn out.

The turnover rate in the force was high. So was drugs, alcohol, and divorce. The pressure was real. If a detective neglected to take into account even the smallest of clues, it was the difference between getting culprits and watching them roam free. It was why people in her line of work were on duty 24/7.

Helen had her own reasons for telling Michael not to go so hard on a case. Her personal life was a mess, and if she didn't solve the cases before her, they would languish even after she retired.

She wouldn't allow that. She would hold the people behind Derek Starr's and Alex Ketchum's murders responsible.

The remains inside the charred GMC Canyon deeply troubled her. This was not how she expected the last couple of months of her career to go. Things were spiraling out of control, and it was up to her to make sure no one else got hurt in the process.

She was about to move away when she spotted the tablet on Michael's desk. He was prone to carrying it around wherever he went. He loved being able to pull it out and start searching for whatever had caught his interest.

Something compelled her to pick up the tablet. She pressed a button on the side of the device, and the screen lit up. A message prompted her for a password. She thought about it and then typed in: "Leslie."

A second screen popped up. It was an image of the bar Derek Starr had gone to on the night of his murder. She saw the image was, in fact, a video Michael had been playing right before he turned off the tablet.

There was a play button at the bottom of the screen. She tapped it.

The camera inside the bar had a wide view of the interior. Derek Starr was at the bottom corner of the bar. He had a pint in front of him. He was staring at his cell phone. Several minutes later, Starr got up and moved to the door. Through the door's glass pane, Helen could see him speaking to someone on the phone.

She had seen this video before. They assumed Starr was speaking to the person he was waiting for.

According to Starr's phone records, it was an incoming call. Which meant someone knew to call him at the exact moment he stepped out of the bar.

As she watched the video, she caught sight of something.

On the other side of the bar, near the windows, another man was on his cell phone.

Helen squinted at the screen. She could see the man's drink had not been touched. And that while the man spoke on his cell phone, his eyes were glued to the bar's front door.

She turned her attention back to Starr. He hung up the phone and disappeared from view. Not a second went by before the man seated by the windows got up and left the bar, too.

For several minutes, nothing happened.

Why were you watching this video again, Michael? she thought. *What made you suddenly leave the tablet on your desk and go to the laundromat?*

She then saw a car drive past the bar. She pressed pause, rewound the footage, and played it again. The Nissan Maxima was clearly visible through the bar's front windows. Helen and Michael had found it abandoned behind Walt Grimsby's barn. It had belonged to Derek Starr.

A moment later, another car drove by. It was a Toyota Corolla. She couldn't tell who was behind the wheel. But when she pressed pause again, she could clearly make out the license plate number.

She then had an idea.

NINETY-SEVEN

SIMON

I rang the doorbell and waited. I was standing outside a red-brick house. There were several cars parked in the driveway, so I knew there were people inside.

I was nervous about my visit. I knew I would be unwelcome. In fact, I was in hostile territory. I would be lucky if I walked away without being cursed at, spat on, or threatened with physical harm. But when you're desperate, you make reckless decisions. This was one of them.

A woman answered the door. She was in her late fifties, and she had strands of gray in her hair and excess skin under her chin.

When she recognized me, her face turned into a scowl. "What do you want?!" she demanded, raising her voice. "You did this to my husband! You put him in the hospital!"

I didn't know the woman's name, but I knew she was married to Dimitris Diakos, the man whose business Gabe and I had taken from right under his feet. We were also responsible for putting so much stress on the man that he'd had a heart attack. In return, his son, Nick, had assailed me.

"Dimitris doesn't want to see you," she said, still with her voice raised. "We don't want you in our house."

"Mrs. Diakos, I'm not here to see your husband," I said. "I'm here to see your son."

A man appeared behind her. It was Nick.

The moment he saw me, he pointed a finger at me and said, "You got some nerve coming here."

"We need to talk," I said as calmly as possible.

"I got nothing to say to you," he said, taking a step closer. "You get the hell off our property before I…"

"Before you what? Beat me up again?" I asked.

He froze. "I… I don't know what you're talking about."

I pulled my hand out of my pocket and held up a watch in the air.

"We either talk like civilized people, or I get Detective Booker to bring you back to the station, where you can answer more of his questions."

Nick's mother looked at him, confused. "What is he talking about?" she asked.

"It's okay, mom," Nick replied. "You go back in the house. I'll deal with this."

He quickly came out onto the front porch and shut the door behind him.

"Let's go down the driveway, okay?" he said. I knew he didn't want his mom, or anyone else for that matter, to hear our conversation.

"Sure," I said.

When we were a good distance away, he turned to me. "What do you want?"

"First off, you and I both know what you did to me."

He looked away.

"I didn't lay any charges back at the station, because I felt bad about what happened to your dad."

He scoffed. "If you felt bad, you shouldn't have screwed us."

"I'm sorry, okay? And I don't plan to be involved in that kind of business anymore."

He stared at me. "How did you know that watch was mine?"

"It's got an inscription on the back, from your dad to you. I assume it's a birthday present."

He nodded.

"I've not shown this to anyone."

Nick's brow furrowed. "Why didn't you?"

"Like I said, I changed my mind when I found out about your father's heart attack."

"Is that why you came here? To tell me you have it?"

"I did, and that I need your help."

He laughed. "I'm not going to help *you*."

"You are because I have this watch as proof of what you did to me."

"I could just take it from you right now."

"You can try, and I'll put up a fight. I have no doubt one of your neighbors will see you beat up a guy on the street. And believe me, if you touch me again, I promise to get the best lawyers that money can buy to put you away for a very long time. Your choice, Nick."

He knew I had him. "Okay, what do you want from me?"

"I need you to get me a gun."

His eyebrows shot up. "A what?"

"A gun."

"Where am I going to get that?"

"You seem like a guy who knows people who know other people, people who can get me what I want."

"I think you have the wrong guy."

"Do you know what my job was at my firm?"

He shrugged. "Stabbing people in the back."

I ignored his slight. "My job was to do extensive research on the companies we invested in. And during this research, I found out that you had been in jail for threatening someone with a gun."

He was stunned that I knew.

I said, "It happened when you were in your teens. I suppose you got involved with the wrong crowd. You wanted to be part of something—a gang even. That explains your tattoos. You thought they made you look tough."

He looked down at his shoes.

"I think that's why your father was so eager to pass the business on to you. He wanted you to take on more responsibilities. As you grew older and realized the thug life wasn't going to get you far, you joined the family business. I know you've still got connections, and I want you to use those connections to get me what I want."

He was silent for several minutes before he said, "Fine. When do you want it?"

"The sooner you get it for me, the sooner you'll get your watch and never see my face again."

NINETY-EIGHT

HELEN

She was surprised to get a response so fast. It was only a little while ago that she had put out an APB for the Toyota Corolla.

She drove to the location and realized she was at the laundromat where Michael had been shot.

An officer was waiting for her when she pulled up to the back of the building. She parked next to his cruiser and got out.

The officer said, "I was already here when I heard the APB on the radio."

The department had stationed an officer outside the second-floor unit just above the laundromat. Forensics had already gone through the apartment. Even the SIU, Special Investigation Unit, had visited the scene. Anytime an officer was hurt or was involved in the shooting of a civilian, the SIU got involved. They wanted to make sure the officer had taken all necessary precautions before going into a dangerous situation.

Michael hadn't, Helen knew. He had gone to the laundromat without telling anyone. The SIU would eventually come knocking at her door. They would want to know what she knew about what happened.

She wasn't concerned about herself. She had deniability. She was concerned for Michael. He was just starting his career, and if the SIU deemed him to be reckless, that would forever be stamped on his record.

Helen would do whatever in her power to make sure that didn't happen. Michael should not be punished for doing his job. There was a reason he had come here. And she wanted to know what that reason was.

"Where is it?" she asked the officer.

"You're standing right in front of it," he replied.

She turned and saw a gray Toyota Corolla parked next to the cruiser.

So that's why Michael had driven all the way here, she thought.

The officer said, "I ran the plate through the computer in my cruiser, and it's registered to a Tyrel Wiggins."

Her face tightened. "I want you to put out an APB for a Tyrel Wiggins," she said.

"Yes, ma'am," the officer said with a nod.

Helen decided to take a look at where Michael had been shot. She ducked under the yellow police tape and proceeded to go up the stairs. There was another strand of tape across the door. She removed a pocketknife and cut through the tape. It was illegal even for her to enter the scene unless she was actively investigating the crime. She felt what happened to Michael, and the cases he and she were investigating were somehow linked. It was all the approval she needed to proceed further. Plus, as a homicide detective and the partner of the officer who had gone down, she knew no one would dare challenge her.

She entered and saw a dark stain in the hallway. *That's where Simon Harris found Michael*, she thought.

She spent a few minutes staring at the spot before she decided to go back down. There was nothing she could learn from being there. She just wanted to see the spot with her own eyes.

All actions had consequences. This included inactions as well.

With her not getting ahead in the investigations, she had let Michael take control. She was the senior detective. She should have been the one to lead them. Her experience would have told her not to make the mistake Michael made: go into a situation ill-prepared.

When she was at the bottom of the stairs, she found the officer waiting for her.

"I didn't touch anything," she said. "You can make a note of my walkthrough of the crime scene for the record if you like."

He shook his head. "That won't be necessary, Detective Sloan. But you need to call the sergeant right away."

Her brow furrowed. "Why?"

"I don't know."

She pulled out her cell phone, speed-dialed his number, and after a few rings, he answered. "Sarge," she said. "I heard you wanted to speak to me."

"I was going to call you," he said.

"About what?"

"It's regarding the APB you just put out."

"Okay."

"I just spoke to the coroner, and they were able to ID the person in the truck."

"How did they manage to do that? The body was in a horrid state."

"Through dental records."

"Okay. And?"

"The victim is Tyrel Wiggins."

NINETY-NINE

BRIAN CHESTER

He took a sip from a glass. The gin and tonic tasted bitter in his mouth. There was a bottle of scotch in his liquor cabinet, but he didn't go for it. He had more urgent things on his mind.

The case against Fast-Card had turned from a nuisance to a serious problem the moment the SEC got involved. They went through all of Fast-Cards' books and records, and they discovered that there was three hundred million dollars' worth of transactions unaccounted for.

When the SEC dug even deeper, they would see that those transactions didn't exist. They were fake. Created in order to inflate the company's earnings and stock prices. This charade had been going on for almost a decade. Brian had come close to seeing it all fall apart once before, and he had somehow managed to fix the problem then.

This time, though, it wouldn't be that simple. Not that what he had done years before was easy. He was not an evil man. He was just desperate. He had come up with several solutions to the issue at hand. Those solutions could only work if the other party was willing to compromise. And when they refused, he had no choice but to take severe and drastic actions.

The moment the scandal regarding Fast-Card exploded in Europe, he felt that, somehow, Chester and Associates would go unscathed. He hoped the CEO of Fast-Card would work out a deal with the European regulators. Pay a fine or penalty. Be banned from holding a management position at another publicly-traded company. Something to make the problem go away.

The European regulators were willing to go down that route. It was embarrassing that they had allowed Fast-Card to go unchecked for so long. The signs were always there. The meteoric rise of a company that never posted a single profit in any year of its operations. It was the speculators who kept the company afloat. They were wowed by the sudden growth in its revenue, and they were swept up by the charisma of its founder. The European regulators were willing to cut a deal, sweep the whole thing under the rug, because it was the lead story on all major news outlets.

However, the US government had other ideas. A majority of the investors were Americans. When Fast-Card's fall inevitably happened, the losses would be borne mostly by Americans. The US government had already prepared an extradition case against Fast-Card's CEO, in order to charge him under US laws.

Brian knew the threat of extradition and the prospect of years behind bars would make Fast-Card's CEO look for a quick plea bargain. The CEO would be willing to throw all parties involved in the scam at the feet of US regulators.

It would not be long before the SEC would come knocking at his door. After all, it was Chester and Associates who had prepared—or more accurately, *cooked*—the books that fooled the investors into believing it was a sound investment.

It was not just regular folks who lost money in the scam, though. It was institutional investors, which included pensions and funds, as well as, some of the largest firms on Wall Street. The pressure was on for the SEC to make an example of Fast-Card.

Brian could be facing a lengthy prison sentence for himself when all was said and done.

He couldn't allow that. He had debated destroying all records he had on Fast-Card. But, he could not merely walk into his office, or ask one of his trusted employees to start shredding documents. There were boxes upon boxes that would need to disappear. It was no small feat, and it was not something that the authorities would take too lightly once they realized what had happened. Additional charges would be laid against him. Obstruction of justice. Destruction of evidence. Tampering. The list went on.

On top of all that, there was another problem that had suddenly reared its ugly head.

Derek Starr.

Derek could see the writing on the wall. He knew Chester and Associates was a sinking ship, and he wanted to jump to the competition.

Brian was aware that Derek had been speaking to Delta Management. It was not uncommon for companies to poach talent. But Derek was no mere employee. He was one of his co-conspirators. Derek knew more about what had happened at Chester and Associates than anyone else, and Brian feared that Derek might throw him under the bus just to save his own skin. He was far more dangerous than Alex Ketchum.

Brian had always found Alex to be weak. Alex should never have been brought into his inner circle. It was Derek who'd vouched for him. They had apparently gone to school together. After the events of all those years ago, Alex suddenly started acting strange. The guilt had started to eat away at him. Brian feared he would crack and go to the police and confess what they had done. It was Brian who had pushed him into a life of drugs and alcohol. Brian loved to party. It was not uncommon for him to charter a private plane, get a bunch of his friends together, and fly over to Vegas for several nights of debauchery. So, he had the right connections to acquire the poison to destroy Alex. It wasn't long before Alex was hooked on heroin. Somehow, over the years, Alex kept overdosing—and surviving.

Derek and Alex, along with the Fast-Card scandal, could one day be the end of him.

One day, he received an unexpected call. The caller never gave him his name. Brian had a feeling the caller was purposely lowering his voice to shield his identity. At first, Brian thought it was a prank call. But, the caller knew about the events that happened years ago, so much so, that Brian knew he had to take him seriously. He thought the caller would try to blackmail him in order to buy his silence.

That was not exactly how things turned out.

In exchange for a lump-sum payment, the caller offered to make all his problems go away. Brian agreed to empty out his life savings, if he could avoid setting foot inside a prison cell.

But first, the caller had to prove he was the real deal. No money would be exchanged unless Brian saw results.

The caller had delivered on the first of his promises.

Derek was gone.

Alex was gone.

And now, the biggest problem, the case against Fast-Card, and his involvement in the scam would be gone, too.

Brian took a sip from his glass and smiled.

ONE-HUNDRED

SIMON

I sat anxiously in my car. It had been an hour since my talk with Nick Diakos. I had asked Nick to get me a gun. It was a request that shocked him and also troubled me. As I've said before, I'm a pacifist. I don't believe in violence. But I do believe in arming yourself in self-defense. I'm not sure why I'd never gone to a gun range or even bothered to take a few lessons on how to use a firearm. It just wasn't something on my radar.

To be honest, I'd never really felt threatened before. Not counting when Nick attacked me. That was, perhaps, the first time I considered keeping a handgun on my person. But other than that, I had lived a relatively harmless life.

Money buys comfort. Money also buys safety. Everyone in my family has life insurance, home and property insurance, motor vehicle insurance, and even business liability insurance. We also have some of the best security systems available on the market.

Naturally, all that money would be useless if someone walked up to me, drew a gun, and decided to shoot me. But even if I had a gun, I don't think I'd be able to pull it out fast enough to defend myself.

If I ever got mugged, I wouldn't bat an eye on handing over all my valuables. My life was worth more than the things I owned. Also, like I said, everything was insured.

I checked my watch for the umpteenth time. The sweat had made my shirt stick to my back. My palms were clammy, and for a minute, I wondered if Nick had stood me up.

He told me to wait for him about a block from his parent's house. I'd been dutifully sitting in my car ever since.

I had thought about getting out and ringing the doorbell again, when I saw him turn the corner and make his way toward my car.

He got in the passenger seat, looked around to see if the coast was clear, and pulled out an object that was wrapped tightly in a black plastic bag.

"I got what you wanted," he said.

"Let me see it," I said.

He handed me the bag, and immediately I felt the weight of it in my hand. I unwrapped the plastic and pulled out a silver handgun.

"Don't ask where I got it or how I got it," Nick said.

"Is it registered?" I asked.

"No. And you can't tell anyone who gave it to you."

"I won't."

I wiped my right palm on my pants and firmly held the pistol by its grip. I was scared and in control at the same time. I was scared at how much damage a weapon like this could do, and I was in control because I would be the one doing the damage.

"Have you fired a gun before?" Nick asked.

I shook my head.

"Disengage the safety and just pull the trigger."

"It's that simple, huh?"

"They make it simple so that anyone can use them."

No wonder we lead the world in gun-related deaths, I thought.

"Why do you need a gun anyway?" he asked.

"It's for protection."

"You're in danger?"

I wasn't about to tell him that I feared for my son's safety. Whoever that man was in the truck, he had shot a police officer, and I had no doubt he wouldn't hesitate to hurt Cole.

I would not let that happen.

I had spent much of my life aimlessly drifting from one thing to another. My sole objective had been to make money so I could buy a bigger house, luxury vehicles, eat at the finest restaurants, dress in some of the best clothes on the market, or go on exotic vacations. It had always been about my needs and my wants.

This was the first time I'd been focused on someone other than me. Now, don't get me wrong, I would've done anything for Vanessa. But I always knew she could take care of herself. If something happened to me, she would find a way to move on with her life.

Cole was in trouble. And if something happened to him, I didn't know if *I* would be able to move on with my life.

"We're good?" Alex asked.

"Yes," I replied.

I pulled out the watch from my pocket and handed it to him. "Again, I'm sorry about your dad. I really am."

He rubbed his fingers over the inscription on the back of the watch. "I'm sorry, too, for jumping you like that outside the restaurant."

Before I could say a word, he got out of the car and hurried away. I watched him disappear around the corner.

My eyes fell on the gun in my hand and, suddenly, I felt exposed holding it.

I stuck it in the glove compartment, started the BMW, and drove off.

ONE-HUNDRED ONE

COLE

When the call finally came, Cole was resigned to it. He knew he was no longer in control of his fate. Leo, and whoever else he worked with, were in the driver's seat. Cole was a mere puppet in whatever game they were playing, and they were pulling the strings.

He was standing outside his apartment building when a white cargo van drove up. He was surprised to find Leo behind the wheel.

"What happened to your truck?" Cole asked, getting in the passenger seat.

"We need more space for what we are about to do," Leo replied, jerking his thumb behind him.

Cole turned and saw half a dozen steel drums lining the back.

"What's inside the drums?" Cole asked.

Leo grinned. "C4."

Cole's eyes widened. "That's a lot of explosive."

"You need that much if you want to bring a building down to the ground."

Cole swallowed. "Where did you get it?"

Leo stared at him. "Does it matter?"

"I don't know," Cole said. "I'm just trying to make small talk."

"Don't bother," Leo said. "You should be focused on the task ahead."

Cole was already feeling uneasy. He hadn't eaten anything all day. He knew even if he tried, he wouldn't be able to hold it down. But knowing that he was sitting next to hundreds of pounds of C4 made him want to throw up whatever was left in his stomach.

"Do you mind if I open the window?" Cole asked.

"Be my guest," Leo replied.

The air was cool, but it didn't help him feel any better. If he wasn't scared stiff, he would've opened the door and jumped out. Do anything to get away from the predicament he was in.

Leo was a murderer, but Cole never thought the man would actually go through with something as insane as blowing up an entire building. The drums in the van were proof of how far he was willing to go.

They were on the highway when Cole said, "There's got to be another way."

"Another way for what?" Leo asked.

"Another way for you to actually get paid without hurting anyone."

Leo smiled. "I told you already. No one's going to get hurt."

Cole wanted to say something about workers—other than the security guard—who would be inside the building, but he held his tongue.

If Cole had been bold, he would've tipped off the police by now. They would have been waiting for them at the office tower. The moment he and Leo pulled up, the police would swarm in and arrest them.

Maybe they would go easy on me for what happened at Tent City, considering I had prevented mass murder, he thought wistfully.

Cole turned to Leo. "After this is over, I don't ever want to see you again."

Leo shrugged. "No problem. Whatever you say."

There was no conviction in the man's voice. Cole wasn't sure what lay ahead for him. All he knew was that he had to follow Leo's instructions. There was no telling what he would do if Cole tried to deviate from the plan.

Up ahead, he saw the office tower. The lights were on inside. People were still in the building.

"I told you it wouldn't be empty," Cole said.

"Relax," Leo said. "We don't plan to blow it up right now. We wait until it's the right time."

"What are we doing here then?"

"We're laying out the groundwork for later when the real fireworks begin."

The cargo van drove up to the front of the building, but instead of stopping, Leo kept going until they were in the back.

They pulled up to the underground parking entrance. Leo stuck out his hand and tapped a white card next to a card reader.

"You have access to the building?" Cole asked.

"I know the right people," Leo replied. "These people want to see this place go up in flames."

They drove down a winding tunnel. They kept moving until they were several levels below the building. They came to a halt at a set of metal doors.

Leo put the van in park. He checked his watch and then turned to Cole. "Okay. This is it. We don't have much time. The guard is probably doing his rounds right now, so he won't be monitoring the cameras."

Leo got out. So did Cole. Leo walked up to the set of metal doors and, using the key in his hand, quickly unlocked them.

"You even have keys?" Cole asked.

"Everything's been set up for us," Leo replied.

They then spent several minutes carefully removing the heavy steel drums from the van and placing them inside what looked like a storage area.

When they were done, Leo grabbed a backpack from the van and said, "Wait for me in the van. I have to set up the detonator."

Leo disappeared into the storage room. A couple of minutes later, he returned, and they quickly drove out.

ONE-HUNDRED TWO

HELEN

When Leslie called her, Helen drove straight to the hospital. She found her in the hallway, just outside Michael's room.

"He wants to speak to you," she said.

Helen gingerly went inside. Michael still looked the way he did the last time she'd seen him. He was hooked up to a variety of monitors, and his face was swollen. This time, however, his eyes were open, and he was alert.

"How are you feeling?" she asked, walking up to his bed.

He gave her a weak smile. "This sounds corny, but I feel like I've just been shot."

She smiled. She reached over and held his hand. "I feel like this is my fault," she said.

"Leslie told me you were here throughout the time I was in the operating room," he said. "Thank you for caring so much."

"I'm your partner. I'm supposed to be worried about you."

His grip tightened around her hand.

"Why didn't you call me, Michael?"

"I didn't want to bother you. You said you had an urgent family matter to attend to, so I figured I would run down this lead on my own."

"Michael, you could have at least told me where you were going."

"Yes, and you would have either talked me out of it or dropped whatever you were doing to meet me at the location."

He's right, she thought. *I would have done either of those things.*

"But that's not the reason I wanted to speak to you," he said.

"Okay."

"I owe you an explanation about my visit to the laundromat."

Before he could say more, she told him about the tablet on his desk and that they had found Tyrel Wiggins's charred body.

"I know why you went to that laundromat, Michael," she said. "And I want you to know the person who shot you is dead."

"You're right. I did go to the laundromat to speak to Tyrel Wiggins. But you're wrong that it was Tyrel who shot me."

Her eyes narrowed. "What?"

"Tyrel didn't shoot me. It was someone else."

"Are you sure?"

"Positive," he replied. "I was standing in the hallway of his apartment when I heard a noise from inside. Before I knew it, I was spun around like a ragdoll, and the next thing I remember, I was on the floor, and my entire body was in shock."

"Did you get a look at the shooter?"

He shook his head. "I wish I had, but I didn't."

Helen was silent for a moment.

"What I can tell you, though—" he then said between breaths. He was getting exhausted talking to her.

"We'll discuss this later," she said.

"No. When I pulled up to the laundromat, I saw Tyrel Wiggins's Toyota Corolla. But next to it was another vehicle. It was a GMC Canyon. I know the license plate number…"

She gently said, "Michael, Tyrel Wiggins was found dead in a GMC Canyon."

He went quiet for several minutes. His eyes were fixed on the ceiling.

Even though he was badly hurt, his mind was still trying to put all the pieces together. He wanted to give her the clues so that she could continue the investigation.

Once a detective, always a detective, she thought.

She patted his hand and gave him a reassuring smile. "It'll all be over soon. I promise," she said. "Now, you get some rest. Okay?"

He stared at her and then nodded.

She left the room feeling worse than before. She now had another shooter to look for.

ONE-HUNDRED THREE

COLE

Throughout the drive back from the office tower, Cole felt uneasy. It wasn't the fact they had unloaded enough C4 to level the entire building. It was the fact that the entire process took less than half an hour. There was no tension. Nothing that got his adrenaline pumping. It was all anti-climactic.

Maybe that was how reality worked.

The building would go down, and to make it happen, it would be as simple as a walk in the park.

It helped that Leo had access to everything: the underground parking garages, the door to the storage room. And he even knew when and where the security guard would be when they made their delivery. Cole doubted his sole purpose was just to deliver the C4. It was something Leo could have done on his own. All he had to do was bring a moving cart to do it. The work would've required some extra effort, but it was entirely doable by one person. Leo didn't need him.

And that's what bothered Cole more than anything else.

"What about the photo and the knife?" Cole asked, turning to Leo.

"Once the job is finished, they'll be destroyed."

"How can I trust you to do that?"

"You have no choice, kid."

"I've done whatever you asked of me. I just want to know that I won't be in any trouble later on."

"Your biggest concern should not be what happened at Tent City," Leo said. "Your biggest concern should be that *I* don't come knocking at your door down the road."

"What's that supposed to mean?"

"It means you keep your head low. You go about your life as if you've never met me. In fact, after tonight, I don't exist. So, you wipe everything you know—or think you know—about me from your memory. Because if you don't, I will find you wherever you are, and I will hurt you."

Leo lifted his jacket up. Cole saw a gun tucked under his belt. Leo wanted to make a statement.

You keep your mouth shut, or else you get a bullet in your head.

Cole did not utter another word for the rest of the ride.

ONE-HUNDRED FOUR

SIMON

After my talk with Nick Diakos, I had gotten a call from Gabe. He wanted to see me right away.

I told him I was busy. But he pleaded with me, something he had never done before. I decided to turn the BMW around and drive over to the office. I found Gabe and our lawyer waiting for me in a conference room.

Gabe was troubled by our discussion in my house. Gabe understood there was friction between us, and he didn't want that friction to roll over to the business. Through our lawyer, Gabe had come up with a proposal. He would be willing to buy half of my share of Harris & Harris. All I had to do was sign a few documents, pick up a check, and never set foot in the firm again.

I knew this tactic very well. Gabe was trying to ambush me so that I made an impulsive decision. It was the same approach we had used against other business owners.

Gabe feared my anger toward him and mother would push me to sell my stake in the firm to our rivals. That would force Gabe to liquidate his share, just to get out of a difficult situation.

Also, the firm was started by our father. It was always his baby. He cared more about the firm than he cared about us. And Gabe, who idolized our father, would not let the firm go to a stranger.

He had some sort of twisted loyalty toward the old man.

I didn't care anymore. My loyalty wasn't to a person who had always been cold with me. My loyalty wasn't to the two people who had betrayed me. My loyalty was now to my son.

I wanted nothing to do with the firm.

Gabe's offer was very generous. He knew if he tried to lowball me, that would only make me more resentful toward him. I would surely look for the next highest bidder, regardless of who they were.

I signed the documents, grabbed my check, and left the office.

I drove straight to the apartment building, took the elevator up, and knocked at the door.

A moment later, Annabelle answered. "Simon, what are you doing here?" she asked, surprised.

"I came to see you," I replied.

She quickly adjusted her robe and her hair. She looked weaker than the last time I'd seen her. But if you asked my honest opinion, my heart still skipped a beat just seeing her.

"Do you want to come in?"

"I can't stay."

I pulled out an envelope and held it out for her.

Her eyes narrowed. "What is it?"

"Take it, please."

She did, and opened the envelope and pulled out the check Gabe had given me.

"I've signed the back," I said. "There is also a business card in the envelope. I want you to call the bank manager on that card. I've already spoken to him. He knows you will be coming into the branch to deposit the check, so there shouldn't be any issues with getting it cashed."

She looked confused. "Cash for what?"

"For your surgery, Annabelle," I said.

Her eyes widened. "That's a lot of money, Simon."

"It should be more than enough to cover all your medical expenses."

"I can't accept this," she said.

"I'm not trying to buy your silence like my mother tried to do years ago. I'm just trying to pay for my share of the responsibilities of raising our son."

"But…"

I stopped her. "You've done everything for Cole. And I mean everything," I said. "Please. Let me do this. I want to. Cole needs you now more than ever. And you have to get better for him."

Her lips quivered, and the envelope shook in her hand. She looked up at me, her eyes moist. "Why… why are you giving this to me now? Why don't you wait until…?"

"I don't have much time. Cole is in trouble, and I have to somehow get him out of it."

"What kind of trouble?" she asked, suddenly concerned.

"I don't know. Just take the money and take care of Cole."

"Simon, you're scaring me…"

"Promise me, Annabelle, that you will deposit the money and use it for your treatment."

She took a step forward and hugged me. I hugged her back.

I don't know how long we held each other, but then I released her and walked away.

I knew if I stayed too long, I would lose the courage to do what I was about to do next.

ONE-HUNDRED FIVE

COLE

When Leo dropped Cole off in front of his building, Cole went inside but didn't take the elevator up to his unit. He waited until Leo disappeared from view and left the building.

Cole didn't have the heart to face his mother after what he had done. She'd called him several times already. She was probably worried about him. He'd been acting strange the last couple of days, and she wanted to know if he was okay.

I'm not okay, he thought. *And nothing will make me feel better once Leo goes ahead with his plan.*

Cole walked down the street until he saw a bar up ahead. He went inside and ordered a drink.

After he showed his ID, the bartender placed a glass of beer in front of him. Cole needed something to calm his nerves. The next few hours would be intense. He didn't want to be anywhere near a TV when the news broke about the events at the office tower.

The bar had an old television that was always on one channel. It played reruns of old shows over and over again. Patrons complained and asked the bar owner to put something else on. But the owner didn't care. It was the only channel the antenna picked up for free.

Cole took a sip of his drink.

He saw someone sitting at the far end of the bar.

He picked up his glass, walked over, and sat across from Buddy.

Buddy looked up from his cell phone and smiled. "Hey, man, what're you doing here?"

"I was about to ask you the same thing," Cole said.

Buddy leaned closer and whispered, "Can I tell you a secret?"

"Sure, I guess."

"You know, at night, I sell weed at the park, right?"

"Yeah, so?"

"Well, I can't do that during the day, cuz that would raise a lot of eyebrows, you know. So, I sit here during the day, and I wait for my customers to come to me. I do this until the place closes."

Cole's eyes narrowed. "You sell weed at the bar?"

Buddy grinned. "Genius, isn't it?"

"Doesn't the bar owner kick you out for dealing drugs on his property?"

"He takes a cut."

"He does?"

Buddy nodded. "He figured he might as well make some extra money, considering a lot of deals occur just around the corner from the bar anyway."

Cole took another sip from his glass. "I never asked you, but how did you end up meeting Leo?"

"What do you mean?"

"How did you find him?"

"I didn't. He found me."

Cole blinked. "What?"

"Yeah. One night I was working at the park—doing my thing—when he came up to me and asked to buy some weed. I thought he was a cop. But he assured me he wasn't. After he bought what he needed, he started chatting me up. He asked me a whole bunch of questions."

"Like what?"

"I don't know. About who my friends were. Who I hung around with. About my family life. I told him I had a girlfriend who was pregnant. I think that kind of soured his mood. He then asked me if I knew anyone who wanted to make fast money. I told him I didn't. But then you showed up at the park, and you had just lost your job. So, I called Leo and told him about your situation. Leo then started asking about you. Who you hung around with. Who your friends were. About your family."

Cole felt a sharp pain in the back of his head. "What'd you tell him?"

"I told him you had nobody else but your mom. And that she was very sick."

"Why do you suppose he wanted to know so much about me, or even about you?"

Buddy shrugged. "I got the feeling that he wanted people who weren't going to be much trouble."

"Or maybe, he wanted people who didn't have a support system," Cole said. "Someone who wouldn't be missed if something were to happen to them."

Buddy stared at him. "I never thought about it too deeply."

Cole suddenly realized he was being set up, and it had nothing to do with what happened at Tent City. The destruction of the office tower would be placed upon Cole's shoulders.

That's what this is all about! he thought.

Leo wanted a fall guy. Someone who was desperate to do whatever he asked of him. Someone who didn't have big social ties or family who would push the authorities to dig deeper about what had happened.

There was never a way out for him. He was never supposed to be free. Once the office tower went down, he would go down along with it.

Cole left his drink and rushed out of the bar. He ran across the street and found one of the last remaining payphones in the city.

He dialed nine-one-one.

ONE-HUNDRED SIX

BRIAN CHESTER

He was behind the wheel of his Mercedes Benz. He rubbed his hands nervously and looked around. He was parked in an alley, just behind an empty retail store. The sign above the store indicated that it used to be a comic book shop. The owners had long ago closed the business and left.

The alley had little to no lighting, which made it dark inside the Benz. Brian pulled out his cell phone to check the time again. He had received the call he had been waiting for about an hour ago. The caller had instructed him to drive to this alley.

Brian was eager to get this done, so he had arrived early. But now, the designated meeting time had elapsed. The person he was waiting for was late.

Brian couldn't just ring him up. He never initiated contact. The person on the other side of the call did. Plus, the call was blocked, so there was no way for him to just hit call-back.

He took a deep breath to compose himself.

Everything will be all right, he reminded himself. *I just have to be a little more patient.*

He heard the car door open as someone entered the vehicle.

"Don't turn around," a man's voice said.

Brian glanced at the rearview mirror. He saw a silhouette just behind his seat.

"Do you have my money?" the man asked.

Brian pointed to a briefcase in the backseat. "It took me weeks to withdraw that much without any alarms going off."

"Is it all there?"

"Half a million dollars, like you asked."

Brian heard the man reach over and open the briefcase. He then heard him ruffle through some papers. Brian didn't dare look back. He didn't want to anger the man. He knew what the man was capable of. Also, the job was still not complete. Brian needed the man more than the man needed him.

Brian said, "Are you sure that all my worries will be gone after tonight?"

"Have I failed you yet?"

"No, you haven't. But that's a lot of money. I just want to be certain everything will go according to what we agreed to."

"Everything is already set up. Once I give you the trigger, you do the rest."

"Okay," Brian replied eagerly. "So, where's the trigger?"

"In a moment," the man said. "I have a few questions I'm curious about."

"What do you want to know?"

"What did you do with Joseph Elliott's body?"

Brian's eyes narrowed. "Why is that so important to you?"

"Isn't *he* the cause of most of your problems?"

"I thought you said you knew," Chester asked.

"I know you, Derek Starr, and Alex Ketchum had something to do with Joseph Elliott's disappearance. He was last seen getting on a boat with the three of you. And as I understand, he was later seen driving his car through a ticket booth. Was it you behind the wheel? Derek Starr? Or perhaps, Alex Ketchum?"

Brian was quiet.

ONE-HUNDRED SEVEN

BRIAN CHESTER

The man said, "I think I've done enough for you so that you can indulge me a little."

"Derek drove the car," Brian admitted.

"And who killed Joseph Elliott?"

"We all did."

"You mean we as in you, Alex Ketchum, and Derek Starr?"

"Not exactly."

"So, who did?"

Brian was beginning to get even more nervous. He didn't like where this conversation was going. "I don't think I want to talk about this anymore," he said.

"Do you want the trigger or not?"

"I do."

"Then tell me."

Brian sighed. "None of us had planned to hurt Joe. We had taken him on the boat, so we could discuss the problem we were facing without anyone listening in."

"And what problem would that be?" the man asked.

"Joe was our in-house accountant, so he had caught on early that Fast-Card was manipulating their books and records. I knew what Fast-Card was doing, as well. People think I was complicit in the scam. I just chose to ignore the obvious and go along with Fast-Card's narrative that they were more successful than they really were."

"A lot of people are going to lose a ton of money, because of the fraud at Fast-Card."

"I know, but it was one of our largest accounts at the time. I knew the firm couldn't survive if we lost Fast-Card as a client."

The man said, "Joseph Elliott wanted no part in the scam. Is that right?"

"Yes," Brian said, feeling deflated. "He was going to go to the SEC. He was going to warn all the investors what Fast-Card was up to."

"And so, you had to silence him."

Brian looked away. "Joe was my best friend. I've known him since we were kids. I tried reasoning with him when we were on the boat. I told him if we got investigated, our reputations would be ruined. But Joe always had a strong ethical backbone. He wouldn't budge. He wanted to do the right thing. I don't know what came over me. Desperation. Self-preservation. Something. I picked up an oar that I kept in the boat in case of emergencies, and I swung it at him. I hit him across the side of the head, and Joe instantly fell to the bottom of the boat. He was bleeding from the back of his head. Once I realized what I'd done, I knew there was no going back."

"Did the others join in hurting Joseph Elliott?"

"Alex and Derek were appalled by what had happened," Brian said. "Derek threw up over the side, and Alex broke down in tears. I had to convince them we had no choice. That Joe was going to destroy us all. Reluctantly, they helped me wrap him in a tarp and hurl his body into the water."

"I assume he was dead by then. Is that correct?" the man asked.

Brian's body shook at what he was about to say next. "No, he was still alive when we threw him overboard."

The man shifted in his seat. Brian could hear the man breathe heavily. The man then said, "It now makes sense why you would want to get rid of the witnesses who could point to *you* as the mastermind behind Joseph Elliott's death."

Brian felt anger rise in him. He began to turn.

He felt something cold touch the base of his skull.

"I warned you not to turn around," the man said calmly.

Brian put his hands up. "Okay, okay. My mistake. I'm sorry. I've already told you everything I know. I swear. Can I please have the trigger now?"

"Course you can," the man said, pulling the gun away from Chester's head. He then held out an object to him.

Brian grabbed it.

At first glance, it looked like a walkie-talkie. It had an antenna and several buttons.

"How does it work?" Brian asked.

"The range on the trigger is only a couple miles. So, you need to be within that range if you want it to work. The C4 blocks are attached to the support beams of the building. They will explode the moment you activate the trigger. The building will crumble, and all your worries will be buried with it."

"It's that simple?" Brian said, surprised.

"Would you have preferred it be complicated?"

"No," Brian said with a smile. "This is exactly what I wanted."

The man opened the door on his side. "Now, don't bother looking behind you. It's best you don't know who I am. Unless you want to end up like your friends."

The door shut with a heavy thud.

Brian sat still for several minutes. When he was certain the man was gone, he started the engine and pulled away from the alley.

ONE-HUNDRED EIGHT

SIMON

Earlier, after my conversation with Annabelle, I walked back to my BMW. I was about to get inside when I saw a cargo van pull up to the front of the building. My face turned hard when I realized the person behind the wheel was the same man I had seen driving the GMC truck that had gone to the laundromat.

To my dismay, I saw Cole in the passenger seat next to the man. They exchanged a few words before Cole got out of the van and went inside the building.

The cargo van pulled away.

I followed behind.

Whatever mess Cole was in, this man was responsible for it. I had no doubt about that. And I was going to do everything in my power to get my son out of it.

Night had fallen, so it wasn't easy keeping track of where the van was headed. But I did my best. After about twenty minutes of driving, the van slowed and parked at the curb. I did so, too, about half a block away from the van.

I looked around. We were in a quiet neighborhood. There were a few shops scattered around. Most were closed, and many were vacant.

I watched as the van idled for several minutes, the exhaust pipe blowing. And then, the engine shut off. The man got out, looked around, and walked across the street, and disappeared into an alley behind a comic book shop.

I debated whether to follow the man. But I had no idea where he had gone or why he was there, to begin with. I knew for sure that going behind another building was a bad idea. I was reminded of the police officer who'd been shot.

I knew if I wasn't careful, my fate could be worse than the officer's. No one would show up in the nick of time and get me the help I would need. I would end up succumbing to my injuries.

I shook the thought away and focused my attention back on the alley.

As minutes ticked by, I started to get anxious. What if the man lived in one of the apartments above the comic book shop? If that were true, I could end up spending the entire night in my car.

I decided to take a look. I wouldn't put myself in any situation I couldn't get out of. But I had to do something. Waiting was not going to cut it.

I got out of the BMW and slowly made my way toward the cargo van. Once I got close, I took a peek inside. There was nothing that caught my attention. I then crossed the street and moved toward the alley.

I placed my back to the wall of the comic book shop and then glanced into the alley. It took a few seconds for my eyes to adjust, but I could see a car parked in the middle of the narrow space. The car's taillights were facing me. I could make out two silhouettes inside the car. One in the front and one in the back.

What's going on? I thought.

The back door suddenly opened, and someone got out.

I quickly turned and started walking away. I shot a glance back and saw the man walk across the street in a hurry. He was carrying a duffel bag over his shoulder as he got back in the cargo van.

I hoped the man hadn't seen me. Even if he had, I doubted he knew who I was or what I was doing here.

I could be a random guy out for a walk.

I reached the BMW. I saw the cargo van's engine start. The exhaust fumes billowed out of the tailpipe.

I quickly got behind the wheel and started the engine as well.

I expected the van to pull out, but it sat there as if it was waiting.

Several minutes went by, and nothing happened. And then, I saw a white Mercedes-Benz pull out from the alley and drive away.

Instead of following the Benz, the cargo van did a U-turn and headed in my direction. I lowered myself in my seat as the van moved past me. I had caught a glimpse of the driver. He was on his cell phone. His eyes were focused on the road ahead.

I quickly did a U-turn and began tailing him again.

ONE-HUNDRED NINE

BRIAN CHESTER

He drove straight to the office tower. He was eager to finish the task and put all his worries behind him. The authorities were circling like sharks. They could smell blood. After all, Chester and Associates were accountants for Fast-Card. They had audited Fast-Card's financial statements. They had given their stamp of approval that the documents presented by Fast-Card could be relied upon. Investors had used those audited statements to make a rational decision. When the truth came out that those documents were, in fact, fraudulent, all hell would break loose. No one would be spared, especially not him.

For security purposes, all records were stored in a storage room in the tower's basement. His firm used a private computer network where everything was backed up to external hard drives, which were also located in the room. This was on top of all the banker's boxes that were kept there.

Brian knew that the moment the building came down, it would destroy any and all incriminating evidence against him and his firm. All the documents he had personally signed as true and factual would be history.

As he approached the office tower, his heart began to beat faster. He saw flashing lights and dozens of vehicles just outside the building.

What's going on? he thought.

He slowed across the way and then came to a complete halt. He squinted in the distance. He could see officers from the SWAT team mobilized just in front of the building.

What are the police doing here? he thought with horror. *Did someone find the explosives?*

He reached over and picked up the trigger on the passenger seat. The man said to get close and then activate the explosives with a switch of a button.

He looked up at the building and saw that the lights were on in some of the floors. There were still people working away at this time of the night. He expected the building would be empty. The man assured him that no one would get hurt.

Brian hesitated, his finger hovering over the button. He wasn't a mass murderer. He just didn't want to end up in prison for the Fast-Card fiasco.

He glanced back at the office tower. He could see the police were preparing to go inside. If they somehow managed to disarm the explosives, the entire exercise was a failure. After the SEC's investigation, the FBI would get involved and lay criminal charges against him and anyone involved in the scam. The half a million dollars in cash he had given to the man would be for nothing. It was money he could've used to hire the best lawyers in the country to mount his almost-impossible-to-win defense. But with the money now gone, he was essentially broke.

It's now or never, he thought.

ONE-HUNDRED TEN

HELEN

She saw a row of police vehicles as she drove closer to the office tower. Lights were flashing everywhere. Sounds were coming from all directions. She parked behind a fire truck and got out. She made her way up to where all the noise was coming from. A uniformed officer told her to stay back. She flashed her badge, and she was promptly allowed to enter the cordoned-off scene.

She found the sergeant speaking to another man who was dressed from head to toe in tactical gear.

"Sarge," she said, approaching them. "I heard it on my scanner. What's going on?"

"We just got a call about a bomb threat inside that building," the sergeant said, pointing to the office tower. He then introduced the other man as the SWAT leader.

The SWAT leader said, "We have to get everyone out of the building now."

"Do we even know how many are inside?" the sergeant asked.

The SWAT leader waved another man over. The man was wearing a security guard uniform. He looked completely out of his depth. Sweat marks were visible under his armpits.

The SWAT leader asked him the same question the sergeant had asked. The security guard was holding a binder, and he quickly flipped through the pages. "Right now, there should only be a couple of people in the conference room on the eighth floor. The rest inside should be the cleaning crew."

"Are you sure?" the SWAT leader asked.

"At six pm, the building is locked. People are allowed to enter and leave after that time, but they have to sign in and out at the front desk."

"What about anyone staying behind after work?"

"They notify us in advance," the security guard replied. "We do get people working overtime. But based on the list for today, there should be no one inside other than the people I mentioned on the eighth floor."

The SWAT leader turned to the building. "We will still have to sweep each floor. We can't take the risk of leaving anyone inside," he said.

"How many men do you have?" the sergeant asked.

"I've got eight guys on my team."

The sergeant shook his head. "Not enough. We need more."

Helen jumped in. "We can get a couple of the uniformed officers and some of the guys from the fire department to assist. I don't mind helping out, either."

"Thanks, detective."

A van pulled up close to them and came to a halt.

"The bomb squad is here," the SWAT leader said.

A man walked over. "We came the moment we got the call. Where is it?"

The sergeant said, "According to the anonymous tip, it's in a storage room next to the underground parking."

"All right," the man said. "I'll get my guy ready."

"Is he good?" the sergeant asked, concerned.

"This isn't his first rodeo, sir. If anyone can disarm a bomb, it's him."

The sergeant turned to Helen. "Wrangle up some officers and see if you can get everyone out as fast as possible."

"Yes, sir," she said and hurried off.

ONE-HUNDRED ELEVEN

BRIAN CHESTER

He watched in amazement as more and more vehicles descended on the office tower. The news had spread like wildfire. He saw vans of all shapes and colors from media outlets surround the scene. If it weren't for the yellow police tape, the media would have been in the middle of the action.

So far, no one had noticed him. He was close enough to see what was going on, but far enough to be ignored in all the chaos.

He knew time was running out. He had seen a black armored truck drive up to the building. Obviously, the van had brought members of the bomb squad. Sooner, rather than later, they would find the explosives and deactivate the detonator.

Brian took a deep breath and pressed a switch on the side of the trigger. A red light started blinking, indicating the trigger was active. He shut his eyes tight, bracing himself for the explosion.

He pressed the button.

There was no explosion.

He pressed again.

Nothing.

Frantically, he smashed the button repeatedly.

The building did not crumble.

What the…? he thought in confusion. *Maybe I need to get closer.*

He was about to get out when his cell phone rang.

He saw it was a blocked number. Reluctantly, he answered.

"Did you press the trigger?" It was the man who had set everything in motion for him.

"It didn't work," Brian said with desperation.

"It was never meant to work."

"What?"

There was a moment of silence before a familiar voice came on the speaker.

It was his voice.

"*I hit him across the side of the head, and Joe instantly fell to the floor of the boat. He was bleeding from the back of his head.*"

Brian's eyes widened. "You… you were recording me?"

"Every word was caught loud and clear."

"Why… why are you doing this?" Brian was now in full panic mode.

"This is for my brother."

"Brother?"

"Joseph Elliott."

The blood drained from Brian's face. "Danny?"

"That's right, Brian."

"You set me up?" he said with disbelief.

"You're ruined. Not only will you go to jail for the Fast-Card scam, but you will also go to jail for my brother's murder."

Brian's entire body shook. He couldn't believe this was happening. His life was over.

"There is a way out," the man said.

"What?" Brian blurted. "What is it? You want more money?"

"Thanks to you, I have enough money to get me where I want to go. But I'm not as evil as you. I've left a gift for you in the backseat. What you do with it is your choice. Goodbye, Brian."

The line went dead.

Brian turned and leaned over toward the backseat. He moved his hand around in the dark space until his fingers touched something. It was metallic. He grabbed it and brought it closer.

It was a handgun.

Brian looked at the bedlam in front of the office tower. It would be a matter of time before the police realized it was a hoax. There was no threat. There was no bomb. There was nothing to be concerned about.

Life would go on for the people in the office tower. But his life would never be the same. If the SEC didn't get him for his involvement in the Fast-Card scam, the FBI would get him for the murder of Joseph Elliott.

Brian placed the gun against his right temple and pulled the trigger.

ONE-HUNDRED TWELVE

HELEN

She was on the tower's third floor when she got a call. It was the sergeant, and he wanted her to come outside right this minute.

She took the stairs instead of waiting for the elevator. She found the sergeant by the front revolving doors.

"What's going on, sarge?" she asked.

"We've got another problem," he replied, shaking his head.

"What?"

"Follow me."

He led her through a path from the office tower, past a row of news vans, to a vehicle parked across the street.

Helen could see a group of photographers and cameramen surrounding a Mercedes-Benz. An officer was futilely trying to push them away.

"One of the news people heard a loud bang," the sergeant said. "When he went to check, he found this."

Helen pulled out a pocket flashlight and shone it into the vehicle's interior. She blinked when she realized what she was seeing.

There was blood and brain splattered on the window. A man had his head tilted down, his body held in place by the seatbelt. There was a hole in the right side of his head.

"Get all these people out of here," Helen said.

"We're trying," the officer next to her said.

Suddenly, more officers came over and started ordering the group gathered around the vehicle to move back.

Helen's eyes narrowed. "I recognize him," she said.

"Who is he?" the sergeant asked.

"That's Brian Chester. He has an office on one of the floors in the office tower."

"Okay," the sergeant said, confused.

Helen moved her light around the interior of the vehicle some more.

"What's that?" she asked.

The sergeant walked around the vehicle and opened the passenger door. He leaned inside and picked up what looked like a walkie-talkie. A red light blinked on the device.

"What could this be?" he asked.

"I have no idea," she replied.

The SWAT leader came over and said, "There is no bomb, sir."

"What?" the sergeant asked, turning to him.

"We found drums in the storage room next to the underground garage."

"And?"

"They were filled with sand." The SWAT leader then pointed at the device the sergeant was holding. "Where did you get that?"

The sergeant pointed at the Mercedes-Benz. "It was in the passenger seat."

"Looks like a trigger of some sort."

"Trigger for what?"

"Trigger to detonate explosives."

The sergeant's face creased. "But you said there was no bomb in the building."

"There isn't," the SWAT leader said.

"So, why did he have it on him?"

"I don't know, but all I can tell you is, whoever made the anonymous call just wasted a whole lot of our time for nothing."

Helen didn't share his sentiment. She felt they might have escaped a situation that could have been far worse had it turned out to be true.

ONE-HUNDRED THIRTEEN

LEO

His real name was Daniel Elliott. He entered the motel room and shut the door behind him. He placed the duffel bag with the cash on the bed. He took off his coat and placed it on the chair in the corner.

He then sat on the edge of the bed and covered his face with his hands. He had just gotten off the phone. Brian Chester had blown his brains out in his Mercedes-Benz.

Danny would have relished the opportunity to put a bullet in Brian's head himself. Danny had known Brian since they were young. He would see him hanging around with his older brother. A few times, Brian had even had dinner at their house.

What Brian did was not only unfathomable, it was also a betrayal.

He had taken Joe from him.

Danny had never liked Brian. There was always something lurking deep beneath him. Brian was too ambitious for his own good. He always talked about the good life. The fast cars. The huge houses. The model girlfriends. Those were the things that Brian coveted.

Joe, on the other hand, was different. His priorities were far different. Joe only wanted a stable and comfortable life, where he wouldn't be too stressed about money like their parents had been.

Danny remembered the tough times growing up. They always had food on the table and a roof over their heads. But there was always a sense they were one unpaid bill from being out on the streets.

With their parents working from morning to night to provide for them, Joe was left to take care of Danny. Joe did his best. He was only a couple of years older than him, but even so, he became a guardian to him.

When Danny got mixed up with the wrong crowd—gangs were prevalent in the neighborhood they grew up in—it was always Joe who got him out of trouble.

Joe was the first person in their family to get into college. After graduating, he moved to New York. Danny had visited his apartment. It was small, but it had a view of Central Park.

To say that Joe was Danny's hero would be an understatement. Danny had come to idolize Joe. They dreamed of starting a business together. Danny was working as a bartender then, so opening their own bar was not out of the question.

Joe would use his connections to raise the funds needed to get the bar up and running, while Danny would use his experience in the industry to manage and run the place.

All those dreams were gone the moment Joe disappeared.

Danny never believed for a fact that Joe would suddenly walk out on his loved ones without telling them—especially not him. They spoke to each other regularly. Joe rarely mentioned what he did at Chester and Associates. But on the day he was last seen alive, he told Danny he had found irregularities in one of Chester and Associates' accounts.

Danny never thought for a minute that anything would happen to Joe when he went on that boating trip that night. In fact, Joe had gone on multiple trips out on that very boat.

Danny had always thought it was a bad idea for Joe to leave his cushy job in New York and come to work for Brian. But Brian could be very convincing. Plus, Joe felt like he owed it to him.

What most didn't know was that it was Brian who'd gotten Joe the job in New York in the first place. Brian's father worked in private investment, and as such, Brian was able to convince him to open the doors to that world for Joe.

While Danny believed it was a mistake for Joe to work for his best friend, he just never imagined his best friend would end up murdering him.

Danny began to dig into his brother's disappearance. He never once suspected Brian until Brian refused to let the police access the boat. And by the time the police did get the search warrant, the boat was destroyed.

Danny confronted Brian about it. Brian assured him he had no idea where Joe was or what had happened to him. Brian had even gone so far as to put up a reward for any information about Joe's disappearance.

It was all a charade. It was done in order to make him look the least suspicious. To make the police stop sniffing around him for clues.

Danny knew that Brian, Derek Starr, and Alex Ketchum knew more than they were letting on. In a fit of rage, he had procured a weapon and decided to go out and get the answers he needed. But someone had talked him out of it. There was no point for him to rot in prison for something those three men had done. They should be punished. Not him.

It took close to a decade for him to formulate a plan. And with the help of someone he had come to respect and admire, he had executed the plan perfectly.

He had found young men who were desperate. Tyrel Wiggins had no family to call his own. Cole Madsen had an ailing mother who didn't have long to live. As Leo, Danny executed the plan to get the two of them to do the dirty deeds.

He had convinced Tyrel to murder Derek Starr. And he had convinced Cole Madsen to kill Alex Ketchum—even though, in Cole's case, the boy had gotten cold feet. Regardless, he would go down for the crime.

It was for that reason Danny had not pulled the trigger and ended Brian's life with his own hands. He knew once Brian saw there was no way out of the predicament he was in, he would pull the trigger himself.

He didn't take pleasure in using Tyrel and Cole to do his bidding, but it was either them or him. With two murders, he knew the police would not stop looking for the suspects.

By wrapping everything up with a neat bow, he was essentially handing the police a gift. They would have everything to connect the murders to Tyrel and Cole. The thousand dollars Danny had drawn from his savings to pay Cole for the watch was a small price to pay for keeping his hands clean.

For the first time in a long time, he felt immense relief. It was over. All those people who had hurt his brother were gone. On top of that, he had enough money to live a comfortable life somewhere far away.

He had settled on Thailand. The girls were beautiful. The cost of living was low. And no one would bat an eye at a foreigner living amongst them.

Moving the money out of the country would not be easy. He couldn't just carry it on a plane. Instead, he had rented a shipping container. He would ship all his personal belongings, including furniture, to a location in Thailand. Among those items, he would hide the money. If customs decided to inspect his container, they would find his personal items. Plus, he would provide them with documents that he was relocating for work. Starting a new job in a new country was something thousands of people did on a regular basis.

But before he could do all that, he had to tie up a few loose ends. The police already believed it was Tyrel who had shot the officer behind the laundromat. The weapon inside the burned-out GMC Canyon would be proof of that.

He now had to deliver the evidence he had that Tyrel was responsible for Derek Starr's death and that Cole was responsible for Alex Ketchum's death to the police.

He couldn't just walk into the police station and hand it to them. He would send it to an intrepid reporter with a note that he or she forward it to the police. He would sign the note as, "A Good Samaritan."

The police would start their own investigation into who had sent the package to the reporter, but soon, they would give up when their focus would turn to apprehending Cole and wrapping up both cases.

Maybe he should've put a bullet in Cole's head as he had done to Tyrel. It would be far more merciful than what the kid was about to go through. There'd be a quick trial but a long prison sentence.

He rubbed his eyes and shook his head.

What's done is done, he thought. *It's time I finish this and get myself as far away from here as possible.*

There was a knock at the door.

ONE-HUNDRED FOURTEEN

SIMON

I had followed the man in the cargo van to a motel on the outskirts of the city. I saw the man go inside the room and close the door behind him.

I debated what to do next. But whatever I had to do, I knew I had to do it now before I lost the opportunity—and my nerve. I reached over, opened the glove compartment, and pulled out the gun Nick had given me. I checked to see if the safety was on. I then stuck it in my jacket pocket and got out.

I left my BMW in the motel parking lot and walked up to the door. I looked around and then knocked, flicking off the gun's safety with my other hand.

"Who is it?" the man asked.

Using the first thing that came to my mind, I blurted, "Motel management."

A moment later, the door opened slightly. "What do you want?" the man asked.

Before he had a chance to react, I pulled out the gun and pointed it at his head.

"We have to talk," I replied.

The man backed away. I pushed the door in. I glanced around. The room was small. There was a bed in the middle with a TV across from it. Next to the bed was a night table. And in the corner was a chair.

I shut the door behind me.

"What do you want?" the man asked again.

"I want what you have against my son."

The man blinked. "Son?"

"Cole Madsen," I said.

The man laughed. "He doesn't have a father."

"He does now," I said, blood rushing to my head. "And I know you're making him do something bad. Whatever it is, I don't care. I want you to give it to me."

The man was silent. I could see that he was studying me.

"What if I refuse?" he asked.

"I will hurt you."

He shook his head. "No, you won't. You don't have it in you."

I aimed the gun between his eyes. "If you think I'm bluffing, I'm not. I followed you from Cole's apartment to the laundromat where you shot an officer. I was also the one who followed you now to the alley where you met someone driving a Mercedes-Benz."

The man's eyes widened in disbelief.

"Just give me what you have on my son. He's just a kid."

"He's a murderer," the man said.

My eyes narrowed. "What are you talking about?"

"Take a look for yourself."

He lowered his hand.

"No sudden moves!" I said, waving my gun.

"Relax. I'm just pulling out my cell phone."

"Okay. Do it slowly."

He reached into his pants pocket and pulled out his phone. He held it out for me. I grabbed it.

I swiped the screen. "It's password protected."

"Four. Three. Two. One."

I looked at him. "Not very secure."

"Easy to remember," he said.

I entered the four digits, and the screen came to life. "What am I looking for?"

"Go into the photo gallery. There's a folder with the name 'Cole' on it."

I scrolled and saw several folders. "Who's Tyrel?"

"Someone you don't need to be concerned about."

I found the folder under my son's name. I clicked it open and saw two images. They were of Cole holding a knife. He was next to a man who was bleeding. Cole had a look of shock on his face. I wasn't sure if the shock was from the fact that he had just killed someone or that he was surprised someone had taken his photo after he'd killed someone.

"I told you I was telling the truth," the man said with a grin.

I felt like someone had yanked my feet from underneath me. I was lightheaded, but I controlled my emotions. I couldn't get distracted now.

"Cole said he was set up."

"I don't know what you're talking about."

"I believe him," I said.

"The evidence is right there."

"If he wasn't set up, then why do you have the photos on your phone? You were blackmailing him, that's why."

He opened his mouth, but then shut it. I had caught him.

"Are there copies?"

He was silent.

"Tell me!" I said, raising my voice.

He nodded toward the night table. I walked over, opened the drawer, and pulled out two clear plastic bags. The bags contained two cell phones and two sets of knives. The blade of each knife was stained red.

"I'm assuming one belongs to Cole and the other—?" I asked.

"Like I told you, that doesn't concern you."

I squinted. "Does the other bag belong to Tyrel? He's the only other person with a folder on your phone."

The man grunted. "Okay, now what?"

"Now, I walk out of here with these two bags."

"I'm afraid I can't let you do that," the man said. His voice and his face had suddenly changed.

"Watch me," I said.

I took two steps back and reached for the door behind me, all the while keeping my eyes focused on him.

The gun was in my right hand. My left was holding the two plastic bags.

I fumbled for the door handle.

When I took my eyes off him for a second to see where the handle was, I caught him moving toward the jacket hung on the chair in the corner.

"Stop!" I yelled.

The man reached into the jacket pocket and pulled out what looked like a gun.

That's when I pulled the trigger.

The bullet struck the man in the neck, spinning him around as he fell to the floor.

My hand shook, and I nearly dropped the gun. I hurried over and looked down at the man. He was holding his neck, and there was blood spurting between his fingers. His eyes were wide. He tried to speak, but red liquid bubbled out of his mouth.

A moment later, his body went limp, and all life fell away from his eyes.

ONE-HUNDRED FIFTEEN

SIMON

I sat on the edge of the bed and stared at nothing in particular. I knew what I had done. I'd shot and killed a man.

I could just walk out of the motel room, but I knew, sooner or later, the police would come looking for me. The motel had security cameras all throughout the property. Also, my BMW was in the parking lot. It wouldn't take long for the police to run my license plate and find me.

I had no intention of running. Even if the police, somehow, couldn't find the person behind the man's death, I would always know I was responsible for it. That knowledge would eat away at me. I would have blood on my hands forever. On top of that, I would always be looking over my shoulder.

Instead, I dialed a number, spoke a few words, and hung up.

As I waited, I thought about all my hopes and dreams. About all the things I wanted to do and would now never get to do.

I had never planned to hurt the man. I only came to get something that could hurt my son.

What was I thinking bringing a gun with me? I thought.

It was only supposed to have been for my protection. I had warned the man not to make any sudden moves. If I hadn't done what I had done, he would have shot me. I would be the one bleeding on the floor. Not him.

There was a knock at the door.

I stood up, walked over, and opened it.

Cole was standing outside.

I had seen Cole's number on the man's phone, so I called and told him I had what he was looking for.

I held the door for him, and he came inside. The moment he saw the man dead on the floor, he covered his mouth in horror.

"You killed him?" he asked.

"He gave me no choice," I replied.

Cole was stunned.

I then pulled out the man's phone and held it up. I said, "The password is: four, three, two, one. There is a folder with your name in the photo gallery. I didn't delete it. I figured I'd let you do it."

"Did you see them?" he asked.

I nodded. "And I believe you when you said you didn't hurt the man I saw in the photos."

"I didn't," came Cole's fast reply. "I swear."

I smiled and then walked over to the bed and picked up two clear plastic bags. "He had backed up the photos on either of these phones. I'm not sure which one. And one of the knives probably has your prints on them."

"Whose bag is the other one?" Cole asked.

"Someone named Tyrel. There's also an image folder with his name on the man's phone."

Cole stared at the plastic bags and the cell phone in my hand.

"Why are you doing this?" he asked, confused. "Who are you?"

I took a deep breath. My shoulders slumped. "I wish I could say this under better circumstances."

"Say what?"

"This might sound like a line from a movie, but Cole, I'm your father."

Cole blinked and then let out an incredulous laugh. "I don't have a father."

"You do," I said. "You can ask your mother. I didn't know you even existed until the day she came to me and asked me to bail you out."

Cole stared at me. "I thought you said you'd met her in India?"

"We did. Over twenty-two years ago. You do the math, and you will see I'm telling the truth."

Cole shook his head. "I don't believe you. It just doesn't make sense."

"Do you think anyone would risk their freedom unless you were their child?"

His eyes suddenly turned moist. "You... you did this for me?"

"If I didn't do it, that man would have used those photos against you. It would be you in prison instead of me."

"Why don't you leave?" Cole asked. "Why don't you just get out of here?"

I shook my head. "All actions have consequences. You can't run away from them. Take the phones and the knives, and you make sure no one ever sees them. The man doesn't have anything on you anymore. You are free to do whatever you want with your life now."

Cole looked at the man on the floor and then back at me. I could tell the boy was still in shock.

He then said, "Mom told me someone had given her money for her surgery. She wouldn't tell me who. She said that person would tell me himself. Was it you?"

I nodded. "Get her the help she needs. I've given her the instructions about how to deposit the check." I walked over to the bed and picked up the duffel bag. "I didn't bother counting it, but there's a lot of money in there. I doubt it's going to be of any use to him." I nodded in the dead man's direction. "I want you to give it to someone for me."

"Who?" Cole asked.

"Jayson Roberts. He's a lawyer. He defends the wrongfully convicted. But I'll ask him to defend me just this one time. I'll plead guilty, so there won't be too many legal costs. The rest of the money he can use to help people more deserving than me."

I held up the bag.

Cole hesitated.

"Take it," I said.

Cole reluctantly did.

"You have to leave before anyone sees you," I said.

"You don't have to do this," he pleaded.

"There is no other way."

"There is always a way."

"Not this time. Now go!" I said, raising my voice.

This startled him.

"Please," I said, lowering my voice again. "Just go and take care of your mom."

He moved to the door, stopped, and turned back to me. "I don't even know your name."

"It's Simon. Simon Harris."

He paused, absorbing this fact that was monumental to his life. He then walked out and shut the door behind him.

I sat back on the edge of the bed. I put my hand in my pocket, pulled out my wallet, and extracted a card Detective Helen Sloan had given me back at the hospital. I had saved her partner's life. Maybe she would go easy on me.

Maybe.

I dialed her number, and after a quick conversation, I hung up.

While I await my arrest, I want you to know that even though I have killed another human being, I'm still the good guy.

ONE-HUNDRED SIXTEEN

HELEN

She knocked on the motel room's door. A moment later, Simon Harris answered.

"What is this about, Mr. Harris?" she said.

He took a step back and held the door open for her. She stepped inside and saw a man lying on the floor.

She immediately drew her weapon and aimed it at Harris. He put his hands up in response. "I'm not armed," he said.

When Harris had called her and asked her to meet him, she had told him to come to the station in the morning. But he said it was urgent. That it was a matter of life and death. Now she realized it was a matter of someone else's death.

"What's going on?" she asked, confused. Her eyes kept darting from the man's body to Harris.

"It was self-defense," he replied.

"Where's the weapon?"

"On the bed. And his gun is on the floor next to the chair."

She slowly walked over and got a good look at the deceased. She stared at the lifeless body in silence.

"You did this?" she asked, turning to him.

"Like I said, I didn't have a choice. He was going to shoot me."

"Why?"

"I believe he was the one who shot your partner."

Her eyes narrowed. "If what you're saying is true, then I find it difficult to believe that you happened to be at the laundromat where my partner was shot, and you also happen to be where another man was shot and killed."

"I know this doesn't look good, detective," he said. "But if I'd shot your partner, you know I wouldn't have saved his life. And if I'd shot this man, I wouldn't have called you."

She was quiet.

He then said, "My lawyer's already been notified, and he should be on his way now. I just wanted *you* to take me in."

"Why me?"

"You seem like someone who wouldn't jump to conclusions without getting all the facts first."

She stared at him. "All right, turn around." After she had cuffed him and read him his rights, she said, "I'm not sure what's going on, but whatever it is, you should know that you could be looking at life for murder."

At the sound of that, Harris's head lowered, his shoulders slumped, and he suddenly looked defeated.

ONE-HUNDRED SEVENTEEN

COLE

He was across the street as police cruisers descended on the motel. He watched as the detective brought out a cuffed Simon Harris from the room. Cole was still unsure of what to make of the revelation.

Is this man really my father? he thought. *It can't be.*

But what the man said held true. No one would risk going so far as to commit murder if it weren't to protect someone they cared about.

Simon Harris had killed Leo. And he had done it so that Leo could not blackmail him again. Cole was both horrified and relieved to see the state Leo was in. It was never easy when confronted with a dead body. But knowing that Leo was gone, it felt like a giant weight had fallen off his shoulders. He wouldn't have to sit anxiously in his apartment, waiting for the phone to ring, or a knock at the door when Leo would take him on another one of his missions, or have the police finally take him away for good.

When the detective had walked Simon Harris to a waiting vehicle, Cole saw a look of defeat on his face. That cracked something deep inside him.

Simon Harris had sacrificed his life for him. He had given his mom more than enough money to get better.

Cole didn't know why, but he broke down and cried.

He quickly wiped his eyes with the back of his sleeve. The motel area was still an active crime scene, and people would be suspicious if they saw him like this. He pulled out Leo's cell phone and entered the password Simon Harris had given him. The screen came alive. He searched and found the folder with the photos of him in Tent City.

He was about to press delete but stopped. He wasn't ready to do it right now—not out in the open.

His eyes fell on Leo's phone log. He noticed there were several calls to one particular phone number.

He didn't know why, but he speed-dialed it. He placed the phone to his ear and listened. After several rings, a voice came on and asked, "Who is this?"

Cole looked over and saw something that baffled him. He then quickly hung up.

A moment later, the vehicle carrying Simon Harris pulled out of the motel's parking lot and drove away.

He knew where Simon Harris was being taken. Cole had been there only a few days ago. Harris would be booked and charged at the Arlington PD.

Cole watched as the vehicle disappeared from view.

He looked at Leo's phone.

Now what? he thought.

Rachel's voice suddenly filled his head.

You're a smart guy, Cole. You just do not know how to apply yourself.

He thought a moment.

A plan began to form in his mind.

ONE-HUNDRED EIGHTEEN

HELEN

She entered the house and found Paul waiting for her in the living room.

"You look like you had a rough day," he said.

She sighed. "I just had to arrest the man who saved my partner's life."

"That's not something you see every day," Paul said. "Would you like to talk about it over a cup of coffee?"

She smiled. "That would be nice."

She took a seat at the dining table, while Paul put the pot on to brew.

"I thought you said you'd be going back to your place today," she said.

"Well, I was hoping to drive over and talk to Svetlana. But she called me and told me she didn't want to be with me anymore."

Helen's eyebrows shot up. "Why? I thought she was really into you."

"I thought so, too. I guess you're only as good as your last book."

Helen looked at him, confused.

"My publisher just told me they wouldn't be picking up my latest novel."

"I'm really sorry to hear that. About you and Svetlana, and about your new book, I mean."

He shrugged. "Thanks."

He poured the coffee, brought the steaming cups, and placed them on the table.

"If it's any consolation," she said, "I've read all your books."

"You have?" he said, surprised.

"I'm in the middle of your last one, *The Searching Man*. I think it's excellent."

His face brightened up. "I would appreciate it if you can post a glowing five-star review online. Each review helps me to sell a few copies, you know."

She smiled.

There was a moment of silence.

Paul broke it. "I spoke to Emily. She told me about what had happened all those years ago when you were a patrol officer."

She looked away.

"I'm sorry that I dismissed your pain and told you to get over it," he said. "I had no idea you'd been carrying so much guilt inside you."

Her eyes suddenly welled up, and she bit her bottom lip to control her emotions.

He reached over and held her hand. She didn't pull away.

"I'm sorry I cheated on you, Paul."

"I guess we both hurt each other in our own ways."

She sniffled. "I guess we did."

They took a sip from their cups.

Paul then said, with a wry smile, "You really enjoy my writing, huh?"

"If I didn't, after the divorce, I would've gone back to my maiden name. But I like being connected to the famous writer, Paul Sloan."

"In that case, would you care to know what my latest book is about? I mean, I don't think another publisher would touch it after they see the track record of my sales. So, you'll get the unedited version."

She smiled. "I have no doubt someone will pick it up. And yes, I would love to hear it."

ONE-HUNDRED NINETEEN

HELEN

She was at the Arlington PD when she'd gotten the call. She was surprised when the caller had asked her to come to the same motel room where she had found Simon Harris and the body of Daniel Elliott.

She knocked on the door and waited. A moment later, a young man wearing a hoodie, track pants, and runners answered the door.

Helen had her hand on her weapon. "Are you Cole Madsen?" she asked.

Cole nodded.

"Do you have a weapon, Mr. Madsen?"

Cole shook his head.

She pushed the door in and took a peek inside. She saw that the room was empty.

"What is this about?" she asked.

"I just wanted to talk to you in private."

She took another glance around the room and then entered. She shut the door behind her and said, "Okay, what do you want to talk about?"

"Simon Harris."

"What about him?"

"He's my father."

She blinked. "Wait... what?"

"I didn't know it either until recently. But it's true. My mom confirmed it. I'm his son."

"All right, so what does that have to do with me being here?"

"Simon Harris is being charged with first-degree murder. I want to tell you he didn't come here to hurt that man."

"Daniel Elliott?"

He nodded. "I knew him as Leo, though."

"Okay, we'll go with Leo."

"Simon Harris came here to work out a deal with Leo."

"What sort of deal?"

"Leo had something against me."

"Like what?"

Cole paused. "I can't go into it, but I can tell you I wasn't behind it. It was Leo."

Helen shook her head. "Unless you give me specifics, I have no idea what you're talking about."

Cole ignored Helen's words. "I believe Leo had planned this whole thing as revenge on the people who murdered his brother, Joseph Elliot. He used other people to get rid of Derek Starr, Alex Ketchum, and Brian Chester."

"Used. How?"

"I'll cite my Fifth Amendment right, which protects me against self-incrimination."

"You're a smart young man," Helen said with admiration.

"I had to brush up on the law before I decided to speak to you."

"Okay, so why did you want to speak to *me*?" she asked.

"Because Simon Harris wanted you to arrest him," he replied.

"You keep referring to him by his full name and not as your father. Why is that?"

"I'm still coming to grips with everything I've been told."

"Fair enough."

"He called you because he saved your partner's life."

"He did," Helen agreed. "And it's something I'll forever be grateful for."

"And from what I've been told, the state attorney takes into consideration the lead detective's opinion. Simon Harris has not denied his actions here, but he has always said it was self-defense."

"It's his right to plead guilty or not."

"But that's the thing," Cole said. "He's willing to plead guilty, but only to voluntary manslaughter, which the state attorney has refused. I've found out that you are pushing for the maximum. *You* want Simon Harris to be charged with first-degree murder."

Helen's eyes narrowed. "The evidence is overwhelmingly against him. He entered this motel room with a weapon. As you just stated, Simon Harris believed the victim had something against you, and in order to procure this something, he threatened to harm the victim. That could all be conjecture on my part, but I've been doing this long enough that I can tell you Simon Harris was the aggressor. While a second weapon was found near the victim, I believe the victim only went for his weapon because he felt *his* life was in danger—and not the other way around. Simon Harris always had the intention to kill when he went to confront the victim in this motel room."

"If that were true, then why did Simon Harris call you and give himself up?" he asked.

"Maybe he realized he couldn't get away with it. Maybe his conscience got the better of him. Maybe he was trying to protect you. I don't know. And I don't care. Ultimately, he is guilty of the murder of Daniel Elliott."

"I believe the reason you want Simon Harris to be punished, and punished severely, is that you knew Daniel Elliott, and it would burn you to see Simon Harris charged for a lesser crime."

"I'm not sure what you are talking about."

Cole pulled out a cell phone from his pocket. Cole then speed-dialed a number.

There was a buzzing noise inside Helen's coat. She didn't bother answering her phone.

Cole said, "I was outside the motel when I saw you take Simon Harris from the motel room to a waiting vehicle. At the same time, I had re-dialed a number on the phone I'm holding right now. That number kept showing up on the phone's log. The person on the other end was surprised to get a call from this number. It made sense. After all, the person this phone belonged to was Daniel Elliot. And he was dead. When I looked back at the motel, I saw you on the phone, too. When I hung up, you did so, too, at the same time. To avoid any confusion, this phone belongs to Leo, or Daniel Elliott, as you knew him."

Helen's eyes narrowed. "Where did you get it?"

"That's not important."

"It is, because it could be used as evidence in Daniel Elliott's murder."

"I very much doubt you'd want it to be used as evidence because that would show your involvement in all of this."

Helen was silent.

ONE-HUNDRED TWENTY

HELEN

"All right, sure," Helen conceded. "I knew Daniel Elliott, but he's not implicated in any crime, is he?"

"I wouldn't be so sure of that," Cole said. He then pulled out his own cell phone. He scrolled through it and then pressed a button. He held up the phone for her to see.

On the screen, it looked like someone was holding the camera just above their lap. A man was visible behind the steering wheel. He had on a baseball cap, dark sunglasses, and a heavy beard. But with some scrutiny, it was easy to see that it was Daniel Elliott.

Daniel Elliott reached over and pulled out what looked like a serrated knife from the car's glove compartment.

"What... is... this?" Cole's scared voice asked.

Daniel Elliott flipped the knife over so that he was holding the tip of the blade with his fingers. "Take it," he said.

A hand appeared on the screen and grabbed the handle.

"What do you want me to do with it?" Cole's asked.

"I want you to go in Tent City and stab someone," replied Daniel Elliott.

"What!? I can't do that."

"Why not?"

"That's murder."

Cole pressed a button, and the screen went blank. Cole was never once seen on the phone, but it was clear that he was the person next to Daniel Elliott.

Cole said, "That's just one of the conversations I recorded between Leo and me. I have many more if you care to listen to them."

Helen's face was dark.

Cole said, "I always thought Leo worked for some criminal organization. He would always say that *we* want you to do this, or *we* want you to do that. It was never *I* want you to do this, or *I* want you to do that. I now believe the person he was working with was you.'"

"That's a bold accusation," Helen said.

"Is it?" Cole said. "Leo always looked like he was in control. As if he was not concerned about the consequence of his actions. Right after the events at Tent City—which I won't go into in detail for obvious reasons—he didn't seem too worried. He said he had connections in the police department, and the police didn't have any suspects. Of course they didn't, because you were investigating the homeless man's murder. Alex Ketchum, isn't it? Also, I've found out that Leo was playing the same cruel game, that he was playing with me with someone named Tyrel Wiggins. He used Tyrel to hurt another man, Derek Starr. Both Derek Starr and Alex Ketchum were stabbed with the same kind of weapon."

Helen's eyes narrowed. "How would you know the type of weapon? Unless you were behind the murders."

"You have no proof that I was," Cole replied with a shrug.

She opened her mouth, but then shut it.

Cole smiled. "You saw the photos Leo had taken at Tent City of Alex Ketchum and me. I bet it was the same with photos Leo had taken of Tyrel with Derek Starr outside the bus shelter. Those photos showed someone other than Leo committing the murders. I didn't know Tyrel. I never met him. And, from what I've read, that would be impossible now, because he's dead from a gunshot wound to the head. So, I can't say whether he went through with Leo's instructions or not."

Helen, again, said nothing.

Cole scrolled through his phone. "I'm afraid there is no visual, but the audio is pretty clear."

He pressed a button and held the phone up in the air.

Cole's voice came on the speaker. *"If... if that happened... I'll tell them the truth."*

"What truth would that be?" Leo replied.

"That you killed that man."

"What man would you be referring to?"

"The man in Tent City."

"Do you even know my real name?" Leo asked.

Cole shut off the audio. "He was right. I didn't know his name until he was dead."

Helen jumped in. "That audio doesn't prove that Danny was the one who killed Alex Ketchum?"

Cole raised an eyebrow. "*Danny,* is it? I thought you said you didn't know him."

ONE-HUNDRED TWENTY-ONE

HELEN

Cole said, "I agree the audio doesn't have Leo confessing to the crime, but it does prove he wanted me to hurt Alex Ketchum in Tent City. The previous video I showed you confirms what I'm saying is true."

"What's your point?"

"If Leo was involved in Derek Starr and Alex Ketchum's murders, then your constant contact with him during this time would prove you were also involved in the murders."

Helen shook her head. "That's a bit of a stretch, young man."

"It would make sense. Daniel Elliott would commit the crimes, and you would clean them up."

"Why would I be involved in any of this?" she asked.

"I wasn't the only one making secret recordings. I found an audio on Leo's phone. It was a recording between Leo and another man. I believe it's Brian Chester."

Cole held up Leo's phone and pressed a button.

Chester's voice came on. "I hit him across the side of the head, and Joe instantly fell to the floor of the boat. He was bleeding from the back of his head. Once I realized what I'd done, I knew there was no going back."

"Did the others join in hurting Joseph Elliott?" The second voice was heavier, as if the person was trying to shield his identity.

"Alex and Derek were appalled by what had happened," Chester said. *"Derek threw up over the side, and Alex broke down in tears. I had to convince them we had no choice. That Joe was going to destroy us all. Reluctantly, they helped me wrap him in a tarp and hurl his body into the water."*

Cole shut off the recording. "The Joe they are referring to is Joseph Elliott, Daniel Elliott's brother. And the Alex and Derek on the audio are Alex Ketchum and Derek Starr. Leo believed that Derek Starr, Alex Ketchum, and Brian Chester were responsible for his brother's death, and so he used Tyrel and me to get rid of them." Cole paused. "Well, I read in the papers that Brian Chester killed himself. But, I think the fake bombing that Leo got me involved in had something to do with his death."

"But, what does Joseph Elliott's death have to do with *me*?" Helen said. "Danny had a reason to want revenge. After all, it was his brother who had gone missing."

Cole smiled. "You are correct. Joseph Elliott was Danny's brother, but you failed to say that Joseph Elliott was in a relationship with you at the time of his disappearance."

Helen scowled. "You have no proof of that."

Cole held up Leo's phone once again. "Leo used burner phones when communicating with Tyrel and me. But he used this phone just to communicate with you. He was careful not to put any incriminating evidence on the phone. There are no personal messages or photos of any kind that would reveal who he really was. But, Leo failed to realize that when he set up the phone, he had mistakenly agreed to back up the information to an account on the cloud. I'm not much of a techie, but there are people who are experts in stuff like this. They were able to use that to access all of Leo's personal files on the cloud. And, guess what? They discovered photos going back almost a decade of you with Joseph Elliott.'"

Cole scrolled through the cell phone and held up an image for Helen to see. It showed Joseph Elliott smiling at the camera with his arm around a younger-looking Helen. They were both holding colorful drinks on a white sandy beach.

Helen's heart sank at the sight of Joe. Her eyes suddenly welled up.

Cole said, "There are apparently dozens of photos of the two of you together. I don't want to go through all of them because they are personal. But they prove your relationship with Joseph Elliott. Which, as far as I am told, also gives you motive, along with Daniel Elliott, to want to hurt the people who hurt Joseph Elliott."

Helen pulled out her gun.

"That's enough," she said. "You are quite clever for your age. I'm surprised you were able to piece it all together."

"You're right. I am young," Cole replied. "And to be honest, a lot of this stuff is way over my head. But I was lucky to get help in making sense of all of this."

Helen's eyes narrowed. "Who helped you?"

The bathroom door opened, and a man came out.

ONE-HUNDRED TWENTY-TWO

HELEN

Detective Michael Porter had a sling over his left arm. In his right hand, he was holding his service weapon.

Helen's eyes widened. "You were there all along?"

"You should've swept the room after you came in," he said. "And please, lower your weapon. I may look hurt, but I'm more than capable of firing my gun."

She hesitated and then put her gun back in its holster. "You heard everything?" she said.

"Every word," he replied. "Cole came to me and told me what he had seen outside the motel room. Naturally, I was skeptical of him. You were my partner. My loyalty is first and foremost to you. You were smart not to use your regular phone to communicate with Daniel Elliott, or else it would be easy to trace your phone to his. Even so, the burner phone you used sends out a signal. At the time Cole had called the number on the phone, you were in the same vicinity as him. The cell tower was a block away from the motel.

"Obviously, that's not enough to indict anyone for a crime. I interviewed Cole in private. He showed me the videos of his interactions with Daniel Elliott. I saw the photos of Cole with the deceased Alex Ketchum. While I found them troubling, I could see from the photos that Cole was shocked at being photographed. I smelled a set up. Daniel Elliott was caught on video convincing Cole to go into Tent City. And, what a coincidence that on his phone we also caught Cole red-handed."

"If you check the prints on the knife," Helen said, "you'll see that it was *he* who had murdered Ketchum."

Michael smiled. "How did you know we had the murder weapon in our possession?"

Helen opened her mouth, but then shut it.

"You know this because that was always the plan. Have Tyrel and Cole take the fall for the deaths of Ketchum and Starr. But, I couldn't just take someone else's word against a fellow detective. So, I got an IT expert in the department to dig through the contents of Daniel Elliott's phone. They were able to access Elliott's photo gallery on the cloud. And that's where we found photos of you with Elliott's older brother, Joseph."

Helen looked away.

"Once I knew your connection with Joseph and Daniel Elliott, it was a simple matter of elimination. I understood why you had suddenly decided to retire. You wanted to wrap up the Ketchum and Starr case on your watch. After which, you would quietly walk away. You knew you were the most senior detective in the department, so it would be easy for you to convince the sergeant to give you the cases." He paused and shook his head. "Now I know why you asked the sergeant not to take me on as your partner from the very beginning. You wanted to control the investigations. But, the sergeant didn't know your motives. He thought it was best for someone with your experience to mentor me. So, reluctantly, you let me tag along."

"Throughout the investigation, I always sensed I was fighting a battle from both sides. One to solve the crime, the other to convince *you* of my theory that it was never a simple case of two drunks getting into a fight outside a bar. For your information, the toxicology report came back, and Starr's blood-alcohol level was not anywhere near high enough for him to be intoxicated. On the night of Starr's murder, it was Daniel Elliott who told Starr to go to the bar. When no one showed up to meet him, Starr had walked out. He didn't realize Tyrel Wiggins was in the bar watching him the entire time. Wiggins then instructed Starr to go to another location—a remote location. It was behind the barn on Walt Grimsby's property, where we ended up finding Starr's Nissan Maxima. I believe that's where Starr was stabbed by either Wiggins or Elliott. He was then left at the bus stop, in order to make it look like he had gotten into a bar brawl. And, in order to make it look more authentic, they left a beer bottle in his hand. I was right about the shoes. The scuffs were an indication that his body had been dragged to the bus stop."

ONE-HUNDRED TWENTY-THREE

HELEN

"Why would Starr go to the bar in the first place?" Helen asked. "Did you ever answer that question?"

"I did," Michael replied. "Daniel Elliott had a suspicion about what might have happened on the boat involving his brother and Chester, Ketchum, and Starr. It wouldn't be hard for him to call Starr and tell him he knew Starr was responsible for Joseph Elliott's death. Terrified, Starr would do anything to make the problem go away. He probably figured it would be blackmail. Something he could buy his way out of. He never got the chance, because revenge was always the motive."

"You sound crazy, you know that," she said, shaking her head.

"I'm not crazy, but I *was* shot."

Her face softened.

"I know you never meant for me to get hurt. You blamed yourself for what happened to me. You never expected me to end up at the laundromat. You always questioned why I never called you. If I had, you would have talked me out of going there alone. Or you would have warned Daniel Elliott to get Tyrel Wiggins out of there. Wiggins was renting an apartment above the laundromat. He was just foolish enough to register his vehicle at that address. I had used his license plate number to track him down. And, I believe his mistake cost him his life. Daniel Elliott murdered Wiggins, like he had murdered Ketchum and Starr. I have no doubt that he had a hand in what happened to Brian Chester in the end. And he did it all with your help, Detective Sloan."

Helen scoffed. "That's a lot of theories, Michael. And last I checked, we don't arrest people based on theories. We arrest them based on evidence."

"You're right, we don't." Michael checked his watch. "If I'm right, we will have the evidence soon."

Helen's eyes narrowed. "What are you talking about?"

"I would check your phone. Not the burner phone, though, but your regular phone."

She pulled it out and saw several missed calls from Paul. She had put the phone on silent when she had come to the motel. She didn't want to be disturbed.

She quickly re-dialed Paul's number.

He picked up on the first ring. "Helen," he said. "I've been trying to reach you. Where have you been?"

"What's going on, Paul?" she asked.

"There are people here going through your house."

"What people?"

"They had a warrant, and I couldn't stop them from coming inside."

Helen looked up at Michael.

"Paul, let me call you back." She hung up. "You got a warrant to search my house?" she asked, fuming.

"It was the sergeant's idea to stall you here while he executed the warrant. He knew if you got wind of it, you'd have put up a fight."

Michael's phone buzzed. He switched his weapon from his right hand to his left and checked his phone. "Speak of the devil," he said, putting the phone to his ear. He listened, smiled, and hung up. "Guess what they found in the basement, right behind a shelf where you keep your prized bottles of wine? A box filled with intel on Brian Chester, Alex Ketchum, and Derek Starr. Apparently, you and Daniel Elliott had been keeping tabs on them. And what better place to hide the intel, than at a detective's place of residence, where it would be the last place where the police would bother looking?"

Helen's face was pale.

Michael switched his weapon back to his good hand. "Helen, it's over. We have everything we need to arrest you. Either you come quietly, or I shoot you. I would prefer the former over the latter."

Helen's hand moved to her holster.

"You will be charged with conspiracy to murder," Michael said. "You will spend the remainder of your life in prison, but at least you can still see your daughter and your granddaughter. The alternative is not something you should even consider."

Several long minutes went by. Nothing happened.

Helen raised her hands in the air. She knew the drill better than anyone.

"Cole," Michael said. "Do you mind relieving the detective of her weapon?"

Cole walked over and took Helen's gun.

Michael then handed him the handcuffs. "I can only do so much with one working arm, so you do the honors."

Cole smiled. "My pleasure," he said, as he cuffed Helen's wrists behind her back.

EPILOGUE

Six weeks later

SIMON

I sat in my eight-by-ten cell with a book in my hand. Ever since I arrived in the state penitentiary, I had been reading more and more. The prison's library system was filled with books from classical literature to modern mysteries. Growing up, I had always enjoyed the company of books. But somewhere along the line, I had neglected to do things that actually gave *me* pleasure.

I was convicted of Daniel Elliott's death. Instead of first-degree murder, I was charged with voluntary manslaughter. I had taken a loaded weapon to meet Elliott at the motel room, and I had fired my weapon at him. Those facts could not be changed.

However, thanks to Detective Michael Porter's statements, and with the help of my lawyer and my best friend, Jay, the state attorney agreed to reduce my sentence to just three years. Several factors had worked in my favor. One, I had saved Detective Porter's life. Two, I was an upstanding citizen with no criminal record. On top of that, Daniel Elliott also had a weapon in his possession at the time of our meeting. Had I not shot him, he may have shot me.

With good behavior, I could be out in less than a year and a half.

I was taking that time to catch up on my reading.

Vanessa divorced me right before I was incarcerated. I was glad she wasn't going to wait for me to come out of prison, so that we could start our life together again. I never had much hope for the marriage after what had transpired. I wished her all the best in whatever she wanted to do next in her life. I just knew that life did not involve me.

Gabe and mother were at my sentencing, but so far, neither has come to see me in prison. I'm not surprised. They weren't the type of people that like doing anything that made them uncomfortable. Money had allowed them to shield themselves from the ugliness in life, and visiting prison would have been a jarring experience for both of them, to say the least. I had no desire to see them, either, so that was that.

I had spoken to Cole a few times on the phone. Detective Helen Sloan was sentenced to ten years for her involvement in the deaths of Derek Starr and Alex Ketchum. She was also stripped of her police pension. It was sad, because she was only a few months away from retiring.

The police saw the video Cole had taken of Daniel Elliott, coercing him to go into the camp called Tent City and kill Ketchum. They were quickly convinced Cole was telling them the truth, that Elliott had killed Ketchum. Cole also returned the watch Elliott had told him to steal as a loyalty test, so the charge against Cole for that was dropped. Again, Detective Porter was instrumental in making this happen. However, Cole was put on probation. If he broke the law again, he could be looking at more severe consequences. I think the boy had learned his lesson. I had no doubt he would stay on the right path.

Annabelle had had her surgery. The brain tumor was removed without any complications. She was expected to make a full recovery.

There was a knock at my cell door. I looked up. A guard stuck his head inside. "Harris," he said. "You've got a visitor."

"I do?" I said, surprised.

"Let's go."

I was led down the hall, through several locked doors, and to the other side of the building. The guards knew my story—it was front-page news for almost a week—so they chose not to go hard on me. I wasn't strip-searched on a regular basis or verbally and physically abused. Something I had seen happen to other prisoners. I was kind of left on my own. I was also not cuffed as I made my way to an open area.

"You've got thirty minutes, Harris," the guard said.

I thanked him and looked around. I saw tables with visitors and inmates. I just wasn't sure who had come to see me.

I then spotted him in the corner of the room. I walked over.

Cole was seated at a table.

We didn't hug or shake hands. Our relationship hadn't progressed that far. Even our conversations over the phone were very formal.

I sat across from him. "What're you doing here?"

The prison was a good three-hour drive from Arlington, so I knew he'd come a long way.

"I came to see you," he replied.

I was elated, but cautious. I didn't want to get my hopes high. Maybe this would be a one-time visit.

I then asked, "How's your mom doing?"

"The doctors are surprised by how fast she's getting better."

"That's good to hear."

"She wants to come and see you."

My heart swelled. "She does?"

"It's still too much of a drive for her right now, but once she's better, I'll bring her down."

"I'd love that."

He pulled out an envelope from his pocket. "Mom mentioned something about you not getting the chance to read her letters before." My mother had destroyed all the letters Annabelle had written to me all those years ago. "Mom was hoping you could read the letters she wrote to you now."

My eyes turned moist. "Tell her I will read them and that I will write to her."

Cole slid the letter across the table.

I shook my head. "You'll have to give it to the guard. They'll pass it on to me. They search it for contraband, but they don't read the mail."

He pulled the letter back.

He then said, "I've enrolled in college."

"That's amazing."

"It's only a couple of classes a week, but I figured I should start thinking about my future."

"What do you plan on studying?"

"I was thinking of getting into finance," he replied. "Isn't that what you did?"

I was speechless. I only nodded.

He then said, "Also, the college is only about an hour away from the prison, so it'll make it easier for me to visit you on a regular basis."

I was stunned. "You want to see me?" The words barely came out of my mouth.

"Yeah, I figured it would give us time to get to know each other before you got out. I mean, I am your son, after all."

Tears flowed down my cheeks as I was overcome with emotion. I then composed myself and wiped my face. "Okay, what do you want to know about me?"

He smiled. "Everything, dad."

Visit the author's website:
www.finchambooks.com

Contact:
contact@finchambooks.com

THOMAS FINCHAM holds a graduate degree in Economics. His travels throughout the world have given him an appreciation for other cultures and beliefs. He has lived in Africa, Asia, and North America. An avid reader of mysteries and thrillers, he decided to give writing a try. Several novels later, he can honestly say he has found his calling. He is married and lives in a hundred-year-old house. He is the author of the **LEE CALLAWAY** series, the **HYDER ALI** series, the **MARTIN RHODES** series, and the **ECHO ROSE** series.

Made in the USA
Middletown, DE
03 March 2021